ARIFURETA: FROM COMMONPLACE TO WORLD'S STRONGEST

story
RYO SHIRAKOME

illust.
TAKAYAKI

"DON'T CRY, YUE. YOU WON THIS FIGHT!"

"HAJIME!"

HAJIME NAGUMO

"...NHAAH...
HAJIME...
AAAH..."
"WHA...?!"

Hajime kicked
off the sheets
and saw that he
had been
sleeping next
to a beautiful
naked girl.

CONTENTS

ARIFURETA:

ARIFURETA SHOKUGYOU DE SEKAISAIKYOU

FROM COMMONPLACE
TO WORLD'S STRONGEST

#1

Presented by
RYO SHIRAKOME

Illustrated by
TAKAYAKI

Seven Seas

novel club

ARIFURETA: FROM COMMONPLACE TO WORLD'S
STRONGEST, VOLUME. 1

© 2015 Ryo Shirakome
Illustrations by Takaya-ki

First published in Japan in 2015 by
OVERLAP Inc., Ltd., Tokyo.
English translation rights arranged with
OVERLAP Inc., Ltd., Tokyo.

Seven Seas books may be purchased in bulk for promotional,
educational, or business use. Please contact your local
bookseller or the Macmillan Corporate and Premium Sales
Department at 1-800-221-7945, extension 5442, or by
e-mail at MacmillanSpecialMarkets@macmillan.com.

Follow Seven Seas Entertainment online at gomanga.com.
Experience J-Novel Club books online at j-novel.club.

Translation: Ningen
J-Novel Editor: DxS
Book Design & Layout: Karis Page
Copy Editor: J.P. Sullivan
Proofreader: Maggie Cooper
Light Novel Editor: Jenn Grunigen
Production Assistant: CK Russell
Production Manager: Lissa Pattillo
Editor-in-Chief: Adam Arnold
Publisher: Jason DeAngelis

ISBN: 978-1-626927-68-1
Printed in Canada
First Printing: February 2018
10 9 8 7 6 5 4 3 2 1

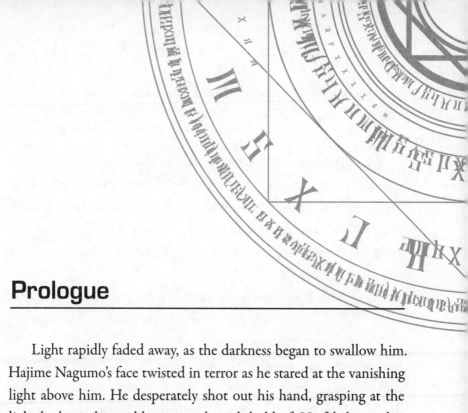

Prologue

Light rapidly faded away, as the darkness began to swallow him. Hajime Nagumo's face twisted in terror as he stared at the vanishing light above him. He desperately shot out his hand, grasping at the light he knew he could never truly grab hold of. He felt his nether regions tense up as he fell freely through the darkness.

The chasm he'd fallen into was so deep that it seemed almost as if he was falling down to the pits of hell. And the light he was staring at was the portal to the world of the living. He'd fallen down a massive tear in the earth while he'd been exploring a dungeon. The hole was so deep that he kept falling long after the tiny pinprick of light had shrunk to nothing. His entire life flashed before his eyes, with nothing but the sound of wind rushing past accompanying his plunge to the hellish depths below.

Let us turn back the clock a bit, and recount how a young Japanese boy found himself in a world that was far too cruel and heartless for the word "fantasy" to be an accurate descriptor. After all, the harsh and unfair events he'd experienced—and was still experiencing—were a bit too bereft of the wonderful hopes and dreams one imagined when they heard that word.

Monday. Quite possibly the most depressing day of the week. Most people were, without a doubt, sighing heavily as they lamented the beginning of the week and the end of their glorious weekend. Hajime Nagumo was no exception. However, in his case, his depression was multiplied by the fact that school was not just a pain, but a veritable hell.

As always, Hajime barely managed to arrive just before the bell for first period rang. He somehow managed to steady his sleep-deprived body and opened the door to his classroom. He found himself on the receiving end of a multitude of scornful glares and annoyed tongue clicks from a majority of the male students as soon as he set foot in the classroom. None of the female students seemed all too pleased to see him either. It would have been fine were they simply ignoring him, but they too gave him stares of contempt.

Hajime did his best to ignore his classmates and went to his seat. But as always, there were a few students who couldn't resist the opportunity to needle him.

"Sup, you gross otaku? Stay up all night playing video games again? I bet you were playing porn games the whole time!"

"Wow, what a creep. What kind of disgusting pervert stays up all night playing porn games?"

The boys all laughed, as if they found that statement somehow hilarious. The student who'd first called out to Hajime was Daisuke Hiyama, the ringleader of Hajime's tormentors. Daisuke never seemed to tire of teasing Hajime, as he went up to him on a daily basis. The ones who were laughing wickedly next to him were Yoshiki Saitou, Reichi Kondou, and Shinji Nakano. It was those four who'd always made Hajime's life miserable.

As Hiyama had stated earlier, Hajime was indeed an otaku. But he wasn't particularly ugly or obnoxious, so the moniker "gross otaku" hardly did him justice. His hair was cropped short and kept tidy. Plus, it wasn't as if he had a communication problem of any sort either. Sure, he wasn't the most talkative guy around, but he had no problem responding to people who talked to him. He was a quiet person overall, but not to the point where it could be considered gloomy. He just happened to have an interest in a very specific set of media—namely manga, novels, video games, and movies.

While it was true that public opinion of otakus hadn't been very positive as of late, at most being an otaku usually earned you a few looks, not that kind of targeted bullying. So why did all the male students hate Hajime so?

The answer was simple.

"Good morning, Nagumo-kun! You barely made it on time today too. I think you should at least make an effort to come earlier." One of the girls smiled softly as she walked up to Hajime. She was one of the few people in the whole school who treated him kindly, and also the reason everyone hated him.

Kaori Shirasaki was one of the most popular girls in school, and beautiful enough to be considered a goddess by many. She had sleek, black hair that went all the way down to her waist, and large alluring eyes filled with kindness. Her small nose sat perfectly upon her face, and her pink lips were the epitome of perfection.

She always seemed to have a smile on her face, and her knack for looking after others, combined with her strong sense of responsibility, made her one of the most respected students at Hajime's school. Moreover, she was tolerant and understanding to a fault, to the point where no one had ever even seen her look unhappy before.

And, for whatever reason, Kaori had taken an interest in Hajime. Most people assumed Hajime was a terrible student because he always slept in class due to his frequent all-nighters (in truth, he had pretty average grades). And, since Kaori was always looking after other students, they believed that was the reason she talked to him.

Had her overtures convinced Hajime to become a better student, or had he naturally been a better-looking guy, the other kids might not have minded Kaori's interest in him as much. As it was, though, he was sadly as average looking as one could get, and his favorite motto was "hobbies over real life," so obviously his attitude toward school had shown no signs of improvement either. As it was, the other average-looking male students of his class couldn't stand the fact that Hajime was so close to Kaori. *Why him and not us?!* they thought. Meanwhile, the other girls simply thought he was being rude to Kaori. They were unhappy that he wasn't even attempting to reform his habits.

"A-ah, good morning, Shirasaki-san." Hajime's face stiffened up as he felt the bloodthirsty glares of his fellow classmates, and he awkwardly returned Kaori's greeting.

In contrast, Kaori smiled happily as she looked at him. *Why do you always look at me like that?!* Hajime despaired as he felt the gazes of his classmates burn into him.

Hajime was honestly bewildered. He didn't understand why the most beautiful girl in school cared about a guy like him. To him, it seemed like there had to have been something more than just her natural disposition to help others.

Of course, he wasn't so conceited as to believe she might possibly have any romantic interest in him. Hajime was well aware of the fact that he'd given up a great deal of things to live a life fully devoted to his hobbies. He knew his appearance, grades, and athletic ability were all utterly average. There was a whole host of guys better than him who were far more suited to be her partner, even just among her acquaintances. Which was why he found her behavior so puzzling.

Honestly, I just wish you'd realize you're the reason everyone hates me right now! Hajime screamed inside his head. However, he didn't give voice to his thoughts. He knew that some of his classmates would no doubt drag him out behind the gym once classes were over if he ever dared to do so... The moment Hajime finished his conversation with Kaori, three new people walked up to them. They'd been watching the two of them like vultures, waiting for him to finish talking. Among this new group was, of course, one of the aforementioned "better guys."

"Good morning, Nagumo-kun. Must be rough staying up that late every day."

"Looking after him again, Kaori? You're really too nice for your own good."

"Seriously. Talking to a failure like him's a total waste of time."

The only person out of the three who'd greeted Hajime was Shizuku Yaegashi, Kaori's best friend. Shizuku's black hair was tied back in her trademark ponytail. Her almond-shaped eyes gave her a rather sharp look, but deep within her gaze dwelled a kindness that made her seem cool rather than cold.

Standing 172 centimeters tall, she was a good deal taller than most of the other girls in his class. That, combined with her well-built body, made her seem like a dignified samurai. And samurai made for a rather apt analogy, as her family actually ran a dojo that taught the Yaegashi style, and Shizuku herself was a peerless swordswoman who'd never lost a single kendo tournament. In fact, she'd been featured in magazines before and had a rather rabid fanbase. The press even took to calling her the "modern samurai beauty." Many of the younger female students had started calling her onee-sama in an almost worshipful manner.

The guy who'd greeted Kaori with that rather clichéd line about her kindness was Kouki Amanogawa. He was perfect in almost every way. Great at sports, handsome, and had outstanding grades to boot. Even his name sounded heroic. Written with the characters for "light" and "radiance," it gave off a rather dazzling impression.

He had flowing brown hair, soft features, stood 180 centimeters tall, and despite his slender frame still had noticeable muscles. He was kind to everyone he met, and had a strong sense of justice (or so he thought, anyway).

Like Shizuku, he'd attended the Yaegashi dojo since he was in elementary school and was skilled enough to have competed in national tournaments. He and Shizuku were childhood friends. Dozens of girls had fallen for him, but because he was always hanging around Shizuku and Kaori, very few had ever worked up the courage to confess. However, he still received at least two confessions a month from girls that didn't go to Hajime's school. A real Casanova through and through.

The last guy, who'd lazily added on his own comments to Kouki's line, was Ryutarou Sakagami, Kouki's best friend. Ryutarou had short, trimmed hair and a gaze that seemed at once both cheerful and stern.

He stood 190 centimeters tall, and had a massive, bear-like frame. As his build suggested, he was a musclehead who didn't have much delicacy.

Because of his love for hard work and hot-blooded actions, he disliked Hajime, who spent all his time in school sleeping. Ryutarou gave Hajime no more than a single glance before huffing disdainfully and ignoring him.

"Good morning, Yaegashi-san, Amanogawa-kun, and Sakagami-kun. Heh, well, you know what they say, you reap what you sow. It's my own fault for staying up all the time." Hajime smiled wryly as he greeted Shizuku and the others. The two guys glared daggers at him, their eyes all but screaming, *"What gives you the right to talk to Yaegashi-san so casually like that, huh?!"* Shizuku was nearly as popular as Kaori, after all.

"If you realize it's a problem, shouldn't you try and fix it? I don't think it's fair to Kaori to keep letting her spoil you. She doesn't have time to always be looking after you, either." Kouki warned Hajime sternly.

Kouki also clearly thought Hajime was a failure of a student who was simply squandering Kaori's kindness. Hajime desperately wanted to shout out *She hasn't been spoiling me! And in fact, I'd really rather she leave me alone!* But he knew that if he did, his classmates would "escort" him somewhere quiet after school. Kouki was the kind of person who always thought he was right, too, so Hajime simply shut his mouth and didn't utter a single response.

Besides, there was really nothing to "fix." Hajime had already decided to make his hobbies the centerpiece of his life. His father was a game designer and his mother a girls' manga author, so he'd worked part-time at both their workplaces to gain experience in the field.

With his experience and interests, employers tended to be interested in him, as he required no extra training, and his plans for the future were all perfectly laid out. Hajime firmly believed he was taking his life seriously already, which was why he saw no need to change his habits, regardless of what anyone said to him. And if Kaori hadn't started poking her nose into his affairs, he would have been able to quietly graduate school without attracting any attention to himself.

"Yeah, I guess. Ahaha..." Which was why Hajime simply tried to laugh off Kouki's words. But, of course, the school's goddess had to go and unintentionally drop another bomb.

"What are you talking about, Kouki-kun? I'm talking to Nagumo-kun because I want to." The whole classroom broke out in an uproar at those words.

If looks could kill, Hajime would have died a hundred times over from the withering glares he received from the male students. They ground their teeth as they glowered at him, while Hiyama's crew took it a step further and began discussing what place would be best to drag Hajime during lunch break.

"Huh...? Ah, I see. You really are far too kind, Kaori."

It seemed Kouki interpreted that as Kaori being nice so as to not hurt Hajime's feelings. Though he was perfect in many respects, or perhaps exactly because of that fact, he had one rather glaring flaw. Namely that he was a little too convinced of his own righteousness. Deciding that correcting him would be too much of a pain, Hajime instead chose to escape from reality by staring out the window instead.

"I'm sorry about that. They don't mean any harm by it..." Shizuku quietly apologized to Hajime, as she was the only one present that was astute enough to grasp everyone's feelings. Hajime simply shrugged his shoulders and smiled wryly in response.

Meanwhile, the bell signaling the start of classes finally rang, and the teacher walked into the classroom. The teacher began the morning announcements, seemingly too used to the turbulent atmosphere in the classroom to care. Then, as always, Hajime drifted off to dreamland as class began.

Kaori smiled as she saw Hajime slumber. Shizuku stared at him, amazed, and mused that Hajime was quite the celebrity in a certain sense. The guys all scoffed at him while the rest of the girls stared, gazes full of scorn.

After a while, the classroom began to grow noisy again. As a habitual classroom napper, Hajime's body had naturally attuned itself to know when to wake up. Which was why his hazy consciousness was able to discern from the surrounding noise that it was lunchtime.

Hajime rummaged through his bag and brought out his lunch, a simple meal that could be finished in ten seconds, but still fully sated him. It seemed that most of the lunch-buying group had already left for the cafeteria, as there were some people missing from the classroom.

A majority of people in Hajime's class usually brought their own lunch, though, which was why around two thirds of the class still remained. Additionally, it seemed that some of the students had questions for the fourth period social studies teacher, Aiko Hatayama, and were milling about the teacher's podium.

Sluuurp! Gulp! Having finished recharging his energy in just ten seconds, Hajime laid back down on his desk, planning to get some more shut-eye. However, the school goddess, perhaps more of a devil in Hajime's case, smiled happily as she scooted her seat closer to his, preventing him from returning to his slumber.

Hajime groaned inwardly. Monday must've made him take leave of his wits. Normally he would've quickly eaten his lunch and bolted out of the classroom to find a secluded place for his afternoon nap, but two straight days of all-nighters had apparently taken their toll on him.

"That's rare, Nagumo-kun. You're still in the classroom. Did you not bring a lunch? If you'd like, you can have some of mine." As the frigid atmosphere descended upon the classroom once more, Hajime screamed internally.

I'm tired a yer crap, his exasperated mind screamed out in some strange dialect. Hajime attempted to resist the inevitable as that thought crossed his mind.

"Ah, thanks for the invitation, Shirasaki-san. But I've already finished eating my lunch, so why not eat with Amanogawa-kun instead?" He showed Kaori the remnants of his packaged lunch as he said that. The rest of his classmates would probably have hated him for refusing too, but at least it was better than spending his lunch break walking over a bed of nails.

However, such a feeble resistance meant next to nothing in the face of the great goddess, so she continued relentlessly.

"Huh?! That's all you had for lunch? That won't do at all; you need to eat a proper meal! Here, I'll give you some of mine!"

Please, please, just give me a break! Why can't you realize already?! Read the mood for once! With each passing moment, Hajime could feel the pressure mounting, and his saviors finally appeared as cold sweat started running down his back. Kouki and Ryutarou.

"Kaori, let's all eat lunch together. It seems that Nagumo needs some more sleep. And I won't allow anyone to eat Kaori's delicious handmade lunch while half-asleep!" Kouki flashed Kaori a dazzling smile as he said that pretentious line, but Kaori simply looked puzzled. Kaori was a bit slow, or rather just an airhead, so Kouki's handsome guy appeal was lost on her.

"Huh? Why do I need your permission to share my lunch, Kouki-kun?" Shizuku let out an involuntary snicker as she heard Kaori ask that question in such an earnest manner.

Kouki began laughing awkwardly and tried to change the subject, but the important point was that the four most famous people in school were sitting together with Hajime and the rest of the class was not at all happy about it. Hajime sighed deeply and continued grumbling to himself.

I wish these guys would all just get summoned to another world or something. I mean, just look at them, they're the perfect party of four. They even feel like the kind of group that'd get sent to another world. Can't some god or princess or priestess or something just summon them away from here? Trying to escape from reality, Hajime sent his thoughts out to whatever other worlds were out there. He stood up and was about to give his usual evasive answer, when suddenly he froze.

There was a glowing silver circle engraved with various geometric patterns glowing in front of Hajime, at Kouki's feet.

The rest of the students all saw the strange circle as well. Everyone was frozen in place, staring at the weird glowing pattern that, for lack of a better word, looked just like a magic circle.

The magic circle began to glow brighter and brighter, until its

light enveloped the entire classroom. The circle itself began expanding as well, and when it finally grew big enough to cover Hajime's feet, everyone became unfrozen and started screaming. Aiko-sensei, who had remained in the classroom, yelled "Everyone! Get out of the classroom!" at the same time the magic circle flared up in a brilliant explosion of light.

After a few seconds, or maybe a few minutes, the light finally began to fade, and color returned to the classroom. However, the room was now deserted. Some chairs were knocked over, half-eaten lunches were sitting on desks, and chopsticks and plastic bottles were scattered across the room. The classroom had everything still left in it except the people.

The mass high school disappearance incident caused quite a stir across the world, but that story is better saved for another time.

ARIFURETA:

ARIFURETA SHOKUGYOU DE SEKAISAIKYOU

FROM COMMONPLACE
TO WORLD'S STRONGEST

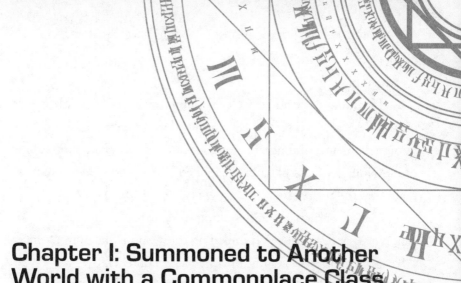

Chapter I: Summoned to Another World with a Commonplace Class

Hajime, who'd covered his eyes with both hands and kept them tightly shut, slowly realized that the people around him were muttering something, and he timidly opened his eyes. He was struck dumb at the sight of his surroundings.

The first thing his eyes registered was a massive mural. The mural, which stretched ten meters long, depicted a faintly smiling figure, whose gender seemed indeterminable, wreathed in a halo, their blond hair flowing freely behind them. Behind them in the background were plains, lakes, and mountains. The figure had both arms spread wide as if trying to grab hold of all of it. It was a truly beautiful, awe-inspiring work of art. But for some reason, Hajime felt chills run down his spine as he gazed upon it, and he soon averted his eyes.

As he examined the rest of his surroundings, he quickly realized that he was in a vast chamber. The entire room was constructed of a gleaming white stone that seemed smooth to the touch. Marble, possibly. Massive pillars with sculptures carved into them rose up to the towering domed ceiling. The room resembled some sort of grand cathedral.

Hajime and the others were standing atop a type of plinth located in the deepest recesses of the room. They were raised above their immediate surroundings. Hajime's classmates were all looking around dumbfounded, just like him. It looked like whatever happened had affected the entire class.

Hajime turned around, looking to see what lay behind him. As he'd expected, Kaori was slumped on the ground. She didn't seem to have any injuries, so Hajime breathed a sigh of relief.

After confirming her safety, Hajime returned his gaze to the crowd of people surrounding him, who he assumed would be the ones to provide an explanation for their current situation.

Indeed, Hajime and his classmates were not the only occupants of the room. Around thirty or so people were standing before the plinth Hajime and the others were on. It looked as if they were all praying, their hands crossed about their chests.

They were all clad in white robes decorated with gold embroidery. At their sides was something resembling a bishop's stave. The tips of their staves opened up into a fan shape, and instead of rings, several flat discs hung from the ends.

Eventually, one of the priests stepped forward. He was an old man in his seventies, dressed even more lavishly than his peers, with a richly decorated monk's cap that stood about thirty centimeters tall. Old was perhaps not the best word to describe him. If not for his deeply wrinkled face and aged eyes, one might think him a man in his early fifties.

His staff jingled as he walked, clear soothing notes reverberating throughout the halls all the while. Finally, he opened his mouth and said,

"Welcome to Tortus, brave heroes. It is our pleasure to welcome you here. I am the pope of the Holy Church, Ishtar Langbard. It is an honor to make your acquaintances." The old man, who called himself Ishtar, broke out into a good-natured smile. He then led the still-confused group of students into another room that was furnished with numerous chairs and long tables, saying it would be easier to speak calmly there.

The new room he'd guided the students to was just as lavishly built as the first. The exemplary craftsmanship of the furniture and the tapestries hanging on the walls was evident even to the students' untrained eyes. The layout of the room implied that it was some manner of banquet hall. Aiko Hatayama and Kouki's group of four all claimed seats at the head of their respective tables, and their followers all arranged themselves around them. Hajime ended up at the very end of his table.

The reason no one had made a fuss so far was because everyone was still too busy processing what had just happened. Besides, Ishtar had just said he would explain what had happened, and Kouki, with his max-level charisma, had managed to calm everyone down. Aiko-sensei had tears in her eyes as she watched a student do what should have been the teacher's job.

The moment everyone had finished seating themselves, a number of carts entered the room, pushed along by a retinue of maids. Actual maids, to boot! Not those sham maids found in a certain electronics holy land, nor those old, plump maids that could still be found in various European countries. They were bona-fide maids, the kind every man dreamed of meeting!

Even in such an incomprehensible situation, insatiable curiosity and libido drove most of the boys to gaze longingly at the beautiful maids. When the girls saw how they melted over the maids, they glared at the boys in a manner cold enough to freeze hell itself.

Hajime was also just about ready to ogle the maid who'd started serving him a drink, but he felt a glacial stare piercing his back and decided to keep his gaze fixed straight ahead. After a moment, he risked a glance back in the direction he'd felt the stare from, only to see Kaori beaming happily at him. He decided to pretend he'd never felt anything odd.

Ishtar finally began talking once everyone had been served their refreshments.

"Now then, I am certain you all must be feeling very confused about the situation you've found yourselves in. I shall explain everything, starting from the beginning. All I ask is that you hear me out until the end." Ishtar's explanation was so generic and unreasonable that it seemed as if it'd come out of a fantasy book template.

In short, this was what he said: First, that this world was called Tortus. Within Tortus lived three different races: humans, demons, and demi-humans. Humans resided in the northern half of the continent, demons on the southern half, and demi-humans far to the east within a massive forest.

Humans and demons had a strained relationship, having been at war for hundreds of years. Though demons lacked the sheer numbers humans possessed, their individual strength far surpassed that of most humans, balancing out the difference nicely. Both sides were currently locked in a stalemate, and a major battle hadn't broken out in decades. However, there had been disturbing movements among the demons as of late. Namely the fact that they had managed to tame monsters.

Monsters were supposedly wild animals that had undergone a magical metamorphosis after having mana poured into them. Though it seemed that humans had yet to fully understand the biology of monsters, so they weren't quite sure. They were apparently very powerful and even capable of using magic, which made them an extremely dangerous threat.

Up until that point, very few people had been able to tame such ferocious beasts. And even those who could were unable to handle more than one or two at a time. However, the situation had changed. Which meant that the only advantage the humans had over the demons, numbers, had been eliminated. As such, humans faced an unprecedented crisis that threatened the existence of their very race.

"The one who summoned you all here was the blessed lord, Ehit. He is the guardian deity of us humans, and the one true god of the Holy Church. The supreme ruler who created the world itself. I suspect Lord Ehit grew aware of our plight. He realized that humanity was doomed to annihilation, so he summoned you here in order to prevent such a disaster. You heroes are humans from a world greater than ours, and therefore carry within you strength that surpasses the humans of this world."

Ishtar paused for a moment before continuing hesitantly. "Or at least, that is what was shown to me in a divine revelation."

"Regardless, I implore you all to do as Lord Ehit has willed you. Please, defeat the demons and save the human race from destruction." He seemed almost in a trance as he said that. He had to have been remembering the time he received that divine revelation.

According to Ishtar, over ninety percent of humans revered the creator god Ehit, and those who received his divine visions were without exception given high-ranking positions in the Holy Church. As Hajime was mulling over how twisted a world must be for people to happily believe in "the will of god" without question, and how dangerous such a belief was, someone stood up and began hotly protesting Ishtar's words. That someone was the teacher Aiko.

"You can't possibly be serious! You're telling these children to go fight in a war?! That's absolutely unacceptable! As a teacher, I cannot allow it! Send us back right this instant! These kids all have families back home who must be worried sick! You can't just kidnap them like this!"

Each of her words dripped with rather evident anger. Aiko, the mid-twenties social studies teacher, was very popular with the kids. She stood only 140 centimeters tall, with a baby face, her hair kept in a neat bob cut. Her childlike appearance, as well as her tendency to run around doing everything she could for the sake of her students (though most of her efforts were for naught), had endeared her to many. The gap between how hard she tried and how helpful she actually ended up being had made most of the students see her as a kid that needed to be protected more than an adult to be respected.

Many of them had taken to calling her by the nickname Ai-chan, though she always grew angry when they did. Since she was aiming to be a respected teacher, she disliked being called by familiar nicknames.

This time too, she flared up at Ishtar to protest the unreasonable forced summoning in order to look like a proper teacher. Unfortunately, the students regarded her the same as always, thinking something to the effect of "Look, Ai-chan's at it again. Always trying so hard," as she tore into Ishtar. However, Ishtar's next words froze everyone's blood cold.

"I understand your feelings, however... I am unable to return you to your world at present."

Silence filled the room. The oppressive atmosphere was felt by everyone present. They all stared at Ishtar blankly, unable to properly process what he had just said.

"Wh-what do you mean...you're *unable*?! If you called us here, you should be able to send us back, shouldn't you?!" Aiko-sensei screamed loudly.

"As I stated earlier, it is Lord Ehit who summoned you here. The only reason we were in that room at all was to greet you heroes, and to offer up our prayers to Lord Ehit. We humans do not possess the power to interfere with other worlds, so whether or not you can return also depends on His will."

"N-no way..."

Aiko slumped back into her chair, all the strength drained out of her. The other students all started yelling as the truth of Ishtar's words sank in.

"You've gotta be kidding me! What do you mean we can't go back?!"

"You can't do this! Please, just send us back somehow!"

"A war?! You can't be serious! Take us the hell back, right now!"

"This can't be happening, this can't be happening, this can't be happening..."

The entire class fell into a panic. Hajime was shaken by this development as well, but because he was an otaku, he had at least seen countless books and games that had the same premise. Which was why he was able to determine that it was not the worst possible scenario.

That was the reason he was at least somewhat calmer than the other students. For reference, the worst-case scenario he was imagining was the one in which they all got summoned as slaves.

Ishtar said nothing and silently watched on as all of the students panicked. Though Ishtar was silent, Hajime thought he could see contempt hidden within the depths of the old man's eyes. Hajime presumed he was thinking, *These people were chosen by god, why are they not rejoicing?* or something along those lines.

Kouki stood up amidst the hysterical group of students and slammed his fist down onto the table with a bang. That managed to get the attention of most of the kids. Once he had confirmed that everyone's eyes were on him, Kouki began speaking.

"Everyone, there's no point in complaining to Ishtar. There's nothing he can do about it now. And... and I, at least, have decided to stand and fight. These people are about to be annihilated. Knowing that, how can I possibly leave them to such a tragic fate? And besides, if we've been summoned here to save humanity, it's possible we'll be allowed to go back once we've saved them... Well, Ishtar-san? Do you think that's possible?"

"It is as you say. Lord Ehit is not so unkind that he would ignore a request from his chosen heroes."

"And we've all gained some amazing powers, right? Ever since I arrived here, it's felt like I've somehow grown way stronger."

"Yes, that is correct. It would be safe to assume that each of you have the equivalent strength of anywhere from a few to few dozen regular men."

"All right, then we should be fine. I'm going to fight. If we save everyone, then we can go home. So just you watch! I'm going to save everyone, including us!" Kouki clenches his fists tightly as he proclaimed his noble intentions, flashing an almost sickeningly dazzling smile at the end.

At the same time, his overwhelming charisma started taking effect. Students who were despairing mere moments ago began to regain their sense of composure. They all looked at Kouki with wonder, as if they were staring at hope itself. Most of the female students had adoration mixed into their gaze as well.

"Heh, knew you'd say that. Still, I'd be worried letting you go off on your own... Which is why I'm coming with you."

"Ryutarou..."

"Looks like that's the only choice we have right now. It pisses me off that we don't get any real say in the matter, but...I'll help too."

"Shizuku..."

"I-If Shizuku-chan's going to fight, then I will too!"

"Kaori..."

The usual group of friends all chimed in with their support for Kouki. Swept along by the flow, the rest of the students naturally all agreed to fight as well. Aiko-sensei was in tears as she ran between her students, imploring them to stop. However, she was ultimately powerless, completely unable to keep Kouki's charisma from infecting the rest of the class.

In the end, everyone agreed to help fight in this world's war. However, most students probably had no idea what war was really like, nor did they even want to fathom it. In a sense, they might have just been trying to escape from reality to preserve their own sanity.

Hajime was considering all of those factors as he observed Ishtar out of the corner of his eye. Ishtar had a rather satisfied smile on his face, something which Hajime took note of.

Ishtar had been discreetly monitoring Kouki as he had given his speech, mentally jotting down how he reacted to which words. Kouki, who had always had a strong sense of justice, had reacted quickly when Ishtar spoke of the tragedy that had befallen the human race. And Ishtar had made sure to emphasize the cruelty and brutality of the demons when he saw Kouki's reaction to his words.

After all, it was obvious that Ishtar had seen right through Kouki. He had realized who among their group held the most influence.

Hajime supposed that as the top leader of a global religious institution, it stood to reason that Ishtar would be so discerning, but he still mentally filed him away as someone to watch out for.

Regardless, since they had chosen to assist the humans in their war, they now needed to learn how to fight. No matter how amazing their newfound powers were, they were still high school students that had been living in the peaceful country of Japan. It would've been impossible for them to just start fighting against demons and monsters without any training.

However, it seemed Ishtar had prepared for that eventuality as well, since he explained to the students that there were people ready to receive them in the Heiligh Kingdom. Said kingdom was apparently at the foot of the divine mountain, and the temple they were currently in was the head temple of the Holy Church that stood at its summit.

The kingdom had very close ties with the Holy Church—according to legend, one of Ehit's progeny, Sharam Vaan, had founded the kingdom. Of all the human kingdoms, it was apparently the one with the richest history. The fact that the Church's most sacred temple was in the kingdom's backyard spoke volumes about how deep their connection ran.

Hajime and the others headed for the temple's front gate. They were about to embark on their journey to the kingdom below. As they walked through the grand triumphal arches that comprised the main gate of the temple, they were greeted by an endless sea of clouds. Because no one had suffered from altitude sickness, they hadn't realized they'd been up so high up. Hajime assumed that magic had something to do with making the environment around the temple habitable. They all stood in wonder as they stared at the clear blue sky and the waves of clouds sparkling in the sunlight.

Ishtar looked on proudly as everyone gawked, before urging them onward. As they made their way forward, they came upon a massive white circular pedestal that was surrounded by a fence. They walked through a lavish hallway made of the same white stone as the cathedral and stepped up onto the pedestal.

Engraved within the stone of the pedestal was a large magic circle. On the other side of the fence lay a steep drop to the clouds below, so most students huddled as close to the center of the pedestal as they could. But they were unable to restrain their curiosity, and timidly glanced around their surroundings despite their fear. As they were looking around, Ishtar began to chant:

"Faith is the key that opens the road to heaven—Celestial Path."

The magic circle began emitting a blinding light as he finished chanting. The entire pedestal began gliding down toward the ground, as if attached to some invisible cable. It appeared that Ishtar's chant had been an activation signal of sorts. It functioned exactly like a fantasy cable car. The students all started clamoring excitedly as they saw their first display of magic. There was quite the ruckus when they passed through the sea of clouds, too.

Once on the other side, the students could finally make out the ground below. Directly below them was a huge city, or rather, a small kingdom. A huge castle that looked as if it were jutting out of the mountainside lay at its center, with the rest of the city spreading outward in a circle. The capital city of Heiligh. The magical cable car seemingly ran from the Holy Church down to the roof of one of the castle's towers via some aerial pathway.

Hajime smiled sardonically at the extravagant theatrics. The entire journey had clearly been crafted to resemble "God's disciples descending down from heaven," or some such feat. It was quite likely that with a display so ostentatious, some of the more ardent believers would come to worship not just Hajime and his companions, but the priests of the order who had escorted them down as well.

Hajime recalled what he had read in history books about pre-war Japan. A time when religion and politics were very closely tied to each other. And it was those very ties that had brought about a great tragedy. In the end, it was quite possible that this world was even more twisted than ancient Japan was. After all, this was a world in which a supernatural being powerful enough to interfere with other worlds existed. It wouldn't have been surprising at all if the whole world literally revolved around God's will.

This entire world, including everyone's chances of returning home, all rested in the palm of God's hand. As the outline of the capital grew more detailed, Hajime felt an inexplicable sense of unease well up inside him. He shook away the oppressive thoughts and reminded himself that he had to focus on doing what he could for the time being.

The moment they landed atop the royal palace, Hajime and the others were escorted to the throne room. The hallways they passed on their way were every bit as ostentatious as the temple had been. Along the way they passed by knights, servants, maids, and government officials. Everyone who passed gazed at the students with a mixture of awe and wonder. It seemed that most people were aware of who the students were.

Hajime's sense of unease continued to increase, and he furtively followed behind everyone at the end of the procession.

Ishtar and the party of heroes finally found themselves standing before a pair of massive double doors, into which numerous beautiful designs had been engraved. Two guards were standing at attention on either side of the door, and they loudly announced the group's arrival to whoever was waiting within. Then, without waiting for a reply, they swung the doors open.

Ishtar leisurely passed through the entrance, clearly at ease. All of the students timidly followed behind him, with the exception of Kouki and his friends, who were seemingly unaffected by the splendor surrounding them.

Within the room stretched a long red carpet that ended at the far wall. At its end lay a magnificent chair—or rather throne. Standing in front of the throne was a middle-aged man who radiated an aura of solemn dignity.

Next to him was presumably the queen, and next to her were a boy and a girl, both with blond hair and striking blue eyes. The boy, who was the younger of the two, seemed no more than ten years old, while the girl must have been around fourteen or fifteen. On the left side of the carpet was a line of soldiers, all clad in armor and uniforms. On the right, a line of civil officers. Altogether, there were probably around thirty people waiting in the room.

Once they were directly before the throne, Ishtar left the students and went to stand beside the king. He then proffered his hand to the king, who took it reverently and kissed it with the slightest brush of his lips. It looked like the pope was even more important than the king. Hajime sighed inwardly, as he was now certain that "God" ran the kingdom.

A flurry of self-introductions followed after that. The king's name was Eliheid S. B. Heiligh, and his wife the queen was called Luluaria. The blond boy was the prince Lundel, and the girl the princess Liliana.

Then came introductions for the knight captain, the prime minister, and other important dignitaries. As an aside, the fact that the young prince's eyes were glued onto Kaori the whole time made it clear that her charm worked on the men of this world as well.

Once the introductions had finished, a huge feast was laid out and the students were able to enjoy the dishes of a parallel world. Though, for the most part, it wasn't very different from Western food back on earth. The pink sauce and rainbow-colored drinks that were sometimes brought out was especially delicious.

Prince Lundel spent most of the meal talking with Kaori, and all the other boys stared on at them worriedly. Hajime secretly hoped the brunt of their jealousy would move away from him and on to the prince instead. Though he didn't really expect a ten-year-old boy to have much of a chance with Kaori.

After they finished their meal, Hajime and the others were introduced to the instructors they would be training with in return for being clothed and fed by the palace. Their instructors had been chosen from the ranks of active duty knights and court magicians.

The king probably wanted to strengthen the relationship between the students and his kingdom for the inevitable war to come.

Once dinner and introductions were finished, everyone was led to their own individual rooms. Hajime was certain he wasn't the only one who was dumbstruck by the huge canopy bed he found in his room. The room was so luxurious that he couldn't fully relax, but he'd already experienced quite the hectic day, so he was tired. He flopped down on his bed and fell asleep almost instantly as the tension drained out of him.

⁕⁕ ⁕⁕ ⁕⁕ ⁕⁕ ⁕⁕ ⁕⁕ ⁕⁕ ⁕⁕ ⁕⁕ ⁕⁕ ⁕⁕ ⁕⁕ ⁕⁕

Training began bright and early the next morning. Everyone was handed a twelve-centimeter by seven-centimeter silver plate. As the students stared at those strange plates, the knight captain, Meld Loggins, began explaining their function.

Hajime wondered if it was really all right to have the knight captain be the one to watch over their training, but he supposed that it would be bad for both their image and lives if the kingdom left the party of heroes' training in the hands of some amateur.

Captain Meld himself seemed to be quite happy to oversee their training, as he laughed heartily and said, "Besides, this gives me a reason to push all the boring paperwork onto my vice-captain!" It seemed the captain was perfectly content with his role, though the poor vice-captain probably was not.

"All right, you kids all got your plates? We call them status plates. As their name suggests, they take various parameters and quantify them for you. They also make for great identification cards. So long as you've got these, you'll be fine even if you get lost somewhere, so hang onto them tight, you hear?" The knight captain had a very informal way of speaking. When asked about it, he had simply said, "We'll be comrades fighting together on the battlefield, so no point in being so stiff with each other!" and even urged them to speak casually with all the other knights.

Hajime and the others found his friendly attitude pleasant. They would have found it awkward to have people far older than them showing them respect, anyway.

"You'll see that one side of the plate has a magic circle inscribed on it. Use the needles I passed out to prick your finger and drip some blood onto the circle. That will identify you as the owner of the plate. Then, if you say 'Open Status,' you'll see your current stats displayed on the plate. Oh, and don't bother asking me how it works. I've got no clue. These things are artifacts left over from ancient times."

"Artifacts?" Kouki asked, stumbling over the unfamiliar word.

"Artifacts refer to powerful magical items that we no longer have the technology to reproduce. They were supposedly all made during the age of the gods, when the creator's descendants still walked the earth. The status plates you all hold are all artifacts from that era as well, but they're the only artifacts that still see widespread use to this day. Most other artifacts are coveted national treasures, but there are enough of these plates that even average citizens own one. It's helpful, since they make for very reliable identification."

It seemed that the artifact that produced these status plates still existed as well, and every year new plates were produced under the strict supervision and control of the Holy Church.

The students all nodded in affirmation as they listened to his explanation. Once it was finished, they all gingerly pricked their fingers and rubbed the blood that welled up onto the magic circle of their plates. The magic circles flared briefly as the blood touched them. Hajime, too, rubbed some blood onto his plate.

His status plate flared up briefly as well, and like ink spreading through wool, his plate was slowly dyed a sky blue. Hajime was taken aback. The other students also looked on in surprise as their plates changed color.

Captain Meld continued his explanation of the plates after that. Apparently each person had their own distinct color of mana, and when their information was entered into their plates, the plates changed color to match it. The reason they were able to serve as such reliable identification cards was because their color and the color of their owner's mana were always the same.

So wait, my mana's light blue? Or I guess closer to sky blue? It's real pretty.

Glad that his mana wasn't pitch black or anything along those lines, Hajime looked around and saw that everyone else was also busy staring at their own colors. Kouki's was, predictably, pure white. Ryutarou's was dark green, Kaori's a very light purple, and Shizuku's the deep blue of lapis lazuli.

"I realize you're all impressed, but don't forget to check your stats, okay?" Captain Meld smiled wryly as he reminded the students to confirm their stats. His voice brought them all back to their senses, and they gave Meld a brief look before hurriedly checking their stats.

Hajime returned his own gaze back down to his status plate. On it, he found written—

HAJIME NAGUMO		Age: 17	Male
Job:	Synergist	Level:	1
Strength:	10	Agility:	10
Vitality:	10	Magic:	10
Defense:	10	M. Defense:	10
Skills:	Transmute • Language Comprehension		

—the above information. Hajime felt that he'd almost turned into some kind of video game character as he looked at his stats. Everyone else was also absorbed in reading their plates. Seeing that, Captain Meld began explaining the different stats.

"Everyone got a good look their stats? All right, let me explain them from the top. First, we have your level. See it? That number grows as your other stats grow. The highest level is 100, and when you've reached that you're at your limits as a human being. In other words, one's current level shows how much of their full potential they've realized. Reaching 100 means unlocking all of your latent potential, and is a cap beyond which you cannot grow. Very few people manage to make it to level 100, though."

So it wasn't exactly like a game, since raising your stats increased your level and not the other way around.

"Your stats will naturally increase as you train, and you can also use magic or magic-imbued items to raise your stats. Also, those with a high magic stat will naturally grow faster than others. No one knows exactly why, but we assume it's because a person's mana assists in the growth of other stats. Later on, you'll all get to choose equipment that corresponds to your individual stats. The items in our treasury will be yours for the taking! You're the heroes who are going to save our kingdom, after all!" Judging by Captain Meld's explanation, defeating a monster wouldn't magically increase one's stats. Everyone just had to train the old-fashioned way.

"Next up, do you all see that little box that says 'job' in it? Put simply, that refers to your natural aptitude. It's directly linked to the skills box in the bottom, and your job determines the kind of skills you can learn. Few people possess a job. Jobs are split into combat-based and non-combat-based disciplines. Combat jobs are exceedingly rare. Only one in every thousand—or, depending on the job, ten thousand—people have a combat-based job. Non-combat jobs are technically rare too, but...well, one in every hundred people has one. Some of them are even common enough that one in every ten people has one, actually. There's a lot of people who have non-combat, production related jobs."

Hajime looked back down at his status plate. His job was "Synergist." Which meant his talents had to do with synergizing, whatever that was supposed to be.

Ishtar had said that Hajime and the others came from a world superior to their own, and that they possessed better abilities than the humans of Tortus due to that fact. *Then it's only natural that I have a job,* thought Hajime, as his lips curled up into a smile. There was no person who wouldn't be happy to be told they were gifted with a special talent.

However, at Captain Meld's next words, Hajime's smile vanished and was replaced by a cold sweat.

"Next...well, your stats are simply what they say they are. The average for most stats at level 1 is around 10. But you're all heroes, so you surely have far higher stats than that! Man, I'm so jealous of you guys! Oh yes, don't forget to report your stats to me. I'll need to know them to decide how to best train you guys." The average stats for someone at level 1 were around 10. And each and every one of Hajime's stats were a perfect 10. His mind raced furiously as cold sweat poured down his back.

Huh? Doesn't that mean that my stats are totally average...? Like completely and utterly mediocre? I don't have any godlike cheat powers? My power level isn't over 9000? Wh-What about everyone else? Maybe everyone's just like this at the start... Hajime clung onto this last sliver of hope as he furtively glanced around at the other students. Everyone's eyes were sparkling as they looked at their stats. Not a single one of them was breaking out in a cold sweat like Hajime.

Kouki was the first to step up and show his stats to Captain Meld. His stats were as follows—

KOUKI AMANOGAWA		Age: 17	Male
Job:	Hero	Level:	1
Strength:	100	Agility:	100
Vitality:	100	Magic:	100
Defense:	100	M. Defense:	100
Skills:	Elemental affinity • Elemental Resistance • Physical Resistance • Advanced Sorcery • Swordsmanship • Superhuman Strength • Armor Proficiency • Foresight • Increased Mana Recovery • Detect Presence • Detect Magic • Limit Break • Language Comprehension		

The guy was a living personification of cheat skills.

"Whoa, you really are a hero. You already have stats in the triple digits at level 1! And most people normally only get two or three skills! You're way beyond normal. What a reliable hero!"

"Well, you know how it is... Ahaha..." Kouki blushed and scratched his head as Captain Meld praised him.

As an aside, Captain Meld was level 62. His stats were all within the 300 range, and he was one of the strongest humans alive. But at just level 1, Kouki was already a third of the way to his strength. If his growth rates were just as high, he'd overtake the captain in no time.

In addition, it seemed as if your skills were basically the innate talents you were born with, so there was no way to increase them. The exception being derivative skills. Those were skills that were acquired by spending a lifetime polishing one's talents, something one acquired by surpassing their limits in a certain field. Put simply, it was when someone suddenly discovered the trick to doing something they'd always struggled to before, and rapidly increased their proficiency with it.

Hajime had hoped Kouki was just somehow special, but everyone else also had overpowered abilities, though none quite matched up to Kouki's. And it looked like everyone else, without exception, had a combat-based job.

Hajime stared at the word—Synergist—that filled his job box. From the name alone, he found it hard to imagine it was a combat-based job. He only had two skills too. To make matters worse, one of them was Language Comprehension, which every summoned being had. In other words, he effectively only had one skill. Even Hajime's stiff smile began vanishing from his face. Finally, it was his turn to show his stats, so he presented his plate to Captain Meld.

Captain Meld was ecstatic after having seen how ridiculous everyone's stats had been. He was probably elated to have so many overpowered allies. But his smile froze in place when he saw Hajime's plate. He muttered "Did I just misread it?" and began rapping the plate with his knuckles, then shone some light on it. After staring at it for a long time, he finally returned the plate to Hajime with a complicated expression.

"Umm, well, you see... A Synergist is basically a blacksmith of sorts. It might come in handy if you plan on opening a smithy, but otherwise..." Captain Meld muttered out a poor explanation of Hajime's role.

Hajime was certain the boys in his class, who all hated him, would jump at this new chance to belittle him. Blacksmithing was clearly not a combat-based job. The rest of his classmates all had combat-based jobs, and he highly doubted his particular job would be of much use in battle.

Daisuke Hiyama grinned wickedly as he hollered out to Hajime, "Hey Nagumo. Don't tell me you seriously got a non-combat job? How's a blacksmith gonna fight monsters? Hey Meld, is this Synergist or whatever a rare job?"

"No, not particularly. One in every ten people has it. In fact, all of the craftsmen the kingdom employs have the job."

"Gimme a break, Nagumo. You're gonna fight with something like that?" Hiyama folded his arms provocatively as he said those words. As Hajime looked around, he could see that most of his classmates, the boys especially, were all laughing at him.

"Who knows. You never know until you try."

"Show us your stats then, if you're so confident. They better be way high to make up for your crappy job."

Hiyama had most likely already guessed Hajime's stats from Captain Meld's expression, but he simply wanted an excuse to bully Hajime some more. He possessed quite a nasty personality. His three flunkies all jeered at Hajime as well. They were the kind of stereotypical thugs that bullied the weak and groveled before the mighty. Their actions were so clearly malicious that Kaori and Shizuku both glared at them, eyes full of disdain.

Despite how smitten they were with her, none of them seemed to realize she disliked such bullying. Hajime lazily handed his plate over to Hiyama.

When he saw the stats engraved on it, Hiyama burst out laughing. He passed the plate down to his other underlings and they all sneered or laughed at Hajime as well.

"Bwahahaha... What the hell, man! You're like totally average! Actually, 10's exactly average, so I bet there are even some babies out there stronger than you!"

"Hyahahaha, you've gotta be kidding me! This guy's not even gonna last ten minutes! He'd die so fast that you couldn't even use him as a meat shield!"

Unable to stand it any longer, Kaori opened her mouth to give them a piece of her mind. But before she could get out a single word, someone else began yelling at them. That someone was Aiko-sensei.

"Hey! Stop laughing at him! I won't allow anyone to laugh at their classmates on my watch! As a teacher, I absolutely will not condone it! Now return Nagumo-kun's plate this instant!"

The boys were all taken aback by how much anger was visible in

Aiko-sensei's small frame. They hurriedly returned Hajime's plate in order to avoid her wrath. Aiko-sensei turned to Hajime and gave him an encouraging pat on the shoulder.

"Nagumo-kun, don't worry about your job! Look, I got a non-combat job too! And aside from my job, most of my stats are pretty average too! You're not alone!"

Aiko-sensei then showed her pink colored plate to Hajime with a "Here, look!"

HATAYAMA AIKO		Age: 25	Female
Job:	Farmer	Level:	1
Strength:	5	Agility:	5
Vitality:	10	Magic:	100
Defense:	10	M. Defense:	10
Skills:	Soil Management • Soil Restoration • Large-scale Cultivation • Enhanced Fertilization • Selective Breeding • Plant Appraisal • Fertilizer Production • Mixed Breeding • Auto Harvesting • Fermentation Proficiency • Wide-area Temperature Control • Farming Barrier • Fertile Rain • Language Comprehension		

Hajime's eyes resembled a dead fish's once he finished reading Aiko's plate.

"Huh? What's wrong, Nagumo-kun?!" Aiko asked as she shook Hajime back and forth.

It was true that her overall stats were low, and that she did not possess a combat class, but her exceptional magic stat and large number of skills meant that she would reach the level of other heroes with just a little training. And lest everyone forget, an army marches on its stomach. Aiko-sensei's job was nothing like Hajime's. His was so commonplace that there were myriad others who were more proficient in it. In other words, even Aiko-sensei was plenty overpowered.

Hajime felt doubly betrayed by her getting his hopes up, even a little.

"Oh my, Ai-chan, that was the final nail in the coffin..."

"N-Nagumo-kun! Are you all right?!"

Shizuku smiled sadly as she watched Hajime shut down, while Kaori worriedly ran over to him. Aiko-sensei tilted her head in confusion. As always, she tried her best, but ended up being completely unhelpful. The students smiled at her unchanging ditziness. Aiko-sensei had managed to achieve her initial goal of preventing Hajime's bullying, but he still smiled emptily as he thought of the difficulties that lay ahead, and the treatment he would definitely receive.

❖ ❖ ❖ ❖ ❖ ❖ ❖ ❖ ❖ ❖ ❖ ❖ ❖ ❖

Two weeks had passed since Hajime was labeled the weakest and most useless member of the class. He was currently in the library using the break time he had between training sessions to investigate something. In his hands was a book labeled *Monsters of the Northern Continent, a Picture Book.* As its name suggested, it was a picture book about monsters.

As for why he was reading such a book, that was because he had not grown at all after two weeks of training. In fact, the past two weeks had only served to highlight how pathetically weak he was. Hoping to cover his physical deficiencies with knowledge, Hajime spent most of his free time in the library.

He perused the picture book for a while before suddenly breathing out a sigh and throwing it down on the desk. The librarian happened to be passing by right as he did that, so Hajime was met with a glowering stare.

Hajime jumped, as he was clearly startled, and hurriedly apologized. The librarian's angry glare implied that he wouldn't tolerate it happening a second time. *What on earth am I doing?* Hajime thought with a sigh.

Hajime suddenly took out his status plate and stared at it, his hands resting on his chin.

HAJIME NAGUMO		Age: 17	Male
Job:	Synergist	Level:	2
Strength:	12	Agility:	12
Vitality:	12	Magic:	12
Defense:	12	M. Defense:	12
Skills:	Transmute • Language Comprehension		

That was all the growth he had to show after two weeks of harsh training. *I can't even say I've gotten much stronger!* Hajime screamed internally. For comparison, Kouki's stats had grown at an astronomical rate.

KOUKI AMANOGAWA		Age: 17	Male
Job:	Hero	Level:	10
Strength:	200	Agility:	200
Vitality:	200	Magic:	200
Defense:	200	M. Defense:	200
Skills:	Elemental Affinity • Elemental Resistance • Physical Resistance • Advanced Sorcery • Swordsmanship • Superhuman Strength • Armor Proficiency • Foresight • Increased Mana Recovery • Detect Presence • Detect Magic • Limit Break • Language Comprehension		

His growth rate was roughly five times as fast as Hajime's. And to make matters worse, Hajime had discovered he had no real affinity for magic.

What exactly did having no magical affinity mean? Well, it had to do with how magic functioned in this world. In the world of Tortus, magic functioned in a very specific manner. By chanting an incantation, one could transfer their mana into a magic circle, and the spell inscribed within that circle would activate, thus casting magic. It was impossible for anyone to directly manipulate their mana, so each spell needed its own corresponding magic circle.

Additionally, the length of an incantation was directly proportional to how much mana one could pour into a magic circle, so the effectiveness of a spell was directly proportional to the amount of mana used to cast it. And the more complicated a spell was, or the larger an area of effect it had, the more inscriptions were needed in the magic circle to complete the spell. Which naturally meant that the magic circle itself needed to be larger too.

For comparison, the standard fireball spell that appeared in most RPGs and the like normally required a magic circle about ten centimeters in diameter. Every spell needed the basic inscriptions for the element, strength, range, span, and magic absorption (the amount of mana someone needed to provide the magic circle in order to activate the spell). If one wanted to add additional parameters such as length the spell is maintained, then extra inscriptions were needed for that as well.

There was, however, an exception to this rule. And that exception was magical affinity.

Magical affinity was basically a measure of how well one's natural constitution allowed them to shorten inscriptions. For example, someone with an affinity for the fire element would no longer need to add the element portion of the inscription to their spell as long as it was a fire-based one. People with an aptitude for something were able to use a mental image to take the place of the inscription. They didn't need to carve the inscription anywhere into the magic circle. By simply imagining flames while chanting the spell, they were capable of adding the fire element to it.

Most people had some level of magical affinity, which meant that the aforementioned ten-centimeter magic circle would generally be smaller. However, Hajime had absolutely no affinity for magic whatsoever, meaning that on top of inscriptions for the basic five properties, he had to include inscriptions for the trajectory, spread, and even conclusion for each of his spells. For him, the standard fireball spell required a magic circle two meters in diameter, making magic completely impractical in combat.

On a somewhat related topic, magic circles came in two different types. The more common of the two were magic circles drawn onto a special kind of disposable paper. The other type were magic circles carved into specific minerals. The former allowed for many different variations of spells, but they burned out after one use and their power was generally on the low side. On the other hand, the latter were bulky and limited in the spells they could cast, but they were reusable and far more powerful than their paper counterparts. The staves Ishtar and the other priests carried all had mineral-type magic circles engraved into them.

Because of his low stats, close combat was impossible, and because of his lack of magical affinity, he could not rely on magic either. The only skill his job had provided him, Transmute, simply allowed him to transform the shape of various ores, or forge them together into alloys. It was effectively useless. He was also told there were no useful artifacts for Synergists, and was simply given a pair of gloves with related magic circles inscribed into them.

After a lot of training, he was finally able to make pitfalls and protrusions in the ground, and the more he trained, the larger he was able to make their sizes, but...he had to be in direct contact with the target to activate them. Running up in front of an enemy and then squatting down to put his hands on the ground was no better than suicide, so even those skills were of no real help to him in combat.

Over the past two weeks, Hajime had come to be treated as a complete waste of space by his classmates. He had attempted to increase his knowledge as a last-ditch attempt to somehow become useful, but even that prospect seemed to have dim hopes, so he sighed more and more frequently as time went on.

If I'm going to be useless around here, I might as well just go out on a journey or something, Hajime thought, as he stared out the library window. He had reached the end of his rope. Hajime had spent the last two weeks devoting himself more than anyone else to the lectures they were being given about the world, spending all his time thinking of where to go.

I'm thinking the land of demi-humans would probably be best... I can't really say I've been to another world if I haven't even seen a single pair of animal ears. But supposedly their territory is really deep within the sea of trees. And they're apparently discriminated against everywhere, so aside from a few slaves, you don't really see many of them outside their homeland.

According to what Hajime had learned so far, the demi-humans were harshly discriminated against, so they lived deep within the Haltina Woods to avoid contact with other people. They were supposedly discriminated against because they didn't possess any mana.

Legend stated that starting with Ehit, each of the gods shaped the very foundations of the world with magic. The magic everyone used now was supposedly a deteriorated version of the power the gods once held. For that reason, it was common belief that magic itself was a gift from the gods. Of course, said belief was strengthened by the fact that the Holy Church preached it as the truth. Because of that, demi-humans, who didn't possess mana and were unable to use magic, were seen as wicked creatures who'd been abandoned by the gods.

This had naturally led Hajime to question, "But what about

monsters?" However, it seemed that monsters were simply thought of as natural disasters, so no one considered them creatures who had received "God's blessing" or anything along those lines, and they were seen as nothing more than wild beasts. *What a convenient interpretation,* Hajime thought, clearly disgusted.

Even worse, though the demons all worshiped a god different from the humans' "Lord Ehit," they too discriminated against the demi-humans.

Demons supposedly had a far higher magical affinity than humans, so they were able to cast spells with much shorter incantations and smaller magic circles than them. They resided in the center of the southern continent, in the demon kingdom of Garland. Though few in number, it seemed that even children in the kingdom were capable of wielding powerful offensive magic. So, in a way, every single citizen of the kingdom was a soldier.

The humans of this world saw the demons who worshiped a different god as their mortal foes, thanks to the teachings of the Holy Church, and despised the demi-humans as godless vermin. And apparently the demons were no better. Though he couldn't be sure, Hajime guessed the demi-humans just wanted to be left alone. It made sense, considering how exclusive the other two groups seemed to be.

Hmm, if navigating the huge sea of trees seems impossible, then maybe I should try for the western ocean instead? If I'm remembering right, there's a city called Erisen that sits by the sea. If I can't get my fill of animal ears, then I at least want to see some mermaids. Fantasy creatures like those are every man's dream. Plus, I want to see what the seafood's like in this world.

The coastal city of Erisen was home to a group of demi-humans known as seamen, and rested on the shores of the western ocean. They were the only group of demi-humans that the kingdom sheltered. The reason being that the city produced about eighty percent of the kingdom's seafood. Such a practical reason.

What happened to them being a godless race? Hajime had thought sarcastically when he had first heard about them.

But in order to get to the western sea from his location, one first had to cross the Gruen Desert. Two important locations that were used as waypoint markers for traders in the desert were the oasis Dukedom of Ankaji and the Grand Gruen Volcano. And the Grand Gruen Volcano was one of the seven labyrinths of the world.

The seven labyrinths referred to the seven highly dangerous locations scattered throughout the world. To the southwest of the Heiligh Kingdom, between the capital and the Gruen Desert, lay another one of them, the Great Orcus Labyrinth. The previously mentioned Haltina Woods was also another one of these labyrinths. Though they were called the seven labyrinths, in truth, only three of them had ever been documented. The rest were places that were believed to exist due to evidence provided in ancient books and other such manuscripts.

Though their existence had not been confirmed, they'd still been provisionally marked on maps. The Reisen Gorge that divided the northern and southern continents was one such place, while the Frost Caverns that lay in the Schnee Snow Fields were another potential candidate.

I probably won't be able to make it across that desert... In that case, the only way I'll ever get to see demi-humans is if I go to the empire and see the slaves they have, but I'm not sure I could bear to see those poor animal-ears suffering as slaves. The empire he'd referred to was the Hoelscher Empire. It was a country that had been formed three hundred years ago, during one of the larger wars between the humans and demons. It had been formed by a certain mercenary group, and was a militaristic country that boasted a large population of adventurers and mercenaries. They held to the doctrine that might makes right, and were a country of rather unsavory repute.

The country's citizens believed in using everything they could to further their own ends, whether that meant demi-human slaves or anything else, so the slave trade flourished there.

The empire lay to the east of the kingdom, and sandwiched between them was the independent merchant republic of Fuhren. As the name suggested, they were a neutral city that didn't rely on either country for support. Being a merchant republic, they boasted a vast amount of wealth, and the flow of money played heavily into their politics. It was also what allowed them to remain neutral. It was said that anything one's heart desired could be bought in that city, such was its economic clout.

Haaah, but if I ever want to get back home, I can't just run away... Wait, crap, it's almost time for training! Realizing that he was simply trying to avert his eyes from reality, Hajime shook his head and quickly left the library so as to not be late for training. It was only a short distance from the library to the palace, but the bustle of the capital could be seen even in such a short trek. The voices of merchants hawking their wares mingled with the happy laughter of playing children and the angry scolding of their parents. The capital was a quaint, peaceful city.

Since it doesn't look like a war's going to break out anytime soon, maybe I can just convince them to send me back... Hajime dreamed of the impossible as he walked back to the palace. He'd just wanted to avoid thinking about the despair that awaited him once he arrived.

•/• •/• •/• •/• •/• •/• •/• •/• •/• •/• •/• •/• •/•

When he arrived at the training grounds, Hajime found a few other students already there, chatting with each other or getting some early practice in. It looked like he had arrived surprisingly early. Hajime decided to pass the time doing a bit of practice of his own, so he took out the slender longsword he'd been given.

As he did, he felt a sudden impact hit him square in the back, and he stumbled a few steps forward. He managed to avoid falling, but chills ran down his spine as he saw how close he had been to impaling himself on a drawn sword. He frowned as he turned back and saw the usual group of four all wearing the same obnoxious expression.

As always, Daisuke Hiyama was standing behind him, together with the rest of the Petty Four, as Hajime liked to call them. Ever since they'd started training, the four of them had taken every opportunity they could to bully Hajime. They were half the reason he found training so depressing, with the other half being how pathetic his stats were.

"Yo, Nagumo. What are you doing? You know that sword's totally useless in your hands anyway, right? I mean, come on, you're a total weakling!"

"Hey, man, that's going too far. I mean, you're totally right though, Hiyama... Gyahaha!"

"Why do you even bother coming to training every day? I'd be way too embarrassed if I were you!"

"Hey, Daisuke. He's just so pitiful... Don't you think we should help him out with his training a little?" Hiyama and the others laughed hysterically, as if Shinji had actually said something funny.

"Huh? Come on, Shinji, don't you think you're being a bit *too* nice to him? Well, I'm a nice guy too, so I guess I don't mind helping out."

"Yeah, that sounds like a great idea. I'm also a super nice guy, so I'll pitch in. Man, you better thank us, Nagumo. We're spending some of our precious time to help out a weakling like you." They put their arms around Hajime's shoulders in a false gesture of kindness and dragged him away to an inconspicuous location. Most of his classmates noticed, but they pretended not to see anything.

"Oh no, I'm fine by myself. You don't have to waste your time on me." Hajime tried to refuse, though he knew it was pointless.

"Huh?! Here I am going out of my way to train your sorry ass, and this is what I get? I can't believe you! You should be on your knees thanking me!"

As he said that, Hiyama punched Hajime in the side, hard. Hajime groaned in pain as he felt Hiyama's fist sink into his soft flank. Hiyama's group had steadily been getting more and more violent with him as of late. While it might've been natural for hormone-driven boys in puberty to go mad with power once they got their hands on some, that made it no easier for the one who had to bear the brunt of their lapse in sanity. Though it was not as if there was anything Hajime could do to fight back. All he could do was grit his teeth and try to bear it.

Eventually, they brought him all the way to a secluded corner of the training grounds that couldn't be easily seen. Then Hiyama thrust

Hajime down to the ground.

"Come on, get up. It's time for some fun training." Hiyama, Nakano, Saitou, and Kondou all surrounded Hajime at those words. Hajime bit his lip in frustration as he stood up.

"Gwah?!"

He felt something crash into his back as soon as he rose to his feet. Saitou had hit him with the sheath of his sword. He flew forward, groaning in pain, and was met with another attack.

"Hey now, you can't sleep there. You'll get burned if you do! Incinerate all that stands in my path—Fireball."

Nakano unleashed a fireball at Hajime. As the impact he'd just received made it impossible for him to get back up right away, Hajime frantically rolled to the side, barely avoiding the incoming fireball. However, Saitou had predicted Hajime would dodge, so he'd cast another spell in his direction.

"Rend my foes, O wind—Wind Sphere." The clod of hardened wind hit Hajime just as he was getting up, which made him double over in pain as he was blown back. He collapsed to the ground once more, throwing up.

The magic they had cast were all low-level spells with simple incantations. But even weak magic like that hit as hard as a pro boxer's punch. The reason even their weak spells hit so hard was because of their magical affinities, combined with the rare artifacts they had received from the king.

"Tch, I can't believe you're so weak. Are you even trying, Nagumo?" Hiyama lazily kicked Hajime in the stomach as he said that. Hajime desperately tried to keep his stomach from emptying itself entirely.

The hazing disguised as "training" continued for a while longer.

Hajime bit his lip, cursing his own powerlessness. Maybe he should have fought back, even if he knew he was too weak to truly achieve anything.

But Hajime had always been averse to violence. He even had trouble really hating people. He'd always folded when cornered into a situation that seemed as if it might devolve into a fight. Always believing that it would end eventually, as long as he could put up with it. And that bearing it was always better than fighting back. Some people thought him kind for it, while others simply saw him as a loser. Hajime himself wasn't sure which he was.

Around the time the pain had grown nearly unbearable, Hajime suddenly heard a girl's angry voice.

"What do you think you're doing?!"

Hiyama and the others paled when they heard that voice. It was only natural. After all, it belonged to the girl they were all smitten with, Kaori. And not just her. Shizuku, Kouki, and Ryutarou were all with her.

"Umm, please don't misunderstand anything. We were just helping Hajime with his training..."

"Nagumo-kun!"

Kaori ignored Hiyama's excuses and ran over to Hajime, who was huddled on the ground, coughing. Hiyama and the others had ceased to matter at all to Kaori when she saw the state Hajime was in.

"Training, huh? Wouldn't you say that was a bit too one-sided to be called training?" Shizuku uttered those words in an icy tone.

"We were just..."

"Save your breath. No matter how unfit for battle Nagumo-kun may be, he's still our classmate. Make sure you don't do it again," Kouki calmly interjected.

"If you've got time to be messing around, then work on your own damn skills instead!" Ryutarou bellowed.

Hiyama and everyone else started giving different excuses as they smiled awkwardly and beat a hasty retreat. Kaori cast some healing magic on Hajime, and he gradually felt the pain recede.

"Th-thank you, Shirasaki-san. You saved me."

Hajime smiled painfully and Kaori shook her head at his words, her eyes filled with tears.

"Do they always do things like that to you? If so, I'll..." Kaori glared angrily in the direction Hiyama and the others ran off to, but Hajime hurriedly stopped her.

"No, no, it's not always this bad! I'm fine, really, so please don't mind me!"

"But..."

Kaori didn't seem fully convinced, so Hajime smiled and said, "I'm fine, really." At those words, Kaori reluctantly gave in.

"Nagumo-kun, if anything else happens, please, for Kaori's sake too, tell us right away." Shizuku said that with a sidelong glance at Kaori, a strained expression on her face all the while. Hajime was about to thank her for her concern, but the resident hero had to go and ruin the mood.

"But you know, Nagumo, you need to put in some effort of your own. You'll never grow strong if you keep using your weakness as an excuse. I've been hearing that you're spending all your time in the library when we're not training. If I was in your shoes, I'd spend every spare moment training to get stronger. I really think you need to start taking this more seriously, Nagumo. Don't you think Hiyama and the others might have done this because they were trying to fix that frivolous attitude of yours?"

No matter what Hajime did, Kouki always interpreted it like that. Hajime was dumbstruck for a moment before he remembered that Amanogawa-kun was the kind of person who believed that all people were inherently good, and filtered everything he saw through that worldview.

To Kouki, it was actually unthinkable on a fundamental level that humans could be so cruel. If that was how he saw everything, then it stood to reason that he believed there was a proper reason behind all cruel acts. "Maybe the problem was with the person they were attacking!" was a natural conclusion to draw with that kind of mindset.

Kouki's words contained no real ill will. His warnings toward Hajime were actually sincere, in fact. That was why Hajime no longer possessed the strength to even try and correct Kouki. Besides, it was pointless to say anything to someone so convinced of their own righteousness.

Shizuku knew that as well, so she put a hand over her mouth to stifle a sigh before apologizing to Hajime.

"Sorry about that. Kouki at least means well."

"Ahaha, yeah, I know. Don't worry about it." Hajime smiled and replied with the same reassuring words he always did. He slowly stood up, brushing the dust off his clothes.

"Anyway, it's almost time for training to start. Shall we head back?" They all walked back to the training grounds together at Hajime's insistence. Kaori kept shooting him worried glances, but Hajime pretended not to notice. As a man, it felt somewhat wrong to let himself be doted on by a girl the same age.

As they returned to the training grounds, Hajime breathed a sigh for the umpteenth time that day. The road ahead certainly looked grim for him.

Normally the students were given free time after training until dinner, but Captain Meld held them back after training had ended on that day. The students all looked at him curiously, and once he had their attention, he proclaimed loudly,

"Tomorrow, as part of your practical training, we will be going on an expedition to the Great Orcus Labyrinth. I'll prepare all the equipment you guys will need, but don't think this is going to be anything like the monster hunts you've been going on outside the capital! You guys better prepare yourselves! Get as much rest as possible tonight so you're ready! That's all—dismissed!" He kept his announcement brief, then left right after he had delivered it.

Hajime stood at the end of the line of chattering students and looked up at the sky. *Very grim indeed.*

•¦• •¦• •¦• •¦• •¦• •¦• •¦• •¦• •¦• •¦• •¦• •¦• •¦•

The Great Orcus Labyrinth. It was a massive dungeon said to span a hundred floors. As it was one of the seven great labyrinths, the deeper one went, the stronger the monsters they faced. Despite the dangers, it was a very popular training spot for adventurers, mercenaries, and new troops alike. The main reasons for that were because it was easy enough to measure the relative strength of the monsters one would have to face based on the floor they were on, and because the mana crystals contained within the monsters were of a higher quality than the ones harvested from monsters on the surface.

A mana crystal was the core of a monster; it was what made a monster a monster. The more powerful a monster, the bigger and purer a mana crystal it held inside. Mana crystals were an important component in magic circles. A magic circle only needed to be drawn to be able to cast the spell inscribed within, but it would have reduced effectiveness without powdered mana crystals used in the engraving of the circle. In fact, it would only be one third as powerful.

Mana crystals allowed for more efficient transfer of mana, which was why they improved effectiveness so much. In addition, most commonplace magical tools used mana crystals as a power source. Because they were used by the common folk and not just the military, mana crystals were always in rather high demand.

However, monsters that possessed high-quality mana crystals were also capable of using powerful specialized magic. It was specialized because while they had large quantities of mana, monsters were incapable of using magic circles or chants, meaning that they could only ever use a single type of spell. Still, being able to unleash that spell without needing a magic circle or incantation was a powerful asset. It was the number one reason one could never let their guard down when fighting a monster.

Hajime and the others arrived in the outpost town of Horaud, together with Captain Meld and a few of his knights. It was a small town that primarily existed to service the adventurers who traveled there wishing to challenge the Great Orcus Labyrinth. As the labyrinth was also used as a training arena for new soldiers, the kingdom maintained a state-run inn at the town, which was where the students were all staying.

Hajime was glad to see a normal room for once, and happily dived into his bed with a relieved sigh. Every other room had at least two people in it, but Hajime had one all for himself.

"Wow, lucky me," Hajime muttered, somewhat disappointed. He did feel a little lonely being in a room alone, after all.

Tomorrow they would all enter the labyrinth. The plan was to go no further than floor twenty, which according to Captain Meld was still high enough that the knights would be able to protect him. All Hajime could say in response were apologies for how much of a burden he was. He honestly would've preferred if they left him behind and went on by themselves...but he didn't have the courage to say that to Captain Meld, considering the atmosphere, and all.

Hajime started reading the picture book he had borrowed that described some of the monsters that inhabited the lower levels of the dungeon. After a while, however, he decided he would need as much rest as he could get, so he planted himself down in bed despite the early hour. The skills he'd developed in school to allow him to sleep in any situation still worked even in another world.

But just as he was dozing off, he heard a knock on his door that broke him out of his stupor. Though he had thought it was still a little early, that had meant early for him, who was used to pulling back-to-back all-nighters. It was actually quite late for the people of Tortus. Suspecting the unexpected late night visitor might be Hiyama and the others, Hajime tensed up. However, his fears vanished when he heard the voice on the other side of the door.

"Nagumo-kun, are you awake? It's me, Shirasaki. Can we talk for a bit?"

What on earth? Hajime stiffened up for a second before hurriedly

rushing over to the door. He quickly unbolted and opened his door. Standing on the other side was Kaori, wearing nothing but a cardigan over her pure white negligee.

"...What in tarnation?"

"Huh?" Hajime was so shocked that he unintentionally slipped into an odd accent for a moment there. Kaori looked at him blankly, so she must not have heard him right.

Hajime composed himself as best he could and asked what she wanted, while trying to avoid looking at her as much as possible. As much of a 2D advocate as he might've been, Hajime was still a teenage boy. Kaori's appearance was a bit too stimulating for him.

"Ah, umm, it's nothing. Anyway, what's up? Do you have a message for me or something?"

"No. I was hoping we could talk for a bit, Nagumo-kun...but I guess I'm being a bother, aren't I?"

"...Come on in." Hajime asked what he thought was the most likely reason for Kaori's appearance, but she bluntly refused and gave a most unexpected reply. And she had asked him with such pleading puppy dog eyes too. The combination was super effective! Before he knew it, Hajime had already thrown the door wide and invited Kaori in.

"Thanks!" Kaori happily stepped inside without any hesitation, then sat down at the table by the window.

Still somewhat confused, Hajime began reflexively brewing her some tea. Brewing might have been a bit of an overstatement, however, as it was just some crappy black tea he made by dumping some teabags into a pot of water. He made enough tea for the both of them and offered Kaori a cup. Once the tea had been served, he sat down across from her.

"Thank you." Despite the terrible quality of the tea, Kaori still accepted it graciously. She gently brought the cup to her lips, and the moonlight illuminated her figure as she did. Her black hair glowed faintly in the silver light, wreathing her in a halo. She looked almost like an angel.

Hajime stared, captivated in a purely platonic manner by her mysterious aura. He finally returned to his senses after Kaori put the cup down with a clink. In an attempt to calm himself down, Hajime downed his cup of crappy black tea in one big gulp. He choked a little as the deluge of liquid poured down his throat. Well, that was rather embarrassing.

Kaori chuckled as she saw him sputter. In order to distract himself from the embarrassment, Hajime quickly started talking.

"So, what was it you wanted to talk to me about? The dungeon trip tomorrow?" Kaori nodded in affirmation, and her smile was replaced by an unbelievably grave expression.

"I want you...to stay here when we go to the labyrinth tomorrow. I'll convince the instructors and the rest of our classmates, so please, don't go!" Kaori grew more and more heated as she spoke, and by the end she was leaning forward into Hajime, pleading with him.

For his part, Hajime was utterly bewildered. She seemed a bit too desperate to be someone who just wanted him out of the way because he would be a burden.

"Umm... I do realize I'd just get in your way, but...I don't think they'll let me skip out after I've come this far already."

"That's not it! It's not because I think you're a burden or anything!" Kaori hurriedly tried to correct Hajime's misunderstanding. Realizing she'd gotten a bit too heated, she placed a hand on her chest and took a deep breath. After calming herself down, she softly muttered, "I'm sorry," and began talking once more.

"Umm, you see, I just have this really bad feeling. I was sleeping just a moment ago, and...I was having this dream... You were in it, Nagumo-kun...but you wouldn't answer even when I called your name...and no matter how much I ran, I could never reach you... Then at the end..." Kaori faltered, afraid to say what happened next, but Hajime calmly pushed her to continue.

"And then at the end?"

Kaori bit her lip and looked up at Hajime with tears in her eyes.

"...You vanished..."

"I see..."

Silence filled the room. Hajime stared at Kaori, who was hanging her head again. That certainly sounded like a sinister dream. But in the end, it was still just a nightmare. Hajime doubted he could get permission to stay behind for a flimsy reason like that, and even if he could, his classmates would have all condemned him for it. Regardless of how it turned out, he would've had nowhere left to go if he asked. Which was why, sadly, Hajime had no choice but to go.

He spoke as gently as he could, trying his best to reassure Kaori.

"It was just a dream, Shirasaki-san. We'll have Captain Meld's veteran knights with us, along with some ridiculously strong people like Amanogawa-kun. Or rather, a ton, since all of our classmates have pretty broken skills. So much so that I actually pity our enemies a little. You probably just had that kind of dream because you've been seeing just how weak I am up close recently." Hajime's words only seemed to make Kaori even more worried.

"And... and if you're still worried..."

"Then what?"

Hajime felt a little embarrassed, but he still looked Kaori in the eyes, then muttered—

"Why don't you protect me?"

"Eh?"

Hajime realized that it was embarrassing for a man to ask such a thing of a girl. In fact, he was blushing bright red from how embarrassed he felt. The moon was shining bright, so the inside of the room was lit well enough that Kaori must've easily been able to see how red he was as well.

"Your job was Priest, right, Shirasaki-san? That's a job that excels in healing magic, isn't it? So no matter what happens to me...even if I get mortally wounded, you should be able to heal me, Shirasaki-san. So will you protect me, please? That way I'll be fine no matter what happens." Kaori stared at Hajime for a long time after hearing his words. Hajime knew he couldn't turn his eyes away in a situation like that, so he held Kaori's gaze, despite nearly dying from the embarrassment of what he'd just said.

Hajime had once heard that people's worst fear was the unknown. At the moment, Kaori was scared because she didn't know what it was that was going to attack Hajime. So even if it was just for her own peace of mind, Hajime wanted to give her the confidence that she could handle anything that came at him, regardless of what it was.

Kaori and Hajime stared at each other for a few moments, but she finally broke the silence with a smile.

"You never change, do you, Nagumo-kun?"

"Huh?" Hajime tilted his head quizzically at Kaori's words, and Kaori chuckled at his confusion.

"Nagumo-kun, you met me for the first time in high school, right? But you know, I've known you since the second year of middle school."

Hajime's eyes went as wide as dinner plates when he heard that. He racked his brain, trying to remember where he had met her before, but turned up blank. Kaori chuckled again when she saw him groaning to himself.

"I knew you, but you didn't know me... I first saw you when you were kneeling on the ground, so it's natural you didn't see me."

"Kn-kneeling?!"

She saw him in such a pathetic state?! Hajime squirmed in embarrassment for a totally different reason when he heard that. Frantically, he tried to remember where he could've possibly kneeled like that in public. Kaori continued her tale while Hajime went through a pantomime of weird expressions.

"Yep. You were prostrating yourself in front of a bunch of delinquents. You didn't stop even when they spat on you, or poured juice on you...or even stepped on you. Eventually they just gave up and left."

"S-Sorry you had to see something so unsightly..."

Hajime wished he could just melt into the floor. That was almost as bad as having someone's angsty teenage middle school past brought up again. He could only smile weakly. It was the same awkward smile he'd had when his mom had found his porn collection and neatly organized it on his shelf.

However, Kaori looked at him kindly, with not an ounce of scorn in her gaze.

"That's not true. It wasn't unsightly at all. In fact, when I saw it, I thought you were a really strong and kind person, Nagumo-kun."

"...Huh?" Hajime couldn't believe what he had just heard. It certainly didn't seem like the proper impression to get from watching a scene like that. *Don't tell me Shirasaki-san has some kind of weird fetish for that?!* Hajime thought, rather rudely.

"I mean, you did all that for the sake of a little boy and his grandmother, didn't you, Nagumo-kun?"

At those words, Hajime finally remembered. Something like that had indeed happened during his middle school days.

A little kid had bumped into some delinquents, and the takoyaki he'd been eating had spilled over their clothes. The guys he had bumped into all snapped, and the boy started crying, while his grandmother cowered in a corner. It had been quite the scene.

Hajime was just passing by at the time, and he'd planned on ignoring the commotion. However, even after the boy's grandmother gave the delinquents some money, most likely as an apology for ruining the shirt, they continued harassing them. In fact, they got even worse, and by the end of it, just snatched the poor lady's wallet right out of her hands. It was at that point that Hajime's body had moved instinctively.

But of course, he was someone who hated violence. The only killer moves he knew were the cringey ones he practiced at home after watching action shows. So he did the only thing he could: prostrate himself before them and beg for mercy. It was, of course, unbelievably embarrassing for him, but also surprisingly embarrassing to the ones he was kneeling to. In fact, it was so embarrassing that they couldn't stand it. And as planned, the delinquents did eventually just leave.

"It's easy for strong people to solve things with violence. People like Kouki-kun can easily fling themselves into trouble and just fight their way out of it...but few people who're weak have the courage to stand up for others, and even fewer could bow down like that for someone else... You know, I was always scared back then... I always made excuses for not helping other people by telling myself things like 'I'm not strong like Shizuku-chan,' so when I got in trouble, I always waited for other people to come save me instead."

"Shirasaki-san..."

"That's why I think you're really the strongest out of everyone here, Nagumo-kun. I was really happy when I saw you again in high school, you know... I wanted to become more like you. I wanted to talk to you more, to learn more about you. Though you always just fell asleep whenever you were at school..."

"Ahaha, sorry about that." Since he'd finally realized why Kaori always hung around him, and why she held him in such high regard, Hajime blushed and smiled awkwardly.

"That might be why I'm so worried. You might do something reckless again for someone else's sake, Nagumo-kun. Just like you did when you took on those delinquents... But, fine." She gazed at Hajime resolutely.

"I'll protect you, Nagumo-kun."

Hajime looked Kaori in the eyes, then nodded, accepting her resolve.

"Thank you."

Hajime smiled bitterly at the exchange. Their roles as boy and girl had been completely reversed. Though Hajime had to admit, Kaori made for a great hero. That would've made Hajime the heroine, though. As a guy, he wasn't quite sure how to feel about that, so all he could do was smile.

They chatted for a while longer, and then Kaori went back to her room. When Hajime finally sank down into his bed, his mind was working furiously. He had to find something he could do at all costs, and rid himself of the "worthless" stigma. He couldn't stay the protected princess forever. Hajime renewed his resolve as he drifted off to sleep.

Kaori had returned to her own room after leaving Hajime's. A figure hidden in the shadows watched as she left his room and headed to her own. No one was there to see...when his face twisted into a horrifying expression.

※ ※ ※ ※ ※ ※ ※ ※ ※ ※ ※ ※ ※ ※

The next morning, everyone reported to the plaza that served as the entrance to the Great Orcus Labyrinth early enough that the sun had still yet to rise.

The students were all filled with equal parts trepidation and curiosity. Hajime, however, had a more complicated expression on his face. He was also somewhat excited and nervous about his first excursion into a dungeon, but when he saw what the entrance to the Great Orcus Labyrinth looked like, some of his excitement faded.

What Hajime had expected was the standard cavern entrance leading into unknown dark depths. However, the sight that greeted him was something that looked more akin to the entrance to a museum, complete with its own receptionist counter. A girl in uniform was checking over the people going in and out of the labyrinth with a smile. It appeared that everyone's status plate was checked at the entrance. That way, the number of casualties could be accurately tallied. With the threat of war looming overhead, the government wanted to avoid losing too many men, so they implemented that policy as one of their countermeasures.

Numerous stalls were lined up on the plaza surrounding the entrance, the merchants all competing with each other to show off their wares. It felt almost like a festival.

Shallower labyrinths that didn't have as many floors were popular with merchants, since people naturally gathered there. The people present ranged from boisterous adventurers who talked big but quickly lost their lives in the labyrinth, to criminals who operated out of back alleys and other unsavory locations. As the government was preparing for war, they didn't want to waste too many resources handling those problems, so they cooperated with the local adventurer's guild to keep the area safe. People were selling their wares all the way up to the receptionist's desk at the entrance, which in a sense made life easier for the adventurers who were setting out into the labyrinth's depths.

Hajime pulled himself together and scratched his head as he looked around, seeing all of the other students gawking like country bumpkins as they followed Captain Meld in single file, like a row of little ducklings.

Once inside, the lively atmosphere that had surrounded them mere moments ago vanished. In front of them was a passage that was a little over five meters wide. Though there was no obvious light source, the entire labyrinth was dimly lit, enough that one could vaguely make out their surroundings without the help of a torch or magical item. In truth, the passages were all lit by a special mineral called green glowstone that was buried in the walls. The entire Great Orcus Labyrinth was actually an excavated vein of green glowstone ore.

The party all filed into ranks and slowly advanced through the labyrinth. After a few uneventful minutes, the passage they were walking down opened up into a wide plaza.

Towering seven or eight meters above them was a dome-shaped ceiling. The students were all looking around curiously, when suddenly a number of gray creatures resembling furballs burst out from cracks in the wall.

"All right, Kouki, your team's up front! Everyone else fall back! I'll have you switch in after some time, so stay sharp! These monsters are called Ratmen! They're quick on their feet, but not all that strong. Keep your cool as you fight!"

As Captain Meld had said, the Ratmen were quite fast, and rushed at them with alarming agility. Pairs of dark red eyes gleamed with a ghastly light from within the balls of fur. Their name was rather fitting, as they looked like giant, muscular rats...that stood on two feet. Only the area around their corded chests and impressive eight-packs was bereft of fur, almost as if they were trying to show off their muscles.

Everyone in Kouki's group, who were facing them head on, grimaced when they got a better look—especially Shizuku, who was standing up front. They certainly did look disgusting.

Once the Ratmen entered into range, Kouki, Shizuku, and Ryutarou all attacked at once. In the meantime, Kaori and two of her close female friends, the glasses-wearing Eri Nakamura and the childish and energetic Suzu Taniguchi, started chanting their spells. They were preparing their magic already. That was the basic formation they'd practiced during training.

Kouki swung his bastard sword faster than the eye could follow, and slaughtered a score of them with his first swing. His sword was one of the artifacts that had been resting in the Heiligh treasury, and had the rather clichéd name of "The Holy Sword." It was blessed with the light element, which had the sickeningly efficient properties of simultaneously weakening enemies that were hit by the light it emitted, while also increasing one's own physical strength. It sure played dirty for a "holy" sword.

Ryutarou, on the other hand, had the job of Monk, which was a martial arts class that fought with its fists. He was equipped with a pair of gauntlets and greaves. Those were also artifacts, and were capable of unleashing enchanted shockwaves. They were also unbreakable. Ryutarou took up a stance and splendidly beat down any enemy that came close with punches and kicks, not letting a single one pass. Despite being practically bare-handed, his massive frame made him seem like an armored heavy knight.

Shizuku, meanwhile, possessed the job of Swordsman, which was fitting for a samurai-esque girl like her. She wielded a blade that was midway between a katana and a shamshir, and made short work of any enemies that got within reach of her sword with her quick-draw skills. She had refined her swordplay even further since arriving in Tortus, and had even earned the admiration of many of the knights. While everyone was busy watching Kouki and the others fight, the girls in the back line finished their chants.

"Flames blacker than pitch, swirl about thine enemies! Burn until naught but their ashes remain—Spiral Blaze!"

They cast the spell in unison, and a huge whirlwind of flames enveloped the Ratmen, burning them to a crisp. The Ratmen screeched in pain, flailing wildly until the flames pouring down on them reduced them to ash. In the blink of an eye, all of the Ratmen had been annihilated. The other students didn't even get a chance to fight. It looked like monsters on the first floor were far too weak to even put up a fight against Kouki's party.

"Wow, well done! All right, the rest of you will be up next, so don't relax just yet!"

Captain Meld reminded the class not to let their guard down, though he was smiling, impressed at their prowess. Still, he couldn't prevent the students from getting pumped up about their first dungeon monster elimination expedition. He shrugged his shoulders helplessly as he saw the students breaking out into smiles.

"Oh, and...while you don't have to worry about it this time since it's training, in the future, try and kill your enemies in a way that preserves their mana crystals. What you did back there was overkill."

Kaori and the others blushed at Captain Meld's words, realizing they may have gone too far. From then on, the class smoothly advanced through the floors of the labyrinth, rotating the vanguard between battles.

Eventually, they arrived at the twentieth floor, the floor that separated skilled adventurers from rank amateurs. Currently, the deepest floor people had managed to reach was floor sixty-five. However, that was a legendary feat that hadn't been replicated since, so in recent times anyone who made it past the first twenty floors was considered a highly skilled fighter. Anyone who made it past the first forty was superhuman.

With Kouki at their head, the students were able to easily advance through the floors. Though they had little combat experience, their overpowered abilities more than compensated. The most dangerous enemy the students faced was actually the traps scattered about. Some of them were even lethal.

The most common countermeasure for traps was something known as a Fair Scope. A Fair Scope was a handy tool that detected traps by reading the flow of mana. Most of the traps in the labyrinth were magical in nature, so a Fair Scope detected around eighty percent of them. However, the Scope possessed a very limited range, so it was only effective in the hands of an experienced user.

Therefore, the real reason Hajime and the others were able to descend so smoothly was because of how well their knight mentors were guiding them. Captain Meld also often reminded the students to never enter a room that hadn't been scoured for traps first.

"All right everyone, from this point on, monsters won't come at you just one species at a time. They'll coordinate with each other and attack in large groups. Don't let your guard down just because we've had nothing but easy victories so far! Today's training will conclude once we clear the twentieth floor, so let's end things with a bang!" Captain Meld's voice echoed throughout the room.

Up until that point, Hajime hadn't done much of anything. He'd once taken on a monster the knights had weakened for him, trapping it in a pitfall and stabbing it to death with his sword, but that was all.

Essentially, he had just spent his time standing by in the rear, protected by the knights, without being able to join anyone's party. It was honestly rather pathetic. However, using his skills in combat helped increase his magic stat, so it wasn't completely useless. Hajime's magic stat grew enough to raise him two levels, so the combat practice had helped some.

But man, I totally feel like a leech for doing this. Haaah... The knights sent another weakened monster Hajime's way, and he approached it with a sigh, placing his hands on the ground to transmute the earth around it. He immobilized it in a pitfall on the off chance that it might still pose a threat, then skewered it with his sword.

Well, at least my transmutation skills are growing a little... I'll just have to keep at it. Hajime swallowed a mana pill and wiped the sweat off his brow. He didn't notice that the knights were all staring at him in admiration.

In truth, the knights hadn't been expecting much of anything from Hajime. They were just having such an easy time of it that they decided to send a few monsters over to him, since he'd seemed so bored. Weakened, of course.

They'd all thought he would just flail his sword around helplessly for a bit. However, he had effectively used his transmutation skill to immobilize the enemy before dispatching it, a tactic the knights had never seen before. They had assumed Synergists were only good for blacksmithing, hence their belief that their skills would be useless in combat.

Hajime only had his single transmutation skill, so he had trained it diligently, assuming that his ability to transmute ore could extend to the earth as well. It had worked, but with how difficult it was for him to take down a single weakened monster, and how strong everyone around him was, he still thought himself weak.

That was the first time he'd shown this ability to people. He'd made an utter fool of himself during their previous excursion to slay monsters outside of the capital, and this was the solution he had come up with.

While he was taking a short break, Hajime glanced over to the front lines, and his eyes met Kaori's. She was smiling at him. She had taken her promise to "protect" him quite seriously, and Hajime looked away, embarrassed, as he realized she had been watching over him the whole time. Kaori pouted a little when she saw him look away. Shizuku chuckled softly as she watched their little exchange out of the corner of her eye, then quietly spoke.

"Kaori, why do you keep staring at Nagumo-kun? Don't you know it's wrong to pick up guys in a dungeon?" Shizuku said that in a teasing manner, but Kaori blushed, and angrily rounded on Shizuku.

"Oh, come on, Shizuku-chan! Could you please not say strange things like that?! I was just wondering if Nagumo-kun was okay!"

That's basically you trying to pick him up then, isn't it? Shizuku thought, but not wanting to make Kaori sulk, she decided to keep quiet. Still, she was unable to hide the mirth in her eyes, and Kaori just pouted and said "Jeez" when she saw Shizuku's expression.

Hajime had been watching their little exchange when he felt someone's gaze on him and reflexively straightened up. It was a glare dripping with hatred. He was used to getting such gazes from his classmates, but the intensity packed in that one was on a completely different level.

That wasn't the first time he had felt this gaze either. He'd felt it multiple times since that morning, but whenever he tried to look for the one who was doing it, they seemingly calmed down. Hajime was growing tired of it.

What's going on...? Did I do something to someone? Though all I've been doing is trying my best despite my incompetence... Wait, could that be the reason? Maybe they were thinking, "The hell do you think you're playing at, acting like you can be helpful?!" or something...

"Haaah..." Hajime sighed deeply. He had started to think there might've been some wisdom in heeding Kaori's warning.

The class continued exploring the twentieth floor.

Each of the labyrinth's floors spanned a few kilometers in every direction, and new floors usually took a team of dozens anywhere from half a month to a month to fully search and map out.

However, at present, all the floors until the forty-seventh had been mapped out, so they were in no danger of getting lost. Nor should they have been in any danger of falling into a trap.

The deepest room in the twentieth floor was like a limestone cave, but made of ice. Icicles protruded from the walls, some of them melted, creating a complex topography. The stairs leading to the twenty-first floor were just past it.

Once they made it that far, their training for the day would be over. Sadly, while teleportation magic had existed during the Age of the Gods, it no longer did, so they had to walk back to the entrance. The students had already begun to relax when a protrusion in the wall prevented them from advancing in formation, forcing them to continue in single file.

Eventually, the two people at the head of their procession, Kouki and Captain Meld, came to a halt. Puzzled, the students prepared for battle as they looked around. It seemed they had encountered a monster.

"It's camouflaging itself! Keep a close eye on your surroundings!" Captain Meld yelled out a warning to everyone.

An instant later, the thing everyone had mistaken for a protrusion suddenly changed color and began to move. The creature that had assumed the shape of a wall was actually a dark brown color, and it stood there on two legs. It began beating its chest. Seemingly, the monster was a gorilla that could camouflage itself like a chameleon.

"A Rockmount! Watch out for its arms, they pack quite a punch!" Captain Meld's voice resounded throughout the cavern as Kouki's party prepared to engage the enemy.

Ryutarou repelled the Rockmount's enormous arms with his fists. Meanwhile, Kouki and Shizuku shuffled to either side to flank it, but were unable to properly surround it because of the rough terrain.

Realizing it couldn't get past the human wall that was Ryutarou, the Rockmount fell back and sucked in a deep breath.

"Graaaaaaaaaaah!!!" Seconds later, it looked back and roared so ferociously that the entire room shook.

"Guh?!"

"Uwaaah?!"

"Kyaaah?!" Though the shockwave of sound that hit the students did no harm, it made everyone stiffen in fear. That was the magic Rockmounts were capable of using: Intimidating Roar. It was a mana-infused roar that could temporarily paralyze all who heard it.

Kouki and the others, who took it head on, found themselves unable to move an inch. They expected to be attacked while stunned, but the Rockmount sidestepped past them, picked up a nearby boulder, and hurled it at Kaori's group. And what a spectacular throw it was! It flew cleanly over the heads of the immobile front line and headed straight toward its intended target.

They all pointed their magic circle-amplified staves at the boulder and prepared to intercept. There was no space to dodge.

However, they stopped their chant midway, the sight of what was coming toward them shocking them into inaction.

The boulder the Rockmount had thrown was a second Rockmount! It somersaulted in the air and spread its arms wide, heading straight for Kaori. The way it spread its arms out resembled the Lupin Dive. The resemblance was so uncanny that one almost expected it to scream "Kaori-chaaaan!" as it hit her. It even had the bloodshot eyes and heavy breathing down pat. Kaori, Eri, and Suzu all screamed in terror and forgot to keep chanting.

"Oi, what do you think you're doing in the middle of a fight?!" Captain Meld swiftly cut down the Rockmount that was diving toward the girls.

They all quickly apologized, but that must've been quite the disgusting sight to see, as their faces were still pale. A certain someone completely snapped when he saw how rattled the girls were. Amanogawa Kouki, the class's resident self-styled hero of justice.

"Bastard... How dare you hurt Kaori and the others...? I won't forgive you!" He must have mistakenly thought their paleness came from their close brush with death, and not how disgustingly creepy the Rockmount had looked.

How dare you frighten a girl like that! Kouki flew into a rage over that rather clichéd reason. Pure white mana began leaking from his body, and almost as if in response, his holy sword began to glow.

"Soar unto heaven, O divine wings—Celestial Flash!"

"No, stop, you idiot!" Kouki ignored Captain Meld, raised his sword up high, and swung down with all his might.

He finished chanting his spell the same instant, and his holy sword unleashed a dazzling blade of light. There was no escaping it. The curved light passed through the Rockmount with only the slightest hint of resistance, cutting it cleanly in two, and stopped only after crashing into the wall.

There was a loud rumbling, and pieces of the wall began to rain down. Kouki breathed a deep sigh, then turned to the girls, a ladykiller's smile on his face. He had defeated the big bad monster for them. Just as he was about to say "It's okay now!" Captain Meld, who was smiling angrily with veins popping out of his forehead, walked up to him and delivered a punch.

"Hobwah?!"

"You damn fool! I understand why you got angry, but you can't use skills like that in a narrow passage! You could've brought the whole cave down on us!" Kouki's complaints died in his throat at Captain Meld's chastising words, and he apologized awkwardly. The girls all smiled wryly and tried to comfort him.

Then suddenly, Kaori turned to look at the crumbled section of the wall.

"...What is that? It's all sparkly..." At her words, everyone turned to look in the direction she was pointing.

There was a strange mineral emitting a pale blue glow, protruding from the wall like a flower in bloom. It looked like a crystal with indigolite buried in its center. All of the girls, including Kaori, were entranced by the beauty of the gem.

"Oh, that's a glanz crystal. And a pretty big one to boot. How rare," Captain Meld said.

Glanz crystals were basically a type of raw gemstone. Though they held no special properties, their luster and radiance made them popular among the noble ladies and their daughters. They were often processed into rings, earrings, pendants, and such other jewelry to be given as gifts. Apparently, most girls were overjoyed to receive glanz jewelry as gifts. It was among the top three jewels used in proposal rings.

"That sounds so lovely..." Kaori blushed when she heard Captain Meld's explanation, and was further entranced by the stone. She then stole a glance at Hajime. It was so quick that it almost went unnoticed. However, Shizuku and one other person most definitely did take note.

"In that case, I'll go grab it for us!" Hiyama suddenly ran forward after saying that. He swiftly climbed up the debris of the crumbled wall, heading toward the glanz crystal as fast as possible. Captain Meld hurriedly tried to stop him.

"Hey! Don't just run off on your own! We're not even sure it's safe yet!" However, Hiyama pretended not to hear, and he was standing in front of the crystal before long.

Captain Meld chased after Hiyama in an attempt to stop him. At the same time, one of the knights pulled out his Fair Scope and scanned the area around the crystal. A moment later, his face went pale.

"Captain! It's a trap!"

"What?! Stop!" However, both Captain Meld's and the knight's warnings arrived a moment too late.

The second Hiyama touched it, a magic circle appeared in the center of the crystal. The trap had been set for anyone foolish enough to touch the glanz crystal. "If it seems too good to be true, then it probably is." That was one of the world's golden rules.

The magic circle glowed bright, then grew large enough to encompass the entire room. It was just like the day they had been summoned.

"Crap, retreat! Everyone get out, now!" Captain Meld's words spurred everyone into action, and they all scrambled for the exit...but they didn't make it in time.

Light filled the room, and before long white was the only thing anyone could see. Everyone was assailed by a momentary sensation of weightlessness.

Hajime and the others could feel the atmosphere shift. A moment later, they all fell to the ground with a thud.

Hajime groaned in pain as he felt his aching butt, then looked around. Most of his other classmates were still on the ground, but Captain Meld and his knights, along with Kouki and the other vanguard fighters, were already on their feet, examining their surroundings.

The magic circle from earlier must have contained a teleportation spell. Magic from the Age of the Gods was remarkable because it could easily do things that no modern-day mage could.

Hajime and the others had been teleported onto a massive stone bridge. It was around one hundred meters in length. The ceiling also towered a full twenty meters above them. Below the bridge was not a river, but instead a dark abyss with no visible end. The gaping chasm resembled the very pits of hell.

Though the bridge was ten meters wide, it had no railing at all, so if someone slipped, there would be nothing to catch their fall. Hajime and the others had been sent to the middle of the bridge. One side of the bridge was a passage heading further in, while stairs leading upward were at the other end.

After confirming the situation, Captain Meld curtly barked out orders.

"Everyone, get up and head for the stairs! Now!" His voice boomed louder than thunder, and the students hurried to follow his orders.

However, labyrinth's traps were not so easy to escape. They would not be allowed to retreat so easily.

New magic circles suddenly appeared on either side of the bridge, accompanied by a swirling torrent of dark red mana. The magic circle on the passage side of the bridge was ten meters wide. The ones on stairway side were only one meter each, but there were many.

The dark red magic circles resembled pools of blood, and gave off an ominous feel. They pulsed once, and waves of monsters began pouring forth.

From the countless magic circles near the stairs came a horde of skeletons wielding swords—Traum Soldiers. Their empty eye sockets gleamed with the same blood-red light as the circles they came from, and they rolled around like real eyes too. Within seconds, the stairs were teeming with nearly a hundred of the creatures, and more were still pouring out.

Despite their numbers, Hajime thought what was coming out on the passage side of the bridge was far more of a threat.

From within the ten-meter-wide magic circle emerged a monster as big as the circle that summoned it. It stood on four legs and had some kind of helmet on its head. To Hajime, the closest thing it resembled was a triceratops. However, unlike a triceratops, its eyes glowed bright red, and as it clacked its wicked sharp claws and fangs together, flames sprouted from the horn on its helmeted forehead.

Everyone stared at it in slack-jawed horror, and Captain Meld's terrified whisper resounded surprisingly clearly throughout the room.

"Oh my god...it's...a Behemoth..."

A wave of unease washed over the students when they saw Captain

Meld, the reliable captain who'd always been their reassuring pillar of support, break out in a cold sweat.

Kouki realized he was up against a truly fearsome opponent, and turned to ask Captain Meld about its properties.

However, the Behemoth, a monster that had even the kingdom's strongest knight quaking in his boots, refused to grant Kouki the luxury of time. It sucked in a huge breath, then let out a guttural roar, signaling the start of the battle.

"Graaaaaaaaaaaaaaaaaah!!!"

"Huh?!" The roar brought Captain Meld back to his senses, and he quickly began barking orders.

"Alan, take the kids and break through the line of Traum Soldiers! Kyle, Ivan, Bael, create a barrier! We have to stop that thing, no matter what! Kouki, head to the stairs with the rest of the students!"

"Please wait, Meld-san! We'll help too! That dinosaur thing is really bad news! We'll also—"

"Idiot! If that thing really is a Behemoth, you kids don't stand a chance! It's a monster that shows up on the sixty-fifth floor! Even the legendary adventurer, who everyone called the strongest in the world, couldn't stand against it! Now get out of here! I definitely won't let you kids die!"

Kouki faltered momentarily at the intensity in Captain Meld's gaze, but he refused to leave. Captain Meld opened his mouth to yell at Kouki, but before he could say anything, the Behemoth roared again and charged...straight toward the retreating students.

In order to protect their summoned heroes, Heiligh's strongest warriors chanted together in an attempt to form a barrier.

"Grant thine protection to your beloved children, O God! Reject all malice and let this be a holy ground that denies thine enemies passage! Hallowed Ground!" The spell was four verses long, inscribed on a magic circle two meters long, and drawn on the highest grade of magical paper. On top of that, it had been invoked by three people in tandem. Though it had only one use, and lasted for only one minute, it created an impenetrable barrier that could not be broken.

A glowing dome of light materialized, stopping the Behemoth in its tracks. A huge shockwave spread out as it crashed into the barrier, pulverizing the ground near the impact. Despite being made of stone, the entire bridge shook precariously. The retreating students screamed, and some of them fell over.

Traum Soldiers were powerful monsters that appeared on the thirty-eighth floor and deeper. They were far stronger than anything the students had faced so far. With their path forward blocked by a horde of ghastly skeletons, and a lumbering beast at their backs, the students fell into a panic.

All semblance of formation crumbled as everyone scrambled for the stairs, trying their best to escape. The lone knight that stayed with the group, Alan, tried to calm everyone down, but they were all far too terrified to listen.

Amidst the panic, someone shoved one of the female students from behind, and she fell forward. She groaned in pain and looked up, only to see a Traum Soldier brandishing its sword right in front of her.

"Ah!" At the same time she let out that gasp, the soldier swung its sword down at her head.

I'm going to die, she thought, when the ground at the Traum Soldier's feet suddenly bulged upward.

It lost its balance, so the swing went wide, hitting the ground with a clang. The protrusion in the ground then swelled forward, taking a few Traum Soldiers with it, and drove them to the edge of the bridge, where it then tipped them into the abyss.

About two meters from the edge of the bridge squatted Hajime, panting heavily. He'd transmuted various parts of the ground in quick succession, dragging the soldiers to their deaths on an earthen slide. His transmutation ability had grown rapidly, and before he knew it, he'd been able to transmute in quick succession. The total area he could transmute had increased as well.

However, he could still only transmute a short distance from where he was touching, so Hajime trembled in fear as he squatted within range of the Traum Soldier's swords.

He popped a mana pill into his mouth and ran over to the collapsed student, grabbing her with his gloved hands and pulling her up to her feet. She silently let herself be pulled up, still in shock, and Hajime smiled reassuringly at her.

"Come on, we've gotta hurry. Don't worry, as long as we stay calm, these piles of bones are nothing. After all, everyone but me is OP as hell!" Hajime confidently slapped her on the back, and she stared at him for a minute before saying "Yeah! Thanks!" cheerfully, and running off.

Hajime continued creating pitfalls and protrusions to immobilize and unbalance the Traum Soldiers, while keeping an eye on his surroundings. Everyone was still panicking, swinging their weapons wildly and firing their spells off at random. If that kept up, it was possible someone might die. Alan was trying his best to reorganize the students, but it wasn't going well. And all the while, soldiers continued pouring out of the magic circles.

"I've gotta do something... What everyone needs right now is a leader...someone with enough strength to blow open a path for us... Amanogawa-kun!" Hajime started sprinting toward Kouki and the Behemoth.

The Behemoth was still ramming the barrier over and over. A huge shockwave accompanied each charge, and the stone bridge began creaking ominously after his repeated assaults. Cracks were forming along the barrier, and it was only a matter of time before it shattered. Meld was adding his incantations to the barrier as well, but it didn't appear that it would last long.

"Agh, blast! It won't hold much longer! Kouki, you need to retreat! The rest of you as well!"

"I refuse! I can't leave you guys behind! We're all going to make it back together!"

"Kuh, now's not the time to go on an ego trip..." Captain Meld grimaced as those words left his mouth.

In such a cramped space, it would be difficult to dodge the Behemoth's charge. Which was why the best course of action was to run while the barrier was still up. However, the knights only realized that fact because they were veterans of numerous battles. For the students, it was still a difficult order to swallow.

Unfortunately, though, Meld had tried to explain the situation to Kouki, who absolutely could not accept the idea of "abandoning" anyone. Plus, to make matters worse, he still thought he could take the Behemoth head on. The glint in his eyes clearly showed that he wanted to fight.

Captain Meld realized it was the overconfidence of someone who was still wet behind the ears. It appeared that praising Kouki and the others for their skills to make them feel more confident had backfired.

"Kouki! You have to listen to the captain and retreat!" Shizuku had grasped the situation, so she grabbed Kouki's arm, urging him to retreat.

"Eh, this isn't the first time we've had to put up with your dumb antics, Kouki. I'm with you all the way!"

"Ryutarou... Thank you." However, Ryutarou's words solidified Kouki's resolve. Shizuku clicked her tongue impatiently at the exchange.

"You're letting the situation get to your head, stupid!"

"Shizuku-chan..." Kaori worriedly looked over at the irritated Shizuku. It was then that a certain boy ran up in front of Kouki.

"Amanogawa-kun!" Hajime screamed.

"N-Nagumo?!"

"Nagumo-kun?!"

"You need to retreat! You have to go back to where everyone is! They need you! Now!" Hajime yelled angrily at the surprised party.

"What do you mean? And more importantly, why are you here?! You shouldn't be here! Leave this to us, Nagumo, and—"

"This isn't the time to be saying that!" Hajime cut off Kouki, who was implying that Hajime would be of no use and should retreat, and yelled with a vehemence he had never expressed before. Kouki unconsciously stiffened up. He didn't expect the guy who was usually so quiet and mature, the one who generally blew everything off with a smile, to yell so angrily.

"Don't you see what's happening behind you?! They're all panicking because their leader isn't with them!" Hajime grabbed Kouki by the collar and pointed behind him.

Kouki saw his panicking classmates slowly being surrounded by the Traum Soldiers. All of their training had flown out the window. The students were all fighting wildly. Because of their inefficient fighting style, the steady rush of reinforcements had kept them from breaking through. Their exceptional stats had protected them so far, but it was only a matter of time until someone died.

"They need someone who has the strength to blow all that away in a single attack! They need someone who can blow their fear away! And the only one who can do that is you, Amanogawa-kun! You're their leader, so quit being so focused on what's in front of you! Look at what's behind you for once!" Dazed, Kouki looked from his panicking and screaming classmates back to Hajime, who was furiously shaking his head, and nodded.

"Yeah, I get it now. We're retreating! Meld-san, sorry—"

"Get down!"

Kouki turned to Captain Meld, planning to say "Sorry for retreating without you," but at that moment Captain Meld screamed out a warning as the barrier finally shattered.

A massive shockwave headed toward Hajime and the others. Hajime instantly transmuted the ground to make a stone wall, but the shockwave shattered it with ease, sending everyone flying. His wall had managed to lessen the force a little...but then the Behemoth let out a huge roar and the dust cleared, only to reveal Captain Meld and the other three knights lying on the ground, moaning in pain. The shockwave had robbed them of their ability to move.

Kouki and the others had collapsed too, but they were able to quickly get back up. Since they'd been behind both Hajime's wall and the knights, they hadn't taken as much damage.

"Gah...Ryutarou, Shizuku, can you buy us some time?" Kouki asked. It looked like they were in pain, but they still stepped forward. Since the knights had been defeated, they had to do something about the Behemoth themselves.

"Not like we've got a damn choice!"

"...We'll manage somehow." The two of them charged the Behemoth after uttering those responses.

"Kaori, you need to heal Meld-san and the others!"

"Got it!" At Kouki's command, Kaori ran over to the knights.

Hajime was already kneeling beside them. He created another stone barrier to keep the effects of the fight from reaching them. He doubted it would be of much use in the grand scheme of things, but reasoned that it was better than nothing.

Meanwhile, Kouki began chanting the strongest spell he knew.

"O holy spirit! Bring ruin to all that is evil with thine divine light! By the breath of God, may these clouds of darkness be swept clear, and the world bathed in sanctity! By the mercy of God, may this strike redeem the sins of man! Divine Wrath!"

Auroras of light poured out from the holy sword. The skill Kouki had used was of the same category as the Celestial Flash he'd unleashed earlier, but this one was far more powerful. The bridge creaked ominously as the rays of light gouged furrows through the stone while racing toward the Behemoth.

Ryutarou and Shizuku retreated the moment Kouki finished chanting. They were in bad shape and wouldn't have lasted much longer. Though it had been a scant few seconds, they'd suffered quite a bit of damage in fending off the Behemoth.

The bombardment of light crashed into the Behemoth with

a thunderous roar. It was covered in a coat of white as the light enveloped it. Cracks began appearing in the bridge.

"That should have been enough... Haah... Haaah..."

"Haah... Haaah... Yeah, that had to have killed it, right?"

"I'd like to think so, but..." Ryutarou and Shizuku fell back to where Kouki was standing. He was panting hard after casting such a powerful spell. That last attack had been Kouki's ace in the hole. It had used up almost all of his remaining mana. Captain Meld stood up behind him, his wounds healed.

Gradually the light began to fade and the dust surrounding the Behemoth cleared. And the Behemoth...didn't even have a scratch on it.

It let out a low growl, and the dark red mana that was unique to monsters began pouring out of its body. The murderous glare it aimed at Kouki was so intense that Kouki felt he might die just looking at it. Then it raised its head high, and its horn began letting out a high pitched buzz as it glowed red hot. The red spread to the rest of its helmet until it seemed like its entire head was a glowing ball of magma.

"Don't just stand there! Run!" Captain Meld's shout brought Kouki and the others back to their senses. Finally over the shock that Kouki hadn't managed to even scratch it, they prepared to run. But it was at that moment the Behemoth chose to charge. Before it reached Kouki, it leaped into the air and hurtled toward them, head down, like a burning meteor.

They were able to leap to the side to avoid a direct hit, but the shockwaves from the impact bowled Kouki and the others over. They rolled across the ground like toppled pins, and were covered in wounds from head to toe when they finally stopped.

Captain Meld was still somehow able to move and he ran over to the others. The rest of the knights were still being healed by Kaori. The Behemoth braced its legs and tried to pull its head out of the hole it had smashed into the bridge.

"Can you guys still move?!" The only responses Captain Meld got were groans. Their bodies had been paralyzed by the shockwaves, just like Captain Meld's team had been a while ago. Their internal organs had taken quite a pounding too.

Captain Meld turned around to call Kaori over. But the words died in his throat when he saw Hajime running toward him.

"Kid! Get Kaori to help you carry Kouki out of here!" Meld decided to ask Hajime instead.

He asked Hajime to take Kouki and Kouki alone. In other words, his orders implied that it was impossible to save more than one person in this situation. Captain Meld bit his lip so hard it drew blood and grimly raised his shield, lamenting that he could not save everyone. Still, he resolved to give his life to stop the beast for as long as possible.

However, instead of obeying, Hajime desperately yelled out an alternative plan. It was possibly the only way everyone would be able to escape with their lives. However, it was an insane, reckless plan with chances of success that were beyond slim. And to top it off, Hajime himself would have to play the most dangerous role.

Captain Meld hesitated for a few precious seconds, which was enough time for the Behemoth to get its head unstuck. Its helmet began glowing bright red once more. Meld was out of time.

"...Are you sure you can do it, kid?"

"I am." Meld laughed and broke out into a grin when he saw the resolve in Hajime's gaze.

"Never thought I'd trust my life to you of all people... I promise I won't leave you behind. So...don't let me down, kid!"

"Yes, sir!" Captain Meld finished talking and walked up to the Behemoth. He unleashed a weak spell at it, provoking its ire. It appeared that the Behemoth had a tendency to focus on whatever was attacking it, which was why it had aimed for Kouki earlier. The spell did the trick, and the Behemoth's gaze locked onto Captain Meld.

It finished charging up its helmet, rushed forward, and jumped. Meld was planning on drawing its attention for as long as possible and got into an evasive stance as the Behemoth hurtled toward him. He then whispered a short chant.

"Be swept away—Wind Wall!" Meld quickly jumped back after he chanted that spell.

The Behemoth smashed into the ground, pulverizing the spot Captain Meld had been standing on not even a second before. The shockwave and rubble were blown away by the wind wall, keeping Meld unharmed. With how imprecise the Behemoth's attacks were, even a weak spell was enough to help avoid indirect damage. But if Meld had been forced to defend Kouki and the others he would have been utterly crushed.

While the Behemoth was still stuck in the ground, Hajime jumped up onto it. The residual heat burned his skin as he landed. However, he ignored the pain as he gathered his sky blue mana, and chanted. He said no more than the name of the spell. It was, after all, the simplest, most basic magic.

"Transmute!" The Behemoth, which had been struggling to unstick its head from the ground, suddenly stopped moving. Because every time it tried to dislodge itself even a little, Hajime reformed the stone around it, keeping its head buried.

It braced its legs, attempting to use the weight of its whole body to rip its head free, only to find that the ground around its legs had been transmuted as well. The Behemoth's legs had sunk a full meter into the ground. And to make completely sure it wouldn't be able to break free, Hajime hardened the stone around them as well.

Even then, the Behemoth's strength was fearsome, and Hajime knew even a moment's lapse in concentration would allow the Behemoth break free. It kept struggling, cracks continually forming in its stone prison, but Hajime continued to relentlessly transmute the ground to repair them—the end result being that the Behemoth was unable to free its head. Were this not a matter of life and death, it would have looked rather comedic.

In the meantime, Captain Meld gathered the recovered knights and Kaori together, and they began carrying Kouki and the others to safety. It seemed that some of the students had finally regained their composure, as they were working in tandem to push the Traum Soldiers back. The one that had rallied them was actually the female student Hajime had saved earlier. Despite his weakness, he had still contributed greatly.

"Wait! Nagumo-kun's still over there!" Kaori started arguing with Meld, who was trying to get everyone to retreat.

"This is all a part of the kid's plan! We're going to break through the soldiers and set up a defensive line so the mages can bombard the beast with spells! Of course, that comes after he's out of our line of fire! Then he's going to run back to us while we keep the Behemoth busy with a barrage of spells. We're all retreating together!"

"Then I'll stay behind with him!"

"No, you can't! Once we've made it to safety, you have to heal Kouki, Kaori!"

"But—" Kaori's angry protests were cut short by Meld's next words. "What you're doing is nothing more than spitting on his resolve!"

"Ah—"

After Captain Meld, the strongest member of their party was without a doubt Kouki. They would need every bit of firepower they could get to hold the Behemoth at bay with just magic. Kouki's condition meant the difference between life and death for Hajime, which was why Kaori needed to be healing him the whole time while they retreated. The Behemoth would be free the moment Hajime's mana ran out and he could no longer transmute.

"O breath of life, grant succor to this injured soul—Heaven's Blessing!" Kaori began chanting, tears in her eyes. Her artifact, a white staff, glowed faintly, and wrapped Kouki in a gentle light. Heaven's Blessing was a high-level healing spell that restored mana on top of healing wounds.

Captain Meld gripped Kaori's shoulders and nodded encouragingly to her. Kaori nodded back, then turned around to look at Hajime, who was still desperately transmuting the ground. Then, she began retreating from the bridge, together with Captain Meld and the knights, who were carrying Ryutarou, Shizuku, and Kouki.

The Traum Soldiers were still increasing in number. There were more than two hundred of them crowding the landing by that point. There were so many that a chunk of them had spilled over onto the bridge itself.

However, that was actually a blessing in disguise. Had they spread themselves out properly, they would have easily been able to surround and then subsequently slaughter the students who charged through the ranks. After all, a good number of the students had done just that when the initial hundred had appeared.

The only reason no one had died yet was because of the knights. It was only because of their excellent skill, which covered for the students' inexperience. However, because of how much it had taxed them to keep all the students safe, they were all covered in wounds.

And so, with the knights' support flagging and the army of monsters only increasing, the students were slowly falling into a panic once more. They forgot all about using magic and swung their weapons blindly. In a few more minutes they would've surely been annihilated.

The students had realized the gravity of their own situation as well, and despair painted their faces. The girl Hajime had saved continued trying to coordinate her small knot of students, but they too were reaching their limits, and there were tears in her eyes.

Everyone was on the verge of giving up, when suddenly—

"Celestial Flash!" A blade of pure light tore through the center of the Traum Soldiers, obliterating the enemies in its path.

The ones that weren't instantly destroyed were blown away by the force of the spell, and tumbled to their deaths in the depths below. A new wave of Traum Soldiers rose to take their place, but for an instant the students caught a glimpse of the stairs that led to their salvation— the hope that they had been unable to see even for a second, no matter how hard they had fought.

"Everyone! Don't give up! I'll carve open a path for us!" Kouki accompanied his shouts with a second Celestial Flash, mowing down yet another group of Traum Soldiers. His overwhelming charisma bolstered the students' flagging morale.

"You morons! Did all your training just fly out the window?! What the hell has gotten into you! Get back in formation this instant!"

The ever reliable Captain Meld unleashed an attack that was arguably even more powerful than Kouki's Celestial Flash, annihilating another line of Traum Soldiers. The students' depression was blown away as their pillar of support returned to assist them.

The haze of panic was lifted from their eyes, and strength returned to their limbs. Though part of that was due to Kaori's magic. She had cast a mental focus spell. Normally it would do no more than help someone relax a little, but its effect multiplied exponentially when combined with Kouki's morale-boosting speech.

The healers began healing the injured, while the mages fell back and started chanting their most powerful spells. The vanguard got into a proper line, and focused on defending the backline.

Once healed, the knights returned to the fray as well, and the counterattack began in earnest. Everyone's overpowered skills and weapons hit the soldiers in waves, drowning them in a sea of attacks. They began destroying the soldiers faster than the magic circles could pour new ones out.

Finally, a path to the stairs was secured.

"Forward, men! We need to secure the landing!" Kouki ran forward, leading the way.

Ryutarou and Shizuku, who had both recovered somewhat, followed close behind him. Together, they cut through their enemies like a hot knife through butter.

In moments, everyone had escaped the encirclement. The soldiers attempted to make a meat wall, or rather bone wall, and close off the path to the bridge again, but Kouki unleashed another spell to blow a hole open in their lines.

His classmates all stared at him in confusion. That was only natural. After all, the stairs were in front of them, not behind. All of them were only thinking of escape at this point.

"Everyone, wait! We still have to save Nagumo-kun! Nagumo-kun's still out there stopping that monster all by himself!" Her classmates all then stared at Kaori in confusion. That too, was only natural. After all, Hajime was the class's supposed "incompetent."

However, when they looked past the thinned crowd of Traum Soldiers toward the bridge, they saw none other than Hajime.

"What on earth? What is he doing?"

"Is that monster buried *in* the bridge?" As more and more classmates began crying out in surprise, Captain Meld gave his orders.

"That's right! That kid's stopping that monster all by himself. He's the only reason your sorry asses aren't skeleton fodder right now! Vanguard, advance! Don't let a single soldier past you! Rearguard, start preparing long-range spells! His magic won't last much longer! Once the kid's clear, start blasting away to keep it busy!" His deep voice resonated through the room, and the students all refocused their attention.

A few of their gazes lingered longingly on the stairs still. And who could blame them? They had been on the verge of death but moments ago. It was only natural they would wish for the safety of the floor above. However, Meld's "Hurry up!" got even the most reluctant students to finally turn around and return to the battlefield.

Daisuke Hiyama was one of the last to follow. Despite the entire mess being his fault, he was still overcome by terror and wanted to escape as swiftly as possible.

However, in the back of his mind, he remembered the events of the previous night.

He recalled the night before they had entered the labyrinth, and what he had seen at Horaud's inn. He had been too nervous to sleep, so Hiyama had stepped out for a bit to go to the bathroom and feel the night breeze. He had been enjoying the cool night air and was about to return to his room when he spotted Kaori in a negligee. He had been so surprised by her sudden appearance that he had reflexively hidden himself in the shadows and held his breath. Kaori hadn't even noticed he was there as she passed by. His curiosity piqued, he'd followed Kaori and watched as she'd knocked on the door of a certain room. More specifically...Hajime's room.

Hiyama's mind had gone blank when he saw Hajime answer the door. Hiyama, like most other guys, was completely infatuated with Kaori. However, he did not think himself worthy enough to stand beside her, and had decided that if his competition for her affections was someone like Kouki, who lived in a totally different world, he might as well give up.

But Hajime was different. Hiyama couldn't understand why Kaori would want to be with someone that, at least in his mind, was even lower than him. *If he's good enough, then why not me?!* His twisted mind actually believed that was a logical train of thought.

His dissatisfaction with Hajime quickly gave way to hatred. The reason he had jumped at the opportunity to get the glanz crystal was also because he wanted to impress Kaori.

Hiyama remembered the events of that night as he watched Kaori gaze worriedly at Hajime, and a wicked grin formed on his lips as the beginnings of a plan took shape in his mind.

Hajime's mana finally began to run out around the same time the students all turned back to the bridge. And he was all out of mana pills. He stole a quick glance back at the bridge and saw that everyone had safely managed to retreat. They had turned back around and were lining up to start firing their spells.

The Behemoth was still struggling against its restraints, but at that point they would only last a few seconds without constant transmuting. He would have to get as far away as possible in that time. Sweat beaded down his forehead. His heart was pounding louder than it had in his entire life, and he was so nervous he was trembling.

He was going to need impeccable timing to make it out alive. After cracks started appearing for the dozenth time, he transmuted the ground once more, and strengthened the Behemoth's restraints for good measure. Then he jumped.

A scant five seconds after Hajime had started running for his life, the ground behind him shattered, and the Behemoth roared menacingly as it freed itself from its restraints. Hajime risked a glance back and saw pure rage in its eyes.

It looked around wildly, searching for the one who had forced it into such an unsightly struggle, and quickly found Hajime. It roared again, angrily, bringing its head down to prepare to charge Hajime. However, before it could move, a barrage of spells slammed into it.

It was like a bizarre meteor shower, where each meteor was a different color. The various spells didn't do any damage to the Behemoth, but they definitely slowed it down.

I can do this! Hajime thought, and sprinted forward, his head bowed low. Despite the procession of spells flying inches above him, Hajime wasn't afraid. He was certain his cheat-level classmates wouldn't miss. Within a few seconds he was already more than thirty meters away from the Behemoth.

He unconsciously broke out into a smile.

An instant later, however, that smile froze in place.

Among the multitude of spells flying at the Behemoth, one of them had a slightly lower trajectory...and it was heading straight for Hajime. Someone had clearly aimed their attack right at him.

But why?! A moment of surprised confusion passed through his mind.

He quickly braced his legs in an attempt to stop, so the fireball merely exploded inches in front of his face. The shockwaves blasted him back toward the Behemoth. He had avoided a direct hit, and suffered no lasting damage, but his semicircular canals had been thrown into disarray, and he completely lost his balance.

Hajime staggered to his feet, trying to put as much space between him and the Behemoth as possible, but the Behemoth was tired of being bombarded. Right after Hajime managed to find his bearings, it let out another roar. He glanced back and saw it gathering its dark red mana for the third time as it finished heating its helmet. It was glaring squarely at him.

It then used its heated helmet as a shield against the spell barrage and charged at Hajime. He was still somewhat disoriented, his vision still blurry, so he could only hear the Behemoth closing in behind him, and his classmates screaming and yelling ahead of him.

Hajime gathered the last remaining dregs of his strength and jumped to the side. A second later, the Behemoth smashed into the ground, using all of its hate and rage to fuel its attack. The entire bridge shook as it fell. Massive cracks spread out from the point of impact. The bridge groaned in protest one last time, before...collapsing entirely.

The repeated attacks had finally driven it past the point of endurance.

"Graaaaaaaaah?!" The Behemoth roared angrily as it desperately tried to find purchase on the crumbling bridge with its nails. However, every spot it latched onto crumbled as well, and after a final, fruitless struggle, it fell to the depths of hell. Its final screams echoed throughout the chamber.

Hajime too, crawled desperately across the collapsing bridge, trying to find somewhere to grab, but all of his handholds crumbled away just as quickly.

Ah, I'm not gonna make it... He muttered those words inside his head as he gave up. Looking over to his classmates one last time, he saw Kaori desperately trying to run over to him, while Shizuku and Kouki had both of her arms and were holding her back. His other classmates were all pale as well, covering their eyes or mouth with their hands as they watched. Captain Meld and the other knights all watched with painful expressions on their faces as they saw Hajime fall.

ᐧᖺ ᐧᖺ ᐧᖺ ᐧᖺ ᐧᖺ ᐧᖺ ᐧᖺ ᐧᖺ ᐧᖺ ᐧᖺ ᐧᖺ ᐧᖺ ᐧᖺ

Finally, the entire bridge fell away, and Hajime plummeted down to the depths of hell, face staring blankly upwards. His outstretched hand grasped uselessly at the fading light.

ᐧᖺ ᐧᖺ ᐧᖺ ᐧᖺ ᐧᖺ ᐧᖺ ᐧᖺ ᐧᖺ ᐧᖺ ᐧᖺ ᐧᖺ ᐧᖺ ᐧᖺ

He listened to the screams of the Behemoth that grew fainter and fainter. He listened to the bridge crumble away into nothingness. And then, all too soon, Hajime was swallowed up into the darkness along with the last of the rubble.

Time itself seemed to slow down as Kaori watched Hajime fall into the depths of the earth, despair evident in her eyes. The conversation she had last night with Hajime played back in her mind over and over.

They had talked under the moonlight, drinking Hajime's subpar excuse for black tea. That was the first time she had ever had such a leisurely conversation.

She remembered the nightmare that had prompted her visit, and how surprised Hajime had looked when she'd suddenly showed up in front of his room. He had even taken her silly dream so seriously. And before she'd realized it, her fears had vanished and they had been talking happily about anything and everything.

She had returned to her room on cloud nine, until she remembered she had visited him in a rather daring outfit, and squirmed with embarrassment. Then seconds later she felt a little depressed, thinking she must not have much charm since Hajime hadn't reacted to her appearance in the least. And then, she also remembered how she'd tried to forget the whole thing had ever happened when she saw Shizuku's exasperated expression.

But most importantly, she remembered the promise she made to Hajime that night. The promise to protect him. The promise Hajime had suggested to ease Kaori's fears. She repeated that promise in her head over and over and over again as she watched Hajime get swallowed up by the murky abyss.

She heard a faint, distant scream, and then realized it was her own, before returning to her senses. Her face twisted in anguish as the reality of what happened hit her again.

"Let me go! I have to go to Nagumo-kun! I promised him! I promised I'd protect him! Let me goooo!" Shizuku and Kouki struggled to restrain Kaori, who looked about ready to jump into the chasm herself. She struggled more fiercely than anyone would have thought possible given that slender frame of hers.

If that kept up Kaori would end up hurting herself. However, they definitely couldn't afford to let go either. If they did, she would most certainly jump off the cliff without hesitation. She was already beyond any sense of rationality. Grief had completely overtaken her mind.

"Kaori, stop! Kaori!" It was precisely because she understood how Kaori felt that Shizuku was unable to find any words to comfort her friend. All she could do was keep calling her name.

"Kaori! There's no point in throwing your life away too! Nagumo is already beyond help! Calm down! You'll hurt yourself at this rate!" Those were the best words that came to Kouki's mind. However, they were also the worst words he could've said to Kaori at that moment.

"What do you mean 'beyond help'?! Nagumo-kun's not dead! I have to go save him! He needs me!" It was clear to everyone else present that there was no saving Hajime. He had fallen off a cliff so deep that no one could even see the bottom.

However, Kaori wasn't in a state of mind where she could accept that fact. Anything anyone said would simply backfire and double her resolve to jump down there herself. Ryutarou and the other students were all looking at her worriedly, at a complete loss for what to do.

It was then that Captain Meld walked up to Kaori and gave her a hard chop to the back of her neck. She spasmed once, then fell unconscious. Kouki caught Kaori before she fell, glaring angrily at Captain Meld all the while. Before he could say anything, Shizuku cut him off and bowed to Captain Meld.

"Sorry. And thank you."

"I...don't deserve your thanks. But I cannot allow anyone else to die. Everyone, we're heading back to the surface as fast as possible... I'll leave her in your care."

"I would have taken her myself, even if you tried to stop me." Kouki unhappily watched Captain Meld walk off, but he remained quiet. As Shizuku was taking Kaori from him, she softly told him the following.

"We couldn't stop her, so Captain Meld did it for us. You realize we don't have much time, right?"

"Kaori's grief might have affected the entire class's morale, and more importantly, someone had to stop her before she hurt herself... Now get your butt up front and open a path for us. You have to take the lead until we all make it out of this... Nagumo-kun said the exact same thing, remember?"

Kouki nodded reluctantly at Shizuku's words. "You're right, let's get out of here."

One of their classmates had died right in front of their eyes. That had shaken the whole class a great deal. Everyone was staring at the chasm where the bridge had been in a daze. A few of the students even sat down where they were, proclaiming things like "I'm done with this crap!" Just as Hajime had told Kouki earlier, they needed a leader to guide them.

Kouki turned to his classmates and raised his voice.

"Everyone! Right now we need to focus on surviving! We have to retreat!" His words slowly spurred the class into action.

The magic circles were still spitting out more Traum Soldiers. Their numbers were gradually being replenished. A head-on battle would've been dangerous, and besides, there was no need for them to fight anymore. Kouki yelled as loudly as he could, urging his classmates onward. Captain Meld and the other knights all tried to inspire some vigor into the students as well. Finally, everyone had made it onto the staircase.

It was a very long staircase. They kept climbing through the darkness, unable to see where the stairs truly led. Judging by their pace, they must have climbed over thirty floors already. Even with body-strengthening magic, the students soon began to grow tired. They were already partially exhausted from their earlier fight, too, so the never-ending darkness of the staircase sapped at their willpower.

Around the time he was thinking he should stop the group for a short break, Captain Meld saw a wall up ahead with a magic circle engraved on it.

The students all began to look a little more hopeful as Captain Meld cautiously approached the door set into the wall and began investigating. He passed a Fair Scope over it as well.

The results showed that it was unlikely to be a trap. The magic circle's purpose was to move aside the wall, or so it seemed. Captain Meld chanted the inscription on the magic circle, pouring his mana into it. Like a ninja's hidden passage, the wall began to turn, until it revealed a short corridor leading to the room ahead. As they passed through, the students found themselves on the twentieth floor once more.

"Did we make it?"

"We made it!"

"We did it... We really did it..."

They all let out relieved sighs as they finally caught sight of the familiar scenery of the twentieth floor. Some of them burst into tears, while others just sat down where they stood. Even Kouki was leaning against the wall, and it looked like he very much wanted to sit down as well.

However, they were still in the labyrinth. Even if this was a floor higher up, monsters could still appear any time. As such, they had to escape the labyrinth proper before they could fully relax.

Captain Meld buried his sympathy somewhere deep inside and yelled at the students to get back up, his face now a commander's mask.

"Hey, you louts! Quit laying around! If you relax here, then you'll be dead before you make it out! Now get into formation, avoid combat as much as possible, and take the quickest route back up! Come on, we've only got a little ways to go!"

Some of the students tried to complain about how he could let them take a short break at least, but his pointed stare cut them short. The group reluctantly staggered back to their feet. Kouki hid his own exhaustion and took up the lead again. The knights did most of the fighting in the few battles they couldn't avoid, and the party took the shortest route they could back to the surface.

Until finally, the nostalgic sight of the main gate and receptionist's desk became visible. Though it hadn't even been a full day since they had entered, many of the students felt as if it had been ages since they last laid eyes on it.

The students all felt relief wash over them as they stepped outside. Some of them just sprawled out on the ground, spread-eagle right outside the gate. Most of them were just glad they made it back in one piece.

However, some of the students, like Shizuku, who was still carrying an unconscious Kaori; Kouki; Ryutarou, who was staring worriedly at them both; Eri; Suzu; and the girl Hajime had saved—all had glum expressions.

The receptionist's gaze lingered on those students for a while, until Captain Meld went up to her to give his report.

The trap they had discovered on the twentieth floor was exceedingly dangerous. Though the bridge had been destroyed, it was possible the trap was still functioning, so it needed to be reported. Along with the fact that Hajime had died. Captain Meld struggled to keep the pain off his face, but he was unable to repress the sigh that slipped through.

None of the students felt like exploring Horaud, so they all returned to the inn. Some of them chatted with each other, but most of them just went straight to sleep, burned out by the events of the day.

Only Daisuke Hiyama left the inn, found an inconspicuous corner of town, and squatted down, hugging his knees. He buried his face into his legs and sat there, unmoving. Had any of his classmates picked that time to pass by, they would have thought he was simply depressed.

However, the truth was...

"Heheheheh... Hee hee hee. I-It was all his fault. Because that damn loser...g-got cocky... I-It was divine punishment. I didn't do anything wrong... It was all for Shirasaki's sake... Now she...doesn't have to waste time with that loser... I didn't do anything wrong... Hehehe." He cackled evilly as he justified his actions to himself.

Indeed, it was Hiyama who had unleashed that errant fireball at

Hajime.

Back when Hajime had been running to the staircase, Hiyama had still been undecided on what to do. But then he had caught sight of Kaori gazing at Hajime, and it felt as if a devil had whispered in his ears, *No one would notice if you killed him right now.*

And so, Hiyama had sold his soul to that devil. He had timed it perfectly, making sure no one would notice, and hurled his fireball at Hajime. It would have been impossible to realize that it was his fireball specifically amidst that storm of spells. And Hiyama's particular affinity was with wind magic. There would be no proof he altered his trajectory, and no one would even notice.

Hiyama kept trying to convince himself he was safe while grinning gleefully to himself. However, it was at that moment that he heard a voice behind him.

"Huh, I should've known it was you. To think the first murderer I'd meet in another world would be my classmate... You're pretty rotten, you know that?"

"Huh?! Wh-Who are you?!" Hiyama turned around in a panic. The person standing behind him was a classmate of his. More importantly, it was someone he recognized.

"Wh-what are you doing here..."

"That's hardly what's important right now. So...how does it feel? To be a murderer? To remove your rival in love, permanently, by killing him in the confusion of our escape?"

The figure snickered, as if watching a particularly funny comedy. Hiyama knew he wasn't really one to talk, as he'd committed the murder, but it was amazing how unfazed his classmate was at the death of another person. Until just moments ago, that person had seemed just as exhausted and shocked as his other classmates, but there was not even a trace of that any longer.

"...So this is what you're really like?" Hiyama muttered, utterly dumbfounded.

The shaded figure sneered haughtily at Hiyama.

"What I'm really like? Please, there's no need to make such a big deal out of it. Everyone masks their true selves somehow. But we're getting off topic here... What do you think would happen if everyone found out? What would she think of you?"

"Wha—?! N-no one...would believe you... You don't have any proof..."

"You're right, I don't. But everyone trusts me, so they'd still believe me. Especially if I'm accusing *you*, who caused this whole disaster in the first place."

Hiyama suddenly found himself cornered. His adversary was just teasing him at that point, playing with an already-trapped rat. No one would've imagined this hidden side of their classmate, so they would never have sided with Hiyama. It would've been far more believable if someone had just told Hiyama that the person standing in front of him had multiple personalities. The sadistic expression he saw looking down at him sent shivers down Hiyama's spine.

"Wh-what do you want with me?!"

"Hm? Now now, don't be like that. You're making it sound like I'm blackmailing you. I actually don't want anything from you right this minute. I guess if I had to say, I'd like for you to become like my hands and feet."

"Y-you can't mean..."

Hiyama was practically being asked to become a slave, so he

naturally hesitated to agree. He wanted to refuse, of course, but he knew if he did that the figure in front of him would tell everyone Hiyama had killed Hajime in cold blood.

Trapped between two unacceptable choices, Hiyama slowly began thinking, *Someday, I'll kill you, too.* However, it appeared his adversary had anticipated even that, and tempted him with the one thing Hiyama couldn't resist

"Don't you want to make Kaori Shirasaki yours?"

"Huh?! Wh-whatever do you..."

His dark thoughts vanished in an instant, and Hiyama stared in slack-jawed shock. The figure grinned wickedly, then continued pouring out honeyed words.

"If you swear your loyalty to me...I'll give her to you. I had originally planned to give Nagumo-kun this offer, but...well, you killed him, didn't you? Though I guess you're more suited for these tasks than he is, so all's well that ends well."

"...What are you after? What's your endgame?!" Hiyama's words were frantic, as he still couldn't grasp the situation.

"Heheh, my goals have nothing to do with you. Let me just say there's something I want... So? What will it be?"

He'd been made a fool of the whole time, and Hiyama couldn't stand that, but his fear at his classmate's sudden transformation greatly eclipsed his vexation. And either way, he realized he didn't really have a choice, so he nodded, resigned to his fate.

"...I'll listen to you."

"Ahahahaha, perfect! Truth be told, I really didn't want to incriminate my fellow classmate. Well, let's get along now, Mr. Murderer. *Ahahaha.*"

The blackmailer spun around and headed back to the inn, laughing heartily. Hiyama watched as his living nightmare walked away, then softly muttered, "Damn it..."

No matter how much Hiyama wanted to forget it, to pretend it didn't happen, the memory of what he'd done refused to leave him. And the same could be said for the sight of Kaori's face when she had seen Hajime fall. Her expression had shown her feelings more clearly than any words ever could.

Once his tired classmates had rested up, they too would calm down a little, and the reality of Hajime's death would hit them. And then, they too would realize Kaori's feelings. That she had hung around Hajime out of more than just goodwill.

Once they realized how hard it had hit Kaori, they would focus their anger on the cause of it. On the person who'd carelessly ensnared them in that trap.

Hiyama would have to tread very lightly. Or else he would lose his place among them. He knew he had already crossed a line, so there was no stopping now. So long as he followed his classmate's orders, a future he had thought no longer possible, a future where he made Kaori his own, might still exist.

"*Hehehe...* I-It'll be all right. Everything will work out. I didn't do anything wrong..." He buried his face in his knees once more, then went back to muttering.

This time, no one interrupted him.

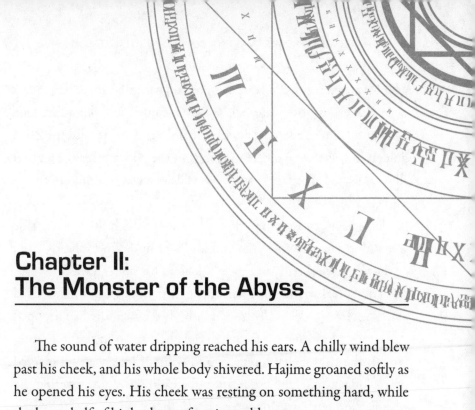

Chapter II:
The Monster of the Abyss

The sound of water dripping reached his ears. A chilly wind blew past his cheek, and his whole body shivered. Hajime groaned softly as he opened his eyes. His cheek was resting on something hard, while the lower half of his body was freezing cold.

Groggily, he pushed himself up off the ground, an aching pain running throughout his entire body all the while.

"Owwww, where...I thought I..." He steadied his head with one hand, then tried to recall how he'd ended up in that position.

His surroundings were relatively dark, but thanks to the green crystals scattered about, it wasn't pitch black. He looked behind him and saw a river five meters wide, and noticed that he was still half submerged within it. His upper body was resting on a boulder that jutted out from the riverbank.

"Oh, yeah...the bridge broke, and then I fell. And then..." A haze lifted from his mind, and his brain finally started working again.

A stroke of luck had saved him from falling to his death.

Halfway down the cliff he had seen an opening in the wall from which water was flooding out. A waterfall, basically. There had in fact been numerous little waterfalls as he continued to fall, and Hajime had found himself swept away by them, until eventually they had guided him into one of the openings in the cliff, much like a water slide from hell. The fact that he was still alive was nothing short of a miracle.

Especially considering that halfway through his water ride, something smacked into him and knocked him out. Honestly, even he didn't comprehend just how miraculous his survival was.

"I don't really remember what happened, but I guess I'm not dead at least... *Achoo*! I-It's really cold." His body temperature had dropped dangerously low due to how much time he'd spent in the cold water. He ran the risk of developing hypothermia if he stayed submerged much longer, so Hajime quickly pulled himself out. Shivering, he stripped and started wringing out his clothes.

Then, in nothing but his underwear, he cast a transmutation spell. He used it to carve a magic circle into the hard earth.

"Gah, I'm so cold that it's hard to concentrate..." He was trying to inscribe the "flare" spell. It was a very basic spell that even kids could cast with a ten-centimeter magic circle.

However, not only did Hajime have no mana crystals with which to enhance the magic circle, he also had a magical affinity of zero. As such, he needed a complicated magic circle over one meter in diameter just to cast a simple flare spell.

After ten grueling minutes he finally finished his magic circle and chanted the incantation.

"Mine desire is fire. Fire, imbued with the essence of light—Flare... Gah, why does such a simple spell have such an exaggerated incantation? Can't believe I have to chant something so embarrassing... Haah..." He sighed again, something he'd been doing quite frequently as of late, and brought himself closer to the fist-sized flame. He also laid his clothes out next to it to dry.

"Where am I...? I fell pretty far down, so can I even make it back up?" Worry gripped his chest as he calmed down and considered his situation while warming himself by the fire.

He felt like bawling his eyes out, and tears did form in the corners of his eyes, but Hajime knew he would break down completely if he let himself cry, so he held them back. He stubbornly wiped his tears, then slapped his cheeks.

"I'm gonna do this. I've gotta get back to the surface somehow. It'll be fine. I'm sure I'll figure something out." He gave himself a pep talk and renewed his determination, wiping the sullen expression off his face. After that he simply gazed into the flames, mulling over his options.

After about twenty minutes he had warmed himself sufficiently and his clothes were mostly dry, so he decided to head out. He didn't know what floor he was on, but he was clearly deep in the labyrinth, and it wouldn't be strange for monsters to pop out at any time. Hajime walked as cautiously as he could down the long passageway.

The path Hajime was going down resembled a cave of sorts.

It was nothing like the orderly rectangular passageways he'd been on in the upper floors. Boulders and other obstructions showed up at random intervals, and the path itself was twisting and winding. Much like the path they had found at the end of the twentieth floor.

However, the size of this one was on a completely different scale. Even with boulders and the like obstructing parts of the path, it was twenty meters wide. In fact, even the "narrow" stretches were still at least ten meters wide. Though it slowed his progress, Hajime moved from cover to cover, making sure to stick to the shadows as he advanced.

He had no idea how long he walked for. Around the time Hajime was starting to grow tired, he found himself at a fork in the road. Though it was more like a street intersection than a fork. Hajime hid behind a boulder as he deliberated which way to go.

While he was thinking, he saw something move out of the corner of his eye, and he hurriedly shrank back, behind the safety of the boulder.

He timidly peeked out from behind the boulder and saw a giant white ball of fur hopping down the passage directly across from him. It had rather long ears and looked just like a rabbit. However, it was the size of a dog, and it also had very thick hind legs. Plus, there were veins of pulsing dark red mana trailing down its body. It looked quite disturbing.

It was clearly deadly, and Hajime decided to go down one of the paths to avoid running into it. Judging by the position of its ears, Hajime determined that it would have a harder time spotting him if he went right.

He held his breath and waited for the perfect moment to run. Eventually the rabbit turned around and lowered its head, busily sniffing the ground. It was at that moment that Hajime attempted to leap out from behind the boulder.

But then the rabbit suddenly twitched, rising back up as it did. It warily looked around, its ears twitching.

C-crap! Did it see me? O-or am I safe? Hajime had quickly retreated behind the safety of the boulder, and he tried to calm his pounding heart as he clung to the rock face for dear life. He broke out in a cold sweat, afraid the rabbit's exceptional hearing would be able to pick up on his pounding heartbeat.

However, it was not Hajime that had spooked the rabbit.

"Graaaaaah!" With a bestial roar, a white-furred wolf monster leaped out from behind a different boulder, heading straight for the rabbit.

The wolf was as big as a large dog, and had two tails sprouting from its behind. Just like the rabbit, pulsing veins of dark red mana ran down its body. Then, out of nowhere, two more Twin-Tailed Wolves suddenly leaped out into the open.

Hajime peeked out from behind the boulder once more to see what was happening. The wolves were clearly attacking the poor bunny, though the creature was nowhere near cute enough to warrant a description like "bunny." Hajime slowly got to his feet, planning on escaping during the confusion of the fight. However...

"Kyuuu!" The rabbit let out a cute squeal, then leaped up, did a turn in midair, and caught one of the wolves with a powerful roundhouse kick.

Boom! It didn't sound anything like how a kick should, and connected squarely with the face of its target.

A second later—crack! Together with a very ominous sound, the wolf's head was turned to a very unnatural angle.

Hajime stood stock-still as the battle raged on.

The rabbit then used the centrifugal force of its spin to turn itself upside down and hurtle toward the ground like a meteor. Then, a mere instant before impact, it righted itself once more. A powerful axe kick came down on the wolf standing at the rabbit's point of landing.

Smash! The second wolf didn't even have time to cry out before its head was pulverized.

Two more wolves came out of hiding and charged the rabbit.

Hajime thought that was the end for the rabbit, but it flipped itself upside down, and like a breakdancer, stood on its ears while spinning, legs spread out. The two new wolves were sent flying by the tornado kicks and slammed into the wall. And they hit that wall with a splat, spraying blood everywhere, then slid to the ground, unmoving.

The last wolf growled menacingly, its tails standing straight up. Suddenly, electricity began running down its tails. It looked like that was the magic the wolves could use.

"Graaaah!!" The wolf roared, and bolts of lightning flew toward the rabbit. But with nimble steps, the rabbit swiftly dodged the incoming bolts of lightning. Then, at the moment the lightning attacks stopped, the rabbit hopped forward and hit the last wolf with a somersault kick. The wolf's head bent back with a sickening crack, and it fell to the ground, utterly still. It was yet another wolf with a broken neck.

The Kickmaster Rabbit let out another squeal.

"Kyu!"

Is that supposed to be a victory cry? After that, it started scratching its ears with its leg.

You've gotta be freaking kidding me. Hajime smiled in disbelief, his body still completely still. "Dangerous" didn't do the beast justice. That thing made the Traum Soldiers Hajime and the others had fought earlier look like nothing more than toy skeletons. In fact, it might've even been more dangerous than the Behemoth they had fought, since the Behemoth's attack patterns had at least been easy to read.

Hajime trembled in fear, knowing that his life was forfeit if he were discovered. Due to his fear, he unconsciously took a step back. But that was a mistake.

Clatter. The noise reverberated throughout the cavern.

He had accidentally kicked a pebble when he'd stepped back. He couldn't believe he'd made such a basic blunder. Rivulets of cold sweat were pouring down his forehead after the fact. The rabbit's neck creaked like a badly oiled machine as it turned to look in the direction of the kicked pebble.

The Kickmaster Rabbit clearly saw Hajime. Its glowing red eyes glared at him. His entire body stiffened, like a deer caught in headlights. His brain was yelling at him to run, but it felt like his nerves had all been cut, so his body refused to listen.

The rabbit turned its whole body around, then began gathering strength for a leap. *Here it comes!* Hajime instinctively managed to guess the moment of the rabbit's leap. The speed of its jump was so ridiculously fast that it left afterimages behind it.

Driven purely by instinct, Hajime threw himself to the side. An instant later, a kick with the force of a cannonball slammed into the ground Hajime had been standing on. The force of it gouged the earth below. Hajime rolled over and over on the hard ground before coming to a stop in a sitting position. His face paled when he saw the pulverized ground and he quickly started running.

The rabbit leisurely got back up and dove toward him with another earth-shattering leap. Hajime hurriedly transmuted a wall behind him, but the rabbit easily blew it away and aimed another kick at Hajime. He instinctively brought up his left arm to shield himself from the blow. That somehow helped him avoid getting his face blown apart, but the shockwave of the kick sent him flying backward. Waves of excruciating pain ran down his left arm.

"Gaaaah!" When he looked down, he saw his arm was dangling at a very unnatural angle. His bones had been completely shattered. He crouched down in pain, then looked over at the rabbit. This time it wasn't lunging forward, but leisurely hopping toward him. He wasn't sure if it was just his imagination, but it felt almost like the rabbit was looking down on him. It was *toying* with him.

But even then, all Hajime could do was unceremoniously continue backing up. Finally, the Kickmaster Rabbit stopped right in front of him. It glared down at Hajime as if it were looking at a worm. It then raised one of its legs up high, as if to show off before slaughtering its prey.

So this is where I die... Hajime thought, sinking into the depths of despair. He looked up at the rabbit with defeated eyes. Its leg came swinging down, together with a whoosh of wind.

Hajime closed his eyes, terrified of what was coming.

"......"

However, the blow he was expecting never came.

Hajime timidly opened his eyes to the sight of the rabbit's foot inches from his face. The rabbit had stopped just before hitting him. Hajime despaired, thinking the rabbit intended to toy with him further, but then he noticed there was something off about it. A closer glance revealed that the rabbit was trembling.

Wh-what? Why's it shaking? It almost looks like it's scared... It wasn't "almost"; it actually was scared.

A new monster had appeared from the right-hand corridor Hajime had tried to escape into. And said monster was massive. It stood over two meters tall, and like everything else on that floor so far, had white fur. And just like the others, it had veins of dark red mana running down its body. The closest thing it resembled was a bear. However, unlike a bear, it had massive forearms that went all the way down to its feet, which ended in wicked sharp claws over thirty centimeters long.

The Claw Bear had closed in while the rabbit had been focused on Hajime, and it glared down at both of them. A moment of silence enveloped the corridor. The rabbit had gone stiff out of fear and stopped moving. Rather, it couldn't move. It was in the exact same situation that Hajime had been in mere moments ago. It was staring up at the bear, completely immobilized.

"...Grrrrr." The bear let out a low growl, as if tired of watching two unmoving statues.

"Wha—?!" The rabbit quickly did an about-face and began hopping away as fast as possible. The explosive jumps it had used to annihilate its foes were instead being used to rapidly jet it to safety.

However, its escape was still unsuccessful.

The Claw Bear rushed forward, surprisingly fast for its large frame, and swiped its paw at the Kickmaster Rabbit. The rabbit nimbly dodged, twisting its body to avoid the paw's sharp claws.

It looked to Hajime like the rabbit had somehow managed to dodge perfectly, avoiding even a glancing blow.

However... The moment the rabbit landed, a fountain of blood spurted forth, and the two halves of the rabbit fell in different directions.

Hajime watched on in shock. That overwhelmingly powerful rabbit had been killed so easily. It hadn't even had time to put up a fight. Hajime understood why it had been so scared and tried to run earlier. That monster was on a completely different level. Even the rabbit's Capoeira-esque martial art skills had been of no use in the face of its might.

The bear leisurely walked up to the rabbit's corpse, speared one chunk of it with its claw, and began scarfing it down, making sickening squelching noises.

Hajime was rooted to the spot. The combination of fear and the bear's sharp gaze kept him pinned in place. It kept its eyes on Hajime even as it chewed on the rabbit.

It finished the rabbit off in three huge bites, then turned its body around and roared at Hajime. Its eyes told Hajime everything he needed to know. The bear's next meal would be him.

Panic gripped his mind as he stared into the eyes of the predator.

"Eyaaaaaah!!!" He let out a garbled scream and momentarily forgot about the pain of his broken left arm as he mounted a desperate escape attempt.

However, it was impossible for Hajime to escape from an enemy not even that rabbit had been able to flee from. He heard the sound of rushing wind, and an instant later something hard hit his left side. He was flung against the wall.

"Gahaah!" Hajime coughed violently as all the air was pushed out of his lungs, before sliding down the wall to fall in a heap on the ground. His vision blurred over, but he could still make out the bear chewing on something.

But he couldn't quite make out what it was. It had already finished eating the rabbit, so it couldn't have been that. Then he realized the bear was chewing a very familiar looking arm. Still confused, Hajime looked over to his left side, which had become inexplicably lighter. Or, more specifically, to where his left arm should have been...

"H-huh?" His expression stiffened, and he tilted his head in bewilderment. *Why don't I have an arm? Why is there so much blood spurting out?* His mind—no, his entire being—was rejecting the reality his eyes saw. But he could only feign ignorance for so long. The excruciating pain of having his arm ripped off finally hit, which brought him back to reality soon enough.

"Agaaaaaaaaahh!!!" Hajime's scream of anguish echoed throughout the labyrinth. His left arm had been torn cleanly off from the elbow down.

That was the bear's particular magic ability. Its claws were wrapped in blades of wind, and could cut thirty centimeters past what their length would suggest. All that considered, it was a miracle Hajime only lost his arm. Hajime wasn't sure if it was because the bear was toying with him too, or if he was just lucky, but that last attack should have cut him in half.

After it finished wolfing down his arm, the bear slowly started walking toward Hajime. Unlike the rabbit, it didn't seem to be looking down on Hajime. Instead, it merely saw him as food, nothing more.

It slowly extended one of its claws toward Hajime. The fact that he wasn't ripped to shreds by it told Hajime the bear meant to eat him alive.

"Aaaaaah! Gaaaah! T-Transmute!" His face covered in tears, snot, and drool, Hajime screamed out his transmutation spell and set his right hand against the wall behind him. He was barely even aware of his own actions any longer.

He had been ridiculed as incompetent and had no magical

affinity or physical talents to speak of, so Hajime, the weakest of them all, relied on the only power he did possess. A skill that was normally only used to craft armor and weapons.

Hajime, who possessed a job normally only meant for blacksmiths, desperately fought back. Because he'd been ridiculed for his lack of strength, he'd used all of his knowledge to think of unique ways to put his power to use. His results had been so unorthodox that he'd surprised even the knights, and his fervent devotion to his lone skill had even made him somewhat useful to his other classmates. This was why, even in the pits of hell, Hajime instinctively relied on this skill, and it was also why that skill was able to save him.

His sky blue mana shone briefly, and a depression opened up in the wall behind him. Hajime barely avoided the bear's outstretched paw and tumbled back into the hole he had created behind him.

The bear roared, furious that its prey had managed to escape from right under its nose.

"Graaaaaaaaaah!!!" It wrapped wind blades around its claws once more, then thrust its paw into the hole Hajime had made for himself. The wall screeched angrily as the bear's claws gouged furrows into it.

"Aaaaaaaaaaaaaaah! Transmute! Transmute! Transmute!" Hajime's panicked mind registered the bear's roar and the sound of the walls being gouged away, so he continued transmuting continuously, trying to put as much distance between him and the bear as possible.

He didn't dare look back for even a second. He just kept transmuting, and crawling forward into each new opening he made. The pain of losing his left arm was temporarily forgotten. His survival instincts had kicked in, and he transmuted like his life depended on it. Which, frankly, it did.

He had no way to tell how far he'd dragged himself. Hajime had no idea; he just knew he could no longer hear the bear thundering behind him. In truth, he had not actually traveled all that far. Transmutation was only effective within two meters of his target (this was still double what it had been initially), and blood loss had slowed him considerably. He wouldn't be able to keep moving for much longer.

In fact, he was already on the verge of unconsciousness. Still, he squeezed every last ounce of strength out of himself to keep crawling forward. However...

"Transmute... Transmute... Transmute... Transm..." He kept chanting the incantation, but the wall in front of him remained unchanged. His mana had run out before his consciousness. Drained of all his strength, his hand fell away from the wall, and he collapsed on the ground.

Hajime used every ounce of his willpower to keep himself conscious, rolling himself onto his back. He gazed blankly at the dark ceiling above him. There were no green crystals there to light his surroundings.

Hajime began recalling events from his past. *Guess this is what they mean when they say your life flashes before your eyes.* He went over his life, from preschool, to elementary, to middle school, and then finally to high school. Memories flew by, until at last they stopped... on the night he had talked with Kaori. He recalled the moonlight spilling in from the window, and the promise she had made to him.

His consciousness finally faded as he recalled that fond memory. But before he sank fully into unconsciousness, he felt water dripping onto his cheek. It felt like someone's tears.

Drip... Drip... The water trailed down his cheek and dripped into his mouth. Hajime's faint consciousness slowly began to grow brighter. Bewildered, he sluggishly opened his eyes.

I'm alive...? Did someone save me? He raised himself up, only to bump his head on the low ceiling.

"Agah?!" He remembered too late that he had made the ceiling above him a mere fifty centimeters tall. Hajime raised his arms up to the ceiling to transmute a larger hole. However, only a single arm entered his line of sight, and he cried out in surprise.

He stared at the stump of his left arm in disbelief for a moment before remembering he had lost it recently. A sharp pang of pain ran down the place where his left arm should have been. He was experiencing phantom pain for the first time. His face twisted in anguish, and he reflexively gripped his left arm, only to realize—that there was slight swelling where his arm had been cut off, and the wound had already closed.

"H-how...? It was bleeding so much..." It was too dark to see, but if there had been any light it would've been clear that Hajime was lying in a pool of his own blood. In fact, Hajime had lost so much blood that he should by all rights have been dead.

He felt around with his right hand and felt the sticky sensation of blood all around him. It was recent enough that it hadn't dried yet. With that, Hajime was able to confirm that his bleeding out had not been just a dream, and that it had been only a few minutes since he'd lost consciousness.

And yet his wound had completely closed up, and as Hajime pondered how such a thing was possible, he felt water drip onto his cheeks and mouth once more. He felt somewhat revitalized as the drops slid down his throat.

"Don't tell me...this is what saved me?" Hajime was still a little lightheaded from the blood loss and phantom pain pangs, but he reached his hand out to the source of the water and transmuted the earth around it.

Still somewhat unsteady, he continued transmuting deeper and deeper into the wall. The strange liquid that he now realized couldn't possibly have been water, continued oozing out of cracks in the rock. Interestingly enough, it restored his mana as well, so Hajime was able to continue transmuting without running out of energy. Hajime deliriously continued transmuting, single-mindedly seeking out the water's source.

Eventually, the slow trickle transformed into a faster stream, and Hajime finally arrived at the source of the liquid.

"This... is..." The source of the liquid was a basketball-sized crystal that emitted a pale blue light.

The crystal was buried into the wall around it, and the liquid was pouring out from underneath it. It had an aura of wondrous beauty about it. The light it emitted was just a shade darker than an aquamarine's. Hajime stared at it in wonder, his pain momentarily forgotten. Then, as if drawn to it, he put his mouth to the crystal.

As he did so the, the pain, the haze that had fallen over his mind, and the fatigue—it all left his body. As he had suspected, it was the liquid from this crystal that had saved Hajime's life. Which meant that the liquid contained some kind of healing agent. His phantom pain could never be cured for good, and the blood he'd lost wasn't coming back, but the rest of his wounds and all of his mana were restored in an instant.

Though Hajime didn't know it, the crystal was actually a "Divinity Stone." Divinity Stones were rare crystals, and considered to be one of the world's greatest historical treasures. Modern day people thought them a lost legend.

Divinity Stones were created when a large clump of mana pooled together and crystallized over the course of a thousand years. They ranged from thirty to forty centimeters in diameter, and then over the course of a few hundred years their saturated mana liquefied and poured back into the earth.

The liquid they secreted was known as Ambrosia, and it healed all wounds. It couldn't regrow missing limbs, but supposedly it extended one's life so long as they continued to drink it. It was also referred to as the "elixir of life." Legend claimed that Ehit healed the masses with this very Ambrosia.

He realized he'd just narrowly escaped a very painful death, and Hajime slumped down against the wall. He hugged his trembling body, then buried his face in his knees, the fear of death still fresh in his mind. He no longer had the energy to try and escape. The constant stress and fear had finally broken him.

If it was just enemies he had to face, then he might have managed somehow. He would have rejoiced at the fact he was still alive, then gotten back up.

But the baleful gaze of the bear had broken him. Those were the eyes of a predator that saw Hajime as nothing more than food. The eyes most humans, who stood at the top of the food chain, never even had to dream about. Those eyes, and the sight of the bear chewing on his own arm, had completely crushed Hajime's spirit.

Someone...anyone...please save me... But he was deep within the pits of hell, so there was absolutely no way his thoughts would reach anyone. He didn't know how long he sat there. But for the longest time, he just huddled in a fetal position, begging for salvation he knew would not come.

٭ ٭ ٭ ٭ ٭ ٭ ٭ ٭ ٭ ٭ ٭ ٭ ٭

Four days had now passed since Hajime had fallen from the bridge. In that time he had barely moved, drawing the sustenance he needed from the Divinity Stone. However, while Ambrosia could keep a man alive through all but the most heinous of conditions, it could not sate his hunger. Though he couldn't die, Hajime suffered constant pangs of hunger, along with the phantom pain that ran down his missing left arm.

Why is this happening to me? That question had been something he constantly thought about.

He couldn't sleep because of the pain and hunger, and if he drank more Ambrosia, all it did was clear his mind to let him feel the pain more vividly. Over and over, his fatigue brought him to the edge of consciousness, only for the pain and hunger to draw him back. And then to escape the pain he would drink more Ambrosia, which only invited further pain. He had repeated that cycle more times than he could count.

At some point, Hajime stopped drinking the Ambrosia altogether. He had unconsciously chosen the fastest way to end his pain.

"If all that awaits me is eternal pain...then I might as well..." He muttered to himself, clearly defeated, and let his consciousness slip away.

Three days went by.

The pain, once it passed a certain threshold, abated for a while, but that was simply the calm before the storm. His starvation came back in full force, and excruciating hunger pangs continuously wracked his stomach. The phantom pain continued as well, tormenting Hajime all the while. It felt as if his fingernails were slowly being peeled off one by one, only for salt to be dumped in the open wounds.

I'm...still not dead yet...? Aaah... Please, please...I just want to live... While craving death, he still instinctively clung to life. His thoughts began to contradict themselves. Hajime was no longer capable of rational thought. His delirious mumblings no longer made any semblance of sense.

Yet another three days passed.

Without the Ambrosia's aid, he would expire in another two days. He had drunk nothing for all this time, as well, so his thirst mingled with his hunger.

However, a short while earlier, around the eighth day since discovering the Divinity Stone, a strange shift in his mentality had begun. Hovering between wishing for death and praying for salvation, his mind had begun to warp, and dark thoughts began welling up from Hajime's subconscious.

Like slime, they had oozed into the cracks in his heart caused by his suffering, and slowly eaten away at his soul.

Why do I have to suffer so much...? What did I ever do to deserve this? Why me...? Why did it end up like this? God just kidnapped me and dropped me off at this place... And then my classmates betrayed me... I was looked down on by a rabbit... And then that bastard ate my arm... His thoughts continued to grow darker. Like black ink slowly spreading through white parchment, Hajime's pure heart slowly grew sullied.

Someone was at fault, someone had pushed this unfairness on him, someone had hurt him like this... His mind started searching for an enemy to hate. The pain and hunger and darkness all slowly eroded away Hajime's sanity. His dark thoughts continued to grow.

Why isn't anyone coming to save me? If no one's going to save me, what should I do? How can I make this pain go away? By the ninth day, Hajime was trying to find a way out of his predicament.

Thoughts of how to escape the pain were all that filled him, and even anger and hatred were slowly being worn away. There was no time to be trapped by such petty feelings. Because no matter how much he raged against his foes, Hajime's pain never lessened. In order to escape the absurd and unreasonable situation he was stuck in, unneeded feelings had to be discarded.

What is it I want? I want to live. And what's stopping me from living? The enemy. And just who is the enemy? Everyone and everything that gets in my way, everything that pushes this unreasonable fate onto me. So what is it I should do? I should... I should...

The tenth day. Both hatred and anger had vanished from his heart. The unfair god that thrust him into this world, the classmate that betrayed him, the monsters that wanted to kill him...even the smile of the girl who said she would protect him...they all ceased to matter.

Compared to the pressing need for survival, such tiny feelings meant nothing. Hajime's will resolved into a hardened point. Like the tip of a sword forged from the fires of hell. Sharp, strong, and able to cut through anything.

And his will desired to... *Kill them.* There was no hatred, hostility, or anger in those words. Just a simple statement of fact. In order to live, he had to kill.

Anything that threatened his life was an enemy. And all enemies were to be... *Killed. Kill kill kill kill kill kill kill kill kill kill kill kill kill kill kill kill kill kill kill kill kill kill kill kill kill kill kill kill kill kill kill kill kill kill kill kill.* In order to escape the relentless hunger, he had to *kill them and eat them.* It was at that moment that the kind, quiet Hajime Nagumo, the Hajime who blew everything off with an apology and a smile, the Hajime Kaori had come to admire, ceased to exist.

And a new Hajime Nagumo, one who was willing to mercilessly slaughter anything that stood in his path, was born.

His shattered soul had re-formed once more. And it was not as a mere patchwork, hastily repaired soul. No, this was a soul reforged in the darkness and despair of hell, a soul tempered in pain and instinct. A soul harder than steel.

Hajime dragged his weakened body over to the cavity where the Ambrosia had spilled, then lapped it up like a dog. His hunger and pain still remained, but his body regained its vigor.

Then he roughly wiped his mouth, his eyes sparkling ferociously as a wicked grin spread over his face. His canines peeked through his cruel smile. It was a complete about-face from the kind of person he had been before.

Hajime stood up, and began muttering while he transmuted the ground.

"I'll kill them."

•/• •/• •/• •/• •/• •/• •/• •/• •/• •/• •/• •/• •/•

Twin-Tailed Wolves made their dens in certain parts of the labyrinth floor. They usually moved together in packs of four to six. Alone, they were among the weakest of the monsters that roamed the floor, so they always acted in groups. This pack was no exception, and was a group of four.

They skirted from boulder to boulder, vigilant of their surroundings, searching for a suitable hunting ground. Twin-Tailed Wolves generally preferred to ambush their prey.

They wandered the corridors for a while until finding what they deemed a suitable hunting spot and all hid behind different boulders. All that remained was to wait for prey to fall into their trap. One of the wolves slipped between a small crack in a nearby boulder and the wall, then erased its presence. It licked its lips in anticipation, imagining the flesh it would soon feast on, when suddenly it felt a rather odd sense of unease.

As the wolves' key to survival was their cooperation, the members of a pack all shared a peculiar link with each other. It wasn't as straightforward as telepathy, but they were basically able to tell what the rest of their pack was doing and where they were. And it was that link that tipped the wolf off. They were a pack of four, and yet the wolf could only sense two of its other companions. The wolf that should have been lying in wait on the other end of the corridor suddenly vanished.

Suspicious, the wolf slowly rose on its haunches, when suddenly another one of its comrades howled. The wolf that was hiding on the same side of the wall as the one that had disappeared was feeling a sense of impatience. It was caught in something and trying to escape, but seemed unable to do so.

The two wolves on the other side of the corridor rose to go to its aid. But then the struggling wolf's presence suddenly vanished as well.

Confused, the two wolves rushed over to the far side, but found no one there. Bewildered at the turn of events, the two wolves put their snouts to the ground and began sniffing the area where their pack members had been moments ago.

Suddenly, the ground under them began to cave in, and the walls jutted out to encase them. They tried to jump out, but before they could, the ground around their feet rose up and hardened around them. Normally, the wolves would have easily been able to shatter such frail shackles. Had they not been confused by this unusual situation, they would never have even fallen for such a simple trap.

However, their assailant had predicted their confusion, as well as their hesitation. And their precious few moments of confusion were enough for him to trap them.

"Graaaah?!" The two wolves howled angrily as they found themselves stuck fast inside the wall... Then the wall swallowed them whole, and only the echoes of their screams remained.

It was, of course, Hajime who had trapped the four wolves. Ever since he had resolved to strike back, he had spent each day in ceaseless training, ignoring his pain and hunger. The Ambrosia extended his life and restored his mana, so he was able to focus on his transmutation twenty-four seven. He worked on his speed, his precision, and his range. He knew then that had he gone outside with his current level of skill, he would have died instantly. So he made his base where the Divinity Stone was, and honed the only weapon he possessed. That weapon was, of course, transmutation.

Though he had ignored his pain while he trained, it only continued to grow as time passed. But that pain only spurred his determination, and he redoubled his efforts to improve his transmutation. Thanks to his focused training, his skills increased far more rapidly than they had been up to this point, and he was now able to transmute from over three meters away. Unfortunately, his talent for earth magic itself had not grown at all.

Once he had decided he'd trained enough, he created a small stone container in which he scooped up some Ambrosia, and began wandering the dungeon, transmuting, searching for his first target.

That was when he had found the pack of Twin-Tailed Wolves. He had followed them silently for a while. Of course, he was nearly spotted numerous times, but every time he managed to transmute walls around him and remain inconspicuous. Then, the moment the four split up to head to their ambush points, he had transmuted the wall and dragged one of the wolves into it.

"Now then, still alive, are we? Well, I can't kill anything directly with transmutation, I suppose. I could maybe make spikes come out of the earth, but they wouldn't have enough force to kill monsters this deep in the labyrinth." Hajime grinned wolfishly as he peered down at the trapped monsters through a small hole at his feet. The wolves were all trapped within the wall itself, and couldn't budge an inch. They were all whimpering softly, panic evident in their eyes.

He had, in fact, tried to attack a monster by transmuting a spike to stab it from underneath before, but it hadn't even had enough power to penetrate its hide. That was, after all, something more in the domain of earth magic and not transmutation. In the end, it was still a skill used for mineral processing and production, so it would be impossible for a production skill to have any real power. Which was why trapping them was the best he could do with it.

"I could just suffocate you in here...but I'm not patient enough to wait that long." Hajime's eyes had the glint of a predator to them by that point.

Hajime put his right hand up against the wall and transmuted it. He cut away parts of the boulder little by little, focusing on the image in his mind to make sure his work stayed precise. Eventually, he was able to make a spiral-tipped spear. He then began working on the shaft. He added a handle where the grip would normally be.

"Now then, time for a little digging!" Hajime pointed his spear down at the wolves as he said that. He thrust down, and felt their tough fur and skin deflect his spearhead.

"So I can't stab through, huh? Well, I expected that, though." Why had he not just crafted himself a knife or sword? That was because the stronger a monster got, the tougher its outer hide was, usually. Obviously there were species that were exceptions to the rule, but as Hajime had spent all his time at the castle studying, he knew that a normal knife or sword wouldn't penetrate the hides of monsters at this level.

And that was why he began to twist the handle he made for himself, while applying a steady downward pressure. The spiral-shaped tip began to rotate as he twisted. He had made a drill to pierce the thick hide of monsters.

He pushed the weight of his entire body down into the drill as he turned it with his right hand. Slowly but surely, the drill began to penetrate the wolf's thick hide.

"Graaaaah?!" The wolf howled in pain.

"It hurts, doesn't it? Well, I'm not gonna apologize for it. Gotta do this to live, after all. You'd eat me if you had the chance, so we're even." He spoke to the wolf while continuing his slow drilling. The wolf tried to struggle, but it was unable to move at all due to the stone tomb.

Finally, the drill pierced the flesh of the wolf. And Hajime mercilessly gouged out its insides. The wolf screamed in agony as it died. Its howls lasted for a while, until suddenly, it spasmed and grew still.

"All right. With this, I finally have some food." Hajime smiled happily as he drilled the other three wolves to death. Once they were all dead, Hajime transmuted their corpses up to him, then began awkwardly peeling away their fur with one hand.

After that, driven by his hunger, he began to devour them. He cut a ghastly figure as he tore into their flesh, illuminated dimly by the green light of the crystals. The green light that defined his hell. He greedily devoured the wolf, every bit of the animal he had just killed.

"Agah... Gah, tastes like crap!" He spat curses, but that didn't stop him from eating the wolf. His entire mind was focused on his meal.

The flesh was tough and stringy, and the fresh blood clogged his throat, but he tore at the meat and swallowed it all happily nonetheless. It was his first time tasting food in two weeks. His stomach protested at the sudden infusion of flesh, and resisted its ingestion. But Hajime didn't care what his stomach thought, so he continued wolfing the wolf down.

He looked just like a feral monster. Any modern human would have found his current figure repulsive.

The meat smelled raw and disgusting, bringing tears to his eyes, but Hajime felt the food relieve his excruciating hunger pangs, and compared to those, such minor inconveniences were nothing. He had never imagined eating meat could be such a euphoric experience. He ate and ate and ate.

Hours passed, and still he continued to consume. He washed it all down with Ambrosia, and had the priests of the Holy Church known his barbaric meal was accompanied by such a sacred drink, they would have fainted. However, around the time he was finally starting to feel full, Hajime began to notice a change occurring within his body.

"Ah? Gah?! Agaaaah!" Searing pain shot through him. It felt as if something were eating away at him from within. As time passed, the pain only grew worse.

"Guaaaaaaaah!!! Wh-what's—gaaaaaaah!!!" It was unendurable agony. The pain was trying to eat him from the inside out. Hajime writhed on the ground, screaming in terror. This pain was far, far worse than the hunger pangs he had been feeling previously.

With a trembling hand, Hajime pulled a stone vial out of his pocket, ripped the cap off, and poured its contents down his throat. The Ambrosia did its work, and the pain began to recede, but then, eventually, it returned once more.

"Gyaaaaaaugh! Why...won't it heal... Gaaaaah!" Along with the pain, Hajime began to feel his body *throb*. It began to pulse, like one big organism. In fact, he could hear his body creaking, too.

However, an instant later the Ambrosia kicked in again and began repairing his body. Once the healing finished, the pain returned. Then he was healed again.

Thanks to the Ambrosia, he couldn't even faint. Its healing powers had backfired on him.

Hajime screamed incoherently, smacking his head against the wall over and over, but the pain showed no signs of ending. He begged for someone to end his pain, but of course no one granted his wish.

Eventually, Hajime's body began to morph.

The color was bleached from his hair. He was unsure whether it was from the pain or for some other reason entirely, but his distinctively Japanese black hair slowly turned white. Then, his muscles and bones began to grow slightly, giving him a toned appearance. Red veins ran down the inside of his body, though he wasn't aware of that at the time.

There exists a phenomenon known as overcompensation. When one attempts muscle training, the muscles actually tear, and the body simply regrows them a bit stronger to overcompensate. And that same thing was happening to Hajime.

A monster's meat was poison to humans. Because of the mana crystals distilled into their blood, a monster's specialized organs allowed them to directly interface with magic, and gave them superior physical strength. The mana that circulated through monsters affected even their bones and muscles.

This transformed mana allowed monsters to use magic without incantations or magic circles, though no one knew exactly how. Regardless of the particulars, a monster's mana was poison to humans, and killed any who tried to ingest it. It would eat a person away from the inside, destroying their very cells.

There were people who had tried to eat monsters in the past and they had all, without exception, died. In fact, Hajime had read all about this, but his extreme hunger had led him to forget.

Had Hajime just eaten the wolf's flesh, he would have died an agonizing, but swift death. But there had been something that prevented that. And that was the Ambrosia. It healed him every time his body was destroyed. As a result, his body was forced to evolve at an unnaturally rapid pace.

It was broken, then repaired. Broken, then repaired. With each cycle, his body slowly changed. Almost like a reincarnation of sorts. His frail human body was forcibly transformed into something stronger, and he went through a ritual of rebirth. It could be said Hajime's screams were akin to the cries of a newborn.

Finally the pain receded, and Hajime slumped to the ground. The hair on his head had turned white, and underneath his clothes, veins of dark red mana ran down his body. Just like the Twin-tail Wolves, or the Kickmaster Rabbits, or the Claw Bears.

Hajime's right hand twitched. He slowly opened his eyes, then groggily looked down at his right hand, and finally clawed at the ground, slowly curling his fingers into a fist.

He clenched and unclenched his hand multiple times, confirming that he was indeed still alive, and that his body still listened to him, before slowly getting up.

"Come to think of it, you aren't supposed to eat monster meat... I can't believe I did something so brain-dead... Well, I wouldn't have lasted much longer without food, either..." Exhausted, Hajime smiled self-deprecatingly.

His hunger had faded, and the specter of his left arm no longer pained him either. For the first time in what felt like an eternity, he was free of pain. In fact, his body felt surprisingly light, and power was overflowing from within him.

Despite how much the constant pain had exhausted him mentally, he still felt better than he ever had in his life. He looked over at his arm, then down at his stomach, and saw very prominent muscles. He had grown a little taller too. He had originally been a mere 165 centimeters tall, but he had grown a full ten centimeters.

"What happened to my body? I feel different somehow..." And it wasn't just the outside. The inside of Hajime's body somehow felt different as well. It was at once both hot and cold, an indescribably strange feeling. If he focused, he could make dark red veins float up to the top of his arm.

"Whoaaa, th-that's gross! It's like I turned into a monster or something... I better not have, that would make for a terrible joke. Oh yeah, I should check my status plate..." He fished around for the status plate he had completely forgotten about, eventually pulling it out of his pocket. It appeared he hadn't lost it yet. He examined his current stats, imagining it would give him some insight to the changes in his body.

HAJIME NAGUMO		Age: 17	Male
Job:	Synergist	Level:	8
Strength:	100	Agility:	200
Vitality:	300	Magic:	300
Defense:	100	M. Defense:	300
Skills:	Transmute • Mana Manipulation • Iron Stomach • Lightning Field • Language Comprehension		

"What in tarnation?" A little of the old Hajime returned as the shock made him slip into his peculiar accent. His stats had all risen astronomically, and he had three new skills. But his level had only risen to eight. Since a person's level represented the proportion of the total potential they had reached, it would seem that Hajime's growth limits had increased as well.

"Mana Manipulation?" If he took it literally, that would mean Hajime had gained the power to directly control mana.

Could that weird sensation I've been feeling be mana? Hajime thought, and attempted to activate his Mana Manipulation skill.

When he focused, Hajime saw those dark red veins come up to the surface of his skin again. He concentrated on an image of that sensation rushing to his right hand all at once. As he did so, the strange sensation, or rather his mana, began slowly flowing down to his hand.

"Oh? Oooooooh!" He unconsciously cried out at the inexplicable sensation of mana moving throughout his body. Then, suddenly, his mana poured into the magic circle inscribed on the glove he was wearing without him having to say anything. Surprised, Hajime attempted to transmute something. The ground rose up without him saying a word.

"No way. I didn't even need to chant an incantation? I thought direct mana control wasn't supposed to be possible for anyone except monsters...? Does that mean I absorbed a monster's special abilities by eating it?" That was indeed the case. Hajime had acquired the power of monsters. He then moved to try out another of his new skills, Lightning Field.

"Umm...how am I supposed to use this? Since it says Lightning Field, it must have something to do with electricity, right? Could it be? Do I have the same skill the wolf used when it gathered electricity in its tail?" He tried various things, but none of them seemed to do anything. Unlike Mana Manipulation, he couldn't physically feel the skill inside him, so he wasn't exactly sure how to go about activating it.

While pondering to himself, he remembered that when he was transmuting, he always needed a mental image of the effect he was trying to produce. The less one relied on a magic circle to define the characteristics of a spell, the more they needed a mental image to guide its creation.

Hajime formed an image of crackling static electricity in his mind. Suddenly, red lightning started trailing down his fingertips.

"Oooh, I did it! I see. So to use a monster's magic, I need a good mental image of its properties. And now that I take a closer look... my mana's become reddish, just like the monsters." He continued practicing making electrical discharges over and over. However, unlike the Twin-Tailed Wolves, he was unable to fire off the electricity he could generate. From the sound of the name "Lightning Field," Hajime surmised that he could only wrap himself in lightning, and transfer it via direct contact. So he practiced adjusting the flow of the current, as well as the voltage of the electricity he could produce.

The skill Iron Stomach most likely did exactly what its name suggested. Hajime most certainly didn't want to suffer that hellish pain of eating monster meat ever again. However, there didn't appear to be any other source of food in the labyrinth either. Which would have meant that he would be forced to choose between starvation and agonizing pain. Fortunately, he assumed that skill of his prevented him from having to make such a choice.

He took another strip of wolf flesh and seared it with his

Lightning Field. Since he was no longer half-mad with hunger, he realized there was no need to eat the meat raw. He tried to ignore the pungent odor of burning flesh as he cooked the meat. Then he steeled himself, taking a bite of the meat.

A few seconds passed...a minute...ten minutes...and still nothing happened. Hajime grilled some more meat and ate it. And still there was no pain. He wasn't sure if it was due to his Iron Stomach, or if his body had just adapted to monster flesh. He also didn't care too much. He was just glad he could eat again, without having to suffer every time he did.

After he had eaten his fill, Hajime returned to his base. As he was, he might even have had a chance against that bear. He decided to spend some time training his new skills first, though.

He went back to where he'd left the wolves' corpses and cut their meat into strips. He had a much easier time peeling their fur off this time. He piled as much meat as he could hold into another one of his stone containers, and carefully took it back to his base.

Once safe in his base with a supply of food, Hajime spent the next few days diligently training his skills.

All of his skills grew at a fast pace. His transmutation skill underwent a change as well. It appeared that he had mastered it to the point where derivative skills began to pop up. The derivative skill he had learned from it was "Ore Appraisal." It was a high-level derivative skill that was rare even among royal blacksmiths.

Appraisal magic was generally far more complex than offensive magic, and therefore required suitably large magic circles to activate. For that reason, only certain academic facilities and large institutions had appraisal magic circles. However, people with appraisal skills could appraise anything within their domain of analysis with a small magic circle and simple incantation, as long as they were touching their target. It was a derivative skill, so it was by definition impossible to innately possess. Only through long years of transmutation training could one obtain the skill.

When he acquired it, Hajime made sure to appraise every single ore and mineral he could find. When he appraised the green glowstones, the following appeared on his status plate:

◊ GREEN GLOWSTONE

This ore can absorb mana. When it is saturated with mana, it emits a faint green light. If you break a saturated glowstone, the light it has contained within explodes out all at once in a brilliant flash.

A very simple explanation. However, it was still very useful information. Hajime grinned wickedly as a plan came to mind. He wandered the labyrinth, looking for other stones to appraise, and ran into a certain mineral that gave him the idea for a weapon that would soon become his trump card.

◊ BLASTROCK

A combustible ore. When exposed to fire, it burns like oil. As it burns, it slowly decreases in volume until it finally burns to cinders. Burning large quantities of blastrock in a confined space will make it explode violently. Depending on its quantity and pressure, it's possible to create flames as strong as those created by fire magic.

Hajime could feel all the pieces coming together when he read that explanation. *Blastrock is just like gunpowder back on earth. With something like this, I can make a weapon out of Transmutation, even!*

Hajime stared at the stone excitedly. It would take a great deal of trial and error to get things the way he wanted them, but he was still overjoyed. He finally had a combat use for the transmutation that had saved his life so many times before.

He began zealously working on his project, so focused on his transmuting that he didn't eat or sleep for days. After thousands of failed attempts, Hajime finally completed it.

A modern weapon that boasted immense strength and fired projectiles that traveled faster than the speed of sound. The weapon was about thirty-five centimeters long, made of the hardest and densest material he could find—taur—and it boasted six chambers. The barrel was rectangular. The bullets were made from the same super-hard taur stone, and each shot was packed with powdered blastrock.

He had made himself a revolver. But the difference was that it used more than just the power of blastrock combustion to propel its bullets. Hajime was able to use his Lightning Field skill to electrically accelerate his shots like a railgun. The combination made his bullets pack more of a punch than an anti-tank rifle. He decided to name it Donner. It was going to be his partner moving forward, so he reasoned it needed a name.

"With this, both those monsters...and the exit...are in my sights!" Hajime stared proudly at Donner, the weapon he had made by using the guns he remembered from his old world as a reference.

The most common class in the world, Synergist, which was

thought to be good for nothing more than crafting swords and armor, had brought forth modern weaponry into this fantasy world with the power of its sole skill, Transmute.

◊ TAUR STONE

A black, hard rock. On the Mohs scale, which goes up to 10, it would rank an 8 for hardness. It is able to handle heat and direct impacts well, but is weak to the cold. Cooling the stone makes it brittle and fragile. However, reheating it will restore its hardness.

"Munch... Munch... Man, even rabbit meat tastes like crap..." A few days after he had finished crafting Donner, Hajime was sitting outside his base eating rabbit meat. By rabbit meat, he of course meant Kickmaster Rabbit meat. The same powerful rabbit that had looked down on Hajime before was nothing more than his prey. Hajime had hoped the rabbit's meat might taste a bit better, but it was every bit as disgusting as the wolves he had eaten. It was still monster meat, after all.

Despite its disgusting taste, he still ate it with gusto. Thanks to his Iron Stomach skill, he was able to eat as much as he wanted whenever he felt himself getting hungry. Using the magic he had acquired from monsters made him grow hungry quickly, and since he had used that magic to take down the rabbit, he had eaten it all to replenish his energy.

If he overused his magic, his hunger pangs would flare up again, and while he wouldn't die, thanks to the Ambrosia he carried with him everywhere, he still needed to be careful about how much magic he used.

Incidentally, he had killed the Kickmaster Rabbit by luring it into a trap. He had drawn water from the river he had first woken up in, and lured the rabbit close. Once it had dashed forward into the wet surface he had created, he had used Lightning Field to transmit a powerful electric shock. Once the electricity passed, smoke started rising from the rabbit's body, and as he had expected, its movements had been slowed. Hajime had finished the weakened rabbit off with Donner.

Just as he thought, his railgun-powered revolver was able to obliterate the rabbit's face, the bullet moving three kilometers per second as it punched through its head. Donner was even more powerful than Hajime had imagined.

"Now then, that was my first time eating rabbit meat, so let's see how my stats changed..."

HAJIME NAGUMO		Age: 17	Male
Job:	Synergist	Level:	12
Strength:	200	Agility:	400
Vitality:	300	Magic:	350
Defense:	200	M. Defense:	350
Skills:	Transmute [+Ore Appraisal] [+Precision Transmutation] [+Ore Perception] • Mana Manipulation • Iron Stomach • Lightning Field • Air Dance [+Aerodynamic] [+Supersonic Step] • Language Comprehension		

As he had thought, eating monsters increased his stats. Though he hadn't gotten much stronger by eating more Twin-tail Wolves, his stats had taken a huge leap when he ate a new type of monster.

Guess I'll test out what this "Air Dance" does. What first came to Hajime's mind was the way that rabbit had moved. It had rushed forward so fast that he'd only been able to make it out as a blur. He inferred that that was most likely the Supersonic Step skill at work. *Come to think of it, it's a lot like the fast movement stuff you see in anime.*

Hajime kept the image of explosive power gathering in his legs and dashed forward. He felt mana gather within his legs. The ground underneath his feet exploded in a shower of rubble as Hajime leaped forward...and slammed face first into the wall.

"Owww! C-controlling my acceleration is harder than I thought." However, his experiment was still a success. He imagined that if he trained it a little, he too would be able to move like the rabbit had. Used in tandem with his revolver, those skills would be a powerful weapon indeed.

Next, he tried to use Aerodynamics. However, he found himself unable to activate it. He had a hard time figuring out just what kind of skill it was from the name alone. After testing a bunch of different things, Hajime suddenly remembered how the rabbit had sometimes looked to be standing in midair. And so, he quickly stuck his foot out and imagined there being an invisible shield supporting it from below. Then he jumped forward.

He found himself face-planting magnificently into the ground.

"Gwaahh?!" He cradled his face in his hand as he rolled around in pain. After the aching subsided a little, he sullenly drank a bit of Ambrosia.

"Well...at least it works..." The reason he had faceplanted into the ground despite jumping forward was because he hadn't properly formed his footing. That was why he had effectively stumbled and fallen in midair. Aerodynamic was apparently a skill that allowed him to create footholds in midair. He had obtained multiple skills at once from the rabbit, though they were all derivative skills branching from Air Dance.

Pleased that he had obtained multiple skills at once, Hajime began training them immediately. He wanted to be strong enough to take down that Claw Bear. He figured he'd be able to defeat it at long range with Donner easily enough, but he wanted to make completely sure, just in case. And there was always the possibility of even stronger monsters showing up. Optimism in the labyrinth got you killed. Once he was certain he could kill even Claw Bears, it would be time to start searching for an exit.

Hajime redoubled his resolve, training harder than ever before.

•/• •/• •/• •/• •/• •/• •/• •/• •/• •/• •/• •/• •/•

A figure sped down the labyrinth corridors so fast that he appeared to be no more than a blur.

That figure was, of course, Hajime. Having completely mastered Air Dance, he was using Supersonic Step to dash off the walls, while sometimes also using Aerodynamic to create mid-air footholds for himself. He traversed the labyrinth at high speed, seeking out his mortal foe, the Claw Bear.

In all honesty, searching for an exit should have taken priority, but Hajime was consumed by the desire to get revenge on the bear. He wouldn't be able to move on unless he was able to prove to himself that he was more than a match for the monster that had once crushed his spirit.

"Graaaaah!" He ran into a pack of Twin-Tailed Wolves, and one of them leaped at him. Hajime calmly vaulted into the air, did a mid-air somersault, pulled out Donner (which was strapped to his right leg with a holster made of transmuted threads), and fired.

Bang! The sound of combusting blastrock echoed down the corridor and Hajime's Lightning Field-accelerated bullet pulverized the head of the first Twin-Tailed Wolf.

He then used Aerodynamic to do a double jump in the air, before taking aim and firing a volley of shots at the other wolves. They didn't all hit their mark, but he was still able to annihilate the pack with only a single barrage.

Hajime held Donner in the crook of his left armpit and quickly began reloading. Then, without so much as a backward glance at the fallen wolves, he dashed off once more.

After a while spent killing any Kickmaster Rabbits or Twin-Tailed Wolves that he came across, Hajime finally spotted his prey.

The Claw Bear was in the middle of a meal. It was chewing on the remains of what appeared to have been a Kickmaster Rabbit. Hajime grinned triumphantly and began leisurely walking closer.

The Claw Bear was the strongest monster to appear on this floor. In other words, it was the king. While there were hordes of Twin-Tailed Wolves and Kickmaster Rabbits, the Claw Bear was the only one of its kind.

Thus, it stood to reason that there was nothing stronger inhabiting the floor. The other monsters all took great pains to stay out of its way, and if they ever encountered it, they ran as fast as they could in the other direction. No creature dared oppose it. The thought of anyone approaching it of their own free will was patently absurd.

However, that very absurdity was currently unfolding before the bear's eyes.

"Sup, bear? Been a while. Did you like the taste of my arm?"

The Claw Bear narrowed its angry eyes. *What is this creature? Why doesn't it run? Why is it not trembling in fear? Why does despair not fill its eyes?* The bear was confused, having never seen something like this before.

"I'm here for my revenge match. But first, I'm going to make you see me as your enemy, and not just prey."

Hajime pulled Donner out of its holster and pointed it at the Claw Bear. He then slowly asked himself a question as he took aim.

Am I scared? The answer was a definitive "No." He wasn't shivering in fear, nor was he in the grips of despair. No, the only emotions roiling within him were a fierce will to survive, and a burning desire to kill his enemies.

Hajime's lips curled upward into a ferocious grin.

"I'm going to kill you and eat you, you bastard." He pulled Donner's trigger. With a resounding bang, a hardened bullet of taur sped toward the Claw Bear at three kilometers per second.

"Gaaaooo?!" It instantly dropped to the ground with a roar, narrowly avoiding Hajime's bullet.

It had started moving even before Hajime had pulled the trigger. It was of course impossible for the bear to see the bullet Hajime had fired, but Hajime's bloodlust had made it reflexively dodge. It wasn't this floor's strongest monster for nothing. It had reacted far faster than its massive two-meter-long frame would have suggested. However, even then it hadn't been able to completely avoid the attack.

The bullet had grazed its shoulder, gouging out a slice of it.

The Claw Bear angrily glared at Hajime, blood staining the white fur around its shoulder. It looked like it finally saw him as an enemy and not just food.

"Graaaooooo!!!" With a furious roar, it charged Hajime. The ground thundered as its tree-trunk-sized legs pounded down the corridor, making for a truly awe-inspiring spectacle.

"Hahaha! That's right! I'm your enemy! Not just some prey to be hunted!" Despite how foreboding the Claw Bear looked as it bore down on him, Hajime's smile didn't waver.

This was the moment of truth. It was the moment that would decide if Hajime could overcome the monster that had eaten his left arm, crushed his soul, and been the impetus of his transformation. A necessary ritual he needed to overcome, if he was ever to move forward. Something deep inside made him feel that he would give up for good if he failed at that point. He couldn't explain how or why, he just knew.

He took aim, firing Donner once more at the charging bear. He had aimed squarely at its forehead, but the Claw Bear somehow managed to roll to the side, even while charging forward. It made no sense for something so big to be so fast.

It barreled its way into range of Hajime and swiped at him with one of its massive claws. The edge of its claws looked slightly warped as they swept down. *Is that related to its special magic?*

Hajime recalled that the rabbit that had supposedly dodged the bear's swipe had still been cut in half. So instead of just barely dodging to the side, he leaped back with all his might.

"Hah." An instant later the bear's claw swiped past where Hajime had just been standing, followed by a ferocious gale. He gasped in pain, then looked down and saw shallow cuts running down his chest. He hadn't been able to completely dodge it. His reaction time wasn't able to keep up with the rapid increase in his physical abilities.

The Claw Bear roared, angry that its prey still lived, and in the blink of an eye, swiped down a second time at his enemy.

"Damn, you're fast!" Hajime cursed without realizing it as he saw a second set of wind blades bear down on him. He instantly used Aerodynamic to flee into the air while firing off a third shot. However, the Claw Bear immediately changed directions the moment it saw the red flash from Donner, completely ignoring the laws of inertia. Upon closer inspection, Hajime saw deep ruts in the ground and realized it must have used its claws as a fulcrum to pivot off of. It was certainly far more intelligent and far more agile than a normal beast.

"Gaaaaaaoo!!!" It roared again, then swung its foreclaws in a cross at Hajime, who was still up in the air. Warning bells went off inside Hajime's head. Without sparing a moment to think, Hajime activated both Aerodynamic and Supersonic Step at the same time, then dashed away from that spot.

He felt a gust of wind brush past his thigh, and a second later the wall behind him had a crosshatched lattice of furrows gouged into it.

"Guh. Damn bastard. You can do that, too?" Hajime groaned as he fell to the ground. He hit the ground off-balance, and collapsed. He righted himself instantly, but staggered as a sharp pain ran through his thigh. It seemed that the Claw Bear could throw its wind claws too.

Hajime's expression twisted into a pained grimace, but he took no time to dwell on it and fired Donner once more. He didn't have time to nurse his wounds, as the bear had already started closing in. He pulled the trigger again, firing twice in quick succession. Even with its inhuman agility the Claw Bear wasn't able to dodge both bullets, and took two hits, one to the temple, and the other to its flank. Though it had managed to avoid fatal injuries, it had still been blown off the course of its charge. The distraction proved enough to stop the next barrage of wind claws from going off.

However, though it had veered a little off course, the Claw Bear still charged forward like a cannonball. Though he wasn't directly in the bear's trajectory any longer, his wounded leg prevented him from dodging, so the bear still managed to hurtle into him. It felt like being hit by a truck. Hajime was blasted backward from the force of the bear's charge.

"Gahah?!" The impact forced the air out of his lungs, which made Hajime snarl ferociously.

Donner's chamber held six bullets. He had fired five, but he still had one left. There was no way he would be able to reload in the middle of this fight, and his own stats weren't high enough that he could beat the Claw Bear without Donner's overwhelming firepower. Each shot that missed was a shot that had brought him that much closer to death. And yet, Hajime still grinned. Because, with this, his victory was now assured.

As he slammed into the ground, he flung Donner into the air. He then pulled something out of his pocket and threw it at the injured Claw Bear.

"I'm quite proud of how this one turned out. You'd best be careful if you don't want to die." Though there was no way for the bear to understand Hajime's words, it still looked down at the object that rolled to its feet when he mumbled that. What lay there was a small emerald ball, about five centimeters in diameter. And that ball suddenly burst in an explosion of light.

It was Hajime's makeshift flash grenade. The principle behind it was simple. He had taken a piece of green glowstone and filled it to the brim with mana. After that he had applied a thin coating over it to keep the light from leaking through. He had then packed a small quantity of blastrock in the rock's center, and created the blastrock fuse that led all the way to a coated surface.

Finally, he had lit the fuse by using Lightning Field. The blastrock on the outside burned slowly until it reached the packed center, at which point it exploded violently. With the crystal shattered, the glowstone released its light all at once in a brilliant emerald flash. He had set the fuse to explode three seconds after he lit it. Though it had taken a great deal of effort to make, he was proud of the end result.

The bear, who had no knowledge of modern weaponry, naturally found its gaze drawn to the grenade, and when it exploded, it blinded the Claw Bear. It roared in pain, wildly swinging its front paws. Being blinded had sent it into a panic.

And Hajime planned to take full advantage of that. He scooped Donner off the ground, took aim, and fired. The electrically accelerated bullet hit the rampaging bear squarely in its left shoulder, and ripped it clean off.

"Graaaaaaooooo!!!" Its roar was loud enough to crack eardrums. The Claw Bear had never suffered such pain before. Gouts of blood spurted from the stump that had once been its arm. The blown-off left arm spun in the air a few times before losing its inertia and flopping back down to the ground with a wet thud.

"What an ironic twist of fate." Hajime had not actually aimed for the Claw Bear's left arm. He just wasn't that good a shot yet. He had enough practice from fighting Twin-Tailed Wolves and the like to hit an enemy that was charging straight at him, but he certainly wasn't good enough to hit a flailing enemy with pinpoint accuracy. So the fact that Hajime had taken the bear's left arm, just as it had done to him, was a complete coincidence.

Hajime kept a close eye on the bear, which was still flailing around blindly, and pushed Donner up against his body with his stump of a left arm and reloaded.

He fired once more. Though the bear was still disoriented, its beastlike sixth sense let it perceive Hajime's bloodlust, and it leaped to the side. It seemed it was Hajime's bloodlust that gave the Claw Bear enough forewarning to dodge railgun-accelerated bullets. Once he realized this, Hajime narrowed his eyes, and used Supersonic Step to dash past the bear, over to where his severed left arm lay.

The bear turned to look at him with its furious, hate-filled red eyes. It seemed it had finally recovered its eyesight. As it was watching, Hajime lifted up the bear's left arm, and bit down on it. His jaws had been greatly strengthened from eating monster meat for so long, so he easily tore through the tough skin and sinew. It was a repetition of the time when the Claw Bear had eaten Hajime's arm in front of him, except this time it was Hajime doing the eating.

"Hamf, mmf, no matter how many times I eat it, monster meat still tastes like crap... Though for some reason this is just a little bit better than the others." Hajime looked down at the bear, who was watching him warily by that point. It didn't move. There was fear in its eyes, but the shock of seeing its own flesh eaten in front of it, combined with its still-blurry eyesight, prevented it from moving.

Glad for the reprieve, Hajime continued chewing. Suddenly, he felt something. Sharp pains pulsed through his body, just like the first time he had eaten monster meat.

"Wha—?!" He quickly pulled out a vial of Ambrosia and ingested it. The pain wasn't as bad as the first time, but it was still sharp enough that he fell to one knee, unable to keep himself upright. It appeared the Claw Bear was a different species entirely when compared to the Twin-Tailed Wolves or Kickmaster Rabbits, and absorbing its power brought with it the old pain.

Of course, the bear wasn't about to let that chance slip past. It roared in defiance and charged forward. Hajime was still on one knee, unable to move. At this rate he would be trampled by the bear, and it would just be a repeat of their first encounter. But when that thought crossed his mind, something suddenly occurred to Hajime, and he smirked.

He put his right hand on the ground...and wrapped it in lightning. All of the lightning released by his full power Lightning Field raced down the liquid coating the ground, and zapped the bear standing on the other end.

The liquid was of course the bear's blood. The sea of blood that had poured out of its stump of a left arm. When Hajime had brandished the Claw Bear's arm right in front of it, he had spilled drops of blood everywhere, and created a small puddle of it around where he stood.

He was not so arrogant that he would eat in the middle of a fight just to show off. He hadn't predicted the pain of eating monster meat to return, but the rest of it had all been part of his trap. Even eating the arm right in front of the bear had been to goad it into charging headlong at him. The pain had thrown a bit of a wrench in his plans, but everything had still ended up working out just fine.

The moment the bear had stepped into the pool of its own blood, thousands of volts of electricity fried its entire body. The electricity burned the Claw Bear's flesh, scorching some nerves as it did. However, though he had unleashed Lightning Field at full power, its might was still a far cry from the actual thing. Unlike the Twin-Tailed Wolves, he was unable to shoot lightning bolts, and his Lightning Field could only put out half the power of the original. But even that much was still enough to paralyze the bear for a few seconds.

"Graooooo!" The Claw Bear let out a low growl, then collapsed to its knees, shivering in a puddle of its own electrically charged blood. Even down on all fours—or rather all threes—it still glared murderously at Hajime.

He glared right back at it, and painfully got to his feet. He slowly pulled Donner out of its holster, and walked over to the Claw Bear. He pushed the muzzle against its forehead.

"You're my prey now," he said with finality, pulling the trigger one last time. The taur bullet fulfilled its duty, utterly pulverizing the Claw Bear's head.

One final gunshot echoed throughout the empty corridor.

Up until the moment of its death, the Claw Bear never took its gaze off Hajime. Similarly, Hajime never took his gaze off the Claw Bear.

The exhilarating rush of joy he had expected never came. But there was no sense of emptiness, either. He had simply done what was necessary. Necessary in order to live, in order to earn the right to survive.

Hajime closed his eyes and rethought his mindset. After a moment of quiet deliberation, he resolved to continue living like this. He did not enjoy fighting. He just wanted to avoid pain. He just wanted to be able to eat his fill.

He just...wanted to live.

Overthrowing his unreasonable fate, killing everything that opposed him, they were all simply steps he took in order to survive.

He swore to himself. That he would survive...and...make it back home.

"That's right... I just want...to go home. I don't care about anything else. I'll make it home, no matter what I have to do. I'll grant this one wish of mine, by my own hands. And no matter who they may be, anyone that tries to stand in my way..." Hajime opened his eyes and smiled viciously.

"Will die by these hands."

HAJIME NAGUMO		Age: 17	Male
Job:	Synergist	Level:	17
Strength:	300	Agility:	450
Vitality:	400	Magic:	400
Defense:	300	M. Defense:	400
Skills:	Transmute [+Ore Appraisal] [+Precision Transmutation] [+Ore Perception] [+Ore Desynthesis] [+Ore Synthesis] • Mana Manipulation • Iron Stomach • Lightning Field • Air Dance [+Aerodynamic] [+Supersonic Step] • Gale Claw • Language Comprehension		

❖❖ ❖❖ ❖❖ ❖❖ ❖❖ ❖❖ ❖❖ ❖❖ ❖❖ ❖❖ ❖❖ ❖❖ ❖❖

Let us turn back the clock a few weeks.

Shizuku Yaegashi gazed sorrowfully at her still-sleeping friend. The summoned heroes had all been granted private rooms in the Heilig Palace, and Shizuku was currently resting in one of them.

It had been five days since their desperate life-and-death struggle in the labyrinth. They had rested one night in Horaud's inn before taking an express carriage back to the palace. After having tasted death and despair, the students were in no condition to continue their practical training course. Furthermore, even if he had been treated as a useless hanger-on, a member of the hero's party had died, and that fact needed to be reported to the king and the Holy Church.

And though they knew they were being cruel, the knights couldn't allow the heroes' fighting spirits to break. They had to restore the mental stability of the students before their psyches shattered completely.

As Shizuku recalled the events that had transpired since Hajime's death, part of her wished that Kaori would wake up quickly, while another part of her hoped that she might just sleep forever.

Every single person who heard the report of Hajime's death was first shocked that a member of the hero's group could have died, and then relieved when they heard it was just the "worthless" Hajime.

Even the king and Ishtar reacted similarly. One of the powerful heroes who would save this nation couldn't be allowed to die in a dungeon. Someone who couldn't survive a dungeon excursion would stand no chance against the demons, and would only serve to spread further unease among the people. The messengers of Ehit, the heroes brought forth from another world, had to be invincible.

At least the king and Ishtar had been somewhat respectful. There were some nobles within the palace that had insulted and belittled Hajime behind his back instead.

Of course, they said nothing incriminating publicly, but when they were talking privately among fellow nobles, many of them had whispered their scorn for him. They all abased him with statements like "Thank God it was the worthless one that died," and "I'm so glad the incompetent got weeded out from God's messengers." Shizuku had trembled with rage when she had heard such snide comments, and had nearly come to blows with those nobles multiple times.

And had Kouki not flown off the handle before her, she probably would have beaten them to a pulp. Because of Kouki's heated protests, the king and the Holy Church seemingly decided that it would be dangerous to let a negative opinion of Hajime spread. Therefore, they quietly dealt with anyone who badmouthed him... However, all that served to accomplish was increase Kouki's popularity. Most people saw Kouki's anger as proof that he was kindhearted enough to care for even the weakest of his party, and the general opinion that Hajime had been nothing more than a burden to such a noble hero remained cemented in the minds of the people.

Despite the fact that the only reason the rest of them were still alive was because Hajime had held back a monster not even the great hero Kouki had been able to touch. Despite the fact that he was only dead because some idiotic classmate had fired a stray fireball that had hit him.

However, as if by some unwritten agreement, the students all agreed not to talk about that stray fireball. Everyone was sure they had kept perfect control over their magic, but it had been a veritable storm of spells, and no one wanted to consider the possibility that it could have been their misaimed fireball that had led to Hajime's demise. Because if it had been them, they would become a murderer.

As a result, they all closed their eyes to reality, choosing instead to pretend that it was some mistake on Hajime's part that had led to his death. After all, dead men tell no tales. Rather than worry about who had killed Hajime, it was far easier to pretend he had died due to his own mistakes. That way none of them would have to worry. Without any collusion on their part, the students all came to that conclusion, and thus the topic was not discussed.

In order to uncover the truth behind Hajime's death, Captain Meld decided it would be necessary to interrogate the students. He did not think the truth was something as innocent as a stray fireball. And even if it were, that was all the more reason to uncover the truth, so he could give the student who had accidentally killed Hajime the counseling they needed.

The longer the matter remained unsettled, the more problems it would cause down the line. And most importantly, Captain Meld simply wanted to know. Even though he had promised to save Hajime after they had fled to safety, his words had turned out to be as hollow as he now felt.

However, Captain Meld was not allowed to go through with his plan. Because Ishtar had forbidden him from questioning the students. He had protested the ban hotly, but even the king forbade him from meeting with them, so he had no choice but to comply.

"If you knew...you'd be furious, wouldn't you?" Shizuku whispered quietly, then took Kaori's hand. She had not woken since that day in the labyrinth.

According to the doctor, there was nothing wrong with her physically. She had apparently just fallen into a self-imposed slumber to protect herself from the mental shock. The doctor had said she would awaken on her own eventually.

Shizuku tightly gripped Kaori's hand and prayed to no one in particular, "Please, please don't let any further harm come to my kind and gentle friend." And at those words, Kaori's hand twitched slightly.

"Huh?! Kaori?! Can you hear me?! Kaori!" Shizuku yelled out her name over and over. Eventually, Kaori's eyelids began to flutter. Shizuku kept calling out her best friend's name. As if responding to her words, Kaori's fingers curled around Shizuku's hand. And slowly, she opened her eyes.

"Kaori!" Shizuku leaned over the bed and looked down at Kaori, tears in her eyes. Kaori looked around dazedly, before her mind finally started working again, and her eyes fell on Shizuku.

"Shizuku-chan?"

"Yes, it's me. Shizuku. How do you feel, Kaori? Does it hurt anywhere?"

"N-no, I'm fine. My body does feel a bit heavy...but that's probably because I slept for so long..."

"That's right, you slept for five whole days...so it's normal to feel a little numb." Shizuku hurried to help Kaori, who was trying to rise, and smiled sadly as she told her how long she'd slept for. Kaori started acting odd when she heard that.

"Five days? How did I sleep...for that long...? I thought I was in the labyrinth...and then I..." As she saw Kaori's eyes grow more and more distant, Shizuku panicked and quickly tried to change the subject. However, Kaori's memories returned before Shizuku could get even a word out.

"And then... Ah... What happened to Nagumo-kun?"

"...Well..."

Shizuku grimaced, unsure of how to explain. From Shizuku's pained expression, Kaori was able to surmise that the nightmare she saw in her memories was indeed true. However, Kaori was still unable to accept that harsh reality.

"...It can't be true. Please, tell me it's a lie, Shizuku-chan. You guys saved Nagumo-kun after I fainted, right? Right? Tell me you did. I'm in the castle right now, right? We all made it back safely to the castle, right? Nagumo-kun's just...out training, right? He's down at the parade grounds, right? Right, that has to be it... I'm going to go check right now. I have to thank him... So can you please let me go, Shizuku-chan?"

Incoherent ramblings spilled from Kaori's mouth as she tried to get up and go look for Hajime, but Shizuku firmly grabbed on to Kaori's arm and refused to let go.

Despite Shizuku's anguished expression, she kept a strong grip on Kaori's arm.

"Kaori... You understand, don't you...? He's not here anymore."

"Stop it..."

"It's just like you remembered, Kaori."

"Stop it."

"He's...Nagumo-kun's..."

"Stop, I said stop it!"

"Kaori! He's dead!"

"No! He's not dead! I know it! Stop saying such cruel things! I won't forgive anyone for saying that, not even you, Shizuku-chan!"

Kaori kept shaking her head, struggling to break free from Shizuku's grasp all the while. But Shizuku refused to loosen her grip even a smidge. Instead, she hugged Kaori, trying to warm her frozen heart.

"Let me go! Let me go right now! I have to go look for Nagumo-kun! Please, I'm begging you... I know he's still alive somewhere...so please!" She yelled at Shizuku to let her go, but was still sobbing into her chest as she did.

Kaori clung to Shizuku like a drowning man to a rock, wailing so loudly her voice went hoarse. All Shizuku could do for her best friend was hug her as tightly as possible. Praying that she might somehow ease the pain in Kaori's heart.

The two of them stayed like that for hours, until the clear blue sky had been stained blood red by the setting sun. Kaori sniffled in Shizuku's arms, and stirred slightly. Shizuku worriedly looked down at Kaori.

"Kaori..."

"Shizuku-chan...Nagumo-kun...he fell, didn't he...? He's not here anymore, is he?" Kaori whispered in a trembling voice.

Shizuku didn't want to give her any false hope. If she told Kaori he was still alive, that might alleviate her pain in the short run. But it would scar Kaori forever when she finally discovered the truth. And Shizuku couldn't bear to see her best friend hurt any more than she already was.

"That's right."

"Back then, it looked like Nagumo-kun got hit by one of our fireballs... Who cast it?"

"I don't know. Everyone's trying to forget it ever happened. It's too scary to think about for them. Because if they were the one that did it..."

"I see."

"Do you hate them for it?"

"...I'm not sure. If I found out for sure who it was...I'd definitely hate them. But...if no one knows...then maybe it's better that way. Because if I did find out, I wouldn't be able to hold back..."

"I see..."

Kaori spoke haltingly, her face still buried in Shizuku's arms. "Shizuku-chan, I don't believe it." Suddenly, she wiped the tears from her puffy, red eyes, and looked up at Shizuku with renewed determination. "Nagumo-kun has to be alive somewhere. I won't believe that he's dead."

"Kaori, you..." Shizuku looked down sadly at Kaori. However, Kaori cupped Shizuku's cheeks with her hands, then continued speaking.

"I know. I know that it's foolish to think he survived that fall... But you know, there's no proof that he died. So what if the chance of him surviving is less than one percent of one percent? It's still not zero... So I choose to believe."

"Kaori..."

"I'm going to get stronger. Strong enough to protect him even from what's down there, and then I'll go look for him. I won't rest until I've confirmed with my own two eyes...what's happened to Nagumo-kun... Shizuku-chan?"

"What is it?"

"Will you help me?"

Shizuku met Kaori's unwavering gaze. There was no sign of madness or desperation in her eyes. Just an unbreakable will, one that would not rest until she had confirmed the truth for herself. Nothing could change her mind when Kaori got like this. She was far too stubborn for even her own family to deal with, let alone Shizuku.

In all honesty, it was probably safe to say the possibility Kaori was referring to might as well be zero. It would be natural to assume anyone who thought differently was simply trying to escape from reality.

Even her childhood friends, Kouki and Ryutarou, would probably try and tell Kaori she wasn't acting sane. But that was precisely why only a single answer came to Shizuku's mind.

"Of course I will. Until you've found an answer you can accept, at least."

"Shizuku-chan!" Kaori hugged Shizuku and thanked her over and over.

"I don't need any thanks. We're best friends, remember?" Shizuku replied, ever the gallant samurai. The title that the magazines had given her was rather apt.

Just then, the door to the room suddenly burst open.

"Shizuku! Has Kaori woken...up...?"

"Yeah, how's Kaori...doing...?"

Kouki and Ryutarou came hurtling into the room. They had come to check up on Kaori. It seemed apparent that they had rushed straight over after training, as dirt still caked their uniforms.

Ever since the labyrinth excursion, the two had trained harder than ever before. They had both been hit pretty hard by Hajime's death as well. After all, they were the ones who had refused to retreat, which had caused the nearly fatal crisis that Hajime had to save them from. They were both training hard so that they would never do something so unsightly ever again.

Aside from those two, however, there was a third figure hanging back in the doorway. Shizuku directed a question toward them, her voice full of suspicion.

"Why are you—"

"S-sorry! I-I'll leave now!"

The figure hurriedly apologized, speaking over Shizuku's words. Looking as if they'd seen something they shouldn't have, they hurriedly left the room. Kaori looked at them in confusion. However, the clever Shizuku realized what the cause must have been.

Kaori was currently sitting on Shizuku's lap, and holding Shizuku's face in her hands. To an outsider it must have seemed like they were about to kiss each other. Shizuku, too, was holding Kaori by the small of her back and her shoulder, like a lover.

It must have looked like a very romantic scene. Had this been a manga, there would have no doubt been flower petals everywhere in the background. Shizuku sighed deeply, moving away from Kaori, who was still staring blankly in confusion.

"Hurry up and get back here, you moron!"

Chapter III:
The Golden Vampire Princess

"Dammit, why can't I find it...?" It had been three days since Hajime had killed the Claw Bear, and he had spent every waking moment scouring the labyrinth for a staircase leading upward.

At this point he had mapped over eighty percent of the floor. After killing the Claw Bear, Hajime's stats had made another huge jump, so there was no longer anything on the floor that posed even a mild threat to him. As such, even though the floor was vast, his search progressed rapidly, and without incident. Despite that, he was unable to find any stairs, no matter how hard he looked

Actually, that wasn't strictly true. While he had been unable to find any staircases leading up, he had already discovered the staircase leading down two days ago. As the labyrinth was strictly divided into floors, it stood to reason that there had to be a staircase leading up as well, but no matter how he searched, Hajime couldn't find it.

He had already tried transmuting his own staircase up to the floor above, ignoring the rules of the dungeon. The only thing he had discovered as a result was that past a certain point, whether he tried to climb up or down, the walls around him simply stopped responding to his transmute skill. He could transmute as much as he liked within the confines of the floor, but the layers that separated the floors seemed to have some kind of magical protection cast on them. The Great Orcus Labyrinth had been created during the Age of the Gods. So it wasn't that odd for it to have some mysteries still.

Which was why Hajime had spent his time searching for the actual staircase. However, he was soon coming to realize that he would need to make a choice about what to do if he couldn't find it. That choice was whether or not to delve deeper, instead.

"...Another dead end. At this point I've investigated all the pathways. What on earth is going on here?" Hajime sighed tiredly, forced to accept that he wasn't going to find a staircase leading up. Resigned, he began heading back to the room where he'd found the staircase leading down.

The staircase he'd discovered two days ago was very roughly carved. It was closer to a bumpy slope than an actual staircase. Moreover, there was no green glowstone lighting the way, and the descent was steeped in darkness, giving off an ominous atmosphere. The darkness and shape of it made the entrance resemble the gaping jaws of some humungous beast. It felt as if once he entered, he would never be able to come back out.

"Hah! Bring it on! I'll devour anything you throw at me!" Hajime ridiculed himself for his trepidation, and smiled fearlessly. And without any further hesitation, he stepped foot into the darkness.

Once he started down the staircase, the darkness enveloped him fully. While it generally made sense for an underground labyrinth to be dark, every floor he had passed so far had been lit with glowstone.

Even if it hadn't been bright, it had never been so fully dark that Hajime couldn't even see his hand in front of his face.

However, there was no glowstone lining the staircase. Hajime stopped for a while, hoping his eyes might adjust, but no matter how long he waited, all that his eyes took in was black.

Left with no choice, Hajime dug around in his makeshift rucksack, created from bear leather and transmuted wire, and pulled out a green glowstone to light his surroundings.

Carrying a light source in the darkness was tantamount to suicide, but Hajime reasoned that he had no other means of moving forward. However, he decided to make sure to at least keep his right hand free, so he tied the glowstone to the stump of his left arm.

After walking forward a while, Hajime saw something glint in the darkness, deeper down the passageway. He strained his senses, suddenly vigilant.

Sticking to the shadows as much as possible while he advanced, he suddenly felt an ominous feeling approach from his left side. He quickly jumped to the side, then pointed his left stump at the source of the feeling. Illuminated in the ghastly green light was a massive two-meter-long gray lizard, and its golden eyes were staring right at Hajime.

The lizard's golden eyes flashed brightly. An instant later...

"Huh?!" With a strange cracking noise, Hajime's left stump began turning to stone. The fossilization spread to the glowstone, and seconds later the petrified glowstone made a cracking noise and crumbled away. Without his light source, Hajime was once more surrounded by darkness. The petrification had continued, reaching all the way up to his shoulder.

Hajime clicked his tongue, pulled out a vial of Ambrosia from the monster-fur-and-transmuted-thread holster strapped to his breast, and downed it in one gulp. As he had hoped, the petrification came to a stop, and slowly began reversing back down his left arm.

Now you've done it! Hajime pulled a flash grenade out from the pouch at his waist and flung it at the spot where he'd last seen the lizard. He saw another flash of golden light appear from the darkness. Despite his inability to see clearly, Hajime quickly used Supersonic Step to dash away.

When he glanced back, he saw the rock behind where he'd been had changed color, looking far more weathered than it once was. That literally petrifying gaze was going to be quite troublesome. The lizard closely resembled the kind of Basilisk Hajime had seen in RPG games.

Hajime pulled Donner out of its holster, and held it in front of his face while tightly shutting his eyes. A second later, the flash grenade exploded in a riot of green light with a quiet bang.

"Kraaaah?!" The Basilisk probably hadn't ever experienced light so bright before, and writhed around in bewilderment. When he opened his eyes, Hajime could barely make out its silhouette in the darkness.

He fired without delay. His bullet found its mark, tearing through the skull of the Basilisk, pulverizing what was contained within. The bullet passed cleanly through the back of the Basilisk's head and drilled deep into the rock wall behind it with a loud hiss. Because his bullets were electrically accelerated, they came out at a very high temperature and burned everything they passed through. It was only thanks to taur's resistance to heat that he was able to fire such powerful rounds.

Wary of his surroundings, Hajime carefully approached the Basilisk. Once he confirmed it was dead, he quickly cut up its flesh and retreated to safety. He could hardly eat it there, where he couldn't even see what was around him. Hajime decided to prioritize scouting the new floor first.

He continued walking through the darkness. He searched for dozens of hours, but was unable to find a staircase leading down. He continued defeating enemies and picking up the rocks he found on the way, and before long he found himself laden with more things than he could easily carry. That was when he finally decided that it was time he made a base for himself.

He put his hand on a nearby wall and transmuted it. The wall opened up easily enough, and he walked into the passage he had made for himself. Hajime continued transmuting the area around him until he had a space about six tatami mats wide. Then, before he forgot, he took the basketball-sized pale blue crystal out of his rucksack and placed it onto a cavity he had carved out for it. He had, of course, brought the Divinity Stone with him. He had also brought along containers to hold the Ambrosia. These he set underneath the stone.

As Hajime was unaware of the stone's real name, he had taken to calling it the "potion rock" and the Ambrosia that spilled from it "potions." While it was true that potions were the standard healing items in most games, Ambrosia's effects far surpassed that of a measly potion. The insultingly basic moniker he had chosen just showed how little thought Hajime had put into naming it.

"Now that I'm all settled in, it's time for a feast." Hajime took all the meat he had collected out of a stone container he had fitted to his rucksack using transmutation. Then he grilled it all with Lightning Field. The day's menu consisted of roast Basilisk meat, roasted whole owl with half its feathers still sticking on, and roasted whole six-legged cat thing. There were no seasonings.

"At least I *have* food." As he worked through his meal, he began feeling that familiar pain in his body. The pain meant his body was being forcibly strengthened once more. Which meant that the monsters here were at least as powerful as the Claw Bear had been, if not more. That made sense, as the combination of their special magic and the darkness had made each of them quite difficult foes to face. However, Donner was able to pulverize anything it hit, so Hajime hadn't really noticed that they were that much stronger than their counterparts on the floor above.

He drank some more Ambrosia and ignored the pain as he continued eating. He had suffered so much since losing his arm that such a measly level of pain didn't even faze him.

"Mmmf, haah, thanks for the meal. Now then, let's see how my stats changed..." Hajime took out his status plate as he said that. His current stats were as follows...

HAJIME NAGUMO		Age: 17	Male
Job:	Synergist	Level:	23
Strength:	450	Agility:	550
Vitality:	550	Magic:	500
Defense:	350	M. Defense:	500

Skills:	Transmute [+Ore Appraisal] [+Precision Transmutation] [+Ore Perception] [+Ore Desynthesis] [+Ore Synthesis] • Mana Manipulation • Iron Stomach • Lightning Field • Air Dance [+Aerodynamic] [+Supersonic Step] • Gale Claw • Night Vision • Sense Presence • Petrification Resistance • Language Comprehension

As he had expected, his stats had risen dramatically. And he had learned three new skills. As he looked around, he realized he could indeed see a little better in the darkness.

Must have been the effect of Night Vision. It might not have been a very useful skill for the rest of the monsters in this hell, but for the floor he was on at least, it was a godsend. His other new skills did as their names suggested. Though Hajime was somewhat disappointed that he had gotten Petrification Resistance, and not the Basilisk's actual petrification skill. He wondered why that was.

"Man, it would have been so cool to get 'Basilisk's Eye' or something..." Hajime lamented dejectedly.

Once he finished his meal, Hajime began transmuting new supplies for himself.

Crafting even a single bullet took a great deal of concentration. His bullets needed to be extremely precise. In order to make use of Donner's rifling, he had to get the size and shape exactly right. And he couldn't make a single mistake in compressing the blastrock packed within them. Each bullet took about thirty minutes to make, but Hajime was still proud of his skill with the craft. *Humans really are creatures that display a terrifying amount of strength when they're desperate,* Hajime thought, impressed with himself.

Besides, though it took time, his bullets were powerful enough that he had no reason to complain, and each one he made trained his transmuting ability to new heights, so it really wasn't a waste.

Thanks to his training, he was now able to purify any mineral or ore of impurities, and he could even decompose an alloy into its composite parts. He also had the power to fuse ore together to create new alloys. Hajime's current transmutation skill was on par with the kingdom's best blacksmith.

He silently continued his work. So far, he had only descended a single level from his starting point, and he had no way of knowing how much further this abyss continued for. He planned on returning to his search the moment he finished transmuting. If he wanted to get home, he couldn't afford to waste time lounging around.

Once he resumed his search, Hajime stopped only when he needed to return to base and replenish his supplies. He had no way of knowing how long his search would take if he let himself rest while searching. Thanks to his Night Vision, he no longer had any problem seeing in the dark, and Sense Presence let him know when there were any monsters within a ten-meter radius. His scouting of the floor progressed swiftly.

Finally, he discovered the stairs leading down to the next floor. He stepped forward without hesitation.

The ground of the floor below was sticky, like tar. In fact, the entire floor resembled a huge swamp. His legs easily got stuck in the ground, and Hajime had a hard time moving. He frowned as he saw how difficult it was to move, then proceeded to climb up a protruding boulder. From there he used Aerodynamic to advance through the sky.

As he continued moving forward he constantly used Ore

Perception to look for new minerals. Among the ones he discovered on this floor, one was of particular note.

◊ FLAMROCK

A glossy black mineral. When heated, it melts into tar. It melts at 50 degrees Celsius, and catches fire at 100 degrees Celsius. When it burns, it can reach temperatures of up to 3000 degrees Celsius. The length it burns depends on the quantity of tar.

"...Seriously?" Hajime grimaced and raised one of his legs. As he did so, the tar he had stepped in numerous times since setting foot onto this floor squelched loudly as it dripped off his shoe.

"N-no fire, got it..." He doubted it would ignite that easily, since 100 degrees wasn't so easily reached, but on the off chance it did, it would set off a chain reaction that would literally have this floor engulfed in fires hotter than hell. Even the Ambrosia wouldn't be able to save him from that.

"That means I can't use my railgun or Lightning Field, either..." Donner was one of his most powerful weapons. Even without Lightning Field to accelerate his bullets, the combustive power of blastrock alone was still quite formidable.

However, that was only as far as normal monsters were concerned. For example, Traum Soldiers would easily be pulverized with just the power of blastrock. Even the Behemoth would have taken a considerable amount of damage from it. However, the monsters that inhabited this deep abyss were different. They were of a completely different caliber than the monsters on the floors above. Which was why Hajime wasn't sure blastrock alone would be enough to kill them.

Despite this predicament, Hajime still grinned eagerly.

"So what if I can't use Donner? What I need to do hasn't changed. I just have to kill and devour my enemies." He pressed on, even with his Lightning Field and railgun sealed.

Eventually, Hajime found himself at a three-way fork. He marked the wall and began walking down the left-hand path.

But just as he moved forward... *Fwoosh!*

"Wha—?!" A shark-like monster suddenly leaped out of the tar, countless rows of razor-sharp teeth visible in its mouth. It snapped down, aiming to take Hajime's head in one huge bite. He managed to duck in time, but a shiver of fear still ran down his spine as that horrifying mouth closed inches from his head.

Sense Presence wasn't able to pick up on it! Ever since he had acquired it, Hajime had been using Sense Presence constantly. And the skill was supposed to be able to sense anything within 10 meters of him without fail. Despite that, he had been unable to sense that shark until just before it had attacked.

Having failed to take out Hajime with its first bite, the shark plopped back into the sea of tar with a splash.

Crap, I can't tell where it is at all! He ground his teeth at his lack of information. However, he realized standing still would get him killed, so he quickly used Aerodynamic to keep himself moving.

As if it had predicted his actions, the shark leaped high this time, reaching all the way up to him.

"Don't underestimate me!" Hajime somersaulted in the air and while hanging suspended upside-down, he fired directly at the shark. The bullet fired from Donner's muzzle rushed forward, eager for blood. And with perfect aim, hit the shark square in its back. However...

"Tch! It doesn't have enough power to penetrate!" The bullet created a small dent in the shark's skin, and then, as if it had encountered a wall of rubber, it bounced off. It appeared the shark's skin was resistant to physical attacks.

"Guh!" It nimbly leaped past and dived back into the sea of tar. Then, with that same agility, the shark aimed for Hajime's landing point, jumping at him once more after he finished his somersault.

He managed to twist his body at the last minute, avoiding being torn in half, but the shark still managed to gouge a tiny chunk of flesh from his side. The impact caused Hajime to fall into the sea of tar. His entire body was covered in black goo, but he quickly leaped back to his feet and jumped into the air. A second later, the shark's jaws opened up where Hajime had just been lying, then closed down with a snap.

Cold sweat ran down Hajime's back as he kept himself in the air with consecutive uses of Aerodynamic. But his fearless smile never left his face, despite how easily he was getting cornered.

"Bring it!" He kept himself aloft with Aerodynamic, always moving from place to place, while he waited for the shark to attack once more.

His powers of concentration, which he had honed through weeks of relentless transmutation, served him well here. As he focused, his surroundings slowly came into clearer view, and he could even make out colors.

So what if I can't find it with Sense Presence? To begin with, I handled myself just fine even when I didn't have it. Even if I can't see where it is, it has to show itself when it attacks. Focused, Hajime moved to leap into the air once more, but as he did so, his footing grew unstable, and he lost his balance as he jumped. The shark wasn't one to let that opportunity go past. It leaped out from behind Hajime, right where his blind spot was.

"Well, I'm glad you're so simpleminded!" His supposedly failing balance suddenly recovered, and he jumped to the side, avoiding the shark's attack. At the same time, he swung his right hand, with Donner still held tightly in it, at the shark.

A huge gash appeared in the shark's side, and blood sprayed everywhere as it fell back into the tar. It floundered around in the tar, flailing in pain.

Hajime had purposely pretended to lose his balance, in order to lure the shark into attacking from his blind spot. Then he had wrapped the Claw Bear's special magic, Gale Claw, around Donner as he had swung it.

Hajime swooped onto the flailing shark and swung Donner down at its head. The Gale Claw split its head cleanly in two. Though he had only one claw instead of three, its sharpness was unmatched. It was the perfect skill for close combat.

"Now then, time to find out why I wasn't able to sense your presence." Hajime licked his lips in a predatory fashion as he said that.

He stored the shark meat in his bag, then continued searching. He found the exit to the next floor before long, and descended to the level below.

HAJIME NAGUMO		Age: 17	Male
Job:	Synergist	Level:	24
Strength:	450	Agility:	550

Vitality:	550	Magic:	500
Defense:	400	M. Defense:	500
Skills:	Transmute [+Ore Appraisal] [+Precision Transmutation] [+Ore Perception] [+Ore Desynthesis] [+Ore Synthesis] • Mana Manipulation • Iron Stomach • Lightning Field • Air Dance [+Aerodynamic] [+Supersonic Step] • Gale Claw • Night Vision • Sense Presence • Hide Presence • Petrification Resistance • Language Comprehension		

Hajime continued conquering the labyrinth.

He descended down floor after floor, until he had gone another 50 floors past the one that had the Tar Shark. He had lost all sense of time down in the dungeon, and had no way of guessing how many days had passed. Though it still took time, it was clear he was progressing through the labyrinth at a ridiculously fast pace.

While progressing, he had countless brushes with death, and had to fight all sorts of unbelievably powerful monsters.

Among them were a huge rainbow-colored frog that could spit poison and a giant moth that, oddly enough, looked a lot like Butterfree. The frog he had encountered on a floor that had a faint poisonous mist spread throughout it, and the moth had the ability to spread its scales through the air. Scales that paralyzed anything they touched. Had it not been for the Ambrosia he was constantly drinking, Hajime would have died countless times searching through the labyrinth.

The poison spit by the frog had assaulted his nervous system and hurt almost as bad as the first time he had eaten monster meat. It was only the tiny Ambrosia vial he kept attached to his back teeth that had saved him. The vial he had attached there was crafted from a weak rock that would easily break with a single bite. He was eternally thankful that he had prepared that as a last resort for emergency situations.

He had, of course, eaten both the moth and the frog. There had been some reservations involved in eating the moth, but he reminded himself it was to make him stronger, which helped him power through that meal. Hajime had remembered feeling somewhat vexed when he'd discovered that the frog had actually tasted better than all the other monsters so far.

And though he was deep underground, he had even gone through a floor that resembled the Amazon Jungle. It had been incredibly humid, and the air hung thick around him. That had been by far the worst floor he had traversed. The monsters he had faced on that floor had been giant centipedes and living trees.

Hardened as he was to most things, even Hajime had been completely creeped out when a giant centipede had come crashing down from a high-up tree branch. It was the most disgusting sight he'd ever laid his eyes on. And the centipede had split itself into various segments to attack him, too. What he had thought was just one enemy suddenly split into thirty, like an army of cockroaches coming out of a particularly disgusting kitchen.

Hajime had fired Donner as fast he could to destroy them, but sadly there had been too many. As reloading would have taken far too long, he resigned himself to butchering them with his Gale Claw. But even that wasn't enough to take them all out, so he had to resort to kicking, which was not his forte at all. When that battle had finally finished, Hajime had sworn to himself that he would work on improving his reload times and kicking skills. He was tired of being bathed in the centipede's purple, disgusting blood.

The tree monsters of that floor were basically the Treants he had seen in RPGs. They used their roots to attack from underground, while also flinging their branches around like whips.

Though the real strength of those fake Treants didn't lie in such simple skills. When they were in trouble, they would start shaking their heads wildly, flinging crimson fruit at their enemies. The fruit they threw didn't hurt, and just to test it, Hajime had tried eating one. When he had, he had stood rooted to the spot for almost an hour. The fruit had contained no poison. In fact, it had tasted delicious. It was sweet and refreshing, like watermelon. Despite expectations, it was nothing like an apple.

The fact that the floor was the most unpleasant one he had encountered yet completely flew out of Hajime's head. Even his resolve to conquer the labyrinth temporarily left his mind. It was the first time he had eaten anything aside from monster meat in months. His eyes became that of a hunter, and he spent a great deal of time hunting down the fake Treants. By the time his craving for their fruit had finally been sated, the Treants had been hunted to near extinction.

And so, he continued progressing through the floors, until he had passed 50 of them before he knew it. And still the labyrinth continued endlessly downward. For the record, Hajime's current stats looked like this.

HAJIME NAGUMO		Age: 17	Male
Job:	Synergist	Level:	24
Strength:	880	Agility:	1040

Vitality:	970	Magic:	760
Defense:	860	M. Defense:	760
Skills:	Transmute [+Ore Appraisal] [+Precision Transmutation] [+Ore Perception] [+Ore De-synthesis] [+Ore Synthesis] [+Duplicate Trans-mutation] • Mana Manipulation • Iron Stomach • Lightning Field • Air Dance [+Aerodynamic] [+Supersonic Step] [+Steel Legs] • Gale Claw • Night Vision • Farsight • Sense Presence • Detect Magic • Hide Presence • Poison Re-sistance • Paralysis Resistance • Petrification Resistance • Language Comprehension		

He spent some time in the base he had created for this floor, the fiftieth since the Tar Shark, training his shooting, kicking, and transmutation skills. He had already discovered the stairs leading to the next floor, but there was a location on this floor that seemed distinctly different to him. An ominous atmosphere seemed to pervade the space around it.

At the very end of one of the side passages was a room which contained a set of majestic double doors, each three meters tall. On each side of the door was a statue of a Cyclops sunk deep into the recesses of the wall.

When he had tried to step into the room, Hajime had felt chills run down his spine, and had beat a hasty retreat, deciding that room was dangerous. Of course, the retreat was only temporary. He was going back to prepare, and had no intention of skipping past that room. After all, it was the first thing he had run into these past 50 floors that was "different." There was no way he wasn't going to check it out.

He was filled with both expectation and trepidation as he thought about the door. However, once he opened it, he knew some kind of disaster awaited. Still, it was also an opportunity to call forth the winds of change in this never-ending hell.

"It's just like Pandora's Box... Now then, I wonder what I can hope for when I open it?" He mentally ran through his abilities, his weapons, and his skills. He checked over each one of them, making sure he was in peak condition.

When all his preparations were complete, Hajime slowly pulled Donner out of its holster, then slowly pressed its back end against his forehead as he closed his eyes. He had already steeled his resolve long ago, but there was no harm in spending a few minutes to steel it some more. Hajime searched deep within himself, giving voice to his dearest desire once more.

"I want to survive and make it back home. Back home...to Japan. Anything getting in the way of that goal is my enemy. And enemies are to be...killed!" He opened his eyes, and with his ever-present fearless smile, set off toward the unknown.

Hajime's footsteps grew steadily more wary as he attempted to enter the room with the double doors. He made it all the way to the entrance without encountering anyone.

Upon taking a closer look at them, Hajime realized that the craftsmanship of the doors was even more impressive than he had initially thought. And that there was a magic circle carved into a tiny hollow on each of the two.

"Huh? That's odd. I studied quite a bit back at the castle...but I still don't recognize this inscription." Back when he had still been ridiculed as worthless, Hajime had spent all his time studying to compensate for his lack of combat ability. Of course, he hadn't had enough time to learn everything there was to know about this world, but it was still unsettling that he couldn't recognize a single symbol on the circles.

"Does that just mean this spell's really old?" Hajime surveyed the magic circles as he investigated the doors, but he was unable to discover anything of note. The conspicuous placement of the circles just screamed "trap" to Hajime, but he didn't have enough knowledge to derive any hints from his investigation.

"Guess my only option is to transmute them, like always." He had already tried pushing and pulling on the doors, but they hadn't budged. And so, he had turned to his trusty transmutation skill. He placed his right hand on the door's surface and began transmuting.

But the moment he started pouring mana into his hand... Zap!

"Whaaa?!" A bolt of red lightning ran down the door, blasting Hajime's hand away. Tendrils of smoke rose up from his hand. Cursing, he drank some Ambrosia to heal himself. A second later, he heard a deep roar.

"Uoooooooooooooooh!!!" It reverberated throughout the entire room.

Hajime backpedaled away from the door and lowered himself into a crouch with his hand on his holster, ready to draw at a moment's notice. While waiting he heard the sounds of something moving mixed in with the roar.

"Wow, this is a clichéd as it gets." Hajime smiled sardonically as he watched the two Cyclops statues suddenly spring to life and start destroying the wall that held them. Their petrified skin rapidly regained its color, going from gray to dark green.

The Cyclopes fit the fantasy description for them to a T. They each wielded swords nearly four meters long that they had pulled from god knows where. Currently, they were struggling to free their still-entombed lower halves, determined to eliminate the unwelcome intruder.

Hajime fired Donner directly at the right Cyclops' glaring eye. With a ferocious bang, the electrically accelerated taur bullet pierced through its eye, made mincemeat out of its brains, and pulverized the wall behind it as it exited the back of its head.

The Cyclops on the left stared blankly at its now-deceased companion. On the other hand, the dead one twitched for a few seconds before collapsing forward, which made the entire room shake as its huge frame crashed into the ground, raising a massive cloud of dust.

"Sorry, but I'm not a nice enough guy to wait for you to break free." The dead Cyclops hadn't seen that coming, in more ways than one. For Hajime, who had survived through countless life-and-death struggles, it was merely a natural course of action to take. Yet...he still felt a twinge of pity for the Cyclops.

It probably wasn't anything more than a humble guardian that had been sealed and tasked with protecting the doors. It must have spent an eternity waiting for someone, anyone, to pass by.

Then finally, someone capable enough of surviving so long in the pits of hell and looking to delve even deeper had appeared before it. It's quite possible he—if it was a he—had been overjoyed to finally have a purpose. But then, before he could even begin to fight, his opponent crushed his prized eye and killed him instantly. *If that's not pitiful, then I don't know what is.*

The remaining Cyclops had a bloodcurdling expression on its face as it turned to look at Hajime. Though it didn't speak, its face was clearly screaming, "How dare you, you bastard!"

Hajime stared at the remaining Cyclops, completely unmoving as he met its gaze. It was acting cautious due to his unfamiliar weapon and crouched low to the ground, ready to dodge in any direction, as it glared at him. Ten seconds passed, then twenty... Eventually, it grew tired of the staring contest and with a deafening roar, the remaining Cyclops charged Hajime.

But before it even made five paces, it face-planted into the ground.

The moment it had rushed forward, all the strength had drained from its limbs, and it careened to the ground. Confused, the Cyclops tried to struggle back to its feet, but it was able to do little more than flail helplessly on the ground.

It roared, unable to comprehend what had just happened, while Hajime slowly walked over to it. His echoing footsteps were like a countdown to the Cyclops' demise. He stopped inches from its face, and put his gun to its head. Then, without any hesitation, he pulled the trigger.

Bang! The sound of a gunshot echoed throughout the room for a second time.

However, something unexpected happened just then. The Cyclops' body glowed briefly, after which its skin repelled the bullet that should have killed it.

"Hmm?" Hajime guessed that it was because of its special magic. From what he could tell, it temporarily gave the Cyclops a massive defense boost. Though it was still face-down on the ground, the Cyclops smirked contemptuously at him.

Unfazed, he retracted his gun and aimed a kick at the Cyclops' head. Thanks to his Steel Legs skill, Hajime's kicks were as powerful as the Kickmaster Rabbit's had been. His foot traced a neat arc through the air before slamming into the Cyclops and turning it over on its stomach. He then pressed Donner to its eye.

Though he couldn't be sure, it looked as if the Cyclops was panicking. Still, he paid it no mind and mercilessly pulled the trigger. As he expected, the body hardening didn't extend to its eye, and the second Cyclops had its brains blown out just like the first.

"Hmm, it took around twenty seconds this time. That's slower than usual... Is it because it has a larger body?" Hajime mumbled to himself, analyzing the results of his experiment.

Why had that Cyclops suddenly collapsed earlier? That had been thanks to the power of his stun grenade. He had made it using the scales he'd harvested from the Butterfree lookalikes. By utilizing a small, controlled blast, he could spread the scales throughout a room, paralyzing everything in it. The instant the Cyclops on the left had been distracted by the death of its companion, Hajime had thrown it into the air.

"Well, whatever. Guess I'll harvest the meat later..." As he glanced back to the door, an idea sprouted in his mind.

He used Gale Claw to cut open the Cyclopes and extracted their mana crystals. Ignoring the fact that they were dripping with blood, he carried the two fist-sized mana crystals over to the double doors and placed them in the two indents.

They fit perfectly. After a brief delay, they began pouring gouts of dark red mana into the magic circles. The sound of something snapping echoed in the distance and the light began to fade. Mana started diffusing through the room at the same time, making the surrounding walls glow with a bright light. The room was suddenly filled with more light than Hajime had seen in ages.

He blinked at the sudden brightness, then pushed open the door, clearly on the lookout for any traps.

The room on the other side of the door was pitch black, with not a single light source to be found. However, a combination of his Night Vision and the light spilling in from the room outside was enough for him to dimly make out his surroundings.

The interior of the room was composed of the same marble-like substance that Hajime had first seen in the church cathedral. Two rows of thick pillars, spaced out at regular intervals, extended all the way to the end of the room. In the very center of the room stood a huge cubical slab of rock. Its surface was glossy, and it shone from the reflected light coming in from the room behind.

Hajime took a closer look at the cube, noticing there was something that glowed faintly jutting out from the center of its front face. It looked almost as if it was sprouting out of the rock.

Intent on getting a closer look, he threw the doors open wide, and looked for something to hold them in place. He didn't want to make the classic horror movie mistake and enter only to find the door shut behind him.

However, before he could fix them in place, whatever was in the center of the cube stirred.

"...Who goes there?" He heard a faint, hoarse, female voice. Startled, Hajime looked over to the center of the room again. The "something" he had seen earlier was squirming slightly. The light pouring in from the other room revealed that something's true form.

"A...person?" The something sprouting from the rock was indeed a person.

The girl was buried in the rock from the neck down, and her golden-blonde hair dangled limply in front of her face, much like the ghost from a certain famous horror movie. Eyes as red as the blood moon peeked out from between gaps in her hair. She looked to be rather young. Despite her haggard appearance and her hair covering the better part of her face, it was still clear she was quite beautiful.

Hajime stiffened in surprise; he hadn't expected to see another person so deep in the labyrinth. It seemed the girl was just as surprised to see him too, as she was staring at him in dumbfounded shock. After a moment of silence, he took some deep breaths to steady himself, and then resolutely said...

"Sorry. I'll just leave now." He went to go and close the doors again. But before he could, the blonde-haired red-eyed girl hurriedly called out to him once more. Her voice was hoarse and weak, most likely from years of disuse, but the desperation in it was clear.

"W-wait...! Please...! Help me..."

"Don't wanna." Hajime replied curtly, then returned his attention to the doors. A truly heartless reply.

"Wh-why... Please... I'll do anything, so..." She really was desperate. Though she could barely move her neck, she still raised her face up to look at Hajime.

But even then, Hajime only gave an irritated reply.

"You know, I really doubt it'd be a good idea to free someone that's clearly been sealed all the way down here in the deepest pits of hell. That just spells trouble. As far as I can tell there's nothing but the seal in here...and it doesn't look like that'll help my escape at all, so..." It was a fair argument.

However, there were few people so devoid of sympathy that they could so easily ignore a girl's pleas for help. It was clear that the old, kind Hajime had long since perished.

Though he had refused her so bluntly, the girl continued hopelessly calling out for help.

"No! *Cough*... I-I'm not anyone bad...! Please wait! I..." He continued pulling the double doors closed, but just before he shut them completely, he ground his teeth. Had he been a bit faster he wouldn't have had to hear those last words of hers.

"I was betrayed!" He heard, through the tiny crack of the still-open door.

The creaking doors ground to a halt. A miniscule sliver of light was all that illuminated the darkness within. Ten seconds passed, then twenty. Finally, the doors began opening once more. Standing behind them was Hajime, scowling unhappily at the situation at hand.

No matter what she had said, he hadn't planned on helping her. He figured there must have been a very good reason someone was sealed all the way down here, far below the light of the sun. And there was no proof that she wasn't dangerous, either. In fact, it was likely that she was just some evil creature that was trying to deceive him into releasing her. He should have just left her.

Seriously, what the hell am I doing? Hajime sighed to himself as that thought passed through his mind.

"I was betrayed!" ...To think those words would stir his heart, the heart he thought he'd long since buried. He thought he had already forgotten about the classmate who had flung that fireball at him. He thought he had already thrown away paltry feelings like hatred and sympathy. In order to survive in this cruel world, he had to.

But the fact that the girl's words had shaken him so deeply meant that he hadn't completely buried his old self. Enough of the old, kind Hajime still lived that he could sympathize with this girl's circumstances, which were so very similar to his own.

He scratched his head uncomfortably and walked up to the girl. Of course, he still remained vigilant.

"You said you were betrayed? But that still doesn't explain why you're trapped here. If you really were betrayed, how come they sealed you in this rock?" The girl seemed shocked that Hajime had actually come back.

She stared fixedly at Hajime through her dirty golden locks, crimson eyes gleaming in the darkness. He began growing impatient at her continued silence.

"Hey, are you listening? If you don't want to talk, then I'll just head back now," he said brusquely and turned on his heel. The girl came back to her senses with a start and quickly began speaking.

"I am one of the original, atavistic vampires... Because of the extraordinary power I was gifted with...I worked hard for the sake of my country and my people. But then...one day...my retainers all...said I wasn't needed anymore... My uncle...said that he would be king in my place... I...was fine with that...but because I had so much power, everyone was afraid of me. They thought I was dangerous... They couldn't kill me...so they decided to seal me here instead... That's why..."

She spoke haltingly but desperately, her parched throat making speech difficult. Hajime sighed as he heard her tale. She had certainly suffered a cruel fate. However, during the course of her tale he heard some things that nagged at him. He felt an inexplicable, complicated feeling well up within him, so he asked the following:

"So does that mean you were some kind of royalty?"

She nodded furiously at his words.

"What do you mean they couldn't kill you?"

"...I heal automatically. No matter what kind of injury it is, it'll just heal by itself. Even if you cut my head off I'll regenerate eventually."

"Th-that's quite the ability... So that's the power everyone was afraid of?"

"That too, but... the main thing was that I could control mana... directly, without a magic circle."

Hajime nodded and replied with a simple, "I see."

After consuming monster flesh he had become capable of freely manipulating his mana as well. He needed no chants or magic circles to enhance his body, or use the special magic he had acquired. Same with his transmutation skill.

However, Hajime had zero affinity for magic, so even if he could manipulate his mana directly, he still needed a huge magic circle to actually cast anything, meaning he effectively couldn't use it for much.

But with this girl's magical affinity, being able to directly manipulate mana turned into an insanely powerful asset. Because while everyone else had to waste time preparing circles and chanting their spells, she could just blast off magic like nobody's business. Frankly, it wouldn't be much of a fight if she chose to take someone on. And to top it off, she was immortal. It probably wasn't perfect, and there was most likely some way to actually overcome it, but even then it was a cheat-level skill far surpassing that of any hero.

"...Please, save me," she begged softly, as she watched Hajime sink deep into thought.

"Hmm..." He stared unblinkingly at her. She stared right back. They spent what felt like an eternity gazing into each other's eyes. Finally, Hajime scratched his head awkwardly and breathed a long sigh. He then placed his hand on the cube holding the girl.

"Ah." Her eyes opened wide as she realized what he was doing. He ignored her and began transmuting.

His mana, which had turned a dark red since ingesting the wolves—or rather, more of a deep crimson—began flowing down his arm.

However, the cube he was trying to transmute remained unchanged, as if it was resisting the force of his mana. Just like the bedrock that lay between each floor of the labyrinth. However, unlike in that case, it wasn't as if his magic was being completely nullified. Little by little, Hajime's power began seeping into the cube.

"Guh, this thing's tough...but I'm not so weak anymore!" He poured yet more mana into his spell. It was enough mana that it would have taken six verses to chant out, were he not able to manipulate it freely. Finally, he felt his magic start taking effect. The tremendous volume of mana dazzled bright crimson, illuminating the entire room in a fiery red.

And yet Hajime continued pouring mana into his arm. Seven verses worth, then eight. The part of the rock encasing the girl began to tremble at that point.

"I'm not done yet!" He pushed even harder, pouring a ninth verse's worth of mana into the stone. At that point, he had burned enough mana to cast some of the most advanced spells in existence and still have some left over. The girl stared at him fixedly as his mana grew brighter and brighter, determined not to miss a single moment.

Cold sweat poured down his back as he kept going. This was the first time Hajime had tried to cast such a large-scale spell. If he lost focus for even an instant, the massive amount of mana he was wielding would go berserk. But even after all that, the cube refused to budge. Desperate, he threw all the mana he had into the spell.

Hajime wasn't sure why he was going so far for a girl he had just met.

But for some reason, he just couldn't leave her alone. Even though he had sworn to himself to eliminate all obstacles in his path and to live only for the sake of his goal, he still continued transmuting. *Seriously, why the hell am I doing this?* He mentally admonished himself for his actions, but then he reasoned that everyone makes exceptions sometimes and stubbornly thought, *I decided to do this, so there's no way in hell I'm quitting halfway!*

He was burning so much mana that his entire body glowed crimson. He was using up every last drop of mana just to free her. With a doggedness that surprised even himself, he kept resolutely transmuting with every ounce of spirit he had. Finally, the portion of the cube entrapping the girl began to melt like hot butter and dribbled to the ground, slowly releasing her from her stone prison.

As the rock slowly fell away, her modest breasts were fully visible. Next came her waist, then her hands, her thighs, and finally the cube melted away entirely and she was free. Her completely naked body was clearly emaciated, but it still had an alluring charm to it. She slumped to the ground in an exhausted heap as soon as her body was fully free. It seemed she wasn't strong enough to stand.

Hajime sat down in front of her. He was panting heavily. Using up

his entire reservoir of mana had clearly exhausted him greatly.

With a trembling hand, he tried to pull out a vial of Ambrosia, but before he could the girl put her hand over his and grabbed it. Her small, slender, and frail hand trembled as it entwined with his own. He gave her a sidelong glance, and realized she was looking right at him. Though her face was expressionless, a wealth of emotions dwelled within her crimson eyes.

In a small and trembling, but powerful voice, the girl conveyed her feelings.

"Thank you."

Hajime wasn't sure he could ever express the emotion he felt at those words. He just knew that the heart he thought he'd discarded began glowing with a faint, but resolute light.

He sat there quietly, his hand in hers. He wondered how long she must have been trapped there, suffering. As far as Hajime knew, the vampires had gone extinct hundreds of years ago. At the very least, that was what had been written in the history books he had read in the royal library.

Even when she had been talking to him earlier, her face had remained expressionless. Which meant that she had at least spent a long enough time in this solitary dark cell to forget how to speak, and even how to show emotions.

According to her tale, she had been betrayed by someone she trusted, too. It was a wonder she hadn't gone insane. Perhaps that had been due to her healing factor? But if that really were the case, that meant she had been tortured for centuries by her own abilities. Unable to even sink into the release of madness.

Guess drinking the potion can wait, Hajime thought to himself with a wry smile, squeezing the girl's hand back as he did. Startled, she jumped slightly, and then strengthened her own grip.

"...What's your name?" she whispered to Hajime.

His smile grew awkward as he realized they hadn't told each other their names yet. He replied quickly, without a hint of hesitation in his tone. "Hajime. Hajime Nagumo. What's yours?"

She muttered "Hajime" to herself over and over, as if carving it into her memories. After she finished repeating it, she opened her mouth to answer his question, before hesitating for a moment and thinking better of it.

"...Give me one."

"Huh? You want me to name you? Don't tell me you forgot your actual one?"

Considering how long she had been imprisoned here it wasn't impossible, but the girl shook her head slowly.

"I don't need a name from the past... I'm fine with whatever name you give me, Hajime."

"...Haah, It's not so easy to just think up a name..."

The reason she wanted a new name was probably similar to the reason Hajime had reforged his heart. She wanted to throw away her old self and be reborn. Hajime had practically been forced to change by the pain and starvation, but it seemed she wanted to be reborn of her own free will. And the first step toward that transformation was getting a new moniker.

She looked expectantly up at Hajime. Hajime scratched his cheek as he thought, before finally christening the girl with her new name.

"What do you think of Yue? I'm not really good at the whole naming thing, so I can try thinking up a different one if you don't like it."

"Yue...? Yue...Yue..."

"Yeah. Where I come from, it means 'moon.' When I first came into this room your golden hair and red eyes reminded me of the moon, so I just... Well, what do you think?"

She blinked in surprise at his words. It seemed she hadn't expected him to have a reason behind picking the name. And though her face remained as expressionless as always, her eyes were sparkling with happiness.

"...Hmm. Then from today onwards, I will be Yue. Thank you."

"Glad you like it. Anyway..." As the girl, now Yue, expressed her thanks, Hajime untangled his hand from hers and took off his coat.

"Huh?" She watched him in mild confusion.

"Here, wear this. Can't have you running around naked forever."

"Oh..." Yue reflexively took the coat offered to her, and looked down at her own body. As Hajime had said, she was stark naked. Every bit of her was completely exposed. She blushed and pressed the coat against her body before looking up at Hajime and saying, "Hajime, you pervert."

"Uh..." He realized anything he said would only make things worse, so he wisely chose to remain silent. Yue happily donned the coat he gave her. As she was a mere 140 centimeters tall, it was a bit too big for her. Hajime smiled as he watched her try and fold the right sleeve back enough for her hand to poke through.

While she was wrestling with his coat, he drank some Ambrosia. He felt strength return to his body, and his mind began working again. He used Sense Presence to check his surroundings...and instantly froze. There was one hell of a powerful monster in the room with them.

And it was...right above them. The same time he noticed its presence, it chose to drop down from the ceiling.

He quickly got to his feet, scooped up Yue with one arm, and used Supersonic Step to dash away as fast as possible. He looked back just in time to see the monster crash into the ground right where they'd been sitting a second ago.

The monster was nearly five meters long, and possessed four arms that all ended in razor-sharp scissors. It had a further eight legs that clacked noisily as it scuttled around. It also had two tails, each of which ended in stingers. The closest thing it resembled was a scorpion. Hajime assumed the two stingers contained poison. It was clearly far more powerful than the monsters he had faced so far. Cold sweat began running down his forehead.

His initial Sense Presences when he first entered the room hadn't discovered anything, but the one he had used mere moments ago had. Which meant that the scorpion-thing must have entered the room after he had released Yue from her seal.

In other words, this was the one last trap her captors had placed to keep her from escaping her cell. If it was a trap designed for Yue, Hajime could escape if he left her behind.

He spared a quick glance at the girl he held in his arms. She was ignoring the scorpion-thing entirely and looking only at Hajime. Her eyes were a sea of calm, showing nothing but the resolve to accept her fate. They spoke volumes more than words ever could. Yue had decided to place her life in Hajime's hands.

When he saw those eyes, Hajime's lips naturally curled up into his usual fearless grin. Though he had told himself he would never care about other people again, he had ended up sympathizing with Yue anyway. She had lit the fire in his heart, a heart he thought he had long since abandoned. And despite the terrible betrayal she had suffered, she chose once more to place her trust in someone. If he didn't help her, then he didn't deserve to be called a man.

"Bring it, you bastard. Kill me if you think you can." Hajime slung Yue over his shoulder, pulled another vial of Ambrosia out of his bag, and thrust it into her mouth.

"Mmmgh?!" The rejuvenating fluid spread throughout her body. Tears formed in the corner of her eyes at the sudden intrusion of something hard into her mouth, but her eyes opened wide as she felt the Ambrosia heal her emaciated body.

He then skillfully swung Yue around, situating her on his back. Weakened as she was, Yue was nothing more than dead weight, but Hajime knew if he just put her down somewhere the scorpion-thing would probably go for her first. Still, fighting a monster that strong while protecting someone was going to be tough.

"Hang on tight, Yue!" Though she was far from fully healed, she had enough strength in her body that she was able to cling tightly to his back.

The scorpion's legs clacked on the ground as it scuttled over to them. He felt Yue's slender arms clutching tightly to his back, and with the fearless grin still on his face, Hajime boldly proclaimed his intent.

"If you try and get in my way...I'll kill you and eat you!" As if responding to his challenge, the scorpion-thing attacked first. One of its tails swelled up and shot a stream of purple liquid at him. The stream traveled surprisingly fast, and Hajime quickly leaped away.

The purple liquid sizzled as it hit the ground, melting the area around it. Hajime suspected it was some form of acid.

He spared the liquid a brief glance before drawing Donner from its holster and firing it.

Bang! He fired at full power. A bullet traveling at three kilometers per second slammed into the scorpion-thing's skull.

Hajime felt Yue stiffen on his back. She was surprised to see such an unfamiliar weapon, and surprised even more when she saw it fire off an attack that hit instantly. On top of all that, though, she hadn't sensed Hajime use magic. However, there was a small amount of electricity running down his right arm; he had created it without chanting a spell or using a magic circle. In other words, Yue realized that he had the same kind of mana manipulation ability she did.

He was the same as her, and for some reason he, too, was stuck in the depths of hell. Though she knew now was no time to be distracted, she couldn't help but pay more attention to Hajime than the scorpion.

Meanwhile, Hajime continued leaping through the air with Aerodynamic, making sure to constantly stay on the move. For once, his expression was actually grim. The reason being that Detect Magic and Sense Presence had told him that his bullet hadn't fazed the scorpion-thing in the least.

As proof, its other tail was swelling up as it took aim at him. Then, once it had built up sufficient pressure, it shot its stinger out at him. He tried to dodge, but the needle burst in midair, splintering into numerous sharp shards that sped toward him.

"Gah!" He screamed in pain, but continued shooting down the jets of liquid with Donner, kicking them away with Steel Legs, and blowing them off with Gale Claw. He somehow managed to survive the onslaught and returned fire with Donner. He then threw Donner into the air, pulled out a grenade from his pouch, and threw it at the scorpion-thing.

It withstood Donner's second shot, preparing to fire another needle buckshot and set of acid spray in return. But before it could, the eight-centimeter-long grenade that had rolled next to it exploded. And as it exploded, it sprayed burning black pitch all over the scorpion.

This was his incendiary grenade. He had made it out of the flamrock he discovered on the tar floor. Right now the scorpion was being engulfed in 3000-degree flames.

It looked like even the scorpion-thing couldn't withstand flames that hot, as it began flailing around, trying to scrape the tar off it somehow. Hajime used this time to land back on the ground and reload Donner, which he had already caught in the air.

By the time he finished reloading, the effects of the incendiary grenade had died down, and the flamrock had mostly burnt out. However, the flames had definitely succeeded in doing some damage, and the scorpion-thing screeched in rage.

"Kshaaaaaaaaa!!!" It charged Hajime, all eight legs scuttling rapidly across the ground. The four scissors attached to its front legs suddenly extended forward as if they had been shot out of a cannon and sped toward Hajime.

He dodged the first with Supersonic Step, then jumped over the second with Aerodynamic. He managed to kick the third one away with his Steel Legs, but that threw him off balance as the fourth one headed for him.

However, an instant before it collided with him, he fired Donner and used the recoil from the shot to propel himself backward. By twisting his body, he just barely dodged the fourth scissor claw. Yue was groaning uncomfortably at his violent movements, but she just had to bear it, since Hajime was at his limits just dodging.

He leaped through the air again, this time landing on the scorpion-thing's back. He somehow managed to keep his balance on the rampaging beast's back, and fired Donner into its shell at point-blank range.

Bam! With a deafening explosion, the bullet forced the scorpion to the ground.

However, even a direct hit at point-blank range wasn't enough to pierce its shell, so the bullet had merely scratched it. Hajime ground his teeth in frustration, then swung down with a Gale Claw. However, it bounced off with a metallic clang, not even scratching the shell.

Fed up with the human on its back, the scorpion-thing fired a round of needle buckshot at its own back.

Hajime swiftly jumped back up into the air, firing another bullet at the joint where the tail connected with the stinger while he was in motion. The high-speed bullet hit with perfect accuracy and flung the tail back...but even the tip of the tail was protected by the same thick shell, so the bullet did no lasting damage. Hajime just didn't have enough power to damage it.

As he fled into the sky, the four scissor arms attacked him once more. He flung another incendiary grenade in desperation and jumped away to safety. The scorpion was engulfed in flaming tar for a second time, but Hajime knew he was just buying himself time.

He put some distance between him and the scorpion-thing and tried to think of a plan. But before he could even begin, he heard another piercing scream come from its mouth.

"Kiiiiiiiiiiiii!" Chills ran down his spine as he heard that, and he tried to use Supersonic Step to put even more distance between him and the scorpion...but it was already too late.

As the scream echoed throughout the room, the ground around him began to warp, and with a thundering roar, spiked cones flew out one after another.

"Dammit!" This was a completely unexpected attack.

He desperately took to the sky once more, only to discover that there were spikes closing on him from behind too. In order to protect Yue, he twisted his body around, but that completely destroyed his balance. He still managed to repel the remaining spikes with Donner and his Steel Legs, but he was forced to stop moving, giving the scorpion-thing time to aim another round.

His face stiffened in horror.

An instant later, a barrage of acid and spiked needles came hurtling toward him. He made a snap decision. He realized dodging both in his current situation would be impossible.

Using Aerodynamic, he jumped out of range of the acid spray and covered his vitals with his right arm and left stump. His face he protected with Donner's barrel. Then, using his mana manipulation ability, he strengthened his body to the limit and clenched his muscles.

Moments later, dozens of needles pierced through Hajime's body.

"Gaaaaaaaaaaaaaaaaaaaaaaaah!" He screamed in pain once more, but he managed to avoid taking a hit in any vital areas. Because Yue was clinging to his back, he made sure to stop the needles with his body, to keep them from piercing her as well.

The force of the impact flung Hajime backward. Assailed by pain, he slammed into the ground and rolled over and over. The impact threw Yue off his back too.

Ignoring the pain of the countless needles that pierced his body, Hajime clenched his teeth and pulled out a flash grenade that he threw at the scorpion-thing. It flew in a neat arc through the air before exploding right in front of its eyes.

"Kshaaaaaaaaaaa!!!" It screamed in pain as the light seared its retinas, and took an involuntary step back. Considering it had followed Hajime with its eyes this whole time, he had guessed, correctly, that it mainly used sight to track its prey.

Hajime bit down on the vial of Ambrosia he kept in his molar and pulled all the needles out at once.

"Guuuuuh!" He bit down on his lips from the searing pain, and a moan escaped his lips. But he withstood the pain. He had suffered so much already that he was used to it. Something of that level was nowhere near enough to break his spirit anymore.

As he continued to pull needles from his body, he looked around, searching for Yue. But before he could find her, she found him.

"Hajime!" She ran over to him, worry etched on her face. Her usually expressionless mask had crumbled and she looked like she was about to burst into tears.

"Don't worry, I'm fine. More importantly, that thing is way too damn hard. I can't think of any way to beat it. If I try to go for its eyes or mouth, those stupid scissor things'll get in my way... Do I have no choice but to try for a suicide rush and just accept that I'll take some damage?" He put Yue's worried face out of his mind for the moment and concentrated on finding a way to defeat the monster. But he became distracted when he heard Yue's murmured words.

"...Why?"

"Huh?"

"Why don't you run?" Yue's words implied that Hajime should already have realized he could leave her and escape by himself. He looked at her, evidently dumbfounded.

"Don't be ridiculous. I haven't fallen so low that I'd leave you behind to die just 'cause the enemy we ran into's a little stronger than usual."

In order to survive, Hajime would use anything at his disposal, whether it was ambushes, tricks, traps, lies, bluffs, and all sorts of other cowardly tactics. Aside from the one fight he had with the Claw Bear, he honestly thought fighting head-on was just moronic. Hell wasn't so nice a place that you could survive with a code of honor. Nor did he feel guilty about his chosen fighting style. That was just how much he'd transformed over the course of his time here.

Still, he hadn't sunk so far that he'd abandon someone. Even now, after all this time, he still had some semblance of morality. No, rather, it was more accurate to say that he had regained some semblance of morality. And the one who had reminded him of that—of who he really was—was none other than Yue.

Hence why abandoning her was not an option. When she had given him that look, a look that told him she had placed her life in his hands, he had made his decision. At the critical turning point that decided whether or not he became as terrible as the monsters he consumed, he had chosen to remain human.

Yue saw in his expression the words he didn't say, and nodded in understanding, before suddenly hugging him.

"H-huh? What's up?" Hajime stuttered, confused. Considering the circumstances, her actions seemed oddly timed. The effects of the flash grenade would wear off any minute. Plus, Hajime's wounds had finished healing. He needed to return to the fray as soon as possible.

Yet in spite of all that, Yue wrapped a hand around his neck.

"Hajime...trust in me." As she said that, Yue kissed the nape of his neck.

"Wha—?!" No, not kissed. Bit.

Hajime felt a tiny pinprick of pain. Following that, it felt as if the energy was being sucked out of his body. He was about to shake her off, when he remembered Yue had said she was a vampire, and realized she must have been sucking his blood.

When she had said "trust in me," she meant she wanted him to put aside his initial fear and revulsion at having his blood sucked.

Smiling wryly, Hajime wrapped his arms around Yue and supported her tiny body as she drank his blood. She twitched in surprise, but after a moment she hugged him even tighter and buried her face into his neck. It might just have been his imagination, but it looked as if Yue was happy he did that.

"Kshaaaaaaaaaaaaa!" The scorpion-thing's roar echoed throughout the chamber. It appeared the time he'd bought with the flash grenade had run out. It must have found them already, as the ground shook once more and began to warp. This must have been its special magic. It could freely control the earth around it.

"Unfortunately for you, that's my specialty too." Hajime placed his right hand on the ground and began transmuting. The ground stopped warping in a three meter radius around him, and instead rose up to form walls that protected him and Yue.

Myriad spiked cones slammed into the walls, aiming for Hajime, but his barriers kept them at bay. Each wall was only able to withstand a single attack, but he transmuted a new one after each broke.

The scope, strength, and offensive power of the scorpion's earth manipulation were far above Hajime's, but his transmutation speed was far faster. The range of his transmutation ability had stopped growing at three meters, so he assumed it had reached its peak. Also, he still couldn't fling spikes or do anything purely offensive with the skill, but when it came to defense, there was none better.

Hajime focused his all on defense, keeping the monster's attacks at bay until Yue finally removed her fangs from his neck.

Her face was flushed as she licked the last few drops of blood off her lips. Despite how young she appeared, the gesture, combined with her flushed face, looked rather seductive. In the span of a few moments, her emaciated body had become healthy, and her porcelain-white skin glowed with new vitality. Her cheeks, once gaunt, were now a rosy pink. A warm, gentle light dwelled within her crimson eyes, and she caressed Hajime's cheek with a slender hand.

"...Thanks for the meal." Suddenly, Yue got to her feet and brandished a hand at the scorpion-thing. As she did so, a tremendous amount of mana, golden in color, poured out of her tiny body, chasing away the darkness.

Then, clad in a wondrous golden light, with her golden hair fluttering around her, she muttered a single phrase.

"Azure Blaze." A massive blue-white fireball, at least six or seven meters in diameter, appeared directly above the scorpion's head.

Though it didn't score a direct hit, the fireball must have still caused quite a bit of damage, as the beast backed away, screeching in pain.

However, the vampire princess of the abyss did not allow it to

escape. She stuck an elegant finger out, waving it around like a conductor's baton. The fireball then followed her finger faithfully, chasing after the fleeing scorpion...and slammed into it.

"Gagyaaaaaa?!" It screeched in pain, letting out a noise Hajime had not heard before. It was clearly suffering. As the fireball smashed into its target, the entire room was filled with a blinding white light, temporarily robbing everyone of their sight. Hajime covered his eyes with his arm, and gazed dumbfounded at the grand display of magic.

Eventually the magic wore off, and the pale blue fireball vanished. Once the flames disappeared, Hajime could see the scorpion writhing around in pain, its shell pulsing an angry red, and noted that parts of it had fused together from the heat.

Hajime wasn't sure what was more praiseworthy: Yue's magic, which had harmed the shell neither his 3000-degrees-Celsius incendiary grenade nor a point-blank railgun shot from Donner could even scratch; or the monster's shell, which had somehow managed to withstand the blast.

He heard a soft thump and tore his eyes away from the wondrous spectacle to look back at Yue. She was slumped on the ground, breathing heavily. It seemed she had used up all her mana.

"Yue, you all right?"

"Mm... Just very...tired..."

"Haha. But man, you really did it. Thanks for the save. I'll handle the rest, so you just relax."

"Mm, good luck..." Hajime waved at Yue, and then used Supersonic Step to close the distance between him and the scorpion in one bound. It was still in surprisingly good shape. Though it *was* howling in pain and rage at having its shell fused together, and when it saw Hajime approach it instantly fired its needle buckshot.

For his part, Hajime swiftly pulled another flash grenade from his pouch and flung it at the scorpion. He then blew away the buckshot with Donner before it had a chance to separate. After that, he fired a non-railgun-powered shot at the falling flash grenade.

Having gotten used to this move already, the scorpion wasn't fazed this time. It screeched in annoyance at its temporary blindness, but it still continued seeking out Hajime.

But no matter where it looked, it couldn't find him. As it glanced about in confusion, Hajime fell from the sky and landed on its back.

"Kshaa?!" It let out a surprised hiss. That was no surprise. After all, its prey had escaped its senses and suddenly showed up behind it.

Hajime had used Hide Presence and the flash from his grenade to escape the scorpion's senses.

The red hot scorpion's shell burned Hajime's skin. However, he ignored the pain, placed Donner directly above one of the damaged sections, and emptied the gun's entire chamber. Having already lost some of its hardness from Yue's earlier fireball, the scorpion's shell was unable to withstand a barrage of point-blank railgun-enhanced bullets, so it finally shattered.

Heedless of the damage it might cause itself, the scorpion thrust at Hajime with both its tails, but he was faster.

"Take this, you bastard." He pulled another grenade from his pouch, then thrust it deep into the hole he had made with Donner. He ignored his burning flesh as he dug his "present" in as deep as he could. Then, before the scorpion could attack him with its tails, he fled to safety using Supersonic Step. As he fled, it turned around to chase him down with a projectile attack.

However, the moment it finished turning—

Boom! A muffled explosion resounded throughout the room, which made the scorpion-thing twitch. The frozen scorpion and Hajime stared at each other as silence reigned.

Finally, the scorpion crumpled to the ground with a resounding crash.

Hajime finished reloading Donner, and slowly walked up to the unmoving scorpion. Just to make sure it was dead, he fired three bullets into its mouth before nodding in satisfaction. It had become his policy in recent times to make sure he thoroughly finished any foe off.

As he turned around, he found Yue sitting on the ground staring at him, expressionless as always. Despite her poker face, it seemed to him that she was happy. He had no idea when he'd finally escape the wretched labyrinth he was currently trapped in, but at least he'd found a reliable partner to travel with.

According to myth, Pandora's Box had contained all of the world's evil, but also a tiny bit of hope. Though he had jokingly referred to the room as Pandora's Box before, it had turned out to be a more accurate analogy than he had ever expected. Thinking happily to himself, Hajime slowly walked over to Yue.

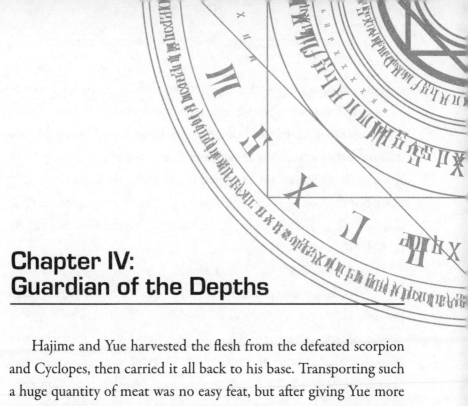

Chapter IV:
Guardian of the Depths

Hajime and Yue harvested the flesh from the defeated scorpion and Cyclopes, then carried it all back to his base. Transporting such a huge quantity of meat was no easy feat, but after giving Yue more of his blood to restore her energy, Hajime was able to enlist her help. With their combined strength, enhanced by her body-empowering magic, they were able to transport the vast quantities of meat to his hideout.

Originally, he had suggested using the room Yue had been sealed in as a new base, but she had rejected the proposal.

He supposed it was understandable. She was probably sick of staring at the walls of what had been her prison for centuries. Even if they were going to be stuck on this floor until Hajime replenished his stock of supplies, it was better for her mental health to have Yue out of that room. Thus, they were both spending the time talking and getting to know each other better while they scavenged for supplies.

"So that means you have to be at least 300 years old, right, Yue?"

"It's rude to ask a girl her age."

She glared angrily at Hajime. It seemed even in parallel worlds asking a girl about her age was taboo.

From what he recalled, the vampires had been destroyed in a massive war that had enveloped the land 300 years ago. Chances were Yue had lost track of time, trapped in the silent darkness as she had been, but it stood to reason that she must have been at least that old. If she'd been sealed at the age of twenty or so, then she was most likely far older than even 300.

"Do all vampires live as long as you?"

"...No, I'm an exception. I don't age because of my regenerative powers."

According to her, she had stopped aging ever since she had awoken to her powers at a young age. Average vampires could still extend their lifespan by drinking the blood of other races, but even then they couldn't live much longer than two hundred years or so.

As a frame of reference, humans in this world lived an average of 70 years, while demons' lifespan was a bit longer at 120. Beastmen had varying lifespans, depending on the specific race. Elves, for example, could live for centuries.

The reason for Yue's exceptional powers was that she had inherited the blood of the ancient atavistic vampires. Her lineage had made her one of the strongest creatures in the world at the time, and she had ascended to the throne at the tender age of seventeen.

I see. No wonder she was able to blast through that scorpion's shell so easily. Better yet, she was nigh immortal. Only gods or devils could aspire to that level of strength. And it seemed Yue had been classified as one of the latter.

Her uncle, blinded by his greed and ambition, had perpetrated the misconception among his fellow vampires that Yue was indeed a devil. He had then used that as justification to try and kill her, but had been stymied by her automatic regeneration. As a result, he had ended up sealing her here in this underground abyss instead. At the time, she had been too shocked by the sudden betrayal to resist capture. By the time she'd regained enough of her composure to understand what had just happened, she had already been sealed inside the rock cube.

Which was why she had no idea how that scorpion had come to dwell there, how she'd been sealed, or even how they'd managed to bring her down here into the depths of hell. Hajime had been a little disappointed when he'd heard that, as he'd hoped she might have known some way out.

She discussed the specifics of her powers with him at length as well. Supposedly, she had perfect affinity with every element. At one point Hajime recalled saying, "What the hell, you're totally overpowered..." to which Yue had replied by saying she wasn't very skilled at close quarters combat. The "best" she was capable of doing was using strengthening magic to increase her physical abilities to run around while firing off spells as fast as she could. Of course, her ability to ignore wounds thanks to her innate regeneration—and the overwhelming might of her spells—meant that was still enough to kill most everything.

An interesting thing to note was the fact that she still said spell names out loud, despite having no need for chants of any kind. It seemed it had just become a habit, since she had started learning that way. Even those with an affinity for magic usually had to say something related to the spell to keep a firm image of it in their minds, and it seemed even Yue was no exception.

Her automatic regeneration appeared to be a kind of special magic similar to what monsters had, and would naturally activate so long as she had mana remaining. Unless she was literally reduced to ashes in an instant, she could come back from any injury. But looking at it from another angle, that meant that once her mana dried up, her injuries would no longer heal. Had she taken any damage in that fight with the scorpion, she would undoubtedly have died.

"Anyway...onto the most important question. Yue, do you have any idea where we are? Or any idea how to get back to the surface?"

"Unfortunately, I don't. However..." It seemed Yue was unsure of their exact location, too. Though her tone was apologetic, the way she trailed off implied that she knew something at least. "According to legend, this labyrinth was built by one of the mavericks."

"The mavericks?'"

On top of being an unfamiliar word, it had a rather ominous ring to it. Hajime stopped his transmutation work and turned to face Yue.

She tore her gaze away from his work as well, and met his eyes before nodding sharply and continuing. "They were rebels that tried to bring about the end of the world."

With how reticent and expressionless Yue was, her explanations always took time. For his part, Hajime had a boatload of transmutation to get through, so he settled back to listen while he worked on replenishing his supply of ammunition. The previous battle had also shown him just how lacking in strength he was, and he had started work on a new weapon to rectify his insufficient firepower.

Supposedly, there had been seven descendants who had colluded together to plot the destruction of the world. However, the gods put a stop to their plans, and they were forced to flee to the ends of the earth. Their bastions of exile were what later came to be called the Seven Great Labyrinths. The Great Orcus Labyrinth being one of them, of course. The maverick who created it was rumored to reside in the deepest depths of this abyss everyone else called hell.

"...It's possible there might be a path to the surface there, in the deepest part of the labyrinth..."

"I see. I can't imagine there being some huge, thousand-story-long staircase at the bottom. But if this whole thing was made by someone from the Age of the Gods, then there's probably a teleportation circle or something." Hajime smiled at this new possibility. He returned his gaze to the work at hand. Yue followed suit. Her eyes were glued to Hajime's hands.

"...Is it really that interesting to watch me work?" She nodded silently. Hajime thought she looked extremely cute just then, sitting there hugging her knees with her fingers barely poking out of the sleeve of his baggy overcoat. He was overcome by a burning desire to hug her.

Man, I can't believe a cute little girl like her is really 300 years old. Parallel worlds really are something. They even have eternal lolis. Even transformed, Hajime never forgot any of his otaku knowledge. As if reading his thoughts, Yue suddenly looked up.

"You just thought something really rude, didn't you, Hajime?"

"What do you mean?" He played dumb, internally sweating at how perceptive her woman's intuition was. Silently, he returned to his work, clearly hoping to distract Yue's attention. He apparently succeeded, as she started bombarding him with questions about himself.

"...Hajime, what are you doing here?" That was the question he had most expected. This was, after all, the bottom of the abyss. The figurative pits of hell. A place no one but monsters called home.

But that was just the first of many questions to come: How are you able to control mana directly? How can you use the special magic of monsters? How are you able to eat monster meat and not die? What happened to your left arm? Are you even human, Hajime? What's that weapon you used earlier?

After the first one it was as if a dam had burst, and she pelted him with questions ceaselessly.

For his part, Hajime too, had been starved of conversation for far too long. He answered each question thoroughly, not at all annoyed by the storm of inquiries. It looked like Hajime had a bit of a soft spot for Yue. He probably also unconsciously realized somewhere that she was the only reason he hadn't truly fallen to the level of an unfeeling monster that cared only for his own survival.

Starting from the summoning, he retold the tale of how he wound up there. He told Yue about how they had been selected as heroes, and how he had been a worthless Synergist with no useful skills, from the labyrinth excursion and his fight with the Behemoth to his betrayal at the hands of one of his classmates and his descent into hell. How he lost his arm to the Claw Bear, his discovery of the potion (Yue later explained to him that it was Ambrosia), how he started eating monsters, how his knowledge from his original world gave him the idea for his weapon, how he won his rematch with the Claw Bear, and finally, how he made his descent through the dungeon until he reached her floor. He talked at length about everything he could remember. And, as his tale wound down, he could hear her sniffling.

"What's wrong?" Hajime asked, the concern evident in his voice. When he glanced back at Yue he saw tears spilling from her eyes. Surprised, he hurriedly wiped the tears from her face and repeated his question.

"What happened? What's wrong?"

"*Sniffle*... Hajime...you suffered so much...just like me..."

She was crying for his sake. Hajime was momentarily taken aback, before he smiled reassuringly and patted Yue on the head.

"Don't worry about it. All that stuff's in the past now. There's no point in getting hung up over it. I don't even really care about my old classmates that much anymore, and I'm not all that interested in getting revenge. All I care about now is polishing my skills, so I can make it out of here alive and find a way to return home."

Still sniffling, Yue closed her eyes and enjoyed the sensation of having her head patted, looking very much like a big cat. However, she suddenly jumped with a start when Hajime mentioned returning home.

"You're going to go back?"

"Hm? You mean to my own world? Of course I am. I miss it... A lot of things have changed now, but I still wanna go home..."

"I see."

She looked down dejectedly, then quietly whispered:

"...I don't have a home to go back to...anymore..."

"......"

Hajime took his hand off Yue's head and awkwardly scratched the back of his own.

He was by no means a dense person, which was why he had already vaguely realized she had started treating him as her new "home," so to speak. It was the same reason she had asked him to give her a name. She was worried she'd lose her home again if he returned to his original world.

Didn't you promise yourself you'd live only for the sake of your own wish? Just how soft can you get? Hajime mentally berated himself, but he still extended his hand to pat Yue's head once more.

"Well, how about coming with me, then?"

"Huh?" Her eyes went wide with surprise as she processed his words. She gazed deeply at him with her crimson eyes, wet with tears. Unsettled by the intensity in her gaze, he quickly began talking.

"I mean, well, back with me to my world. It's a boring place with nothing but humans, and someone with powers as amazing as yours might not find it to your liking, but... Well, at this point, I guess my abilities are just as crazy. Anyway, I have no idea if you'll even like it or not...and it's only if you want to come, but, well, what do you say?"

She blinked at him in confusion for a few seconds before timidly asking, "I can really come with you?" Though her voice was meek, her eyes were overflowing with hope.

Hajime smiled when he saw how vividly her eyes were shining, and nodded. As he did so, Yue smiled so brightly it almost felt as if her expressionless mask until now had just been an act. For a few moments, he was completely captivated by her radiant smile. After a while he realized he was staring like an idiot, and he quickly shook his head.

Unable to keep looking at her, Hajime returned to his work. Fascinated, Yue sidled up to watch. However, this time she stuck much closer to him as she observed him transmute. He had to keep reminding himself not to get flustered.

"...What's this?" She pointed to the mechanical parts Hajime was currently transmuting. There was a thin cylinder about one meter long, red bullets twenty centimeters in length, and a few other strange objects. They were all sections of a new weapon he was developing in order to make up for Donner's lack of power.

"This is, uhh...an anti-tank rifle, railgun-enhanced edition. I showed you my other gun, right? This is basically just a bigger version of it, with special bullets." Once the parts were all slotted together, it would turn into a rifle that was one and a half meters in length. He had pondered earlier how he could possibly increase his firepower, and had come to the conclusion there was no way to increase Donner's explosive force, or the acceleration of its bullets. That simply meant that if he wanted something stronger, he would need to make a new gun.

And said gun would of course need a wider and longer barrel, so it could fit larger caliber bullets and accelerate them for longer.

Hence why he decided to model this one after an anti-tank rifle. Its size made it cumbersome to carry around, and it could only hold one bullet at a time, but its power would be theoretically unmatched. Donner alone was already slightly more powerful than a standard anti-tank rifle, so it stood to reason that a railgun-enhanced rifle would fire with enough force to pulverize most anything. The recoil alone from such a gun would be enough to destroy any normal human's arms.

Theoretically, his new Schlagen would be five to six times as strong as Donner...or at least that was the hope.

He had used parts harvested from the scorpion to make it. After the battle had concluded, he had examined the scorpion's super-hard shell. To his surprise, his Ore Appraisal had been effective on it, and had shown him its properties.

◇ SHTAR ORE

A peculiar ore with a unique affinity to mana. The more mana it absorbs, the harder it gets.

It appeared the scorpion's toughness had come from building its shell from shtar ore. Since the scorpion had probably been able to pour a huge amount of mana into it, it made for a perfect defense.

If it's classified as ore, I should be able to duplicate it myself, right? He had tested that theory and had found he could replicate the ore quite easily. After which, a truly depressing thought had run through his mind. *Wait a minute, if this is ore, I could have just transmuted that stupid scorpion's shell off to save us a ton of trouble.*

In the end, they had still succeeded, and he had gotten his hands on some interesting new materials, so he supposed it was all right. Once he had analyzed the ore's properties, he had instantly gotten to work making Schlagen's barrel. His skills had progressed considerably since the time he had built Donner, and his work went far more smoothly than before.

He was very precise with how he made his bullets too. He used taur for the shell's core, and applied an outer coating of shtar over it to harden it. It was his fantasy version of a full metal jacket bullet. He also made sure his ratio of compressed blastrock for the new bullets was perfect. Thanks to his Duplicate Transmutation derivative skill, he was easily able to mass produce the bullets once he had finished a satisfactory prototype to work off of. He talked Yue through the entire process as he worked, and the time flew by quickly as he finished

Schlagen.

It looked quite intimidating once it was all put together. He gazed at it proudly, satisfied with the quality of his work. Having finally finished, he realized he was quite hungry and grilled some of his Cyclops and scorpion meat.

"Yue, you want some—er, wait, you probably shouldn't eat this, should you? I really don't want to let you experience that kind of pain... Actually, since you're a vampire, can you eat monster meat just fine?" Eating monster meat had become a natural routine for Hajime by that point and he almost invited Yue to eat with him out of habit before correcting himself. He glanced over to her and saw she was fiddling with his new weapon. When she noticed his gaze she put it down for a moment and shook her head, saying, "I don't need any food."

"I guess that makes sense. You survived 300 years without it after all... Still, do you not get hungry at all?"

"I do...but I'm full for now."

"You are? You already ate something?" He tilted his head in confusion at Yue's declaration. She pointed at Hajime.

"...Mhmm. Your blood, Hajime."

"Aah, I see. So does that mean as long as they've got blood, vampires don't need to eat?"

"We can absorb nutrients through food as well, but blood is more efficient."

He supposed it only stood to reason that a vampire would be fine with just blood. *So Yue's full from the blood she sucked out of me.* As he nodded to himself in understanding, Yue licked her lips suggestively.

"...Why are you licking your lips like that?"

"Hajime...you taste good..."

"Th-that's not true. I've eaten so many monsters by now that I probably taste disgusting."

"Your blood tastes very rich..."

"......"

According to Yue, Hajime's blood tasted like a very savory soup. *Come to think of it, she looked pretty happy when she was sucking my blood last time too.* He imagined it must have been akin to eating a first class meal after starving for weeks.

But when she licked her lips like that, she looked eerily seductive, so Hajime wished she would cut it out. It was times like those that he remembered she was far older than him. But her outward appearance was still that of a young girl, which made Hajime feel guilty for thinking dirty thoughts.

"...Delicious blood."

"Please, just give me a break." His new partner was quite dangerous, in more ways than one.

※ ※ ※ ※ ※ ※ ※ ※ ※ ※ ※ ※ ※

The same day that Hajime and Yue had met, and fought off the scorpion, Kouki and the others had returned to the entrance of the Great Orcus Labyrinth. This time, though, it wasn't the whole class, but just Kouki's party of four, Hiyama and his band of thugs, and a judo club member called Jugo Nagayama along with his five burly party members.

Their reason for returning was quite simple. Even if they avoided talking about it, Hajime's death had still been weighing down on most of the students. They had realized they might really die fighting here in this world, and that fact had greatly shaken their confidence in their abilities. Hajime's death had traumatized them.

Naturally, the Holy Church was not happy with the turn of events. They urged the students to go back and gain more practical fighting experience, thinking time and familiarity would heal their wounds.

However, Aiko had vehemently opposed that plan.

She hadn't been present for the fateful excursion where Hajime fell. Because of the rare and valuable job she possessed, the Holy Church wanted her to focus on cultivating the land over building up combat experience. So long as they had her agricultural powers, they could easily solve their food problems.

When she had learned of Hajime's death, Aiko had fainted from shock. She had felt responsible for the students, and couldn't forgive herself for hiding back at the castle where it was safe while one of her students had fought and died. She blamed herself for not being able to bring everyone back to Japan safely. Hence why she firmly refused to allow her students to be exposed to any further danger.

Her job was special enough that she was capable of single-handedly revolutionizing the agricultural standards of this world. So when she protested any further practical training exercises, the Holy Church had no choice but to acquiesce. They couldn't afford to antagonize Aiko.

As a result, only Kouki's party, Hiyama's party, and Jugo's party, who had willingly volunteered to return to the battlefield, were at the labyrinth. In order to grow stronger, they had chosen to once more challenge the Great Orcus Labyrinth. Captain Meld and a contingent of knights were escorting the students this time as well.

Today marked the sixth day of their expedition.

They had made it all the way to the sixtieth floor. After only five more floors, they would arrive at the deepest point humans had ever explored.

However, Kouki and the others were currently stuck. It wasn't that there was no way forward, but rather that the sight before them brought back old fears that kept them frozen in place.

A huge cliff spread out in front of them. Though it wasn't the same one Hajime had fallen from, it was similar enough to bring back unpleasant memories. In order to advance to the next floor, they would have to cross the suspension bridge that spanned the length of the room. Normally that would have been no problem, but past memories bound the students in place. Kaori especially just stood there, gazing intently down into the abyss.

"Kaori..." Shizuku worriedly called out to her friend. Kaori slowly shook her head and turned to smile at Shizuku.

"I'm fine, Shizuku-chan."

"Okay...but don't push yourself, yeah? You don't have to pretend to be strong in front of me."

"Ehehe, thanks, Shizuku-chan."

Shizuku returned Kaori's smile. A powerful light still dwelled deep within Kaori's eyes. She was no longer in the grips of despair. Shizuku, who was gifted with above-average powers of observation and a knack for understanding the feelings of others, realized Kaori was telling the truth when she said she was fine.

Kaori really is strong. It was all but certain that Hajime was dead. His chances of survival were honestly less than hopeless. Despite that, Kaori chose neither to run from that fact nor to deny it. She simply kept going forward, determined to see the truth for herself. Shizuku admired her strength.

But as always, the class's thickheaded hero was unable to realize that. To Kouki, it seemed as if Kaori was doing nothing more than grieving at the death of her classmate. *She truly must be kind, if she's still sad over his death.* Thus, when she smiled to Shizuku, he concluded she must be forcing herself to look cheerful.

He didn't even consider the possibility that Kaori had feelings for Hajime, or that she still thought he could be alive, and walked up to offer some unnecessary words of consolation.

"Kaori...I really admire how kind you are. But you can't let yourself be depressed over your classmate's death forever! We have to move forward. I'm sure that's what Nagumo would want, too."

"Hey, Kouki..."

"Please let me finish, Shizuku! I know she may not want to hear this, but as her childhood friend, I have to open her eyes! Kaori, it'll be all right. I'm still here with you. I won't ever die. And I won't let anyone else die either. I promise I won't let anything make you sad ever again."

"Haaah, this guy never changes... Kaori, I—"

"Ahaha, don't worry about it, Shizuku-chan. Umm... I get what you're trying to say, Kouki-kun, so you don't need to worry either."

"You do? I'm so glad I got through to you!"

Kaori smiled awkwardly, feeling a little guilty for fueling Kouki's misunderstanding. But even if she tried to explain herself to him, she doubted he'd understand.

Hajime was already long dead in Kouki's mind. So it would have been impossible for him to fathom that the reason Kaori threw herself into training so fervently, and was so eager to return to the labyrinth, was because she wanted to look for him. Because he never once doubted that his own beliefs were the absolute truth, he would simply think Kaori was unable to face reality, or that Hajime's death had somehow mentally damaged her, were she to tell him her real feelings.

She'd known Kouki for long enough that she understood how he thought, and therefore decided it was far simpler to just go along with his interpretations.

That having been said, he had no ulterior motives in trying to cheer Kaori up either. He was seriously concerned for her well-being. Shizuku and Kaori were both used to his behavior, so they usually just ignored him, but had that line been directed at any other girl, she would have fallen for him in an instant.

Kouki was smart, kind, handsome, and athletic: the kind of perfect guy that no girl normally thought to resist. However, there was a reason his two childhood friends had no romantic interest in him whatsoever. Shizuku had spent her childhood training in her father's dojo under his strict tutelage, along with many other adults. Her upbringing, combined with her naturally observant disposition, had led her to quickly realize Kouki's fatal flaw: his misguided sense of justice. A sense of justice that had brought nothing but trouble for Shizuku. Of course, she still cared for him as a friend.

For her part, Kaori was naturally dense when it came to matters of love, and she'd heard enough complaining from Shizuku to be more or less aware of Kouki's true nature. She did think he was a nice person, but his clichéd lines failed to set her heart aflutter, and she had no romantic interest in him.

"Kaori-chan, I'm here for you! If there's anything I can do to help, just ask."

"Yeah, we're your friends, Kaorin!"

The two girls, Eri Nakamura and Suzu Taniguchi, walked over to Kaori to try and cheer her up.

Kaori had only met the two of them in high school, but they had hit it off immediately, and were now counted among her best friends. In addition, they were powerful fighters that were strong enough to fight in Kouki's party.

Eri was a beautiful girl who kept her black hair cut in a tiny bob, and wore glasses. She was a quiet and gentle girl who usually observed things from a distance. She loved books, and resembled the stereotypical bookworm. She had, in fact, also been the class librarian.

Suzu, on the other hand, was a tiny girl, barely 142 centimeters tall. Despite her short stature, she had a boundless supply of energy, and always looked like she was having fun. She kept her hair in braids, and was constantly jumping around. Her hyperactive personality had made her into the class mascot.

The two of them had seen how distressed Kaori had been when Hajime had fallen off the cliff, and they both understood and approved of Kaori's decision to see things through for herself.

"Yeah. Thanks, Eri-chan, Suzu-chan." She smiled reassuringly at her two friends.

"Ohhh, you're so brave, Kaorin! Nagumo-kun, you better not make Kaorin any sadder than this. If you're not alive, I'll kill you myself!"

"U-umm, Suzu? You can't kill him again if he's already dead, right?"

"Who cares! Fine, if he's dead, we'll just use your necromancy to revive him, Eririn!"

"S-Suzu, don't say that! Kaori still thinks Nagumo-kun's alive, remember? Besides, my necromancy isn't..." Eri scolded Suzu for her tactless behavior. That interaction was indicative of how the two usually were.

Kaori and Shizuku smiled happily as they watched their two noisy friends. Kouki and the others had gone on ahead, so they didn't hear the conversation between the four girls. Along with his overbearing sense of justice, he was also blessed with the ability to conveniently go deaf whenever someone said something that didn't fit with his worldview.

"It's okay, Eri-chan, I don't mind."

"But Suzu, you should still tone it down a little. You're bothering Eri."

Suzu puffed up her cheeks and pouted at Shizuku's words. Though relieved to hear that Kaori wasn't hurt by Suzu's words, Eri was nevertheless still pale.

"Eririn, are you still uncomfortable with using necromancy? It's such a cool job, too..."

"...Yeah, sorry. I know I'd be more useful if I could use it properly."

"Eri, everyone has their own strengths and weaknesses. You also have a really high magic affinity, so don't worry too much about it, okay?"

"That's right, Eri-chan. The fact that it's your job just means you have an aptitude for it. It doesn't actually mean you have to force yourself to use it if you don't want to. You're already more than helpful enough with just your magic."

"I know, but I still think I should try and master it. I'll be even more helpful that way." She curled her small hand into a fist and solidified her resolve.

Suzu hopped around Eri going "That's the spirit, Eririn!" while Shizuku and Kaori watched on.

Eri's job was Necromancer. It used dark magic to alter the minds and spirits of others, and was primarily a magic debuffer class. The most advanced of its skills involved using dark magic to recall the lingering attachments of the deceased. The Holy Church employed a number of necromancers as mediums, and they used their powers to converse with the dead and relay their final moments to their families and friends. It was regarded as quite the sacred job.

However, necromancy's true strength didn't stop there. The proper way to use a necromancer's magic was to wrap those people's lingering thoughts in magic, then use them to possess their corpses. The corpses revived through this method were capable of using the skills they possessed when they were alive, to an extent. Furthermore, necromancers could possess the bodies of the living, and copy their skills to some extent.

However, the revived corpses were not truly brought back to life. Though they could respond to basic commands, they retained little of their original personalities, and their skin remained pale and lifeless. They were more zombies than anything. Furthermore, Eri's conscience prevented her from doing something as immoral as resurrecting the dead, so she had trained her necromancy abilities very little.

While the girls discussed Eri's powers, a certain figure watched them, or rather Kaori, from the shadows.

Daisuke Hiyama. A few days after their return to the capital, Hiyama began to be shunned by the other students. Once they had calmed down a little, they began to resent him for leading them all into that trap, just as he had expected.

He had planned for this, and once the insults started flying he instantly got down on his knees and begged for forgiveness. He knew trying to argue back would only make things worse. To make sure it had the maximum amount of impact, he had chosen a particular time and place to give his apology.

Specifically, he made sure to do it publicly, in front of Kouki. He knew that Kouki was likely to forgive him if he apologized sincerely, and would then smooth things out with the rest of his classmates.

His plan succeeded perfectly, and people quickly stopped directing their scorn at him. Kaori was fundamentally kind by nature, and even she forgave him when he got down on his knees and begged with tears in his eyes. Everything so far had gone according to plan. However, Shizuku was still vaguely suspicious of Hiyama, and disliked him for manipulating her friends.

Meanwhile, Hiyama began surreptitiously carrying out the orders he'd received from the figure that day. They were quite frightening orders. Orders he would normally have never accepted. But now that he'd crossed a line, there was no looking back. As much as he hated it, he had agreed to carry out his master's orders.

He was terrified of this classmate of his, who was capable of plotting something so dreadful and could still mingle in with the rest of their classmates somehow. Still, mixed in with the terror was a small seed of joy at the sheer brilliance and audacity of the plan.

That monster is totally insane. But if I do what they say, Kaori'll be mine... If he followed orders, Kaori would eventually be his. He felt a surge of fierce joy, and his lips curled up into a wicked grin.

"Hey, Daisuke, what's wrong?" Kondou, Nakano, and Saitou all looked at Hiyama with puzzled expressions on their faces. Those three stooges were still hanging around Hiyama. As the saying went, birds of a feather flock together. Their relationship had become slightly strained when Hiyama had come under attack, but his contrite apology had restored their friendship. Whether it could still be called friendship if they only got along when it was convenient was debatable, but that was just how it was.

"O-oh, it's nothing. I'm just happy we made it all the way to the sixtieth floor."

"Oh, yeah, I get what you mean. Five more floors and we'll be the greatest dungeon delvers in history!"

"We've gotten pretty strong, haven't we? Man, those guys who stayed behind have no balls."

"Now now, don't say that. We're just that much stronger, that's all." The three others had accepted Hiyama's explanation without question.

Believing themselves special just because they won a few fights was the trademark trait of all small-time bullies. And like the bullies they were, they had actually been throwing their weight around among the students who had chosen to remain. Their arrogance had started bothering the others. However, they were still strong enough to make it as far as the sixtieth floor, so no one was brave enough to complain to their face.

Besides, even they couldn't match up to Kouki's party, so they at least remained docile in his presence. Just like the small-time thugs they were.

The party managed to advance without any real difficulty, and before long they stepped foot on the historic sixty-fifth floor.

"Stay sharp, everyone! This floor still hasn't been fully mapped.

There's no telling what might happen!" Captain Meld's loud voice echoed throughout the room. Kouki and the others had grim expressions on their faces as they stepped into the unknown.

After a few minutes of walking they found themselves in a massive chamber. Everyone present suddenly felt a chill run down their spine.

An ominous premonition settled over them, a premonition that proved all too soon to be accurate. A magic circle suddenly began glowing in the center of the room. A very familiar, pulsing, dark red magic circle.

"Y-You've gotta be kidding me... It's that thing again?!" Cold sweat poured down Kouki's forehead. Everyone else was clearly nervous as well.

"Seriously?! I thought that bastard died when he fell!" Ryutarou screamed, the shock evident in his voice. Captain Meld replied to the group in a stern but calm voice.

"We're still not sure what causes monsters to spawn in the labyrinths, but it's possible to have to fight a monster you defeated once before. Everyone, stay sharp! Make sure there's always at least one open path of retreat!" His foremost priority was securing an escape route. The knights under his command all hurried to obey. However, Kouki seemed unhappy with his orders.

"Meld, we're not the same weak kids from before. We've gotten way stronger! I promise we won't lose this fight, so let us take him!"

"Heh, you said it. I can't stand being beaten and having to run away all the time anyway. It's time for our revenge match!" Ryutarou said, a feral grin adorning his face all the while. Captain Meld shrugged with exasperation at their eagerness, but he had to admit that they might have a chance with their current strength. He too, smiled grimly.

The magic circle exploded in a burst of red light and summoned forth the nightmare that haunted all of their dreams.

"Graaaaaaaaaah!!!" The Behemoth roared angrily as it stamped the ground. Those familiar red eyes, dripping with murderous intent, glared squarely at Kouki.

Among the cowering students, one girl glared right back at it with unwavering determination.

Kaori. In a voice so quiet that no one else heard it, Kaori said the following to the Behemoth:

"I won't let you take anyone else from me. I'll trample over you and make my way back to his side." With her determination thus expressed, the battle to overcome their past began.

Kouki made the first move.

"Soar unto heaven, O divine wings—Celestial Flash!" With a thunderous roar, a shockwave of light slammed into the Behemoth.

In their previous fight, even his strongest skill, Divine Wrath, had been unable to scratch the Behemoth. But as Kouki had said, they were no longer the weak kids they had been.

"Graaaaaaah?!" The Behemoth backed away shakily, screaming in pain. There was a long red gash running down its chest, spilling blood.

"We can do this! We've gotten way stronger! Nagayama, you circle around to its left. Hiyama, take it from behind. Meld, encircle it from the right! Rearguard, give us some spells! The strongest you've got!" Kouki swiftly began barking out orders. His quick assessment and judgment were a result of Captain Meld's personal training.

"Heh, you've gotten pretty good at giving orders, kid. You heard the man! Everyone, follow his lead!" Captain Meld confirmed Kouki's orders, then led his troupe of knights around to the Behemoth's right side. Everyone sprang into action at once, surrounding the Behemoth.

The vanguard set up a defensive perimeter, preventing the Behemoth from wreaking havoc on the back lines.

"Graaaaaaaaaaaaaaah!" It decimated the ground as it charged forward, trying to break through.

"Like hell you will!"

"You're not going anywhere!" The class's two burliest guys, Ryutarou Sakagami and Jugo Nagayama, grappled the Behemoth from each side, holding it in place.

"Grant unto your servant the strength to shake the earth! Herculean Might!" Clad in their body strengthening magic, the two boys halted the Behemoth's charge.

"Graaaaaah!"

"Raaaaaaah!"

"Uooooooooooooh!" The three of them each let out a different roar as they squeezed out every ounce of their strength. The Behemoth, enraged that a pair of mere humans had stopped its assault, stamped impatiently on the ground. Seeing this, the other students took advantage of its momentary distraction.

"Peerless swordsmanship that rends even the heavens—Eternal Severance!" Shizuku drew her sword, slicing through one of the Behemoth's horns. Her lapis lazuli-colored mana wrapped around her sword, an artifact with a magically sharpened cutting edge, and increased the speed of her draw. However, her sword failed to cut all the way through the horn, instead getting lodged halfway into it.

"Guh! Why's it gotta be so hard!"

"Leave it to me! Pulverize, shatter, decimate—Bonecrusher!" Captain Meld leaped forward, slamming his sword into Shizuku's own. The speed of Shizuku's slash was enhanced by the sheer strength the captain had put behind his own blow, forcing the sword deeper into the Behemoth's horn. Finally, her sword cut all the way through, and sliced the horn straight off its head.

"Graaaaaaah?!" Infuriated beyond reason, the Behemoth flailed wildly, flinging Shizuku, Meld, Ryutarou, and Nagayama to the corners of the room.

"Enfold the weak with your gentle light—Hallowed Nimbus!" Before they hit the walls, countless rings of light intersected to form a net behind them, cushioning their fall. Kaori had used a rather peculiar defensive spell to soften the impact of their landing.

Her artifact, a white staff, glowed light purple as she fed it her mana. Without pause, she began chanting another spell.

"Heaven's blessing, shine thy grace on all thine children—Succor!" In an instant, all four fighters that had been flung away were healed. Long distance, wide-area healing was on the upper end of the intermediate level of light spells. This particular one was an advanced version of the Heaven's Blessing spell she had used once before.

Kouki shifted stances in preparation to thrust, then charged the beast. He chanted a spell as he ran forward, aiming for the wound he had created earlier.

"Dazzling Eruption!" Vast quantities of mana gathered at the tip of his sacred sword as he thrust deep into the Behemoth, which then exploded from within.

"Graaaaaaaah!" The Behemoth howled in pain as spurts of blood poured out of the new wound gouged into it, but it still managed to land a counterattack while Kouki was recovering from the effects of using a skill.

"Guuuuuh!" Kouki screamed in pain as the Behemoth's clawed paw flung him into the wall. The claws themselves failed to pierce his sacred armor artifact, but the force of the impact still left him gasping for breath. Still, at least the pain vanished almost instantly. Kaori had started chanting another healing spell before Kouki had even hit the ground.

"Heaven's blessing, grant thy progeny the strength to fight once more—Divine Ray!" Unlike the mass heal from earlier, the new spell was only capable of healing one target at a time, but in return it was far more potent. Kouki was momentarily wrapped in golden light as he was fully healed.

Meanwhile, the Behemoth roared mightily and leaped into the air, tired of the other flies buzzing around it. The shockwave sent everyone tumbling back while its broken horn began glowing red.

"...So it can do that even with a broken horn. Brace yourselves, everyone!" Shizuku yelled out a warning as the Behemoth began hurtling down.

Everyone present was familiar with its special magic, and they had already prepared for impact. However, the trajectory of its leap surprised everyone. Rather than aiming for Kouki and the others, it was headed straight for the back line. During the fight on the bridge it had always leaped only toward what was directly in front of it, and the members of the vanguard all panicked when they saw it pass over them.

One of the members of the back line, Suzu Taniguchi, stepped forward and switched over to chanting a new spell.

"Let this be a holy ground that denies thine enemies passage— Hallowed Ground!" A glowing dome of light surrounded them not a moment too soon, and the Behemoth crashed into it. The shockwaves from the impact was so powerful that the rocks on the floor nearby were swept away like cobwebs.

Suzu's barrier successfully ground those shockwaves to a halt as well. But because she forcibly shortened the four-verse spell into only two verses, the shield was imperfect. Cracks had already begun appearing within it. Had her job not been Barrier Master, her improvised barrier wouldn't have done much of anything.

She grit her teeth, and held both hands out before her. Frantically, she supplemented the verses with a mental image of an impenetrable barrier. *A good shield never cracks. My protection is absolute!*

"Uooooooh! Like hell I'll lose to this stupid thing!" The Behemoth's murderous gaze fell directly on Suzu, making her arms tremble in fear. The artifact that she used, a pair of bracelets, went dark for a second before glowing bright orange with her mana once more. She banished the fear from her mind and shouted again.

But unfortunately, her willpower wasn't enough to keep the barrier alive. The Behemoth was attacking relentlessly, and in a few more seconds it would crumble.

No! It's going to break! Suzu lamented.

"Heaven's blessings, grant me thy wonder—Transference!" Suddenly, her body was wrapped in light, and she felt her mana increase exponentially. Kaori must have healed her.

Normally, the spell would only restore a little of the recipient's mana, but by adjusting how much of their own mana the caster used, it was possible to restore all of it. Transference was a very practical spell. And only someone like Kaori, who possessed the priest job, could use it.

"I can make it now! I love you, Kaorin!" Suzu poured her newly replenished mana into the barrier, cementing its strength. With a sharp snapping noise, the cracks in the barriers began mending. Angry at being cut off from its prey, the Behemoth glared at Suzu. She glared right back.

Finally, the red glow started dissipating from its horn. It slumped to the ground now that the force of its charge was completely spent. Suzu's barrier vanished at the same time.

The Behemoth decided to kill that heavily panting girl next, but before it could do anything, the vanguard arrived and began surrounding it again.

"Back line members, retreat!" At Kouki's signal, the rearguard all took a few steps back and the vanguard filled in the space between them. They continued their hit-and-run tactics until finally the back line had finished chanting their strongest spells.

"Everyone, fall back!" Eri, the leader of the rearguard, gave the signal. The vanguard all simultaneously unleashed their strongest attacks and leaped away.

Momentarily winded, the Behemoth was unable to avoid the barrage of fire spells that came flying at it right after.

"Royal Flare!" Five people chanted in unison. A miniature blazing sun bore down on the Behemoth, scorching everything in its path. It grew to eight meters in diameter before colliding with its target.

Blistering heat scorched every inch of the Behemoth. The spell was so powerful that it threatened to engulf even the students, and Suzu hurriedly erected a barrier. Unable to escape, the Behemoth's helmet melted from the heat of the blast.

"Graaaaaaaaaaaaah!" Its dying screams echoed throughout the

chamber. They were the same screams the students had heard when the last one fell off the bridge. The ear-piercing cries slowly faded to a pained gurgle, until finally the Behemoth was nothing but a smoldering pile of ash. Only the blackened walls and charred ashes served to show there had even been a monster there before.

"D-did we get it?"

"We won..."

"We really won..."

"Seriously?"

"Is this real?" Everyone stared dumbfounded at the remains of the Behemoth, tentatively muttering words of disbelief. Kouki was the first to regain his senses. He held his sword aloft, and proclaimed,

"That's right! We won!" His holy sword glittered in the dim dungeon light, declaiming their victory for all to see. The reality of what they'd just achieved finally hit them, and the students all broke out into cheers simultaneously. The guys all slapped each other on the back, while the girls hugged each other with joy. Even Captain Meld was moved by the victory.

Kaori, however, was simply staring blankly at the pile of ash that had once been a monster. Shizuku noticed she wasn't joining in on the celebration, so she walked up to her.

"Kaori, is something wrong?"

"Huh? Oh, it's just you, Shizuku-chan. No, nothing's wrong. I was just thinking...we've made it so far." Kaori smiled wryly as she answered Shizuku. She was even more moved than most that she'd gotten strong enough to defeat the monster that had once haunted her nightmares.

"Yeah. We've gotten a lot stronger since then."

"Mhmm... Shizuku-chan, do you think we'll find Nagumo-kun if we keep going?"

"That's what we're here to find out, isn't it? That's what all of this was for."

"Ehehe, yeah." They could finally move forward. There was finally a very real chance Kaori could find out exactly what happened to Hajime. She suddenly stiffened up in fear, scared the answer might not be the one she wanted. Shizuku noticed the change, and chose to tightly squeeze Kaori's hand in response. Reassured that Shizuku was with her, Kaori banished the fear from her heart.

They stood there silently for a few minutes until Kouki walked up to them.

"Are you two all right? Kaori, that was some amazing healing. As long as you're here, I'm not scared of anything." He flashed the two girls a dazzling smile as he praised Kaori and Shizuku.

"As you can see, I'm perfectly fine. And you... Well, you're obviously all right," Shizuku muttered in a tone full of mirth.

"Yeah, I'm fine, Kouki-kun. I'm glad I was helpful."

They returned his smile. But their smiles slipped slightly at Kouki's next words.

"With this, I'm sure Nagumo can rest easy too. The classmates he protected were able to take down the monster that killed him."

"......"

He was already lost in thought, and didn't notice the two girls' expressions darken. Apparently, Kouki really thought it was the Behemoth that had sent Hajime to the depths of hell. In a sense, that was true. After all, it was the Behemoth's magic that destroyed the bridge. But more precisely, it was the person who had thrown that errant fireball that had killed Hajime.

Even if everyone agreed not to talk about it, it didn't change the fact that it was true. But it seemed Kouki had forgotten that fact, or perhaps simply never been aware of it in the first place, since he seemingly thought killing the Behemoth would be all it took to let Hajime rest in peace.

Kouki, who believed everyone was a fundamentally good person, probably didn't want to keep blaming someone for a mistake. And of course, he couldn't even imagine the possibility that someone might have done it on purpose.

But Kaori couldn't put that thought out of her mind even if she wanted to. She could only hold it in because she didn't know who it was, but she knew for sure if she found out she'd chase that person to the ends of the earth. Which was why it amazed her that Kouki could just forget about it so easily.

Shizuku let out a long sigh. She really wanted to reprimand Kouki, but she knew he didn't mean anything ill by what he said. In fact, he had been thinking only of Kaori and Hajime when he had said that. Sadly, it was his good intentions that made the barb sting even more.

Besides, the other students were still basking in the glow of victory. Shizuku wasn't so tactless that she'd try and start a scene.

After that, the class's most energetic girl jumped into the conversation, dispelling the strained atmosphere.

"Kaorin!" Suzu jumped into Kaori's arms, calling her by her strange nickname.

"Fwah?!"

"Ehehe, I love you sooo much, Kaorin! If you hadn't saved me back there, I would be flat as a pancake right now!"

"Y-you're exaggerating, Suzu-chan... Wait, stop touching me there!"

"Gehehe, do you like it? How about this—you like this?"

Kaori blushed as Suzu started feeling her up like some old pervert.

Shizuku stopped her rampage with a quick chop to the head, though her blow had a little more force behind it than what was strictly necessary. "Cut it out. Kaori doesn't belong to you... She belongs to me."

"Shizuku-chan?!"

"Hmph, I won't let you get in my way. The only one who gets to xxx Kaori's xxx is me, Suzu!"

"Suzu-chan?! What are you trying to do to me?!"

Trapped between Suzu and Shizuku, Kaori could only wail helplessly. The strained atmosphere from earlier was nowhere to be found.

From there on out, they would be heading into uncharted territory. After defeating the specter of their past, Kouki and the others advanced deeper into the labyrinth. Meanwhile...

❖ ❖ ❖ ❖ ❖ ❖ ❖ ❖ ❖ ❖ ❖ ❖ ❖

"Daaaaah! Dammit!"

"You can do it, Hajime..."

"Aren't you a bit too relaxed?!" Hajime was running through a clump of grass, with Yue on his back. Thick, tall grass, coming all the way up to Hajime's shoulders, stretched out in every direction as far as the eye could see. Yue would be completely buried within the 160-centimeter-tall grass.

The reason Hajime was currently whacking weeds out of the way as he ran for his life was—

"Shaaaaaaaaa!!!"

—Because he was being chased by two hundred monsters.

Once they finished their preparations, Hajime and Yue had set out for the bottom of the labyrinth. They'd cleared ten or so floors with ease already. His new equipment and improved skills had been part of the reason, but another important factor was Yue's devastating magic.

She could cast any elemental spell nearly instantly, and supported Hajime from the rear. Though she was unparalleled when it came to offensive magic, it appeared Yue wasn't very skilled with barriers or healing. Perhaps it was because she unconsciously regarded them as unnecessary, since she was able to automatically heal any wounds. Furthermore, Hajime had his Ambrosia with him, so he had no need for healing spells either.

That was why their travels had progressed smoothly until now. When they had first descended onto the floor they were currently on, they had been greeted by a massive sea of trees. Each tree was over ten meters tall, and they were packed together tighter than sardines. The entire floor was extremely humid as a result. However, unlike the jungle floor he had traversed earlier, it wasn't sweltering hot.

As they had been searching for the next staircase, they suddenly felt a huge earthquake. Seconds later, they had found themselves face to face with a huge reptilian monster. It looked just like a Tyrannosaurus rex.

The only difference was, for some reason, it had a beautiful flower adorning the top of its head. Its sharp fangs and overflowing bloodlust clearly marked a dangerous foe, but the sunflower resting atop its head made it seem more comical than deadly. This was quite possibly the most surreal monster Hajime had faced thus far.

The Tyrannosaurus roared angrily and charged the two of them. Unfazed by its onslaught, Hajime calmly moved to draw Donner... only to be stopped by Yue, who raised her hand.

"Crimson Javelin." A spear of whirling flames formed out of thin air, then shot straight through the mouth of the T. rex. The heat melted the T. rex's entire head, leaving him dead in seconds. The ground shook as the beast crumpled.

The flower perched on the remains of its head came off with a plop.

"......" Hajime stared on, speechless.

She'd been asserting her strength more and more aggressively recently. Originally she had just supported Hajime from behind, but as time passed she eventually just started preemptively one-shotting anything that intended to do him harm.

He had fewer and fewer opportunities to show off his skills, and was starting to feel rather useless. *Is she just one-shotting them because I'm nothing but a burden to her in combat?* he began to think worriedly. If she really told him that he'd probably be depressed for weeks. And so, he holstered Donner and awkwardly asked Yue the question on his mind.

"Umm, Yue? I'm glad you're pumped to fight, but...I feel like I haven't been pulling my weight recently."

Yue turned back to Hajime, and despite her poker face, he could tell she was rather proud of herself. "...I want to be useful. Because I'm your partner." It seemed she just wasn't satisfied with only covering

Hajime from behind.

He certainly did recall saying a while back that they would need to rely on each other in fights as partners who shared the same fate. It had been just after one of their fights. Yue had overextended herself and collapsed after running out of mana. Hajime had to rescue her, and she was beating herself up over it pretty bad, so he had told her that to comfort her...but it seemed she'd taken those words to heart. She wanted to show Hajime she was a partner worth relying on.

"Haha, trust me, you're more than useful. But even though your magic is ridiculously strong, you're not good at close combat, which is why I asked you to guard my back. Being the front-liner's my job."

"Hajime... Fine." Yue looked a bit glum as she listened to Hajime lecture her.

Hajime just didn't want her to be hung up on the idea that she had to somehow be useful to him. He smiled reassuringly and gently stroked her soft hair. That was all it took for Yue's mood to improve, and Hajime lost the heart to keep lecturing her when he saw her contented expression.

He didn't want her to end up dependent on him, so he tried to warn her from time to time, but in the end he was just too soft on her. He was actually disgusted at himself for how weak-willed he'd become in that regard.

As the two of them were having their faux lovers' spat, Hajime didn't neglect to continually use Sense Presence, and he suddenly realized there were enemies approaching them.

About ten of them were circling around to surround them. *If they're coordinating their movements, does that mean they hunt in packs like the Twin-Tailed Wolves?* Hajime thought warily to himself as he motioned to Yue and began retreating. If they were outnumbered, it would be in his best interests to at least move to more advantageous ground.

As the enemy began to close their encirclement, Hajime chose a point to break through and charged. Hajime and Yue pushed their way through a dense copse of trees, and as they finally jumped clear, they found themselves face to face with a massive, two-meter-large, raptor-like monster. This one had a tulip blooming on its head.

"...Cute."

"...Are those in fashion or something?" Yue blurted out those words before she could stop herself, and Hajime found it hard to take the raptor in front of him seriously. As he stared at it, an impossible hypothesis came to mind.

Like the T. rex, the raptor's bloodcurdling howl was at complete odds with the cute flower on its head. Everyone began getting ready for combat. The flower fluttered peacefully on the raptor's head, but...

"Shaaaaa!" It paid it no mind, and leaped at the distracted Hajime. The twenty-centimeter-long talons extending from the raptor's feet glinted cruelly in the dim light as it attacked.

Yue and Hajime both jumped in different directions to dodge.

Not content with simply dodging, however, Hajime also used Aerodynamic to leap multiple times through the air, until he was directly above the raptor. As a test, he shot off the tulip poised on its head.

His bullet passed effortlessly through the tulip, scattering its petals in all directions.

The raptor spasmed momentarily, before tripping over itself and somersaulting into the trees, where it lay motionless. A moment of silence descended. Yue tottered over to Hajime, and they both stared at the tulip petals scattered across the ground.

"Is it dead?"

"Doesn't look like it to me."

As Hajime had so astutely observed, the raptor wasn't dead. It twitched for a few seconds before slowly standing up and examining its surroundings. When it noticed the tulip petals, it padded its way over and started crushing them underfoot, as if the tulip had done it some great harm.

"Huh? What on earth is it doing? Why's it crushing the petals?"

"...Maybe someone put it on its head as a prank?"

"I'm pretty sure the monsters around here aren't some elementary school kids that go around sticking 'kick me' signs on everyone they see..."

Once it had finished grinding the tulip into dust, it looked up contentedly at the sky and let out a high-pitched screech. It then finally spotted Yue and Hajime, and jumped with a start.

"Looks like it just realized we were here. Just how absorbed was it with that tulip?"

"...Maybe it's being bullied?" As Hajime marveled at its inattention, Yue looked at it with something akin to sympathy. The raptor stood there for a moment, overcome by shock, before suddenly lowering its stance and bearing its claws. It let out a low roar as it rushed Hajime.

He calmly pulled out Donner, and shot an electrically accelerated taur bullet right into the raptor's gaping maw.

It made mincemeat out of the raptor's head, and bored its way through a few of the trees behind it before vanishing from sight.

Carried by the force of its own charge, the dead raptor slid a few feet across the ground before coming to a stop. Yue and Hajime both stared down at the raptor's corpse.

"Seriously, what *was* all that about?"

"First it was bullied, and then it got shot... Poor thing."

"Can we just drop the bullying part? I'm pretty sure that never happened."

He had no idea what had just happened, but the monsters on this floor made no sense to him anyway, so he just stopped worrying about it. Their encirclement had started closing in on them, so they quickly moved to find more advantageous terrain.

As they pushed forward, they found themselves surrounded by a sea of trees, each five meters wide at the base. The trees were packed so closely together that their branches were entwined, making a natural pathway through the sky.

Hajime used Aerodynamic while Yue used wind magic to hop from branch to branch. He planned to shoot down all the monsters that came after them from above.

In less than five minutes, the ground below became a hive of activity as one raptor after another poured into the area. He was about to throw down an incendiary grenade when suddenly he stiffened. Next to him, Yue also stiffened, her hands still outstretched to cast magic. The reason for their sudden hesitation was none other than...

"Why the hell do they all have flowers on their heads?!"

"It's one big garden."

As Hajime had so eloquently stated, the dozen or so raptors all had flowers adorning their heads. All of varying shapes, sizes, and colors.

His outcry had alerted the raptors to their presence, and as one, they all turned to face him. Each of them got ready to leap.

He quickly threw his incendiary grenade and began shooting down the raptors outside its range. After each gunshot was a brief red flash, signaling that Donner had torn the head off its quarry. At the same time, Yue used her Crimson Javelin to take down raptors one after another.

Roughly three seconds after the battle began, the incendiary grenade exploded. Burning hot tar splashed everywhere, incinerating a swathe of raptors. Hajime breathed a sigh of relief when he saw that his other weapons were still effective on this floor. It appeared that scorpion had just been exceptionally strong.

The entire flock of raptors was taken care of in less than ten seconds. But for some reason, Hajime's expression was still grim. Yue saw the look on his face and tilted her head in confusion.

"...Hajime?"

"Don't you think it's strange, Yue?"

"Hm?"

"They're too weak."

Yue was taken aback by that unexpected response.

It certainly was true that both the raptors and the T. rex had moved in very simplistic patterns and had been easily defeated. On top of that, though they exhibited a fair amount of bloodlust, they had felt almost unnaturally mechanical in their actions. Especially when compared to the raptor whose flower Hajime had blown off. The way it had ground the flower to dust had felt far more natural.

Hajime turned to Yue, but before he could say anything, his Sense Presence detected a new wave of monsters. There was a veritable army of them closing in from all directions. His Sense Presence had a radius of twenty meters, and there were already more monsters than he could count heading their way, with even more pouring into range every second.

"Yue, we're in trouble. There's at least thirty, no, forty monsters heading our way. They're surrounding us from all sides too. It's almost like someone's controlling them."

"...Should we run?"

"No point. With how many there are, we won't escape. It'd be smarter to climb to the top of the tallest tree and pick them off from there."

"Okay... I'll ready a big spell, then."

"Yeah, let 'em have it!"

They sped through the branches, searching for the tallest tree in the area. Once they found it, they hopped onto one of its branches and destroyed all of the surrounding footholds, making it harder for the monsters to follow them.

Hajime held Donner at the ready as he waited. He felt a slight tug at the hem of his shirt, and realized Yue had grabbed onto him. That restricted the movement of his arms a little, so he leaned into her to free them. Her grip strengthened as he did so.

Finally, the first wave of enemies appeared. It was a mix of raptors and T. rexes this time. The T. rexes started ramming into the trunk over and over while the raptors used their claws to make footholds and leaped up the tree.

Hajime squeezed Donner's trigger. Chunks of flesh rained down to the ground below as one of the raptors had its head blown off.

That had been the last of his clip, so he detached the revolver's cylinder and spun it to dislodge the empty shells before sticking it in his left armpit and reloading. The entire process only took five seconds.

But he had still made sure to drop an incendiary grenade in the downtime to keep the raptors busy. A curtain of flame fell to the ground below. Seconds later, a barrage of bullets followed. Hajime had already killed fifteen of them, but there was no time to rest.

A group of thirty raptors and four T. rexes had formed down below, and they were frantically trying either to climb the tree or just topple it outright.

"Hajime?"

"Not yet... Wait just a bit longer," he replied, without taking his eyes off the enemies he was shooting at down below. Trusting in Hajime, Yue concentrated only on pouring more mana into her spell.

Finally, when there were more than fifty creatures swarming around the forest floor, Hajime decided that must have been all of the enemies he'd detected and he gave Yue the signal.

"Yue, now!"

"Okay! Frost Prison!"

The moment Yue unleashed her magic, the ground all around the tree began to freeze. In the blink of an eye, all of the monsters had been encased in tombs of pale blue ice. They dotted the frozen landscape, looking like crystal blossoms.

Trapped in their pretty frozen coffins, the light of life soon drained from their eyes. The field of frost expanded fifty meters in all directions. Her magic really was a weapon of mass destruction.

"Haah... Haah..."

"Nice job. I'm so glad I have a vampire princess on my side."

"...Eeheehee..."

Hajime couldn't help but marvel at the frozen hellscape Yue had created with a single spell. But casting such a high-level spell had drained her of all her mana, and she was panting heavily. She had completely exhausted herself with that attack alone.

Hajime gently supported her with one arm and bared his neck. She'd recover her mana if she drank his blood. The Ambrosia could heal her exhaustion too, but perhaps because she was a vampire, it took a lot of time to fully take effect on her. He supposed it made sense that blood was the best remedy for a vampire.

Yue smiled faintly at Hajime's praise before sinking her fangs into his neck. A slight flush crept up her cheeks as she drank his blood.

Before she could finish, however, Hajime suddenly dislodged his neck and stood back up. His Sense Presence had discovered another hundred monsters heading their way.

"Yue, we've got twice as many as before heading our way."

"Wha—?!"

"There's definitely something strange going on here. We just wiped out a huge group of them, didn't we? But they're still rushing us anyway... It's like they're being controlled. Don't tell me those flowers are..."

"Parasites?"

"You think so too, Yue?"

Yue nodded in agreement.

"...It should have a main body somewhere."

"Yeah. If we can't get the bastard that stuck those flowers on everyone, we'll have to fight our way through every single monster on this floor."

They decided to look for the mastermind behind the flower parasites before they got overwhelmed by sheer numbers. Until they defeated the puppet master, they wouldn't be able to do a proper search of the floor.

As they no longer had time to let Yue leisurely suck his blood, Hajime tried to pass her a vial of Ambrosia. However, she didn't take it. He tilted his head, puzzled. Yue was holding both her arms out to him instead of taking the vial.

"Hajime...carry me..."

"What are you, five?! Wait, don't tell me you expect me to carry you and run while you suck my blood?!"

She nodded emphatically. He supposed Ambrosia would take too long to take effect, and in a pinch, they would need Yue's magic to save them. However, he wasn't thrilled about the idea of fleeing from a monster army while she sucked his blood. *I suppose drastic times call for drastic measures...* In the end, he agreed and lifted Yue into his arm...and then realized that would hinder his movements too much, so he slung her over his back instead. His preparations complete, he leaped down.

And so, we return to the earlier scene, in which Hajime was being chased down by 200 monsters. Hajime hacked his way through a dense clump of weeds with Yue still clinging to his back. Though she had finished sucking his blood, she still hadn't gotten off.

As he ran, he heard a massive rumbling noise behind him. The entire floor shook as the army of dinosaurs charged toward him. The raptors hid themselves in the tall grass and threw themselves at Hajime from all directions. He killed the ones that managed to reach him and ignored the rest as he ran as fast as he could. He was currently making his way to what he thought was the most obvious hiding spot he could think of. Yue launched magic projectiles left and right, keeping the monsters at bay and preventing them from getting completely hemmed in.

Sluuuurp. She sucked his blood again as he ran. Their destination was the dungeon wall located at the other end of the sea of trees. On that wall was a massive fissure that opened into a cavern.

The reason he had chosen to investigate that location first was because of a peculiarity he had noticed in the monsters' behavior. While Hajime had been running through the forest, it was only when he had headed in a certain direction that the monsters' attacks became more frantic. As if they were trying to prevent him from going that way. It wasn't much to go on, but it was all they had. Besides, if they took too long they'd be overwhelmed anyway, so they had no choice but to bet it all on whatever clues they managed to find.

He had hoped to hide among the grass as he made his way over, but that plan had clearly failed. Instead, since his position was already compromised, he decided to speed up and activated Aerodynamic along with Supersonic Step to shoot forward.

Sluuuurp.

"Yue?! Can you please stop sucking my blood at every opportunity?!"

"...I need it."

"Liar! I know you've barely used any mana since the last time you took a sip!"

"Their flowers are...draining my... Ugh."

"Stop playing the tragic heroine card. I know you're just fine, you moron! I can't believe you're screwing around like this when I'm running for my life."

Even in such a tense situation, Yue was more interested in Hajime's blood than their impending crisis. *Man, she's got no shame. Guess I should've figured since she's royalty and all...* And despite her playful attitude, she was still shooting down every monster that leaped in range without skipping a beat.

After a few more minutes of running, they arrived at the cave entrance, with two hundred monsters in tow.

The fissure was narrow enough that two grown men would have trouble walking side by side. The T. Rexes wouldn't fit at all, and the raptors would have to follow single file. One of the raptors leaped at them, claws at the ready, but before it could even make it a few feet, Hajime blew it to bits with Donner. Once they were through the fissure, Hajime transmuted it, closing it behind him.

"Haaah, we can finally take a break."

"...You sound tired."

"If you're worried about me, how about you get off my back?"

"Muhh... Fine."

Reluctantly, Yue slipped off of his back. *She must really like my back.*

"Now then, considering how desperate those guys looked, I'd say we're in the right place. Make sure you stay on your toes."

"Okay."

The inside of the cavern was dim since Hajime had closed the exit, so they proceeded cautiously.

After a few minutes of walking, the path opened up into a wide room. There was a second fissure on the other side of the room. *Maybe that's the path that leads to the next floor?* Hajime started combing the room. Sense Presence didn't detect any enemies, but there was this ominous feeling he just couldn't shake, so he kept his guard up. He had learned the hard way that some monsters could evade his Sense Presence.

It was when they reached the center of the room that it finally happened. A countless number of what seemed like green ping pong balls flew at them from every corner of the room. Yue and Hajime stood back to back and began shooting down the ping pong balls.

However, there were over a hundred coming at them fast, and he realized he couldn't get them all in time. He instantly changed tracks and transmuted a wall to protect himself. The balls all crashed into the wall, unable to pierce through the thick stone. Though fast, they didn't appear to have much force. Yue had no problem taking care of the ones on her side with her superior wind magic.

"Yue, I think that's the main body's way of attacking. Do you have any idea where it is?"

"......"

"Yue?" Hajime asked, inquisitively. Though she didn't possess any perception skills like Hajime, her honed vampire senses provided her with a useful amount of information unavailable to Hajime.

However, Yue didn't respond. Confused, he turned to her and asked again, but the reply he received was completely unexpected.

"...Run, Hajime!" Her hands were pointing at Hajime. Gales of wind whipped dangerously around them. His instincts screamed at him to run, so he leaped away as quickly as possible. Not even a second later, a blade of wind passed through the spot he'd just been standing on and neatly sliced through the wall behind him.

"Yue?!" Hajime could barely believe what he was seeing. He raised his voice in surprise, but then understanding dawned on him when he saw what was above Yue's head. Blooming atop her golden hair was a small flower. It felt almost as if the monster had chosen that flower specifically for her too. After all, the scarlet rose above her head suited her perfectly.

"Dammit, those green balls must've been flowers!" *How stupid can I be? I want to punch myself right now,* he thought, as he evaded another one of Yue's wind slashes.

"Hajime... Unngh..." Her usual poker face was replaced with a grief-stricken expression. When he'd shot the flower off the raptor's head it had stamped on it with a surprising amount of hatred, which meant that it had recalled the time it had spent under the flower's control. The flower controlled only the body, and not the mind.

Fortunately, he already knew how to free her from it. He took aim at the flower and prepared to pull the trigger.

However, it seemed his quarry was aware of what his weapons were capable of, and that he'd shot down a flower before.

It controlled Yue, forcing her to protect the flower. It made her bob up and down, meaning that if he missed he was liable to shoot right through her skull. He ran forward, intending to pluck it off, but Yue pointed a hand at her own head as he did.

"Oh, now you've done it..." The message was clear. If he tried to get close, the monster would force Yue to attack herself with her own magic.

Though she was practically immortal, Hajime couldn't say with confidence she'd still be able to regenerate if she blew herself to smithereens with a powerful spell. And she was more than skilled enough to cast even the strongest of spells in seconds. He wasn't willing to risk Yue's life on a gamble like that.

Sensing his hesitation, the monster slithered out of the crack in

the back of the room.

What crawled out of the depths was a woman-plant hybrid that closely resembled something like a Dryad or Alraune. There was no better way to describe the creature they faced. According to legend, these monsters took on the forms of beautiful women to sap their opponents' will to fight, and if one treated them well, they would be blessed with good fortune. However, the creature standing in front of them didn't seem anything like the legends.

While it did still look like a woman, its face was as ugly as its fighting style was dirty, and the countless vines writhing around it like tentacles only served to make it look all the more disgusting. It might have been better to call it an Alraune wannabe. There was a wicked grin plastered across its hideous face.

Hajime lost no time in pointing Donner at this new opponent. But before he could fire, Yue got in between him and the Alraune wannabe, blocking his line of sight.

"Hajime...I'm sorry..." Yue gritted her teeth in frustration. Not being able to control her own body must have been unbearable for her. Even now, she was desperately struggling to move. As Hajime watched, crimson droplets began trailing down the corners of her mouth. She must have bitten her lips so hard she drew blood. He couldn't tell if it was frustration at her own powerlessness, or an attempt to inflict enough pain that she could break the spell. Perhaps it was a little of both.

Using Yue as a shield, the Alraune wannabe fired another green ball at Hajime.

A bullet from Donner blasted it to bits. Though he couldn't see them, he was sure the ball must have sprayed flower spores everywhere when it burst.

However, Hajime didn't feel a flower blooming on his head. The Alraune wannabe suddenly stopped grinning when she saw Hajime was still unfazed. The spores seemed not to work on him.

Must be because of all the resistances I have. His guess was more or less correct, as the Alraune wannabe's spores were a form of neurotoxin. Hence, his Poison Resistance made him immune to their effects. In other words, the only reason Hajime wasn't a puppet was because of sheer luck. It wasn't as if Yue had let her guard down or anything. Which was why she had no reason to be blaming herself.

Realizing her spores couldn't control him, the Alraune wannabe pouted and commanded Yue to attack him with her magic. Another blade of wind shot out toward him. From how simple Yue's movements had become, and how single-minded the earlier raptors' attacks had been, Hajime surmised that the Alraune wannabe couldn't bring out her controlled subjects' full strength.

I guess that's some consolation at least. When he moved to jump out of the way, Yue pointed a hand at her head again, rooting him in place. Unable to dodge, he activated the Diamond Skin skill he'd taken from the Cyclops to defend himself.

Diamond Skin involved coating the caster's body in mana and then hardening it, so that they were surrounded by a shell literally as hard as diamonds. He hadn't trained it much yet, so it was probably barely even a tenth as strong as the Cyclops' version of it had been. Still, it was enough to stop Yue's wind blades, which were sharp but lacked power.

There is a way I can end this fight right now, but...I'm worried about the aftermath... Should I try throwing an incendiary grenade at it? As

Hajime pondered how best to escape the deadlock, he heard Yue's grief-stricken shout.

"Hajime! Don't mind me...just shoot!" It seemed she'd resolved herself. If she was just going to get in his way and attack him, she'd rather be shot at herself. There wasn't even the slightest hint of hesitation in her crimson eyes.

Normally this would be a scene where the main character said something like, "There's no way I can do that!" or, "I'll save you, no matter what it takes!" and strengthen his bonds with the heroine. And in fact, the old Hajime might have done just that. But the current Hajime was a much harder man.

"Wait, really? Thanks." *Bang!* A single gunshot resounded through at the room.

Upon hearing Yue's words, Hajime had fired without hesitation. Silence filled the room as the gunshot's echoes faded away. The red rose spun through the air before soundlessly falling to the ground.

Yue blinked in surprise. The Alraune wannabe did too.

Yue uncertainly patted the top of her head. The flower was gone, but the hair near it was frizzly and torn. Even the Alraune wannabe, wicked as it was, glared scornfully at Hajime.

"You of all people don't have the right to judge me!" *Bang!* Hajime fired angrily at the Alraune wannabe. Green goop splattered everywhere as it lost its head. Its limbs spasmed momentarily before the whole thing crumpled to the ground.

"Are you all right, Yue? You don't feel weird anywhere, do you?" Hajime casually walked up to Yue. However, Yue glared angrily at Hajime while continuing to flatten down her hair.

"...You really shot me."

"Huh? I mean, yeah, you told me to."

"...You didn't even hesitate..."

"Well, yeah, I was planning on shooting from the start. I have confidence in my skills, but I figured you'd get mad if I just shot without warning. I was just being considerate by waiting for you to say something first."

"...You grazed...my head..."

"It'll heal up right away though, won't it? So there shouldn't be any problem."

"Ughhh..."

Her expression screamed "So what!" as she beat on his chest with her fists.

It was true that she was the one that told him to shoot, and that she would have preferred that to continuing to get in his way. But Yue was still a girl. She had dreams too. She'd hoped Hajime would have hesitated at least a little. She was mad at how lightly he'd taken her resolve.

For his part, once Hajime had realized the Alraune wannabe couldn't control Yue well enough to use more advanced magic, he had thought there was no longer any reason to worry. There weren't many attacks that could overcome her immortality.

Despite that, he had hesitated, the greatest taboo of fighting, until Yue had given him a signal that it was okay. He couldn't understand why she was still so mad. In his mind, he had given her the ultimate amount of consideration. She got even angrier when she heard his explanation, and sulkily turned her back to him.

Hajime sighed to himself and started thinking about how he could improve her mood. Something that proved to be infinitely harder than defeating the Alraune wannabe.

• *•* *•* *•* *•* *•* *•* *•* *•* *•* *•* *•* *•* *•*

It was a few days after they'd defeated the Alraune wannabe and Hajime had soured Yue's mood. She'd nearly sucked him dry before she forgave him. But it had been worth it to make her happy again. Once Hajime had recovered from near-death blood loss, the two of them went back to exploring the labyrinth.

The next floor would mark the hundredth from the one Hajime had started in.

Before they delved into it, he decided to make sure his supplies were in perfect order. As always, Yue watched him work with unbridled enthusiasm. Though it was perhaps more accurate to say she was more interested in watching Hajime than in watching the work itself. Today, too, she was sitting right next to Hajime, watching his hand and his face as he worked. Her expression was far too relaxed for how dangerous a place they were in.

Having lost all track of time, Hajime had no way of knowing how many days had passed since he'd first met Yue, but she'd been showing him that relaxed expression quite often recently. She'd clearly gotten used to being around him.

Especially when they were resting in his temporary bases, she always stuck to him like glue. When they were sleeping she clung to his arm, and when they were sitting she always hugged him from behind. And when she was sucking his blood she'd just hug him from the front. Even when she finished she'd cling to him for a long time after. She particularly enjoyed burying her face in his chest and rubbing against him.

But see, the problem was, Hajime was still a guy.

Fortunately, Yue's childish appearance made her look more cute than sexy, but the fact remained that she was actually quite old. He normally couldn't tell due to the way she acted, but the few times her age shone through she looked so alluring that he had a hard time holding himself back. He was able to control himself only because he was aware of the constant danger that surrounded them at all times, but he wasn't confident he'd be able to withstand the temptation of her once they got back to the surface and they could relax for a bit. If he was honest with himself, he wasn't even sure he wanted to withstand it...

"Hajime... You're being even more careful than usual."

"Hm? Yeah, cause the next floor's going to be the hundredth one. I just get the feeling there's going to be something big waiting for us. They say most of the labyrinths are only supposed to go one hundred floors deep too, so... Well, there's no harm in taking precautions."

Actually, in Hajime's case, he had traversed a further eighty floors after falling past dozens more—starting from a floor that already was most likely deeper than the twentieth. He had long since passed the point where the standard depth of the Great Orcus Labyrinth was thought to come to an end. Considering how much deeper he had delved after already falling into the depths of hell, even he could tell he was far deeper than the endpoint of the "normal" Great Orcus Labyrinth.

Marksmanship, physical abilities, specialized magic, weaponry, and finally transmutation. Hajime had polished his skills in each field to the utmost. His strength was quite formidable as well. However, the truly scary thing about this labyrinth was that even with his strength, it might still throw something at him that could kill him without breaking a sweat. Which was why he made as many preparations as he could before descending. For reference on just how strong he'd become, his current stats looked something like this:

HAJIME NAGUMO		Age: 17	Male
Job:	Synergist	Level:	76
Strength:	1980	Agility:	2450
Vitality:	2090	Magic:	1780
Defense:	2070	M. Defense:	1780
Skills:	Transmute [+Ore Appraisal] [+Precision Transmutation] [+Ore Perception] [+Ore Desynthesis] [+Ore Synthesis] [+Duplicate Transmutation] • Mana Manipulation [+Mana Discharge] [+Mana Compression] [+Remote Manipulation] • Iron Stomach • Lightning Field • Air Dance [+Aerodynamic] [+Supersonic Step] [+Steel Legs] • Gale Claw • Night Vision • Far Sight • Sense Presence • Detect Magic • Sense Heat • Hide Presence • Poison Resistance • Paralysis Resistance • Petrification Resistance • Diamond Skin • Intimidate • Telepathy • Language Comprehension		

Though he received new skills with each monster he consumed, he obtained new magic less and less frequently. Boss-level monsters still gave him new magic, but the standard ones loitering around each floor had stopped granting him new spells. He hypothesized that was because he was becoming more and more monster-like in constitution every time his body strengthened itself from eating monster meat. After all, monsters didn't obtain the magic of the prey they killed and ate.

With their preparations finally complete, Hajime and Yue descended the stairs to the floor below.

The bottom of the staircase opened up into a massive open room, empty save for the pillars that dotted the area. Each pillar had a spiral pattern engraved into its stone face. It gave off the impression that each pillar was a massive tree with vines entwined around its trunk. The pillars were all spaced evenly apart from each other, and extended all the way to the ceiling thirty meters above. The ground was unnaturally smooth, as if it had been paved. All in all, it was a very majestic room.

Hajime and Yue took a step forward as they marveled at the room's design. The moment they stepped inside, the pillars in front of them began glowing faintly. The two of them instantly returned to their senses and warily observed their surroundings. Starting from the pillars nearest to them, each set began glowing, one after the other.

Hajime and Yue both instantly raised their guard, but after a while nothing more happened, so they carefully continued forward. Both of them were on alert for any sign of enemies.

After about two hundred meters of walking, they found themselves staring at the opposite wall. Set within it was a massive set of doors. The ten-meter-tall pair of double doors also had something engraved into them. There was a heptagon carved into each, with a peculiar pattern adorning each vertex of the shape.

"Well, that's quite the impressive entrance. Do you think this is..."

"...Where the maverick lives?" Yue responded.

It really looked like the kind of room that'd have a last boss in it. Though none of his perception skills were picking up on anything, Hajime's instincts were screaming at him nonetheless. "It's dangerous to go any further," they told him. Yue felt it as well, and cold sweat beaded on her forehead.

"Well, if it is, that's just perfect. That means we've finally made it to our goal." Hajime pushed down his instincts and put on his usual fearless smile. No matter what was ahead, they had no choice but to move forward.

"...Yeah!" Yue glared resolutely at the double doors.

They stepped forward simultaneously, walking past the last pair of pillars. The moment they cleared them...a massive, thirty-meter-large magic circle appeared in the air between them and the door. It pulsed malignantly as it shot out gouts of dark red light.

This kind of magic circle was very familiar to Hajime. He could never forget the magic circle that was responsible for trapping his class on the bridge and ultimately sending Hajime hurtling down into the abyss. However, this one was three times the size of the one that had summoned the Behemoth, and the inscriptions on it were far more complex and precise.

"Crap, that size is no joke. We're seriously up against this place's last boss?"

"Don't worry... We won't lose."

Hajime's smile understandably faltered a little, but Yue's determined expression remained unshaken, and she tightly squeezed Hajime's arm. He nodded in response, and smiled wryly as he watched the magic circle finish its summoning.

Finally, it let out one last incandescent burst of light. Yue and

Hajime both covered their eyes to preserve their sight. Once the illumination dimmed, they got their first glimpse of their foe. What stood before them was a monster thirty meters in length. It had six heads attached to very long necks, each of which had a different-colored pattern engraved into its head and a pair of dark red eyes. It resembled the mythical Hydra.

"Graaaaaaaaaaaaaaaaaah!" It let out a peculiar howl and focused all six pairs of eyes on Hajime and Yue. Determined to pass judgment on the foolish intruders, the Hydra unleashed a wave of bloodlust so powerful it would have stopped a normal person's heart on the spot.

At the same time, the red-patterned head opened its jaw and unleashed a torrent of flames. A veritable wall of fire raced toward them.

Hajime and Yue both dove in different directions, and instantly began firing off counterattacks. Hajime pulled Donner's trigger, and a small spark ignited the blastrock inside the bullet, which passed through an electrically charged barrel and accelerated toward the red-patterned head. The bullet slammed into the Hydra, blowing the red head clean off.

As he struck a triumphant pose, the white head let out a long screech, and white light began enveloping the destroyed red head. Then, like a tape rewinding, the red head flew back through the air and reattached itself to the Hydra's neck. *So the white head's the healer.*

Seconds later, Yue's ice spears sheared the green head off, but the white head restored that one too.

Hajime clicked his tongue and contacted Yue with Telepathy.

"Yue, aim for the white one! This'll never end if it keeps healing!"

"Got it!" The blue head opened its mouth next, firing a spray of ice pebbles at both of them. They nimbly dodged the barrage and took aim at the white head.

Bang! "Crimson Javelin!" A burning spear and speeding bullet raced toward the white head.

But just before they hit their target, the yellow head put itself in the line of fire and reared like a cobra. It took both Hajime's bullet and Yue's Crimson Javelin head on. It survived both the impact of a bullet and the heat of the explosion completely unscathed, and gazed coldly down at the two creatures below it.

"Tch! It has a tank too? Quite the balanced party it's got there." Hajime pulled an incendiary grenade out of his pack and threw it at the heads. He then fired a barrage of full power rounds at the white head. Yue fired a salvo of Crimson Javelins to match him. *If she uses her Azure Blaze, she can probably take the yellow and white heads out at once, but it'll be risky since she'll be exhausted afterward. She'll recover right away if she sucks my blood, but I doubt the other heads will give us that much time.* There was also the possibility they were tough enough to withstand Yue's strongest spell. Therefore, Hajime decided it would be too dangerous for Yue to use her strongest spells until at least half the heads were dealt with.

The yellow head managed to perfectly block their barrage of attacks. However, even it couldn't come out of such a bombardment unscathed, and it was clearly wounded in places.

"Graaaaaaaah!" But the white head began healing the yellow one almost instantly. It was disgustingly proficient at healing magic.

However, right as it finished healing the yellow head, the grenade exploded directly above it. A deluge of burning tar fell upon the Hydra's heads. Some of it landed on the white head too, which made the monster screech in pain.

Hajime activated his Telepathy to inform Yue not to let this chance slip by. But before he could say anything, a bloodcurdling scream reached his ears.

Yue's scream.

"Aaaaaaaaaaaah!!!"

"Yue?!"

Hajime tried to rush over to Yue, but the red and green heads unleashed a torrent of flame and wind to block his path. Yue's screams continued, and Hajime gritted his teeth in worry as he tried to piece together what was happening. It was then that he remembered the black head had yet to make a move.

No wait, maybe it already has made its move! Hajime frantically dodged with Aerodynamic and Supersonic Step while he fired Donner at the black head. A hyper-accelerated bullet slammed into the black head, knocking its gaze off of Yue. At the same time, Yue slumped to the ground. He could tell she was pale even from his distant position.

The blue head opened its jaw wide, and rushed toward Yue, intending to eat her.

"Don't you daaaaaaaaaaare!" Heedless of the damage it might do to his own body, he used Supersonic Step to dash right through the storm of fire and wind.

He used Donner and Gale Claw to deflect any fatal blows while ignoring the rest, and just barely made it to Yue before the blue head did. He had no time to mount a counterattack, so he used Diamond Skin to make himself a human shield. When Diamond Skin was active, Hajime couldn't move. That was why he hadn't used it earlier.

A layer of diamond-hard mana enveloped him seconds before the blue head's jaws sunk into him.

"Grrrrr!"

"Guh!"

With a low growl, the blue head tried to swallow Hajime whole. However, he held his ground and used his back and feet to keep it from closing its jaws on him. He quickly pushed Donner up against its upper jaw and fired.

With a bang, the top part of its head popped off like a jack-in-the-box. The strength vanished from its jaws and Hajime kicked the remnants of its head away with his Steel Legs. He then pulled out a flash grenade and sound grenade and kicked them over to the Hydra.

The sound grenade was a new addition he had picked up from a monster on the 80th floor that used ultrasonic waves to fight. He had harvested the organ the monster used to produce those sounds and incorporated it into his arsenal. It hadn't provided him with any new magic, but the organ had been apparently classified as an ore, so he was able to transmute it into a sound grenade.

The combination of light and sound disoriented the Hydra. With the few seconds he'd managed to buy them, Hajime scooped up Yue and hid behind one of the pillars.

"Hey! Yue! Say something!"

"......"

She didn't respond to Hajime's voice at all, and simply sat in his arm, pale and trembling.

"How dare that black bastard do this!" Hajime cursed and started lightly slapping Yue's cheeks. He tried calling out to her with Telepathy too, and even gave her a vial of Ambrosia. After a while, Yue's eyes finally began to regain their former glimmer.

"Yue!"

"...Hajime?"

"Yep, it's me. How are you feeling? Just what happened back there?"

After blinking confusedly for a few more seconds, Yue gently stroked Hajime's cheek, as if making sure he was really there. Once she was sure he really was, she breathed a small, relieved sigh. There were tears welling up in her eyes.

"I'm so glad... I thought I'd been...abandoned again. Alone in the darkness..."

"Huh? What on earth are you talking about?" Hajime asked, bewildered.

Apparently Yue had suddenly been assailed by visions of being abandoned by Hajime and sealed once more in the darkness. The absolute terror of something like that happening to her had paralyzed her thoughts and stopped her from moving.

"Tch! So the black one's a debuffer? Looks like it inflicts a fear status on people. Crap, this monster really is a perfectly balanced party!"

"...Hajime."

Yue looked worriedly up at Hajime, who was busy insulting the Hydra. It must have been quite the terrifying sight for her—being abandoned by Hajime.

From Yue's point of view, Hajime was the man who had risked his life to save her from her three-hundred-year-old prison. On top of that, even after learning she was a vampire, he hadn't shunned her. In fact, he'd happily let her suck his blood every day. The thought that he had abandoned her had stricken her to her very core.

Hajime's side was the only place she had left to return to. She was happy beyond words when he had offered to take her home with him. And the thought of being alone again scared her just as much.

The seeds of fear the head had planted in her mind had begun to sprout, and they were eating away at her even now. Hajime didn't have the time to console her though, as the Hydra had recovered from the flashbang. He rose, intending to return to the fray, but was stopped by Yue, who clutched tightly to his shirt.

"...I..." She was still trembling, and it looked as if she would burst into tears at any moment. Hajime was able to more or less figure out what was going through her mind based on the nightmare she'd just had. And from the way she always acted around him, he could guess what she was feeling too. Regardless, he had promised he'd bring her to Japan with him. He could hardly ignore her plight.

That being said, there was no time to comfort her. Trying to give her any half-assed words of consolation would just make things worse if the black head attacked her again. It was even possible the head would target Hajime, so he needed Yue in perfect mental condition to follow up in case he got hit.

But in the end, he knew he was just trying to make excuses for himself. Hajime awkwardly scratched his head and squatted down in front of Yue. She tilted her head, puzzled, as he looked her in the eyes. And...

"...Ah?!"

He kissed her on the lips.

It was more of a peck than a kiss, and Hajime's lips barely touched hers, but it took her completely by surprise. Her eyes opened wide as she stared blankly at him. Embarrassed, he broke eye contact and pulled Yue to her feet.

"We're gonna kill that bastard. We're gonna make it out of here alive and go home... Together." Yue was still staring at Hajime in a daze, but her usually empty expression was gone. In its place was the most radiant smile he'd ever seen.

"Yeah!"

Hajime awkwardly cleared his throat and switched gears back to battle mode as he outlined his plan. "Yue, I'm going to bring out Schlagen. It can't fire consecutive shots, so I'm going to need you to cover me."

"Leave it to me!" There was more enthusiasm in Yue's voice than usual. Normally, she just mumbled listlessly, but her reply this time was filled with emotion. It looked like she'd been freed from all her old fears. And from the looks of it, her inhibitions. When he recalled just how dependent she was on him, he realized he might have been a bit hasty. *The future's going to be pretty rocky*, he thought, as he smiled wryly.

Tired of their lovers' skit, the Hydra roared angrily, reminding the two of its presence with a barrage of wind, fire, and ice. The two of them leaped out from behind the pillar, then began their counterattack.

"Crimson Javelin! Force Lasher! Glacial Sleet!" Yue unleashed spell after spell. Spears of fire, spiraling whirlwinds created from the force of a vacuum, and needles of ice assailed the Hydra one after another.

She had aimed for the moment right after the heads had finished their attack, when they were at their most vulnerable. A barrage of magic rained down on the red, blue, and green heads. The yellow tried to cover them, but then noticed Hajime was firing on the white, and roared angrily as it was forced back to protect their healer.

"Graaaaaaaaaaah!" It slammed into a nearby pillar, transforming the stone into an impromptu shield. It appeared the yellow head had an ability similar to the scorpion's. Though it was nowhere near as powerful.

The first of Yue's spells pulverized the shield, allowing the latter two to rain down on the unprotected Hydra heads.

"Graaaaaaaaaaaaaaaaaaaaaaah!" The three heads all screamed in unison. The black head turned to Yue the moment her spells subsided and cast its fear magic on her again.

She could feel the same fear and unease creeping up on her. But this time, the memory of Hajime's kiss reassured her. The fear was blown away and replaced by something warm as it tried to take hold of her.

"That won't work on me anymore!" Since her current job was to just cover Hajime, she focused on bombarding the Hydra continually with spells, not worrying too much about their strength. The red, green, and blue heads all recovered and started attacking again, but Yue was able to take all three on at once. She neutralized their barrage with her own magic and often had enough time to slip in an attack too.

Hajime closed in on the Hydra while the three attacking heads were busy with Yue. He couldn't afford to let them block his first shot, since that was likely all he was going to get.

Realizing its fear magic wasn't working on Yue, the black head turned to Hajime. Fear and unease began to well up in his chest, and visions of his early days in hell floated up in his mind. He recalled the pain and starvation he had suffered when he had first fallen into the abyss. However...

"So what!" That was a past he had long since overcome. He had suffered enough that such pain meant nothing to him anymore. He nonchalantly blew the black head off with Donner.

The white head began healing again, but before it could finish restoring the black head, Hajime jumped up to it with a combination of Aerodynamic and Supersonic Step. After that, he pulled Schlagen off his back and nestled it within his armpit.

The yellow head moved to block Hajime, but he had already predicted that effort.

"I'll just get you both, then!" He activated his Lightning Field, and there was brief red spark as the bullet ignited. This specialized bullet was a full metal jacket, made with a taur core and coated with the same material that composed the scorpion's shell, shtar. Since shtar hardened with magic, the Lightning Field further powered up its destructive force. His rifle bullets had far more blastrock packed into them as well, and there was a mini-explosion as the bullet rocketed forward.

Boom! There was the sound of a cannon firing, and his special red bullet rocketed through the 1.5-meter-long barrel, picking up speed as it passed. The electrically accelerated bullet was easily four to five times as powerful as a full-power shot from Donner. That tiny bullet packed more force than a battleship round. The creation of such a fearsome weapon was only possible because of Hajime's special magic and the super-hard minerals found in this other world.

The only thing that could compare would be a very powerful laser. The bullet scorched the very air as it passed, heading straight for the yellow head.

The yellow head had its own powered-up version of Hajime's

Diamond Skin, but the bullet still blasted through it as if it were nothing more than paper. It pierced through the yellow head, pierced through the white one behind it, and exploded against the wall behind that. The entire dungeon floor shook from the impact.

Once the dust cleared, all that remained were the remnants of the two melted heads, which had somehow fused together, and a hole drilled so deep into the wall Hajime couldn't see where it ended.

The remaining three heads momentarily forgot to keep fighting and stared in slack-jawed amazement at what had happened to their comrades.

Hajime landed lightly onto the ground and ejected the spent shell from Schlagen. The empty casing fell to the ground with a clink, and the three heads suddenly remembered the predicament they were in. They all glared hatefully at Hajime, but the opponent they had been engaged with until just now was not one they could afford to take their eyes off of.

"Thunderlord's Judgment." Ribbons of gold mana flew wildly around the regal vampire princess. Hajime bore witness to the overpowering strength her family had feared so much that they'd sealed her away. Her magic rained down on the Hydra like judgment from God.

Six spheres of lightning surrounded the remaining three heads. They hung there in the air for a moment before shooting bolts into each other, connecting the six spheres into one huge ring of lightning. A new sphere formed at the ring's center, larger than all the others.

It hung there, like a Parthenon made of lightning, shining brighter than the sun. The blazing temple of lightning unleashed its power with the force of a thousand suns.

Crackle! The middle lightning sphere pulsed, and everything encased within the temple was blasted with millions of volts of electricity. The three remaining heads desperately tried to escape, but the outer ring acted as a prison, trapping them in their lightning hell. A huge flash was followed by a thunderous boom, and it was as if God's wrath itself had come down on them.

Within seconds, Yue's spell burnt the remaining heads to cinders. They died screaming in agony, unable to do anything to resist.

Yue slumped onto the ground like she always did after casting a powerful spell. She was panting heavily and had returned to her usual deadpan expression, but her eyes glowed with satisfaction. She gave Hajime a thumbs-up. Smiling, he returned the gesture. He fixed his grip on Schlagen, then started walking over to Yue.

However, an instant later—

"Hajime!" He heard her panicked shout. Sensing the urgency in her voice, he turned around to see what she was looking at, and saw that a seventh head had grown out of the remnants of the Hydra's body. It was glaring right at Hajime. He reflexively stiffened up.

The seventh head, which had a silver pattern carved into its forehead, shifted its gaze from Hajime to Yue, and without warning, fired an aurora of rainbow-colored light at her. The aurora ate up the distance between the Hydra and Yue at an alarming rate. She had exhausted all her mana and wouldn't be able to dodge in time.

Hajime shifted his gaze from the head to Yue, and chills ran down his spine. Without thinking, he leaped forward. Just like when he had rushed to save her from the blue head.

Hajime managed to reach her before the aurora could wipe her off the face of the earth.

However, things didn't end as fortuitously as they had with the blue head. The light swallowed Hajime whole. Even after he absorbed most of the attack, the shockwaves were enough to bowl Yue backward.

After the light subsided, Yue forced her aching body to get up. She frantically looked around, searching for Hajime.

She saw him standing in the same spot he had been in before the attack hit. He stood there defiantly, smoke rising from his body. The burnt husk of Schlagen slipped from his fingers, and fell to the ground. The bottom part had already fused with the floor below.

"H-Hajime?"

"......"

There was no reply. Then suddenly, he pitched forward onto the ground.

"Hajime!" Ignoring her body's protests, Yue desperately tried to run over to Hajime. However, her exhausted body couldn't keep up, so she tripped. She curbed her impatience and forced herself to drink a vial of Ambrosia. The moment she felt an ounce of her strength return, she stood back up and rushed over to Hajime.

He was lying face-down on the ground, blood pooling beneath him. His Diamond Skin hadn't been able to protect him completely. Had he not used Schlagen, which was made of the scorpion's shell, as a shield, he most likely would have died instantly.

She gently rolled him over onto his back, then gasped when she saw his injuries. His fingers, shoulders, and armpit had all been burnt to a crisp, and white bone was peeking out from the charred remains of skin and muscle. The entire right side of his face had been scorched too, and blood was dripping from his burnt right eye socket. The only thing that had saved his legs from suffering the same fate was probably the angle of the attack.

Yue hurriedly tried to force some Ambrosia down his throat, but the Hydra was already readying its next attack. This time it fired off a barrage of ten-centimeter-wide balls of light. It was like some kind of rainbow-colored Gatling gun.

Yue picked up Hajime and, squeezing out every last ounce of her strength, managed to carry him to safety behind one of the pillars. Light balls slammed into the pillar one after another. It likely wouldn't last even a minute longer. Each of the balls contained a frightening amount of force.

Yue quickly poured Ambrosia all over his wounds and pulled out a second vial, intending to feed it to him. However, he didn't even have the strength left to swallow, so he weakly choked it back out. Yue filled her own mouth with Ambrosia, then plugged his mouth with her own, forcing it down his throat.

However, while the Ambrosia stopped any more blood from seeping out, it was unable to fully heal Hajime's wounds. Normally it would start healing them right away, but it seemed something was obstructing it from working properly.

"Why?!" Yue was practically in a state of panic at that point. She began pulling out all the Ambrosia vials Hajime had on him.

The reason things were progressing slowly was because the Hydra's light actually contained a poison that melted flesh as well. By all rights, it should have already finished melting Hajime's body.

The fact that it hadn't, in and of itself, showed just how powerful the Ambrosia was. It had managed to overcome the poison, though not by much, and was slowly healing Hajime's wounds. Though it was taking longer than usual, the Ambrosia's effects coupled with Hajime's

naturally strong half-monster body meant he would eventually heal. However, his right eye had already dissolved beyond all repair, and even the Ambrosia wouldn't be able to bring it back.

The pillar was on its last legs too, and would most likely be destroyed before Hajime recovered enough to move. Yue looked down at him, a determined expression on her face, and kissed him. Then, after taking Donner from its holster, she stood up.

"...It's my turn to save *you* this time..." she whispered softly, before dashing out from behind the pillar.

She had very little mana remaining and no more Ambrosia. The only things she could rely on were her body-strengthening magic, her natural abilities as a vampire, her unreliable self-regeneration, and Donner.

The Hydra reared its silver-crested head as Yue ran into its sight, and fired another barrage of light balls. Yue didn't have the mana left to shoot them down with magic and, lacking Hajime's skill with firearms, didn't have the confidence to shoot them all down with Donner, so she opted to run. But physical strength had always been Yue's one weakness. She was backed into a corner almost instantly.

Finally, one of them hit her on the shoulder.

"Agahh?!" Even as she screamed in pain, she used the impact of the attack to roll back on her feet and resume running. She knew the moment she stopped from the pain, it'd be all over for her.

Her automatic regeneration took longer than usual to kick in. The melting properties of the Hydra's head were effective against her self-healing as well. And so, she lost even more mana by healing herself. At the rate things were going, she wouldn't even have enough mana to keep her body-strengthening up.

Every time she tried to get closer, a barrage of light balls drove her back. But she needed to close the gap somehow. She wasn't confident she'd be able to hit the Hydra with Donner from so far back. She needed to create an opening. However, she was unable to find any way to do so, and all too soon she was cornered again.

Desperate, she fired Donner in the hopes of forcing a way out of her predicament. Though she couldn't use Lightning Field, she was proficient enough with thunder magic that she managed to accelerate the bullet. In a stroke of beginner's luck, the bullet weaved neatly between the barrage of light balls and hit the Hydra right in the head.

Unfortunately, however...

"Huh?" Yue let out an involuntary mewl of surprise.

Even if she hadn't gotten the hang of accelerating it yet, she'd still added quite a bit of force to the bullet. Despite that, the silver-crested head had only a tiny scratch on it.

Despair began coloring her expression. But if she let herself be defeated, Hajime would die. Yue gritted her teeth and continued dodging.

Still, she wouldn't be able to keep it up forever. The silver-crested head reared back and fired a second aurora. The spread of bullets restricted her evasive routes until, finally, she was forced to let a ball blow her back to keep her from getting devoured entirely by the aurora's light.

The ball she was forced to take as compensation for dodging the aurora hit her square in the stomach and sent her sprawling to the ground.

"Ugh... Ghh..." Her body refused to move. She knew if she didn't get up she'd be devoured by a barrage of light balls. But no matter how she struggled, her muscles refused to listen. Her auto-regeneration was taking even longer than last time to kick in.

Before she knew it, there were tears rolling down her face. They were tears of frustration. Frustration at her inability to protect Hajime, even after he'd protected her so many times.

The Hydra took a moment to let out a victorious "Graaaaaaah!" before firing the next barrage of light balls.

Yue's death drew closer in the form of rainbow-colored light. She refused to close her eyes. If nothing else, she wasn't going to be defeated in spirit. She glared right at the silver-crested head, determined to go down fighting.

Eventually, the balls filled her vision, and she couldn't even see the Hydra anymore. They were going to hit her. She would die. Inside her head she apologized to Hajime for dying before him. For not being able to protect him. But suddenly...a gust of wind flew by.

"Eh?" By the time she'd grasped what was going on, Yue was in someone's arms and the light balls were passing by to her side. Her expression filled with utter disbelief, she looked up at the person holding her.

It was, of course, none other than Hajime. His body was still covered in wounds, he was panting heavily, and his right eyelid was tightly shut.

"Don't cry, Yue. You won this fight."

"Hajime!"

Overcome with emotion, she hugged him tight. His wounds had barely begun to heal. In reality, he was standing on willpower alone.

But he still glared angrily at the Hydra's silver head. It was looking condescendingly down on the both of them as it fired yet another barrage of light balls. It looked as if it was saying something like "What can a half-dead ape like you do?"

"Too slow." Hajime waited until the last minute before dodging with unsteady movements.

The silver head narrowed its eyes in anger and fired another salvo.

"Hajime, run!" Yue shouted frantically, but Hajime seemed utterly unconcerned. With Yue still held tight in his arm, he spun and danced around the Hydra's attacks. Though at times he stumbled, he never failed to dodge. In fact, it looked more as if the balls were dodging him than the other way around. And Yue watched it all, her eyes full of wonder.

"Yue, drink my blood." He spoke quietly, his silent gaze inviting her. For once, she hesitated. He had lost so much blood already. He dodged with tottering steps, but he still pushed Yue's face closer to his neck.

"Your magic is our only hope, Yue... So do it. Hurry up, and win this for us!"

"...Okay!"

Yue acquiesced to Hajime's powerful words, and nodded. She chose to trust in him and buried her face in his neck. Her body healed rapidly as his blood flowed into her. They danced a dance of death, the two of them, as they weaved their way through a storm of bullets.

For a moment, everything lost all sense of color for Hajime. He was whirling his way through a world of black and white, while everything around him moved in slow motion. Only his movements remained sharp.

He had seen it all. While he had been struggling to remain conscious, he had watched as Yue had battled all on her own. He watched as she desperately fought with his gun, until finally she was backed into a corner. He watched as she was thrown to the floor and bombarded with light.

It was at that moment that a seething anger had welled up. Anger at himself. What the hell are you doing?! How long do you plan to lie here sleeping?! Are you going to let your partner get killed right under your nose?! You're going to give in to that crappy excuse for a monster?! No! No, I won't! Anything that threatens my—that threatens our survival is an enemy! And enemies are to be...

"Killed!" Hajime had felt a tingling run through his body, and suddenly he had awoken to a new skill. He had acquired the final derivative skill of Air Dance, Riftwalk. By focusing all five of his senses to the utmost limits, his other Air Dance derivatives grew that much stronger. The extremity of his situation had forced him to surpass his limits once more.

It was that ability that had allowed Hajime to instantly teleport to Yue's side, and it was that ability that was currently allowing him to dodge the Hydra's attacks.

Yue finished drinking his blood, her strength fully restored.

"Yue, hit him with Azure Blaze when I give the signal. Until I do, just focus on dodging."

"Okay... But what about you, Hajime?"

"I'll be laying the groundwork for your finisher."

He let Yue down behind one of the pillars and then charged the Hydra.

He dodged each of the light balls by a hair's breadth using Supersonic Step, and then fired Donner once he got close enough. Annoyed by the fact that the last shot had still managed to scratch him, the silver head dodged this one. The bullet passed harmlessly through the air and bored a small hole into the ceiling above. Unconcerned, Hajime continued firing as he ran. Sadly, each of his bullets only served to put more holes in the ceiling.

The silver head scoffed at Hajime as it effortlessly dodged. Yue was a little worried about Hajime's uncharacteristically sloppy shooting, but she chose to believe in him and wait.

Once he exhausted a chamber's worth of bullets, Hajime took to the air with Aerodynamic. His leaps had grown more precise and he freely flew through the air, sticking close to the ceiling.

Tired of being toyed with, the silver head began firing auroras off at random. Hajime grinned as he dodged them with ease. He was reading the Hydra like an open book. And he had noticed it had to stop moving to recharge every time it fired.

"This is for hurting Yue. I hope you like it." He finished reloading Donner and fired all six bullets at once, each in a slightly different direction.

Six small explosions dotted the ceiling, and after a moment of silence, a section of it came crumbling down. Ten tons of rock hurtled toward the Hydra. And the Hydra was unable to escape in time as the rock rained down on its head.

"Graaaaaaaaaaaaaaaaah?!" The beast screamed in both surprise and pain. Hajime's timing had been perfect. He had aimed for the moment it stiffened up after firing an aurora to make sure it wouldn't be able to escape.

He had missed originally on purpose, and then had run around the ceiling transmuting it to weaken the foundations while also setting up grenades in various locations. His six shots had been to set off the grenades.

But he didn't stop there. He hadn't done all that just to drop a giant rock on it. He closed the distance to the trapped Hydra in a single Supersonic Step, then began transmuting the rubble around it to make a perfect prison. He transmuted the area around its head specifically to make something like a blast furnace.

He then threw his whole pouch of grenades into the blast furnace and shouted the following:

"Now, Yue!"

"Okay! Azure Blaze!"

A burning blue sun appeared within the blast furnace, consigning the trapped Hydra to hell. Hajime's grenades all exploded at once when the blast hit, dealing a considerable amount of damage to the silver head.

"Graaaaaaaaaaaaaah!" The silver head screamed in pain. It started firing light balls everywhere, desperately looking to free itself. But whenever it managed to break one of the walls, Hajime simply transmuted it back in place. It had just fired an aurora too, so it wasn't able to pull out another right away. Slowly but surely, the blue sun sank deeper into the furnace, purging the monster with a fire hotter than hell.

Sense Presence told him the Hydra was now well and truly dead. Once he was sure it was gone for good, Hajime collapsed on the spot.

"Hajime!" Yue tried to rush over to him, but her body was exhausted too, so she was forced to crawl instead.

"You pushed yourself...too hard..." Yue somehow managed to crawl over to Hajime. He could feel her hugging him as he slipped into unconsciousness.

❖ ❖ ❖ ❖ ❖ ❖ ❖ ❖ ❖ ❖ ❖ ❖ ❖

Meanwhile, as Hajime and Yue were fighting with the Hydra, the party of heroes was taking a short break from their dungeon expedition, and was resting in the capital.

The increased strength of the monsters they faced combined with the strain of scouting out an unmapped floor had of course taken its toll on the students, but that wasn't the only reason they had chosen to take a break. There was apparently also someone waiting at the palace to meet them. The Hoelscher Empire, which had shown no interest in the heroes thus far, had suddenly sent an envoy to greet them.

Kouki and the others were naturally wondering why they would send someone after all this time.

The reason there hadn't been any representative from the Hoelscher Empire, which was allied with the Heiligh Kingdom, when the heroes were first summoned was that there had been very little time between the oracle's message from Ehit and the summoning itself. That being said, the king had assumed even if they had managed to get a message to the Empire in time, they wouldn't have bothered to send an envoy. The main reason being that ever since its founding at the hands of a famous mercenary 300 years ago, the Empire has been a strength-based meritocracy. Adventurers and mercenaries of all kinds called that holy land their home precisely because they could make a name for themselves with the strength of their sword arm alone.

People like them wouldn't accept some summoned humans as their new leaders just like that. While the Holy Church did have a presence there, and most of its citizens were technically believers, they weren't nearly as devout as the citizens of the Kingdom. Since even the merchants and officials generally came from a mercenary or adventurer background, almost all of the citizens valued coin over religion. That having been said, they were still believers, even if they weren't as devout.

However, it was quite likely that they would've spurned the heroes had they met them when they were first summoned. That was why it was fortunate that Hoelscher's emperor had seemingly shown no interest in the heroes until now.

Their sudden change of heart had come about when they had heard the reports that Kouki's party had cleared the sixty-fifth floor of the Great Orcus Labyrinth, something no one else had managed to do before. When news of the historic breakthrough had reached the Empire's ears, they had immediately dispatched a messenger to the Kingdom informing them that they wished to meet these new heroes. Both the king and the Holy Church agreed that it was probably the best time to arrange the meeting.

Captain Meld relayed all of this information at length to Kouki and the others on their return trip to the capital.

As the students were getting off their carriages, a single boy came running toward them from the palace. He was around ten years old, with blond hair and blue eyes. He resembled Kouki in many ways, though he was more of a rambunctious little kid. He was, of course, the prince of Heiligh, Lundel S. B. Heiligh.

The young prince resembled a puppy welcoming home its owner as he ran up to one of the girls and started shouting at her.

"Kaori! You're finally back! I was waiting for you!" Of course, it wasn't just Kaori who had returned. All the other students on the expedition had also come back with her. Most of them were clearly annoyed that Prince Lundel basically ignored their existence.

Lundel had been infatuated with Kaori since the day she was summoned. But of course, he was still only ten years old. Kaori simply thought of him as a little kid who had grown attached to her. She had no reason to suspect his feelings ran any deeper than that. And since she was naturally inclined to look after others, she simply treated him like a cute little brother.

"Prince Lundel, it's nice to see you again." Even Kaori thought he resembled a puppy, with the way he craved her attention. As she smiled kindly at him, Lundel blushed bright red, but he still tried to look as manly as possible in front of his crush.

"Yeah, I haven't seen you in ages! Everything felt so boring while you were gone. You're not hurt, are you? If only I was stronger, you wouldn't have to fight for us..." Lundel bit his lip unhappily. Kaori no longer held any desire to sit back and let others protect her, but she still smiled at the boy's childish resolve.

"I'm truly happy you're so concerned about me, but there's really no need to worry. I'm fighting because I want to."

"No, fighting doesn't suit you, Kaori. Th-There has to be some kind of safer job you can do."

"Like?" Kaori tilted her head slightly. Lundel somehow managed to blush even brighter. Shizuku watched the entire exchange from the sidelines, smiling as she watched the prince's clumsy attempts to woo Kaori.

"W-well, how about being a maid? I could even make you my personal maid so you don't have to work too much."

"A maid? Sorry, but I can't accept your offer. I'm a priest, so..."

"Then how about working at the hospital? There's no need to

expose yourself to danger and fight at the front lines in the labyrinth, is there?"

The kingdom had a state-run hospital in the capital. It was located right next to the palace. It was quite obvious that he wasn't really worried about Kaori's safety. Lundel merely wanted to keep her close to him. Unfortunately, Kaori was too dense to realize that.

"I'm sorry, but it's only at the front lines that I can heal the injured right away. I'm truly grateful you're so worried about me, but I'm going to keep fighting."

"Hmph..." Lundel pouted a little as he realized he would be unable to change Kaori's mind no matter what he said. It was then that the thickheaded bundle of justice decided to butt in and pour oil on the flames.

"Your Highness, Kaori's a very dear childhood friend of mine. I promise I won't let any harm come to her," Kouki said with a grin, intending to assuage the young boy's worries. Unfortunately, he didn't realize that only made matters worse. To the smitten Lundel, it sounded like he was saying "Don't you dare lay a hand on my woman. As long as I'm around, I won't let anyone else have Kaori!" The hero and the healer. They really did seem like a dream couple.

Lundel glared hatefully at Kouki, as if he were staring at his mortal enemy. To his young mind, it seemed as if Kouki and Kaori were already lovers.

"How can you call yourself a man when you take Kaori to such dangerous places with you?! I won't lose! I'll show you that Kaori's better off with me!"

"Umm..." Kaori stared at Lundel, puzzled by his sudden outburst, while Kouki just stared at him blankly. And Shizuku, having watched the entire exchange, just sighed at Kouki's dense attitude.

Lundel ground his teeth angrily, and Kouki opened his mouth to try and smooth the situation over. But before he could make matters worse, a sharp voice rang out across the courtyard.

"Lundel, stop acting like a child. You're bothering Kaori and Kouki."

"S-sister...?! B-but—"

"No 'but's. Everyone's working so hard for our sake, but you're completely ignoring their feelings and trying to keep Kaori here... Don't you think you're being immature?"

"Aww... B-but..."

"Lundel?"

"I-I just remembered something I have to do! Excuse me!"

Unwilling to admit his own mistake, Lundel turned around and ran off. Princess Liliana sighed exasperatedly as she watched him go.

"Kaori, Kouki, I apologize on my brother's behalf. He must have caused you a great deal of trouble." She bowed deeply as she apologized to them, and her long blonde hair fell gracefully over her shoulders.

"There's no need to apologize, Lili. I'm sure Lundel was just worried about me."

"Exactly. I'm not sure why he was so angry, but...if I said anything that offended him, it's me who should be apologizing."

Liliana simply smiled awkwardly. She sympathized a little with her younger brother. The target of his affections wasn't interested in him in the least. Worse, his self-proclaimed rival in love didn't even care that he was around.

There had actually been quite the commotion when Kouki and Lundel had first met, but...that was a story for another time.

Liliana was currently fourteen years old. Her beautiful appearance and flowing blonde hair made her popular both within the palace and among the common folk. She was serious about her duties, gentle, and not too uptight about social standing. Despite her station, she was kind to the servants and maids, and got along well with people of all classes.

She was actually deeply troubled by Kouki and the other students' situation. Not only in her capacity as a princess, but on a personal level, as well. She felt extremely guilty about getting a group of unrelated children embroiled in her country's problems.

It took her no time at all to get friendly with most of the summoned students. In fact, she got along especially well with Kaori and Shizuku, and before long they had dropped formal titles and were calling each other by nicknames.

"There's no need for that, Kouki. Lundel's just a bit wild, so don't mind him. More importantly, welcome back, everyone. I'm glad you all returned safe and sound." Liliana smiled warmly at the students. Even though they were used to seeing beauties like Kaori and Shizuku in their class, the guys were still utterly charmed by her friendly smile. Liliana's beauty was accentuated by the refined air of royalty, something that few other people could hope to match.

The members of Hiyama and Nagayama's groups were both beet red, and even some of the girls were blushing slightly. The students were all overwhelmed by the fact that they were speaking directly to royalty, something they would never have gotten the chance to do in their own world. To them, it was strange that Kaori and Shizuku were able to talk to her like she was just another one of their friends.

"Thanks, Lili. Your smile alone is enough to blow all our exhaustion away. I'm happy to see you again, too," Kouki replied, with his usual set of clichéd lines, accompanied by his trademark smile. However, to reiterate, Kouki had no ulterior motives hidden in his words. He truly was just happy to come back alive and see his friend once more. In reality, he was completely clueless about the effects his words and conduct had on others.

"Eh, r-really? U-umm..." Since she was a princess, Liliana had gotten used to receiving compliments from all sorts of people. Nobles, foreign dignitaries, messengers, and even commoners praised her beauty or her intelligence at every turn. Hence why she had mastered the art of discerning people's true intentions.

And that was precisely why she was able to tell Kouki sincerely meant every word he uttered. The only other people that complimented her sincerely were her family, so she wasn't used to wholehearted praise. She blushed a deep crimson as she scrambled to formulate some kind of reply. That easily flustered side of her was also part of the reason she was so popular.

Kouki just stood there, grinning happily, once again utterly unaware of the effects his words had caused. As always, Shizuku sighed tiredly behind him. It was because she knew him so well that she understood that, even if someone tried to tell him, he wouldn't get it.

"Umm, anyway, thank you so much for everything you're doing for us. There's a warm meal and hot baths waiting for everyone, so please take some time to relax. The Hoelscher Empire's envoy isn't due to arrive for a few days, so there's no need to rush." Liliana managed to compose herself and give a princess-like response.

The students all began winding down, and slowly eased away the exhaustion they'd built up during their labyrinth excursion. They told their classmates who stayed behind that they'd defeated the Behemoth, and shouts of joy could be heard echoing throughout the palace halls. The good news convinced more of them to return to the front lines, and the labyrinth party's numbers quickly swelled. The ones who'd been away also learned from the ones who stayed behind that Aiko-sensei was being called the Harvest Goddess by the citizens because of how amazing her agricultural skills were. Aiko herself was embarrassed by the nickname, and didn't particularly want anyone calling her by it. While most of the students were glad to finally have a break, Kaori alone wished they were still down there fighting.

Three days after the students' return, the Hoelscher Empire's envoys arrived. Five dignitaries stood on the throne room's red carpet. The students who had gone on the labyrinth expedition, all the important nobles, and Ishtar's posse of priests were, of course, all there to receive them.

"Welcome, envoys. You are free to appraise our kingdom's saviors at your leisure."

"Your Majesty, we are truly grateful that you have granted us this audience at such short notice. Pardon my abruptness, but which among them is the hero we have heard so much about?"

"Allow me to introduce him. Sir Kouki, if you would be so kind as to step forward."

"As you wish."

With the necessary formalities out of the way, it was finally time for Kouki's introduction. He stepped forward as requested. Though scarcely two months had passed since his summoning, Kouki's build and expression had both become much manlier.

Had any of the maids, nobles' daughters, or members of Kouki's fan club been present in the hall at the time, they would have wet their panties at the sight of his dashing figure. There were dozens of noble ladies that had approached Kouki already, but his dense mind simply thought they were all nice people who wanted nothing more than to chat with him. He was the very incarnation of a dense harem protagonist.

"You're quite young. Forgive me for being so forward, but have you really cleared the sixty-fifth floor? If I recall correctly, a vicious monster known as a Behemoth guards the exit to that floor." The envoy that spoke watched Kouki carefully. He couldn't be too overt with Ishtar's eyes on him, but he was clearly suspicious of Kouki's abilities. One of his guards sized up Kouki, as if he were evaluating a piece of merchandise.

Kouki found the man's gaze disquieting, but he still answered their questions.

"Umm, would you believe me if I explained how we beat it? Or would it be better to show you the partial map we have of the sixty-sixth floor?" Kouki threw out a number of suggestions, but the envoy grinned boyishly and shook his head to deny them all.

"No, words won't convince me. There's a much faster and more efficient way of making sure, don't you think? How about you have a mock battle with one of my guards here? That'll show us the fullest extent of your skills, Sir Hero."

"Well, I don't mind, but..."

Kouki seemed somewhat unsure and turned to look back at King Eliheid. King Eliheid, in turn, looked to Ishtar for confirmation, who nodded solemnly. It wouldn't have been difficult to invoke Ehit's name and use the force of religion to get the Hoelscher Empire to accept Kouki as the leader of the human resistance, but having them fight him was the fastest way to clear up any doubts about his abilities.

"Very well. Sir Kouki, please demonstrate your strength to our guests."

"Then it's decided. Could you please prepare a suitable location for our bout?"

Once the match was decided, all of the members present shuffled out of the throne room and into the venue of the fight.

Kouki's opponent looked average in every way. Average height, average looks, average build. He was someone that would instantly disappear in a crowd of people. At a glance, he didn't seem all that strong either. The envoy's bodyguard drew his sword lazily and let it hang limply at his side. He didn't bother to take any kind of stance.

Anger started to build within Kouki at being underestimated so blatantly. He started off more vigorously than he had initially intended, thinking a powerful attack would make his opponent take the fight seriously.

"Here I come!" Kouki moved like the wind. With the power of his Supersonic Step, he closed the distance to his opponent in an instant and swung down with his bamboo practice blade.

An average warrior would have had trouble just following his movements. Kouki planned on stopping just before actually hitting his foe. But it seemed such consideration was unnecessary. The one who had been underestimating his opponent was in fact Kouki.

"Ah?!" He let out a surprised cry as he was blown backward.

The bodyguard was simply standing there, glaring at Kouki with his sword half-raised. The instant Kouki had let the strength drain from his arms to pull the swing short, the bodyguard had flicked his sword up and flung Kouki back.

Kouki slid across the ground for a few seconds before somehow managing to recover his stance. After that, he stared at the bodyguard in open-faced shock. Even if he had been focusing his attention on controlling his power, the fact that he hadn't been able to see the guard's attack at all was unbelievable.

The bodyguard lowered his raised sword and returned to his original defenseless stance. *I see. The reason I couldn't follow that attack was because it was so natural and harmless that my body didn't feel any danger from it,* Kouki suddenly thought.

"...Hey, Hero. You don't come from a fighting background, do you?" Kouki squinted his eyes suspiciously, still somewhat physically and mentally rattled from that last exchange. The bodyguard was regarding him with a ponderous expression as he haughtily asked that question. Though he stumbled over his words, Kouki managed to get out a reply.

"Eh? Umm, no, I don't. I was originally just a student."

"...And now you're Ehit's chosen hero, huh?"

He scoffed contemptuously and shot a quick glance over at Ishtar and his priests. Then, with those same unnaturally natural movements, he began closing in on Kouki.

"Prepare yourself, Hero. If you hold back again..." Goosebumps coated Kouki's arms. The bodyguard's tone of voice clearly conveyed what awaited him if he held back. There was a sudden surge of bloodlust, which made Kouki's instincts start screaming at him. He quickly raised his sword over his head, which was the only thing that prevented him from being decapitated right then and there.

"Ugh?!" There was the loud thump of sword against sword as their weapons met. The force of the man's unrefined swing sent Kouki to his knees, and he gazed up into the bodyguard's eyes, his thoughts paralyzed by shock. *How on earth did he get to me so quickly?!*

The bloodlust coming off the bodyguard was dense enough to be palpable.

"Ah... Eyaaaaaaaah!!!" Kouki let out an incoherent roar, and suddenly, large gouts of mana began pouring from his body.

The force of his mana alone was enough to push the bodyguard back, breaking his stance. Kouki took advantage of that opening and thrust forward with his Holy Sword. But milliseconds before it pierced through the man's skin, Kouki's sword suddenly slowed. It had nothing to do with the fact that he was trying to hold back. The slowing of his sword had been due to something more instinctive. The bodyguard suddenly narrowed his eyes. Then...

"Let's stop here," he muttered coldly. At the same time, he recovered his stance almost instantly, and blocked Kouki's desperate attack with a lazy flick of his sword. Following that, he jumped back and sheathed his weapon.

"Eh? Huh?" Kouki gazed at him blankly, and the bodyguard simply stared at him coldly.

"Hey, do you realize what it is you're going to be going up against?"

"U-umm, we'll be fighting monsters and demons and stuff... The ones who are making all these people suffer."

"Monsters and demons and stuff, huh? And you think you can handle that with such cowardly attacks? Doesn't seem like it to me. You're supposed to be the one who'll lead us in battle? Don't make me laugh." The man threw Kouki's words back in his face and criticized his shortcomings with neither an ounce of scorn or ridicule in his voice. He spoke mechanically, stating the simple truth. Even Kouki couldn't take this much abuse lying down.

"Don't you think it's rude to call my attacks cowardly? I'm serious about—"

"A kid who's afraid to get hurt or hurt others can't do anything. Don't go running your mouth when you won't even come at me with the intent to kill. You can't claim you're 'serious' with that half-assed resolve of yours."

Kouki shut his mouth, suddenly at a loss for words. He recovered quickly enough and was about to retort with something like, "I'm not afraid!" but the bodyguard had already turned around and was walking back.

The king and the priests suddenly started shouting, saying things like, "How dare you act so rudely toward our hero!" and, "How can you call the battle over when he hasn't even had a chance to show you his skills!" and so forth. Bolstered by the support, Kouki was about to begin protesting again, but before he could, Ishtar soothed the crowd with his aged voice.

"As you can see, our hero is still in the midst of his growth. It's unfortunate, but he simply does not have enough experience yet. I do not expect your nation to come to a conclusion right away. I shall assume the words you directed at our esteemed hero were for his own sake. I hope we can leave it at that. If not, as the pope of the Holy Church, I may have to sanction an inquisition against you. You understand what that would mean, correct, Emperor of Hoelscher, Gahard?"

"...*Tch,* so you figured it out. What a shrewd old geezer."

The bodyguard kept his voice low, so no one could hear his blasphemy. Then, he turned around and removed the earring on his right ear. As he did so, he was surrounded by a thick gray mist. When it cleared, a completely different person was standing in his place.

The emperor was a savage-looking man in his mid-forties. He had silver hair that he kept cropped short, and piercing blue eyes that reminded one of a wolf's. He was passably handsome and possessed rippling muscles that corded the entire length of his body. The entire room broke out in an uproar.

"L-Lord Gahard?!"

"The Emperor himself?!"

The man Kouki had fought was none other than Gahard D. Hoelscher, the emperor of Hoelscher. Eliheid massaged his temples as he asked a question, seeming nonplussed.

"What on earth are you doing, Lord Gahard?"

"Well well, if it isn't His Highness Eliheid. I apologize for not greeting you earlier. I apologize also for this disguise. I simply wished to ascertain this hero's strength with my own eyes. After all, his existence will play a vital role in our battles to come. Do please forgive my insolence."

Though he apologized profusely, Gahard didn't seem all that sorry for what he had done. Eliheid simply sighed and shook his head as he said "Forget it" in response to the man. Kouki and the other students were utterly confused. Even putting aside the emperor's incredible footwork and combat skills, everyone was treating his surprise appearance like it was an everyday occurrence.

"Ishtar, Your Holiness. As you so wisely discerned, my words were nothing more than advice for our young hero. I would never dream of belittling Ehit's chosen warrior. I apologize if I seemed too brusque; it's simply a bad habit I picked up from my countrymen."

Gahard's reply was so insincere that it could hardly even be considered an apology. Still, Ishtar's calm expression never faltered, and he bowed his head ponderously.

"As long as you understand," was the only response he uttered.

The whole event was then smoothed over, and the two rulers began discussing the affairs of state. Eliheid managed to extract at least a flimsy promise from Gahard that the Empire would support the new hero "based on the promise he'd shown," thus concluding the main reason for his visit.

Later that evening, in his private quarters, Gahard told his subordinates what he really thought.

"Man, that brat's no good. He's barely out of his diapers. The way he talks, it's clear he really believes all that crap he spouts about ideals and justice. What's worse is that he has just enough strength and charisma for people to believe him, too. He's the kind of person that'd kill without hesitation for the sake of his 'ideals.'"

"Agreed. I can't believe he honestly put demons and monsters together on the same level. If it had been a conscious decision, then it wouldn't have been so bad, but..."

"Yeah, he clearly wasn't thinking at all when he said that. In fact, he's the type that probably thinks ignorance is bliss. I'm amazed he's managed to live so long with that mindset. Maybe his original world was just one where that was acceptable, or maybe his strength has simply carried him until now. Either way, he's nothing but trouble. Unfortunately, we can't speak out against him because he's Ehit's chosen warrior. For now, we have no choice but to go along with that brat's whims." As far as the emperor was concerned, Kouki was no hero at all.

Gahard shrugged his shoulders, but when he thought back on how strong Kouki had been, despite only learning how to fight a few months ago, he reasoned there might have been some potential in him yet.

"Well, maybe he'll live up to his name after he's fought a few demons. We can make our final evaluations then. For now, we just have to make sure we don't get caught up in those damn priests' machinations. Be wary of that crafty pope."

"Yes, my lord."

Unaware of the true evaluation he'd received, Kouki stood outside the palace gates along with the others to see off the emperor the next day. It seemed like he was leaving right away, since he'd finished what he'd come for. He really was one spry ruler.

As an aside, it appeared that the emperor had run into Shizuku during her morning training and had grown quite smitten with her. He had even invited her to be his mistress. Shizuku had politely declined, to which the emperor had simply laughed and said, "Well, just think about it." It hadn't blown up into a serious issue, but Kouki had also been there to witness the event. When the emperor caught sight of him, he had just laughed scornfully. It was then that everyone present had realized those two would never get along.

Needless to say, Shizuku simply sighed.

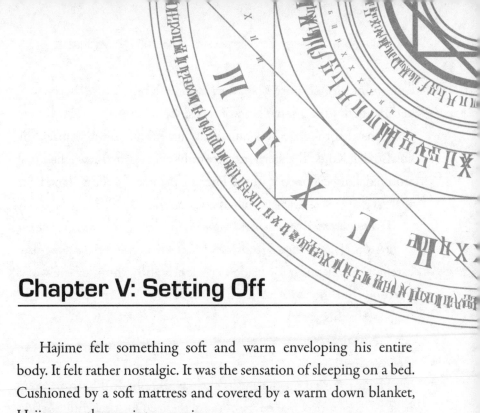

Chapter V: Setting Off

Hajime felt something soft and warm enveloping his entire body. It felt rather nostalgic. It was the sensation of sleeping on a bed. Cushioned by a soft mattress and covered by a warm down blanket, Hajime was thrown into a panic.

What the hell? I thought I was in the labyrinth... What am I doing on a bed? Still somewhat groggy, he blindly tried to grope around his surroundings. However, his right hand refused to move. It was wrapped in a completely different kind of softness than the bed and actually couldn't move.

What's going on? He experimentally tried to squeeze his hand a little. Between his fingers, there was a soft, elastic thing that molded to his touch. He found himself enjoying the sensation and began squeezing the soft object over and over again, when suddenly...

"...Aaahn..."

Huh?! He heard a sensual moan. His hazy consciousness was instantly alert. Panicking, he frantically pushed his body into a sitting position. As he did so, he realized he really had been sleeping on a bed.

A magnificent four poster bed furnished with pure white sheets.

The bed was on some kind of raised stone terrace. A faint breeze blew past his cheek. The view of his surroundings was blocked by thick pillars and thin curtains. It was like a bed had been dumped smack dab in the middle of the Parthenon. Warm yellow light, light that he hadn't seen in ages, spilled into the room.

I thought we'd just gotten done with our death match against the Hydra. Where on earth am I? Don't tell me this is heaven! The ostentatiousness of it all made Hajime instantly think of the worst outcome, but the voice he heard beside him a moment later brought him back to his senses.

"...Nhaah... Hajime... Aaah..."

"Wha—?!"

Hajime kicked off the sheets and saw that he had been sleeping next to a beautiful naked girl. Yue was sleeping peacefully beside him, her tiny body wrapped around his right arm. It was then that he realized he too was naked.

"I see... Guess I've become a harem protagonist... Wait, no I haven't! What the hell am I saying?!" Hajime acted out some kind of weird skit in his confusion. Somewhat disoriented still, he tried to wake Yue up.

"Yue, get up. Yue."

"Mmmf..." Yue mumbled incoherently in her sleep and clung even tighter to Hajime's arm. His right hand was getting dangerously close to a certain part of her lower body.

"Guh... Don't tell me this really is heaven?!" Spouting absolute nonsense, Hajime attempted to disentangle his right arm. But every time he tried to move it...

"...Mmmf... Mmng... Ah..." Yue moaned provocatively.

"Gah, I need to cool it. No matter how old she is, she still looks way too young. I can't let myself get excited over something like this! I'm no lolicon!" He repeated those words to himself, knowing it was this moment that would decide forever whether he was a pervert or a gentleman. Hajime gave up on freeing his arm and instead tried to wake Yue up, but no matter how loudly he shouted her name she simply mumbled in her sleep and continued snoozing.

Eventually, he started getting a little annoyed. How dare that little brat sleep so peacefully while I'm tearing my hair out worrying about where we've ended up!

Unable to bear it any longer, he screamed at her.

"Wake up already, you stupid sexy vampire princess!" After that, he activated his Lightning Field. There was a crackle of electricity and tendrils of lightning raced down his arm.

"Ababababababababababa?!" Yue twitched as the electricity jolted her awake. She quickly let go of Hajime's arm and opened her eyes.

"...Hajime?"

"Yep, it's me, Hajime. Morning, sleepyhe—"

"Hajime!"

"Huh?!"

Yue gazed blankly at Hajime for a few seconds before suddenly opening her eyes wide and leaping into his chest. With the both of them still stark naked, of course. He felt the soft sensation of her skin caress his entire body while a sweet aroma tickled his nose. He couldn't keep himself from getting aroused any longer.

However, when he saw her sobbing into his chest, he couldn't bring himself to peel her off. Instead, he smiled awkwardly and patted her head.

"Sorry. I probably worried you, didn't I?"

"Yeah... You sure did..." She clung to him for a while, showing no signs of letting go. Hajime reasoned that since she was the one who looked after him when he'd collapsed, she deserved at least this much, and so he simply continued stroking her head.

Finally, after Yue had calmed down, Hajime asked her about their current situation. He made sure she wrapped herself up with some sheets too.

"So what happened after we beat that thing? Where are we?"

"After you collapsed..."

According to Yue, she had crawled over to Hajime, exhausted from using up all her mana, and was clinging to him when the door suddenly opened by itself. Prepared to fend off a new wave of enemies, Yue sat there vigilantly, but no matter how much time passed nothing came through the door. Finally, she recovered enough of her mana to be able to stand and went to examine what was on the other side.

Even though the Ambrosia was healing his wounds, Hajime was still on the verge of death and in a very unstable condition. His abnormally powerful half-monster body was keeping him alive, but there was no telling how long the Ambrosia would be able to counteract the effects of the poison. Had new enemies popped out of that door, it would have been the end for them both. Which was why Yue went to go confirm what was on the other side.

What she'd seen on the other side of the door was...

"The maverick's lair." She'd discovered a very comfortable living space. After she had made sure there were no enemies in the area, she had carried Hajime to the bedroom she'd found and given him every last drop of Ambrosia that came out of the now dwindling Divinity Stone. Finally, it appeared that the Ambrosia's power had overcome the aurora's poison, and Hajime had begun healing normally. Exhausted, Yue had fallen asleep next to him.

"...I see. So you saved me back there, Yue? Thank you."

"Mhm!" Yue's eyes sparkled with boundless happiness at Hajime's gratitude. The expressiveness of her eyes made up for the lack of normal expressions by her.

"By the way... Why am I naked?" he asked, genuinely curious. He sincerely hoped it wasn't because they'd had sex. It wasn't that he didn't like Yue... He just wanted to make sure he was mentally prepared before he made that jump.

"You were dirty...so I cleaned you up."

"Why are you licking your lips like that?"

That seductive smile of hers was the same one she always wore after she'd finished sucking Hajime's blood. Shivers ran down his spine.

"Okay, but then why did you sleep next to me? And why...naked?"

"Eeheehee..."

"Wait, what's with that laugh?! What'd you do?! And quit licking your lips like that already!"

Hajime kept questioning Yue, but she simply gave him that same bewitching stare and refused to answer any further. It looked like she was having fun. Finally, he gave up and decided to start investigating the maverick's lair.

As they prepared to leave, Yue pulled out some clothes she had found while exploring earlier. They were men's clothes. Which meant the maverick was most likely a guy. Hajime discovered they fit him quite nicely and began inspecting what remained of his equipment.

One never knew what kind of traps they might encounter in a labyrinth. Yue finished dressing herself as well, and Hajime turned back to look at her.

All she was wearing was...a single long-sleeved shirt.

"Yue, are you trying to tempt me?"

"Hm...? The shirt's just too big."

Hajime supposed a guy's clothes would be too big for Yue, who was only 140 centimeters tall. However, the shirt hugged her body tightly, accentuating her modest breasts, and stretched only down to her thighs, leaving her slender legs exposed. Despite her young appearance, she looked positively alluring. Hajime was unsure where to look.

"...If you're not doing this on purpose, then that's scary too." Hajime couldn't tell if Yue was purposely doing it or not, but that charm of hers was frightening either way.

As he exited the bedroom, he was stunned at the sight that greeted him outside.

The sun was shining brightly into the room.

Of course, they were still underground, so it couldn't possibly have been the real sun. There was a giant conical structure hanging high above the ceiling, with a dazzlingly bright orb hugging the cone's bottom side. The reason Hajime's mind had instantly thought of sunlight was not only due to the light and warmth, but also because it had none of the artificial quality present in lamps or fluorescent lighting.

"...It looks like a moon at night."

"Seriously?"

The sight of the sun was so shocking that it took him a second to realize the sound of rushing water filled the room as well.

The room they were in was about the size of a baseball stadium, with the wall in the far back completely covered by a waterfall. Water poured out of a small opening in the ceiling and fell into a river below that flowed further in, passing through a cavern on the far wall. The rush of falling water created a refreshing breeze that blew pleasantly across their faces. Upon closer inspection, Hajime discovered that there were fish living in the river, too. It was possible the fish had followed the river's current and traveled there from the surface.

A short distance from the river was a miniature farm. There didn't seem to be anything growing there at the moment. Next to the fields stood a cozy looking barn. Though it seemed empty, it was clear that with the supply of water, fish, meat, and vegetables present, they could cook anything they were inclined to. The entire room was covered in greenery, and there were trees scattered about the area.

Hajime decided to explore the side closest to him first, and started walking toward a building located next to the bedroom they'd been sleeping in. It was more a structure carved directly out of the rock wall than a building.

"...I investigated it earlier, but most of the doors were locked."

"I see. Yue, don't let your guard down."

"Okay..."

The rock that the house was carved out of appeared to be some kind of white limestone. It gave off a very clean look, and another one of those light spheres was hanging from the entrance's ceiling. The light was a bit too dazzling for Yue and Hajime, who'd spent a great deal of time surrounded by darkness. The house was three stories tall and well ventilated throughout.

They decided to start by exploring the first floor.

There was a thick rug laid out next to a fireplace, a living room furnished with sofas, a kitchen, and even a bathroom. Interestingly enough, the place appeared brand new. Though they found no presence of other people, it seemed obviously lived in. The appliances and furniture hadn't seen use in quite some time, but it was clear their owner took good care of them. Rather than an inhabited dwelling, it felt more like a house someone simply managed. Hajime and Yue warily continued deeper into the house.

After a while, they found themselves standing outside again. There was an oval-shaped door that led to a backyard of sorts that contained a lion statue. The lion's mouth was open mid-roar. Next to the statue was a magic circle. Hajime experimentally poured some mana into it, and hot water jettisoned out of the lion's gaping maw. Apparently lion fountains were a staple of high-class places no matter which world one was in.

"This is basically a bath, isn't it? Perfect. It's been months since I last took one." Hajime smiled happily. Until that point he had never had the luxury of worrying about hygiene, but now that they were finally able to take a breather he realized he was filthy all over. He used the magic circle to pour out some more water and lightly wiped his body down as a temporary measure.

Still, that wasn't enough to satisfy him. He was Japanese, and like all his countrymen, he loved baths. Once they were sure the area was safe, he was going to take a nice long soak and cleanse himself properly.

Yue watched his growing excitement, and chimed in with her opinion on the matter.

"...Do you want to go in together?"

"I'd prefer to relax alone for a bit..."

"Mrrr..."

Yue was playfully kicking around the water, and Hajime thought that if she bathed with him his bath would be anything but relaxing, so he refused her. She pouted unhappily at his curt rejection.

Their examination of the lion statue complete, the pair made their way up to the second floor. There they discovered a library and a workshop of some kind. But the bookshelves and the door inside the workshop were all locked, so they weren't able to do a thorough examination of the rooms. They tried various means of opening them, but none worked, so they simply gave up.

After that, they climbed the stairs to the third floor and saw a single room set in the back.

There was nothing else on the floor. As Hajime pushed open the door, he saw an eight-meter-long magic circle inlaid on the floor that had some of the most complex and subtle inscriptions he had ever seen. The circle's design and layout were so detailed that it wouldn't have been an exaggeration to call the whole thing a work of art.

But what caught Hajime's eye most was the person sitting in an ostentatious chair right next to the circle.

Said person was clearly dead. The corpse had already decayed until nothing but bones remained, and it was clothed in a grand robe of black and gold. There was not the slightest hint of dust or grime anywhere on the robe. The impeccable cleanliness of the corpse made it seem more akin to a haunted house prop than something actually scary.

It was splayed out on the chair in a relaxed pose, with the skull's empty sockets staring down at its own figure. Almost as if the person it had once been had simply sat down there and died that way. The skeleton and magic circle were the only objects in the room. *Why'd they choose to come here to die, and not their bedroom, or the living room...?*

"Looks suspicious... What should we do?" Yue seemed concerned about the skeleton as well. Hajime assumed it must have belonged to the maverick that was said to live here. The strange thing was that he died peacefully sitting like that, as if he were waiting for someone.

"Well, if we want to find a way out, this room seems to be our best bet. Even Transmutation couldn't do anything to the locks we found in the library and the workshop, so...this is the only thing left to investigate. Yue, be ready for anything. I'll be counting on you if something happens."

"Okay... Be careful."

Hajime tentatively took a step forward. Nothing happened, so he kept advancing slowly. Then, when he reached the center of the circle, the entire room was filled with bright yellow light.

Hajime closed his eyes, unable to handle the intensity. A second later, it felt as if something was invading his head. He began seeing flashbacks of his time in the abyss, starting from when he fell all the way up until he fought the Hydra.

Finally, the magic circle's power began to wane and the light dimmed somewhat. Hajime opened his eyes...and saw a black-robed young man standing before him. He hadn't sensed him enter the room at all.

The magic circle still glowed faintly, filling the room with a mystical light. Hajime instantly shifted into a battle stance, but after a few seconds he lowered his guard. Not only could he not feel any hostility or malice coming from the man in front of him, but the figure himself didn't seem real. When he scrutinized it a little further, Hajime realized the robe he was wearing was the same as the one the skeleton had. That told him enough to guess who the man in front of him probably was.

Hajime silently gazed at the figure, waiting for something to happen. Finally, the apparition began to speak.

"I congratulate you on overcoming my trial. My name is Oscar Orcus. I am the man who created this labyrinth. I suppose to the world I'm known as a maverick." It seemed the dead man sitting in front of them was Oscar Orcus, the creator of the Great Orcus Labyrinth. Hajime and Yue stared—half surprised, half expecting it.

"By the way, please spare me the questions. This is nothing more than a recording I left behind, so I unfortunately cannot answer any queries you may have. I wanted to tell those who made it this far why it was that we, who learned the truth of the world, chose to fight against the gods...so I decided to leave a message. And this was the simplest form to convey that message in. I want you to know...that though we were mavericks, we were not truly rebels."

The story he wove for them was completely different from the history Hajime had learned from the Holy Church's records, or the stories Yue had been told about the mavericks. The revelations Oscar had for them shocked them to the core.

His tale was one of mad gods and their descendants who fought against them.

A short time after the Age of the Gods, the world was engulfed in strife. Humans, demons, and even beastmen all fought against each other in a never-ending war. Their reasons were as numerous as their battles. Land, resources, personal values, greed—but most important among them was theology.

In that age, the races and countries were split up into numerous factions, each of which had their own god. And it was each tribe's god that incited its people to fight against those who worshiped others.

After some time, a group appeared that sought to put an end to this centuries-long war. They called themselves the Liberators.

There was only one thing they all had in common. Each member was a direct descendant of one of the gods. Their leader was someone who had, by coincidence, happened to learn of the gods' true intentions. It appeared that the gods were using the various races like pawns, playing a grand game of chess with the world as their board. The leader of the Liberators couldn't stand their sickening disregard for life, and began looking for comrades who felt the same way he did.

After an arduous search, they were able to discover the location of Asgard, the home of the gods. There were seven among the Liberators who were exceptionally powerful, and they were chosen to be the vanguard in the battle against the gods.

However, their plans were foiled before the battle could even begin. The gods manipulated the sentient races and made them believe the Liberators were trying to destroy the world. They were marked as enemies of the gods, and every human, demon, and beastman considered them their mortal foe.

After a great many conspiracies, events, and dramatic encounters, the Liberators found themselves on the run. They couldn't bring themselves to fight the people they had sworn to protect, but those very people believed they were ungrateful heretics trying to bring about the end of the world. Their true names were forgotten, and they were known simply as "mavericks" in the annals of history.

The Liberators were killed off one by one, until only the strongest seven remained. With the entire world against them, they realized they wouldn't be able to defeat the gods. So they scattered to the ends of the earth and built huge labyrinths to hide themselves in. They created a series of trials, praying that someone who could clear them might one day appear, so they could bequeath their powers unto them, in the hope that these new warriors would carry out their dreams.

After he finished his long speech, Oscar smiled peacefully.

"I have no idea who you are, or why you chose to fight your way down here. Nor do I have any intention of forcing my own dreams of the gods' demise onto you. I simply wanted you to know what it was we fought and died for... As a reward for hearing me out, I shall grant you my strength. How you use it is entirely up to you. I can only pray you won't use it for evil. That's all I have to say. Thank you for listening to the end. May the 'blessings' of the gods never reach you."

Oscar's apparition vanished once he finished talking. At the same time, Hajime felt something strange enter his mind. The sensation was quite painful, but because he knew what was happening, he quietly let it enter inside him.

The pain finally subsided, and the magic circle grew dim once more. Hajime let out a long breath he hadn't realized he'd been holding in the whole time.

"Hajime...are you okay?"

"Yeah, I'm fine... But man, what a tale."

"Yeah... What are you going to do?"

Yue was referring, of course, to Oscar's tale.

"Hm? Nothing really. It was those good-for-nothing gods that summoned me here in the first place and told me to go fight in their war. I hate them as it is anyway. Still, this world's got nothing to do with me. All I care about is making it back to the surface and finding a way home. That's all... Did his story bother you, Yue?"

The old Hajime might have been more sympathetic to this world's plight, but the reforged Hajime discarded Oscar's tale without so much as a second thought. *It's this world's problem, so the people of this world should deal with it.*

That being said, Yue was someone of this world. Which was why, if she said she wanted to do something about it, Hajime might have reconsidered. His bond with Yue wasn't something he could discard as easily Oscar's story.

However, Yue shook her head without hesitation.

"My home is wherever you are... I don't care about anywhere else." She sidled up to Hajime and squeezed his hand. The warmth of her hand told him she wasn't just trying to be considerate.

Yue once devoted her entire life to her country. Despite that, she was betrayed by the ones she trusted most and left to rot in the darkness. None of her subjects came to save her. Three hundred years had passed since then, and all the people she knew were long since dead. For Yue, there was not a single thing left to care about in this world. In fact, much like Hajime, she had started to see the realm as a prison more than her home, after being trapped for so long. And it was Hajime who had saved her from that prison. Which was why she only cared about being by Hajime's side.

"...I see." Hajime blushed a little. He then cleared his throat and dropped a bombshell of an announcement.

"Umm, also, I think I learned a new spell... Some kind of magic from the Age of the Gods, I think?"

"...Really?" Yue said, amazed. Her surprise was understandable. After all, magic from the Age of the Gods was something the gods had once used, magic that no longer existed in the present day. Teleportation magic was from that age as well.

"This magic circle did something to my head, and it's like I suddenly understand how it works, kind of."

"Are you sure you're all right?"

"Yeah, I'm totally fine. Even better, this spell's a perfect fit for me."

"...What kind of spell is it?"

"Umm, it's a creation spell of some kind. It lets me add magical properties to minerals, and create new ore with special traits."

Yue's jaw hung open as she listened to Hajime's explanation.

"You can make artifacts?"

"Yeah, something like that."

The creation spell Hajime had inherited was the same magic people had used to create artifacts in the Age of the Gods. Truly, it was the perfect skill for a Synergist. Though Hajime didn't know it, Oscar's job had also been Synergist.

"You want to learn it too, Yue? You just have to step into the magic circle. It does this kind of thing where it runs through your memories. Oscar said something about a trial earlier too, so since we cleared it together, you should have the right to learn it as well."

"...I can't use transmutation."

"Oh yeah, I guess that's true... Still, it's magic from the Age of the Gods. There's no real harm in learning it either way, right?"

"Okay. If you want me to, Hajime." Urged onward by Hajime, Yue stepped into the magic circle next. It began glowing faintly and started probing Yue's memories. It must have decided Yue had cleared the conditions as well, since the apparition appeared once more.

"I congratulate you on overcoming my trial. My name is Oscar..."

Oscar's disembodied voice rang out for a second time. Having it happen a second time kind of ruined the moment. Oscar repeated the same words he had earlier, so Yue and Hajime ignored him and continued their conversation.

"How'd it go? Did you learn it?"

"Yeah, I did. But artifacts don't make much sense to me."

"Hmmm, I guess even ancient magic is useless unless you've got an affinity for it."

The vision of Oscar smiled as it wrapped up its conversation. It was kind of surreal, really. Hajime couldn't be sure he didn't imagine it, but it felt like the skeleton behind the vision looked somewhat sad.

"Ah, since I guess this house is basically ours now, we should get rid of the skeleton." He had no respect for the corpse at all.

"Yeah... He'll make good fertilizer for the fields." Neither did Yue. Though there was no wind, Oscar's skull fell forward another few inches.

•/• •/• •/• •/• •/• •/• •/• •/• •/• •/• •/• •/• •/• •/•

They buried Oscar's skeleton near the edge of the field and even gave him a modest gravestone. In the end, even they felt enough pity for him that they didn't just make him into fertilizer.

Once the burial was finished, Hajime and Yue returned to the two places that had been locked before. When they had buried him, they'd relieved him of the ring he'd been wearing on his skeletal finger.

It wasn't grave-robbing, since he hadn't been buried yet. The ring had a symbol of a circle with a cross splitting it into even sections engraved on it, which matched the engravings on the locks perfectly.

First, they went to the library. They were hoping some of the books would have knowledge on how to get back to the surface. Hajime and Yue broke the seal on the bookshelves and started perusing the volumes. During their search, they discovered what appeared to be the building's blueprints. They weren't nearly as detailed as a proper set of blueprints, but there were a lot of memos about what would be built where and how the layout of the house would look.

"Bingo! I found it, Yue!"

"Nice."

Hajime let out a whoop of joy. Yue responded happily as well, though with less intensity. According to the blueprints, the magic circle on the third floor connected to another circle that would teleport them back to the surface. It seemed that function could only be activated with Orcus' ring, though. It was fortunate they'd sto—*taken* it from him.

They also learned that cleaning was handled automatically at set intervals by golems that normally rested in one of the workshop rooms, and that the globe hanging from the ceiling possessed the same properties as the sun, so they could grow crops if they wished. *So that's why it's so clean, even though no one's lived here in ages.*

There were a number of artifacts and rare materials Oscar had been working with in the locked room of his workshop, according to the memos. Hajime decided to ste—*take* those, too. It couldn't hurt to have more items to work with, after all.

"Hajime...look at this."

"Hm?"

Yue had been looking through the other books while Hajime had pored over the blueprints, and she came to him with one of them in her hands. It turned out to be Oscar's diary. It chronicled the normal everyday life of Oscar and his six powerful companions. One of the passages in it talked about the labyrinths his six comrades had made.

"...So basically, that means if we conquer the other labyrinths, we can get all the ancient magic the other Liberators possessed too?"

"...Maybe."

According to his diary, his six comrades had also designed their labyrinths so that anyone who made it all the way to their furthest depths would be granted magic from the Age of the Gods. Unfortunately, it didn't go into the specifics of what kind of magic each had.

"One of them might help us get back to your world." Yue definitely has a point there. After all, the teleportation magic that summoned my class here was from the Age of the Gods too.

"Yeah. Now we have an idea of where to look next. Our goal after we get back to the surface is to conquer the other six labyrinths."

"Yeah."

Hajime smiled, glad he'd finally found a lead. He started unconsciously patting Yue's head, at which she closed her eyes happily and let herself be spoiled.

They searched around the library for a while longer, but they couldn't find any books telling them the exact locations of the other labyrinths. For now, they were stuck with the two whose locations were known, the Grand Gruen Volcano and the Haltina Woods. They could also start searching around the Reisen Gorge and Schnee Snow

Fields, where two other labyrinths were said to be hidden.

Once they finished rummaging through the library, the pair headed over to the workshop. There were a number of locked doors in the workshop, all of which Hajime opened with Orcus' ring. Crammed inside were all manner of ore, tools with unknown purposes, and work manuals. The entire treasure trove was a Synergist's dream come true. Hajime folded his single arm as he lapsed into thought. Yue tilted her head, puzzled, and asked him the question on her mind.

"...What's wrong?"

After thinking deeply for a few minutes, Hajime turned to Yue and answered. "Hmm, well I was thinking. How about we stay here for a little while, Yue? Don't get me wrong, I'm eager to return to the surface, too...but since there's all this stuff to explore and learn about, it might be better to make this our base and rest up for a bit. Especially since if we're going to be heading for the other labyrinths next, it'd be best to prepare ourselves as much as possible. What do you think?" Hajime was trying to be considerate of Yue, since he figured after 300 years of darkness she was aching to see the light, but she agreed rather quickly after looking at him blankly for a few seconds. Hajime found that a little strange, but she just gave him a curt reply.

"...As long as I'm with you, Hajime, anywhere is fine." It seemed she didn't harbor any burning desire to see the sun.

Hajime blushed and scratched his cheek when he heard her declare that so boldly.

With that settled, the two decided to stay there to train and prepare as much as possible.

❖ ❖ ❖ ❖ ❖ ❖ ❖ ❖ ❖ ❖ ❖ ❖ ❖ ❖

Soon enough evening fell, and the bright sunlight turned to pale moonlight. Hajime was currently soaking in the bath, letting his entire body relax for the first time in months. He'd been on edge ever since he'd fallen into the abyss. The bath cleansed him in both body and soul.

"Haaaah, this feels great!" This kind of carefree tone was a first for the new Hajime. As he let the energy drain from his body, he suddenly heard the sound of footsteps heading his way. He cursed himself for letting his guard down.

"I told you I wanted to take my bath alone!"

There was a loud splash.

"Hmm... This really does feel nice..." And then, Yue was sitting next to him. She scooted over next to Hajime, completely naked.

Her beautiful, porcelain-colored skin glowed enchantingly in the moonlight. That was the first time Hajime had seen her do up her hair. The exposed nape of her neck only served to increase her charm.

"...Yue, I distinctly remember telling you multiple times that I want to bathe alone, so why are you here?" Hajime knew the flush rising up his body had nothing to do with the heat of the water. He scolded Yue more angrily than usual, trying to hide his excitement.

Yue could easily tell what was going through Hajime's mind at the moment, so she gave him her most seductive sidelong glance yet as she replied.

"...But I refuse."

"Hey! When'd you get the time to read Jojo?!"

"......"

Hajime's retort came reflexively. Which, unfortunately, meant he looked right at her. Her slightly flushed skin filled his vision. There was a subtle blush painting her face, making her look all the more erotic. Her current appearance reminded him that she really was far older than him. He was already unable to stand, but somehow he was far calmer than he had been even when he fought the Hydra.

"At least cover your front. I know this house has a lot of towels."

"I want you to look."

"......" Hajime was at a loss for words. Her unexpected reply left him even more flustered than before. His lower half was raring and ready to go as it peeked out with a *You rang, master?*

"...See? Hajime, don't you want to look?" Yue followed up with another attack. Her pleading voice was slowly whittling away at Hajime's reasoning. *Master! Target spotted at 12 o'clock!* His breathing started growing ragged.

"U-umm, Yue. I'm not sure I..."

"...Am I not pretty enough?"

Hajime tried to reason his way out of the situation, but Yue cornered him with a very depressed-sounding follow-up. When his eyes met hers, he realized the sadness and insecurity in her voice had been real.

"Not at all. Trust me, you're really pretty. There's no way I'd ever think you're ugly!" Before he realized it, Hajime's voice had grown louder and he was nearly shouting. After he finished shouting, he suddenly realized how heated he'd gotten and realized it was too far too late to back out. Yue had the same seductive expression she'd worn at the beginning.

"...I see. That makes me happy. Because I belong to you, Hajime.

So look as much as you want."

"......"

Yue abruptly stood up. Bathwater dripped down her soft skin as she bared herself to Hajime.

Hajime watched a single bead of water trail its way down her body. It passed over her modest breasts, clung tightly to her slender waist, and trailed down her nether regions before finally running down her thighs and rejoining the larger body of water below it.

There was not a single blemish on her pale skin, and her proportions were almost perfect. She wrapped her arms behind her back, not trying to hide any of herself from Hajime. There was no way such an action wouldn't be embarrassing, and she was indeed blushing slightly, but she still stood there proudly, her body trembling slightly. It was the perfect combination of bashfulness and seductiveness.

Framed by the fake moon, her golden hair glowed around her like a halo. The sight was so perfect that she seemed almost divine. At that moment, Hajime wouldn't have doubted her even if she had told him she was a goddess.

At a complete loss for words, he could only continue to stare, clearly enthralled by the sight of her. And as Yue had planned, that was enough to blow away any last traces of reason he had left.

"Heehee..."

"Hah?!"

Yue laughed triumphantly, and Hajime finally returned to his senses. She was staring at the only part of his body that was being honest about his feelings, and he swiftly decided to beat a hasty retreat before his lower half got the better of him.

At this rate, he would get sucked into going at Yue's pace. It was precisely because he valued her so much that he didn't want to do something in the heat of the moment without carefully considering it first. As a man, he wanted to make sure he was ready to commit to Yue before having sex.

However, it was already too late for him to escape from the vampire girl's clutches. She flung herself at him, determined to settle things once and for all.

"Gotcha."

"...I-I can feel your—"

"I know, I'm doing it on purpose."

"Where'd you learn about all these cliches from?! Screw it, I'm getting out!"

He could clearly feel all of Yue's soft bits as she hugged him tight. He didn't think he could hold on for much longer. If he didn't leave, he would turn into a mindless beast and ravish the only person he held dear.

Unfortunately...

"You're not getting away!"

"Hey, wait! Ah... Aaaaah!"

The vampire princess wasn't going to let her prey escape. What happened after was...well, exactly what anyone would imagine.

⁕ ⁕ ⁕ ⁕ ⁕ ⁕ ⁕ ⁕ ⁕ ⁕ ⁕ ⁕ ⁕

Two months had passed since that fateful night in the bathtub.

Both Hajime's body and spirit had been reforged by fighting the monstrosities that inhabited the deepest pits of hell. But no matter how much the abyss might have toughened him up, he still had had no chance of fending off Yue's aggressive advances. So, in the end, he decided to simply accept them.

He'd known for a while that Yue had feelings for him. It was actually part of why he'd promised to bring her back home with him. Plus, he'd realized he loved Yue, but had given himself flimsy excuses—like telling himself he needed to keep his mind focused on the goal or he'd never make it back home—to keep himself from acting on those feelings.

But then they'd managed to discover a safe location to turn into their base, and a hint of how he could find his way home, so even that flimsy pretext had vanished. Without any reason left to turn down Yue, he could no longer resist.

Their idyllic lifestyle in the following months had been so full of coquettish flirtation that anyone watching them would have started tearing their hair out in annoyance. Around the same time, somewhere very far away, a girl was terrifying her best friend with an expression so demonic that it appeared as if the avatar of rage himself had manifested behind her like a Stand. It was an omen of what was soon to come.

"...Hajime, how does that feel?"

"Ahhh, yeah that's perfect."

"Heehee... Then how about this?"

"Aaah, that's good too."

"Then...this will be even better..."

Yue was currently giving Hajime a massage. An honest to goodness, non-erotic massage. They were both fully clothed, too. Hajime had modified some of Oscar's old clothes to fit Yue.

She was currently dressed in a short skirt that left most of her slender legs fully revealed. The reason she was straddling Hajime and giving him a massage had something to do with his left arm. His left arm that ended in a stump below his elbow. Attached to that stump now was an artificial arm. Yue was in the process of massaging the area around it to work the kinks out of it.

The fake arm he had attached to his left elbow was an artifact, and with the infusion of mana, it could be moved just like a real one. The arm had pseudo-nerves installed within it as well, and Hajime could feel things with it like he could with his real arm when he filled it with mana. There were lines of pure silver running down the black surface of his new arm, with magic circles and other engravings carved into the apparatus at odd intervals.

The arm was fitted with all sorts of interesting gimmicks. Some of them had originally been part of the arm when he'd found it in Oscar's workshop, while others were new additions of Hajime's own design. He had used his creation magic to materialize all kinds of specialized ores and added them to his arm. As it was now, his artificial limb was an artifact that rivaled the greatest national treasure of any kingdom. That being said, one needed the ability to directly manipulate their mana to operate the arm at all, so it would be useless for most people. Over the course of the past two months, Yue and Hajime had both improved their strength and equipment far beyond what it had been when they first arrived. These were Hajime's current stats, to put into perspective just how much they had grown:

HAJIME NAGUMO		Age: 17	Male
Job:	Synergist	Level:	???

Strength:	10950	Agility:	13450
Vitality:	13190	Magic:	14780
Defense:	10670	M. Defense:	14780
Skills:	Transmute [+Ore Appraisal] [+Precision Transmutation] [+Ore Perception] [+Ore Desynthesis] [+Ore Synthesis] [+Duplicate Transmutation] [+Compression Synthesis] • Mana Manipulation [+Mana Discharge] [+Mana Compression] [+Remote Manipulation] • Iron Stomach • Lightning Field • Air Dance [+Aerodynamic] [+Supersonic Step] [+Steel Legs] [+Riftwalk] • Gale Claw • Night Vision • Far Sight • Sense Presence [+Precision Sensing] • Detect Magic [+Precision Sensing] • Sense Heat [+Precision Sensing] • Hide Presence [+Illusion Waltz] • Poison Resistance • Paralysis Resistance • Petrification Resistance • Fear Resistance • Elemental Resistance • Foresight • Diamond Skin • Steel Arms • Intimidate • Telepathy • Tracking • Increased Mana Recovery • Mana Conversion [+Stamina] [+Healing] • Limit Break • Creation Magic • Language Comprehension		

A person's level was meant to denote their current degree of growth compared to their max potential, and was capped at 100. However, Hajime's body had undergone so many transformations after absorbing demon meat that after a certain point his level stopped growing even when his stats did, and finally his status plate had simply decided to mark his level as unknown.

It did make sense, considering his current stats would normally be unthinkable given the starting values he had initially begun with. His upper limits as a human had increased with his stats, so it was safe to assume that his status plate was unable to calculate the limits of his potential with his body so transformed.

As a comparison, the hero Kouki Amanogawa's maximum stats were somewhere in the 1500 range. With the Limit Break skill, Kouki could temporarily triple those stats, but even then, they barely came up to one third of Hajime's. And thanks to the Hydra he had consumed, Hajime could use the Limit Break skill too. He had far surpassed his overpowered classmates and become an overpowered cheater himself.

Most average humans had maximum stats of no more than 100 to 200, while those who possessed a job ranged from 300 to 400. Demons and beastmen could have stats ranging anywhere from 300 to 600 depending on the individual race and its characteristics. If the hero, Kouki, was overpowered, then Hajime had to be some kind of monster. With how much he had changed both physically and mentally, "monster" probably was the best description for him.

The artificial arm wasn't the only new piece of equipment Hajime had plundered from Oscar's workshop. Another handy piece of equipment he'd obtained was the "Treasure Trove." This was a ring-shaped artifact that had a small one-centimeter ruby set in its center. The ruby was actually an artificially created dimensional space where things could be stored. It was like a Bag of Holding, basically.

Hajime wasn't sure exactly how big this space was, but it was large enough to hold a decent amount. There had still been space left over even after he had crammed all of his weapons, tools, and crafting materials inside it. It only took a little bit of mana to activate the magic circle engraved on the ruby to add or remove things from it. Anything within one meter of the ring could be deposited, and withdrawn objects could be placed anywhere within the same radius.

It was a very handy artifact by any measure, but for Hajime it was especially useful because of his weapons. Because the ring could transport withdrawn objects anywhere within one meter of the ring, Hajime had toyed with the possibility of reloading with it.

When he had put his theory to the test, he met with limited success. While the ring wasn't precise enough to let him warp the bullets directly into his magazine, it could bring them out perfectly aligned in position to be loaded. So instead he combined his skills together to teleport the bullets into the air above his gun chamber and let them fall into the magazine. It was an impromptu form of midair reloading.

The only type of gun suited to that style was a break-action revolver. Unfortunately, break-action revolvers weren't as powerful as swing-out revolvers. However, reloading a swing-out revolver in midair was also far more difficult.

In order to remedy the situation, Hajime had created a makeshift kind of swing-out cylinder. Part of it swung out to the top to allow for midair reloading. By manipulating his mana, he could discard old shells as well. Then all he needed to do was spin the chamber and let the bullets fall into place.

It had taken him only a month of nonstop training to perfect this technique. And there was a reason he managed to master this superhuman feat in only a month. His Riftwalk ability. Riftwalk not only gave him the ability to heighten his other movement skills, but it also enhanced his five senses to their limit. It made it seem as if the rest of the world was moving in slow motion, which was what made midair reloading possible.

On top of improving his weapons, he had also crafted a two-wheel mana-powered vehicle, Steiff, and a four-wheel mana-powered vehicle, Brise.

As their description suggested, they used mana as fuel. Their frames were covered with Azantium, the hardest metal in existence. Both of them were loaded to the brim with weapons, too. For all his transformations, Hajime was still a boy at heart. He still had a burning passion for all things military. There had been times that he had gotten so focused on his crafting that Yue had started to sulk, and he had all sorts of fluids sucked out of him before she forgave him.

He had also developed something he called the Demon Eye. Hajime had lost his right eye fighting against the Hydra. The heat of the aurora had evaporated his eyeball entirely, so the Ambrosia had been unable to heal what at that point had become a "lost" appendage. Yue had felt guilty about it since he had lost it protecting her, so she had helped him develop the Demon Eye.

Even with ancient creation magic, Hajime was unable to reproduce an actual human eyeball. However, he had instead imbued a piece of the Divinity Stone with Detect Magic and Foresight, which created an artificial eye that saw different things than a normal one.

He then added the same pseudo-nerves that were in his artificial arm into his artificial eye, allowing for the images it captured to be sent directly to his brain. His Demon Eye couldn't see things his normal eye could. Instead, it saw the flow and strength of mana surrounding a person or object, its color, and the element and "core" of the spell they were trying to activate.

The core of a spell was basically the gist of how it was being activated, and the effect it was attempting to enact on the world. He had known that the effects of a spell were governed by the inscriptions inlaid into the magic circle invoking the spell, but until now he had never considered the possibility that the spell and the magic circle must somehow have been linked for the circle to continue directing the spell after it was invoked. None of the books he had read in the palace had mentioned anything of the sort. It was quite possible he had made a new discovery in the field of magic. Especially considering that even Yue, who was an expert in magic, hadn't known anything about it either.

Much like Sense Presence, Detect Magic as a skill only gave Hajime a vague idea of the position and amount of mana being used. It wasn't much better than an alternate way of searching for enemies. However, with the enhanced Demon Eye, he could pinpoint the exact amount of mana being poured into what kind of spell, and because he could see the spell's "core," it was possible for him to shoot it down and nullify the spell entirely. Shooting down a spell's core required an extreme amount of precision, though, so it wasn't always practical.

The reason he had used the Divinity Stone as the base material for his eye was because no other ore would have worked. Hajime's guess was that only the Divinity Stone could hold enough mana to maintain the spells he had imbued it with. He was still unskilled at using his newly acquired creation magic, which was why he had only been able to add two spells to the Divinity Stone so far. But considering how much mana it could hold, he suspected he would be able to add even more spells to it once he got better at using his creation skill.

Since the Demon Eye was made out of Divinity Stone, it was constantly giving off a faint blue glow. In other words, his eye was always glowing. No matter what he did, he couldn't seem to do anything about it, so he gave up and covered it with a black eyepatch.

White hair, a fake arm, and an eyepatch—Hajime looked like

some kind of edgy anime protagonist now. The kind that might have spouted clichéd lines like, "Be still, my sealed left arm!" When he had seen himself in the mirror, Hajime had been so depressed that he had spent an entire day moping in bed. Yue had to resort to some rather... drastic measures to finally cheer him up.

Hajime had upgraded his weapons too. He had remade Schlagen, which had been destroyed in the battle with the Hydra. He used Azantium for the frame and bullets, making it harder than before. And since he no longer had to worry about carrying it around thanks to the ring, he lengthened the barrel as well, increasing its range and power.

He had also added a new gun to his arsenal—Metzelei, a railgun-enhanced gatling gun. The inspiration for it had come from the time they had had to fight the army of raptors and hadn't had enough firepower to take them all on. It was a monster of a weapon, with six rotating barrels capable of firing 12,000 30mm caliber rounds a minute. He had used creation magic to form the barrel out of a special, self-cooling ore, but even then he could only fire consecutively for about five minutes before the gun ran the danger of overheating. Plus, it needed a long time to cool before he could use it again.

Also, as a way to gain complete combat superiority, and simply because Hajime thought it was cool, he had created a rocket launcher called Orkan. It had a rectangular barrel, and boasted a large magazine allowing for 12 consecutive shots. He could fire different varieties of rockets too.

He had also created a sister revolver to Donner, Schlag. Since he had a prosthetic arm, Hajime figured he could use two revolvers at once. His preferred style of combat was close quarter gun combat, gun-fu basically, with Donner and Schlag overpowering his enemies. The reason he had settled on close combat was to work more efficiently with Yue, who was a stereotypical back liner. That being said, he could fill any role in a party with the variety of equipment he had at his disposal.

Hajime had created a wealth of other miscellaneous tools and equipment. However, the Divinity Stone had finally lost most of its original mana, and had ceased producing Ambrosia. He only had twelve precious vials of it left. He had tried suffusing it with mana again, but the stone had refused to produce any more Ambrosia—the reason being that mana had to be concentrated in the stone over centuries in order for it to take effect.

But even then, Hajime didn't throw it away. It was, after all, the person—or rather, stone, that had saved his life. It was a sheer stroke of luck that he had found it at all, and without it, he would have died for sure. Which was why he was so attached to it. He loved it as much as that one plane crash survivor from a certain movie had loved his volleyball.

So instead of discarding it, he had made use of the fact that it could store boundless amounts of mana to make his Demon Eye. He had then carved the remainder of the stone into a necklace, a pair of earrings, and a ring that he decided to gift to Yue.

Yue could use extremely powerful magic, all without incantations or magic circles, but because she could so easily pour mana into her spells, she quickly ran out and became unable to move. But by storing mana in her Divinity Stone jewelry beforehand, she would be able to use them as a battery, allowing her to fire off powerful spells one after another without collapsing.

With those thoughts in mind, Hajime had presented the Magic Stone Accessory series to Yue, but her reaction had been rather unexpected.

"...Are you proposing to me?"

"You wot, mate?" Hajime was so surprised he slipped into some weird accent. "It's to keep you from running out of mana quickly. I made these to protect you."

"So you *are* proposing."

"How many times do I have to say 'no' before you get it? It's just equipment I made for you."

"Hajime, you're so shy."

"Do you just ignore the words coming out of my mouth or something, Yue?"

"...You're shy in bed, too."

"Can we please not go there?! Please?"

"Hajime..."

"Uh, yeah?"

"Thanks... I really love you."

"...You're welcome."

Almost all their conversations devolved into flirting after a while.

They had completed their preparations to the utmost over the past two months. Ten days later, Hajime and Yue finally decided to return to the surface.

As he began activating the magic circle on the third floor, Hajime quietly spoke to Yue.

"Yue...my weapons and our powers are probably considered heresy to the Holy Church. I doubt they, or the various human kingdoms, are going to just let us roam free."

CHAPTER V: SETTING OFF

"Yeah..."

"They'll ask us to give up our artifacts or try and force us to help them in their war."

"Yeah..."

"If it was just humans we had to deal with, it wouldn't be a huge problem, but those crazy gods pulling everyone's strings are probably gonna be after us, too."

"Yeah..."

"We might end up making the entire world our enemy. No matter how many lives we have, it might not be enough to come out unscathed."

"So what?" Hajime smiled at Yue's unconcerned response. She looked up at him, and he gently stroked her golden-blonde hair in reply. He looked deeply into her crimson eyes, and saw that they were glowing with happiness. After a moment, he took a deep breath, then spoke aloud his hopes and convictions in order to carve them into his soul.

"I'll protect you, and you'll protect me. As long as we watch each other's backs, we'll be stronger than anyone. We'll beat down anyone who stands against us and bust our way out of this crappy world!"

Yue held her hands up to her chest, as if carving Hajime's words into her own soul as well. Her deadpan expression crumbled, fading away to reveal the most beautiful smile in the world.

Her reply was the same single syllable she always gave:

"Yeah!"

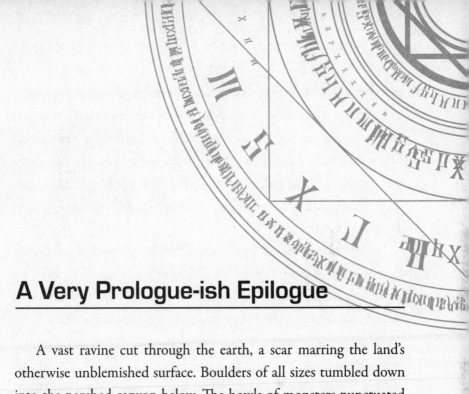

A Very Prologue-ish Epilogue

A vast ravine cut through the earth, a scar marring the land's otherwise unblemished surface. Boulders of all sizes tumbled down into the parched canyon below. The howls of monsters punctuated the air, reminding any who passed by that this was a land where only the strong survived.

This was a land where humanity's prized magic was ineffective, and food was scarce. Climbing out of the ravine required scaling a hundred-meter-tall cliff. A cliff that held no cover, and was filled with monsters waiting to feast on any foolish enough to attempt the climb.

There were staircases leading out on the eastern and western ends of the ravine, but once someone fell, the monsters lurking below had no intention of letting their prey escape.

To most people, the ravine was synonymous with hell. Though for some, it also made for a convenient execution ground.

A solitary silhouette suddenly moved within that godforsaken canyon. A pair of rabbit ears poked out from below a boulder. They twitched a little, as if searching for any noises. Such a cute spectacle was completely at odds with the hellish surroundings of the ravine.

After ascertaining its surroundings were safe, the figure tentatively stuck its head out from behind the boulder. Surprisingly, the rabbit ears were attached not to a rabbit's head, but a human's. The figure was actually a bunny girl in her mid-teens. After poking her head out, she looked around, confirming once more by sight that there were no dangers around.

She was quite beautiful. She was covered in grime and her shabby clothes were in tatters, but that did nothing to mar her stunning looks. She had light blue hair and azure eyes, and gave off this aura of majestic mystery. And that dignified-looking girl was currently...

"Ugh, I'm so scared. I wish I were in bed eating snacks right now." Her rather undignified outburst ruined the entire effect her looks had.

The bunny girl continued muttering complaints for a while, but then she suddenly slapped her cheeks and renewed her determination.

"If I don't do something, then it's my family that'll end up being the monsters' snacks," she muttered to herself, her eyes shimmering with resolve.

"...I've gotta hurry. I need to make it to that future, to that person." She straightened her back and dashed off deeper into the ravine.

A few minutes later, a pathetic scream echoed throughout the gorge.

"Hiiii! I'm not tasty, don't eat meeeee!"

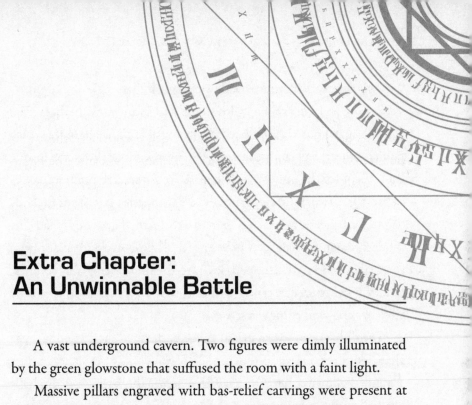

Extra Chapter:
An Unwinnable Battle

A vast underground cavern. Two figures were dimly illuminated by the green glowstone that suffused the room with a faint light.

Massive pillars engraved with bas-relief carvings were present at regular intervals, forming a passage around the two figures.

The moment the two figures stepped out from behind the shadows of the pillars, one of them hurled a burning spear of flame at the other. The burning spear illuminated the room, and bent its course like a homing missile to head straight for the second figure.

An instant later—*bang!* A red flash briefly added to the illumination as an explosive noise echoed throughout the room. A single streak of light passed through the spear, making impact with the core of the spell, and vanished into the ceiling. The spear scattered into a thousand tiny embers and vanished.

Unconcerned, the first figure quickly crafted a second spear, this one of ice, and flung it off to the side. The spear curved in a beautiful arc, heading for the second figure from around the other side of the pillars.

This one, too, was destroyed by a single bullet.

"...Hm. So I can't get you with single attacks anymore. In that case..."

The first figure leaned back against a pillar, her charming voice, golden-blonde hair, and crimson eyes reminiscent of a beautiful bisque doll. Yue—for the figure was, of course, Yue—created numerous balls of fire. One, two, four, eight; finally, she stopped at sixty-four fireballs.

It took her a mere two seconds to form that many. Had any modern-day magician seen how effortlessly she wielded such magic, their jaw would have dropped down to the floor. Being able to bring out so much mana instantly without even an incantation or magic circle was beyond common sense.

Yue didn't even bat an eyelid as she performed such a godlike feat. Then, like an orchestra conductor, she began waving her slender finger around. Following her finger's movements, the barrage of fireballs headed straight toward the second figure. A meteor shower of fire trailed a sea of sparks as it headed toward its target, Hajime.

"Tch. Don't you think that's a little overkill?"

He complained loudly enough that Yue could hear him. There was a sudden barrage of gunshots, and Yue's fireballs began to be shot down one after another. She had staggered her fireballs a little so they wouldn't hit all at once, but even then, it was a difference of milliseconds.

The fact that Hajime was accurately shooting each one down meant he had to be decently skilled as well. Or rather, exceptionally skilled.

About one month had passed since the day Hajime and Yue had conquered the Great Orcus Labyrinth and sworn never to lose to anyone again. They had spent that time preparing better equipment and training their skills. In that time, Hajime had practiced seeing through a spell's core with his Demon Eye, mastering two-handed gun combat, the art of the aerial reload, and the precision shooting required to destroy the spell's core.

He had been training with Yue, getting her to fire spell after spell at him so that he could practice shooting them down. At first, he could barely hit a stationary spell, but now he had reached the level where he could shoot down moving spells in mock battles. If he focused on just a single attack, he could shoot it down with almost one-hundred percent accuracy, and he was able to hit successfully half the time when attempting to shoot down a barrage.

His enhanced stats and Riftwalk's ability to increase his speed and reaction time a dozenfold were what made it possible at all, but the main reason he could acquire such an inhuman skill was because of his dedicated concentration in training that single skill nonstop for an entire month.

His unflagging zeal toward training stemmed of course from his burning desire to make it back home. Along with his wish to stay together with Yue forever. Yue had seen how hard Hajime was working up close, and the fact that part of the reason he was doing it was because of her made her unbearably happy.

"...Hajime, here's the next one." Yue lovingly muttered Hajime's name as she prepared the next attack. However, letting such emotions get the better of her during a mock battle was a grave mistake. Not because she let her guard down, but because she forgot to control the strength of her magic when her emotions were heightened.

"W-wait! That's way too many!"

"...Huh?"

Hajime's words brought Yue back to reality. It was then that she suddenly realized that she'd sent over a hundred fireballs hurtling in his direction. They were dancing around Hajime as they surrounded him, occasionally rushing at him from all directions simultaneously.

It seemed she had gotten a little too into their practice while thinking of Hajime. She had unconsciously created even more fireballs, and her happiness had set them dancing around him. Before she knew it, the attacks that were supposed to be part of training had become an actual barrage meant to hit him.

Unconsciously releasing magic like that wasn't exactly the same as being unable to control it properly, but it was close enough. And Yue, who had spent her life being called a genius of magic, couldn't stand that she had slipped up. But even that was because she wanted to be more useful to Hajime.

"...It's hard loving you this much, Hajime."

"Where on earth did that come from? Also, it's way harder dodging this many fireballs!"

Hajime was desperately shooting down the flames that were closing in on him. He was unable to shoot all of them down, and had to resort to dodging and swiping them away with Donner and Schlag. This was meant to be training that incorporated shooting down magic cores with the rest of his standard combat patterns, so in a sense, it made for very good practice, but...

"Crap—" He had been at it for over ten hours now, and the irregular dancing motions of the flames were bound to cause him to misstep eventually.

The sound of six gunshots echoed throughout the room, and six fireballs scattered into nothing. Hajime twirled Donner in his hands, planning on reloading his now empty chamber. But he messed up his reloading motion.

Another barrage of fireballs closed in on Hajime, and he had no way to intercept them. Because he had been planning on shooting them down and not dodging, he was one step too late in twisting his body away, and he had to resort to using Diamond Skin.

But before they even reached him—

"Okay. Time for a break," Yue muttered softly. She then snapped her fingers, dismissing her army of fireballs.

"Haaah... Haaah... Damn, I still can't get it down perfect." Hajime holstered Donner and Schlag, then rested his hands on his knees as he panted heavily. He ground his teeth in frustration. His real eye was bloodshot, and veins bulged prominently on his forehead from beneath his white bangs.

Yue wanted to congratulate Hajime on working so hard, but she knew words of praise weren't what he was looking to hear. Instead, she walked up to Hajime, sat down beside him, and gently patted her thighs.

She was currently dressed in a frilly dress shirt, a mini skirt, and knee-high socks. In other words, her outfit was currently showing off the strip of exposed skin between the top of her stocking and the edge of her skirt. Her knee socks tightly hugged the soft flesh of her thighs.

Ever since he had his chastity taken from him in the bath, Hajime had grown used to a woman's, or at least Yue's, body, and no longer got flustered over something as innocent as a lap pillow. However, that being said...

"You're not going to assault me, are you?" There was still always that worry. Hajime was currently exhausted from long hours of training. If she pounced on him, he would be helpless. It was only natural for him to be so cautious when he was living with a wolf like Yue. Though normally, the position of the wolf would be reversed.

"...How mean. You make it sound like I'm forcing you."

"You kind of did when you took my first...but well, I'll just stop there. Any more and I'm just asking for it." Hajime shook his head after saying that, then gratefully sunk his head into Yue's lap. Bliss spread throughout his body as Yue gently stroked his hair. *This is what happiness must feel like.*

Yue smiled as she watched Hajime relax, but she still felt a little uneasy about what he had just said.

"...Did you not like it?"

"Are you kidding? If I didn't like it, I would've just stopped you. I'm just worried about stupid things like a man's pride and stuff. You don't have to worry about it."

The unease vanished from Yue's eyes, and she replied with a simple "Yeah." She then gently brought her lips down on Hajime's forehead. Her lips slowly trailed down his head as she kissed his nose, then his cheeks, and finally his mouth. Any man without a girlfriend would have wanted to blow Hajime away with an anti-materiel rifle if they'd caught sight of that scene.

Hajime blushed and averted his gaze. Yue smiled playfully as she saw him shy away.

"...Then did you like it?"

"Hey, Yue, can we just drop this subject already?"

"So you didn't like it?" Hajime tried to change the topic, but Yue sadly lamented her own lack of experience and let out a depressed sigh.

"Umm, well...I liked it." Hajime looked as if he couldn't believe the words that had just come out of his mouth, but the fact that he couldn't bear to see her sad was enough proof that he was already hopelessly in love.

Yue looked relieved and gazed off into the distance as she softly muttered her thoughts aloud.

"Hmm...I should thank Mistress, then."

"I'm not sure if I should thank her or not, personally."

The "Mistress" that Yue was referring to was the one who had taught her about the world back when she was still a princess. Yue didn't know what had happened to her after she was sealed away, but her mistress had taken care of her until the day she was imprisoned.

The reason Yue was thanking her now was because she had also apparently taught her about how to seduce a man. Because she was royalty, though, she had of course protected her chastity for marriage. That being said, as royalty she had still had a duty to produce an heir. Which was why her mistress had taught her how to properly please a man. The reason Yue always had her way with Hajime at night was surely thanks to those lessons.

By the way, this discussion had started because Hajime had initially thought Yue might not have been a virgin. Thanks to her auto-regeneration, he had considered the possibility that even her hymen had recovered, but...Hajime would never forget Yue's expression when he brought the subject up with her. Even the monster of the abyss, the Hydra, hadn't been able to strike fear in Hajime's heart, but Yue's expression at that moment had terrified him beyond belief.

The result being that he of course apologized. What happened after he got down on his knees and begged forgiveness for ever doubting Yue, who had offered up her chastity to him, was of course more of what had occurred prior.

"All right, let's just do one more mock battle. We can go eat dinner after that."

"...Okay. Are you all right?"

"Not really, but if I don't push myself past my limits, there's no point to training, is there? Sorry for dragging you along with me, Yue."

"It's okay."

Yue had burned through a great deal of mana too, but she could still keep going, thanks to her magic accessories. Hajime was the one who was more exhausted, as continual use of Limit Break and Riftwalk had taxed his body immensely, but Yue didn't have the heart to try and stop him after seeing how determined he was.

He pushed himself off Yue's lap and walked a good distance away. He then pulled out Donner and Schlag, and got into his stance.

"Don't hold back! Give it everything you got, you damned monster magician!"

"Okay. Take this: Lots of Fireballs!"

That can't seriously be the actual spell name! Hajime thought, extremely confused. But though crude, the name was rather apt as countless fireballs started chasing Hajime down. The reason she wasn't using her relatively more harmless water balls was because Hajime had told her he couldn't get into it if the danger wasn't real.

The barrage of fireballs closed in on him like a wall of flame, and he quickly activated Riftwalk. The world began to lose all color as things started moving in slow motion. His Demon Eye clearly grasped the location of each ball's core.

Each of his bullets accurately pierced through the center of each spell's core. He teleported bullet after bullet into the air, rotating his chamber to make sure each fell perfectly in place. He fired and reloaded so fast that the movements blurred together into one smooth motion. By the time he finished ejecting one round's spent shells, the next set of bullets was already on its way.

Donner and Schlag's chambers were spinning almost constantly, giving off the illusion that Hajime was holding a round shield in between them.

Both the number and speed of the fireballs gradually began to increase. Hajime inwardly marveled at how much mana Yue possessed, but didn't lose focus for even a second. He ignored his pounding head and eyes, and increased the intensity of his Riftwalk even further.

"Yue, can I ask you something?"

"Sure?"

The two of them didn't let up at all as they began talking. Hajime was slowly getting a headache that had nothing to do with his overtaxed body, but it seemed like Yue genuinely didn't realize she was doing something wrong.

"Why exactly are all your fireballs heart-shaped?"

"......"

Yes, for some reason, all of the fireballs hurtling toward Hajime were shaped like hearts. While she was speeding them up, she also changed how they looked. Each one was crafted with the utmost precision, and it was a marvelous display of useless skill. When asked about her strange proclivity, Yue's response was rather unexpected.

"Aww... You shot them down." She manipulated the hundred-odd fireballs with just one hand while strangely rubbing her cheek with the other. Hajime naturally shot down the fireballs. Each heart-shaped fireball let out a depressed sputter of sparks before being snuffed out.

"I'm taking this training seriously, you know?"

"...So am I. I'm serious about pushing you—ahem—beating you down."

"You were totally about to say pushing me down, weren't you?!"

"...Your body's at its limit from all this never-ending training, Hajime. You need to rest. But I know you won't stop until you collapse."

"...I see. You're just going to ignore my last comment, huh? So?"

"...Yeah. That's why, I'm going to defeat you and make you rest...in bed."

"Quit licking your lips like that! I don't think I'm going to get any rest in bed tonight!"

It appeared Yue was serious about defeating Hajime this time, in order to force him to rest. She still hadn't answered why she was shaping her fireballs like hearts, and the way she was licking her lips suggested to Hajime that while she did mean to put him in bed, she had no intention of letting him rest.

Yue grinned wickedly and started getting serious with her magic. She started mixing in extremely fast wind blades, along with lightning balls that curved along strange trajectories. All of which were heart-shaped.

"Ugh, are you holding a grudge because I've been training this entire past week and haven't slept with you even once?!"

"...I'm not holding a grudge. I'm just a little lonely."

Hajime felt a pang of guilt as he saw Yue pout slightly, and he quickly realized he was going to be beaten around until he couldn't move, and then toyed around with in bed until Yue was satisfied.

Hajime was a healthy young boy, so there was no reason for him not to look forward to sex, but...he still had his pride as a man, and didn't want to be one-sidedly played around with. Therefore, he honed his concentration to the limit, focusing on intercepting each of Yue's attacks. If he could just hold out until Yue ran out of mana, then victory would be his, and he could protect his flimsy pride. However...

"Are you kidding me, Yue?!"

"Nope!"

Since this was still precision training, Yue wasn't using any of her intermediate class spells, but she was clearly giving it her all, judging by the force and speed of her multi-elemental barrage. The barrage of spells already looked like something out of a Touhou game. Yue's breathing was beginning to grow a little labored, but she still smiled seductively as she pushed down on Hajime, and cold sweat began pouring down his back.

"Even I won't stand for getting beaten down every time! I've got my pride as a man too, you know?!" Even he wasn't sure if he meant it in the context of their mock battles, or their nighttime battles.

Hajime's scarlet mana spiraled around him. He activated the skill he'd stolen from the Hydra, Limit Break. His stats all tripled.

"Mngh, you're good, Hajime. This is the first time anyone's stopped my full power barrage."

"I'm honored."

"Yeah... You always take my firsts, Hajime."

"Do you have to turn everything into a dirty joke?!"

Hajime's words were punctuated by short pauses as he fended off wave after wave of spells. Yue was taking this just as seriously, though. Her words had even been calculated to try and shake him mentally. She knew he would fall unconscious before long if he continued to use Limit Break in this exhausted state, so she wanted to defeat him as quickly as possible before he collapsed and needed Ambrosia again.

That being said, constant use of mana was wearing Yue down, too. Thanks to the fact that they were all elementary spells, she managed to keep the barrage going for a decent amount of time, but she'd still been burning mana constantly while keeping up with Hajime's training. And even if her mana could hold out, her stamina couldn't. While Yue's automatic regeneration healed wounds, it didn't recover lost stamina or mana. However, precisely because she didn't want Hajime to burn himself out, Yue pushed her strength to the limit.

"That wasn't your strongest?!"

"Nope. Anyone can use Limit Break as long as they have the power of love."

"I think that's just you!"

Not only was Yue's magic overpowered, her love was overpowered too. A curtain of bullets bore down on Hajime with increased speed.

Hajime still wasn't used to manipulating his prosthetic arm or using two guns, so he was finding himself unable to keep up even with Limit Break. Even if he could still see everything, his body couldn't keep up. There wasn't a single monster in the abyss that could pull off such a feat, so Hajime couldn't even count on past experience to help him. It was, in a sense, the perfect training for him.

Yue's spells slowly drew closer and closer before being intercepted. She began walking toward him, both hands outstretched as she pummeled Hajime with magic. She licked her lips seductively and tottered toward him like some kind of vengeful ghost. Hajime was determined not to lose, but even with her mana-deprived body, the Limit Break granted to her by the power of love made Yue unstoppable. Finally—

"Dammit! Stop alreadyyyyyyy."

"But I refuse."

Hajime was defeated. His slip-up was something he could have covered for in less than a second, but the sexy vampire princess wasn't going to give him even that much time. She stepped into his guard and quickly grabbed hold of him. Then...

"I win. So now I get to take my prize."

"Hey, wai—aaah!"

Hajime's scarlet mana dispersed, and not because he ran out. The barrage of spells scattered into nothingness, leaving only faint traces of mana hanging in the air.

The monster of the abyss added another defeat to his record today. Had he just switched to dodging, he would have easily been able to escape Yue's grasp, but the fact that he didn't showed just how much Hajime cared for her too. In other words, the real reason he could never beat Yue wasn't because he was physically weaker, but because he couldn't bring himself to mentally.

＊＊＊＊＊＊＊＊＊＊＊＊＊＊

The fragrance of meat and the sizzling noise of food being grilled wafted through the air. The pair were currently standing inside Oscar Orcus's kitchen. As one would expect of a master craftsman, Oscar's kitchen was so well outfitted that it seemed more like a modern-day kitchen than a fantasy one. Numerous artifacts that aided in the process of cooking were installed in various locations.

Hajime was currently grilling a massive steak in a frying pan. Next to him, Yue was making a grilled fish salad. She had her hair up in a ponytail and was wearing a white apron.

The vegetables added into the salad had been grown in Oscar's fields. There was some kind of artifact in the soil that grew crops at an accelerated pace, so the seeds Hajime had taken out of the Treasure Trove had borne fruit in only a week. That being said, activating that artifact had required a huge amount of mana, so only someone like Yue or Hajime would have enough to use it often.

Hajime hummed cheerfully as he sprinkled salt and pepper over the nicely browned steak. The spices were another thing he'd found in Oscar's Treasure Trove.

He gave Yue a sidelong glance, and caught a glimpse of her pale neck. He couldn't explain why, but he found the nape of her neck, barely hidden by her golden hair, extremely erotic. Perhaps the aftereffects of their previous "break" were still influencing him.

The word newlyweds suddenly popped into his mind, and Hajime shook his head, trying to banish the idea.

Yue saw him shake his head and tilted her own quizzically. Hajime bashfully turned away, and Yue smiled playfully as she grabbed the hem of her apron and daintily lifted it up.

"How do I look?"

"...Really cute."

Yue twirled around like a ballerina, and Hajime found himself unable to lie to her. Even though she was the one who'd asked, Yue blushed brightly at Hajime's unexpectedly honest response. Happy at being praised so, she decided to give him a little reward.

"...Then how about I only wear this apron?" An electric shock ran through Hajime's body.

Is this the legendary naked apron I've heard so much about? Hajime thought, looking at Yue. She was staring up at him, timidly fidgeting with the hem of her apron. The look in her eyes agitated him even further. At this rate, Hajime would end up taking another "break," so he reluctantly shook his head. Yue didn't seem disappointed at all, and instead muttered, "I'll save this for another night, then." Hajime pretended not to hear her.

Finally, their meal was cooked, and the pair began setting the table. They placed the dishes on a clear table made of crystal and sat down on some nearby sofas. The two sofas had originally sat facing each other, but Hajime and Yue had dragged theirs together so they sat eating next to each other. This wasn't just limited to the dinner table: Yue refused to sit anywhere that wasn't next to Hajime. It seemed she enjoyed being next to him.

"All right, time to eat..."

"Yeah. Good luck, Hajime."

Hajime had a look of deep resolve on his face as he stared down at the meat. Yue was looking at it worriedly too. Hajime bit into the meat while Yue watched.

"Guh... Gaaah." He groaned painfully as his entire body stiffened. He was biting down hard enough to break through his own teeth, and was trembling incessantly. He continued eating despite the pain, and every new bite brought forth new waves of agony. Yue worriedly patted him on the back and poured him a cup of Ambrosia.

"God, it's been a month and it still hurts this much to eat... Just how powerful was that snake bastard?!" Hajime was currently working his way through a piece of Hydra steak.

Every other monster he had eaten thus far had ceased to give him pain after the initial meal, but not only was his body still suffering every time he ate more of the Hydra, his stats continued to grow as well. Considering recent monsters had ceased to increase his stats at all, the Hydra must have been something special.

"...Hm. That monster really was different. I think all the Liberators must have worked together to make something like that."

"Yeah. It's a miracle we even managed to beat the damn thing. Seems to me like this labyrinth was designed to be beaten after conquering some of the others. You'd need magic from the Age of the Gods at your disposal to beat something like that, normally."

Hajime was right. Even with his monster-strengthened body, beating something like that Hydra would normally have been impossible.

The primary reason they had won at all was because of his weapons. His railgun and explosives boasted a strength that far surpassed his actual stats. Had he fought with traditional fantasy weapons like swords or magic, he would have been defeated for sure.

The other huge factor that had contributed to their victory was the Ambrosia. Without it, he wouldn't have even been able to make it to the lower floors. He would have died from the wounds the Claw Bear had given him. If not that, the Basilisk's petrification would have done him in. And even ignoring those, there were countless other situations where he would have died if not for the Ambrosia.

Last, but not least, was the fact that Yue had been with him. She could bring to bear the full force of her considerable mana instantly without having to chant an incantation or use a magic circle. She was the one who had covered for Hajime's weaknesses in wide-area attacks, and had saved him numerous times even before they'd reached the Hydra.

In other words, the three main things that had contributed to his victory were not his stats, but his overpowered weaponry, his overpowered healing rock, and his overpowered ally's magic.

Hajime finally finished his Hydra steak and looked longingly at the normal food laid out before him as the pain gradually faded. The fish had been harvested from the underground lake, while the vegetables were ones they'd grown themselves.

"I've only been eating monster meat until now, so even this tastes like heaven, but..."

"...Yeah. It would be better if we could get some actual food," Hajime said, a hint of longing in his voice as he stuffed his face full of vegetables. Yue agreed wholeheartedly as she stuffed her face full of fish.

Hajime had come from a culture that respected the art of cooking, while Yue was former royalty that had tasted the bounty of this world's culinary arts before. Both of them were getting tired of simple grilled, boiled, or fried vegetables and fish with just salt for seasoning, and had discovered just how hard cooking truly was.

"...I'm sorry Hajime. If only I knew more about cooking..."

"It's not your fault, Yue. You don't have to apologize. Besides, you used to be royalty. No one expects a princess to cook for herself. If anything, I wish I'd spent more time learning how to cook."

Both of them, one because she was royalty and the other because he was a student, had little skill with the culinary arts. Yue, however, was doubly depressed because she couldn't cook for the man she loved. She frowned, wishing her mistress had taught her how to cook too, and not just how to please someone in bed. Hajime scratched his cheek as he watched Yue pout and sink further into depression.

"Well, you know, my mom's a really good cook, so I'm sure you can just ask her to teach you."

"Ah...! Yeah. Yeah! Cooking with your mom sounds like fun, Hajime."

Yue's eyes began sparkling at Hajime's suggestion. She envisioned an idyllic scene where she was cooking with Hajime's mom while Hajime and his dad both watched from the living room. Then they'd all eat together, and his parents would praise their daughter-in-law's delicious cooking. Her fantasy played out for quite some time, and her usual expressionless mouth slowly loosened into a smile.

"Yeah, then I can count on you to make breakfast and lunch. My mom's the kind of person that only cooks dinner, so I always just had leftovers and stuff for every other meal."

"Yeah... Just leave it to me."

Since Hajime's mom was a popular manga artist, she was always sleeping through breakfast time and busy with work during lunch. Hajime was usually busy either helping his parents with their work or playing games until late into the night himself, so for him breakfast and lunch were always a groggy affair he paid little attention to.

But if Yue was willing to learn how to cook and cook him breakfast and lunch, then he could ask for nothing more. Back when he was still a student, he would never have imagined he might one day eat handmade lunches cooked by a blonde beauty.

Though I guess I did once eat a beautiful girl's handmade lunch. She kind of forced it on me, though, so I don't remember how it tasted.

He wasn't sure what kind of life he was going to live once he made it back to Japan, but the idea of going to school and eating Yue's handmade lunch certainly did seem appealing. In fact, the mere thought of it brought back faded memories that felt decades old.

Memories of when Kaori Shirasaki had offered some of her lunch to him when he had been about to take his afternoon nap. She'd also given him some of her lunch on the fateful day that they were summoned. Rather forcibly, too. Her actions broadcasted that bombshell of an announcement to the whole class, in fact.

Hajime had reluctantly accepted the offer. Of course, his classmates wouldn't stand for him eating the school goddess' lunch, but...they would have hated it even more if he had refused. Besides, Kaori had looked rather dejected as she got ready to put away her lunchbox.

He was damned if he did and damned if he didn't. Which was why he had decided to at least accept Kaori's goodwill, and had taken her up on her offer. All he really remembered of the time was cold sweat pouring down his forehead as he hurried to eat Kaori's lunch as fast as possible. That, and how she'd smiled as she watched him eat.

Suddenly, chills ran down Hajime's spine. He awoke from his flashbacks and realized that Yue was staring at him with a very complicated expression on her face.

"...Hajime, who was that girl?"

"......"

He wanted to know how she knew, but he also realized asking that now would be a terrible faux pas. A woman's intuition was one of the seven great mysteries of this world, and all excuses were worthless before it. They would easily be seen through. Without a doubt. Seen through for the flimsy lies they were.

"She's one of the classmates I told you about before."

"...Is she the reason you fell down here, Hajime?"

"Well, I guess she is in a way."

Hajime wasn't sure how to react to Yue's question, but Yue ignored Hajime's confusion and muttered softly, almost as if she were speaking to herself.

"...Have you eaten her cooking?"

"Kind of have, yeah."

"Was it delicious?"

"I honestly don't remember that well... I guess it was? She was known for her cooking."

"...I see."

Yue stared long and hard at Hajime. She then slowly started leaning forward, her gaze still fixed on him.

"Yue?"

"...She knows a part of Hajime that I don't. And she's even fed you her cooking. Plus, you know her well enough to think of her right away when cooking comes up... I'm jealous."

"W-wow, you're rather honest about that. Wait, hold up. What does that have to do with you leaning in to me like that?" Hajime said, feeling cautious, and grabbed Yue by the shoulders to stop her from pouncing on him. But Yue wouldn't be stopped.

"...Everything. I need to fill your mind with nothing but me, Hajime."

"No, no, no, Shirasaki just popped into my head because of the topic, we're not really—"

"It's okay. It won't hurt. We'll just be taking a little break."

"How many times do I have to tell you?! Those lines are the guy's lines! And if a guy does say that, then you know they're trouble. Restrain yourself a little, you stupid sexy vampire princess! Don't think things'll always just go your way! I'm a Japanese man that knows how to assert himself and say no!"

Hajime spouted incomprehensible babble while Yue bore down on him, trying to kiss him. He continued putting up his feeble resistance for the sake of pointless things like his pride or dignity, but in the end it was all meaningless. Somewhere deep down, there might have been a brooding edgy Hajime that was stoic enough to refuse her advances, but even if there was, he would never let it surface. Because he himself had already decided to accept Yue, body and soul, so he knew his complaints were all just for show.

As proof, ever since that night in the bath, he had never once been able to actually refuse Yue. Every time she had come to him this past month, he had always grudgingly ended up giving in. Even when he had been training his Hide Presence and Sense Presence skills, he hadn't been able to escape from Yue.

The one time he had seriously tried to hide from her, Yue had spent hours wandering the darkness of the abyss looking for him, crying from loneliness.

"Hajimeeee, where are youuuu?" she had cried like a child, rubbing her eyes. Hajime, who was surprisingly firm when it came to training at least, had still stopped their impromptu game of hide and seek almost instantly.

Technically he hadn't lost, but he might as well have. Especially considering what had come after.

Once he'd canceled that training, Yue had stuck especially close to him for the next few days. The amount of times she'd pushed him down at night those days were far more than usual, too.

Her mind was filled with nothing but thoughts of Hajime. When he was busy transmuting new weapons and bullets, she was sitting next to him sewing clothes from the cloth Oscar had left behind and the monster hides they had harvested. And she made sure, regardless of whether they were his clothes or hers, to make them conform completely to his tastes.

She made a point of dressing up in all of the outfits she made to show off to him too. At first her sewing skills had been crude and she'd had a hard time making clothes the right size, but before long she had become very skilled with her fingers. With her skills so greatly improved, she had started making very adult underwear to wear at night too.

She would give Hajime peep shows, blushing shyly while wearing the clothes she'd made herself, and those situations always ended in Hajime losing his will to resist her advances. His will thus broken, Yue's next course of action was without fail to then push him down.

There was another time that they went to catch fish in the river together, and Yue's swimsuit had charmed Hajime so thoroughly that she seduced him then and there.

Ever since that first night in the bath, it had become an unspoken agreement that they would always bathe together, too. Hajime was never able to resist Yue's pleadings, and always ended up letting her wash his back. She didn't stop at just his back though, and soon enough she ended up pushing him down every night in the bath.

Also, she grew aroused every time she sucked Hajime's blood, and unable to restrain her instincts, she would invariably always push him down every time she drank it.

He would try and refuse, of course, but...lately, he wasn't sure why he was even bothering to resist, and had stopped even putting up the appearance of rebuffing her advances.

Tonight, once again, Hajime's almost nonexistent pride and reason were overwhelmed by Yue's boundless lust and passion. Her next words were the nail in the coffin that finally killed his will to resist. Yue said, with flushed cheeks:

"...I just want to kiss you. Please."

"Ah."

When his lover looked at him with wet eyes and begged so earnestly, Hajime couldn't do anything to resist. Like a robot with its battery removed, all the power drained from his body. For a moment, his body was afflicted by the charm status, and Yue wasn't going to miss an opening like that.

"C-crap—"

"You're mine."

A man's screams of pleasure echoed throughout the stone house.

The monster born in the abyss had no chance of ever winning this battle.

Hajime walked out to the terrace and flopped onto the couch sitting outside. He mulled over the day's defeat while basking in the rays of the artificial moon. Naturally, there was a little vampire girl nestled snugly within his embrace.

Yue shifted a little in his arms so she was looking up at him. Hajime was breathing softly with his eyes closed. Though he wasn't yet in dreamland, he was quite close to it.

She felt something warm blossom within her chest as she watched him rest peacefully. The warmth grew into a burning heat, but rather than being painful, it felt wonderful. Yue let out an enamored sigh as she continued gazing up at Hajime.

As far as she was concerned, his very existence was like a miracle.

The sight of him glowing scarlet with mana when he had freed her from her stone prison was carved permanently into her heart. Her three hundred years of despair were nothing compared to her meeting with Hajime. When she thought of how wonderful their current life was, and how much more happiness surely awaited her, she felt it was worth suffering all those years of torment if it meant she could be together with him.

Perhaps to another's eyes, she might seem nothing more than overly clingy, or simply dependent on him. They might have thought she was simply exaggerating how much Hajime had done for her. But anyone who had seen the pair's meeting would have agreed it was enough to justify her behavior.

However, regardless of what others might say, Yue would never change her mind. Their opinions meant nothing to her. At that time, he had been willing to die for her, a girl he had just met. During that fight with the scorpion, Yue had decided that she would give herself to this man, the one who had willingly joined his fate to hers.

It was obvious, considering Hajime's circumstances and the situation he was in, that the way forward would be fraught with peril. But something deep inside her still told her he was the one. He wasn't someone who would use her as bait to escape his own predicament, nor was he someone who would end up as just a simple friend.

It was too clichéd for her to ever say it out loud, but if she had to put it into words... she would have said their meeting was fate. To her, at least, it was a fated meeting.

Which was why she wasn't going to stop. She was going to keep showing just how much she loved him. She was going to keep cherishing him. And without hesitation, she was going to offer all of herself to him. To the boy she had met after three hundred years of imprisonment.

Even if Hajime truly loved someone else, even if he made the entire world his enemy, even if he came to hate Yue, she would never stop.

"...Heehee, you'll never be able to escape from this vampire." If one were to sum her feelings up into one sentence, that would be it.

"Hm? Did you say something?" Hajime's eyes fluttered open as he heard Yue mumble something. She was half straddling him as she gazed up at his face. Hajime gently brushed a few stray strands of hair off her mouth.

He trailed his fingers across her lips and rested them against her cheek. As he did so, Yue's neck shivered a little.

"Nope, nothing," she replied.

Finding her reaction entertaining, Hajime started tickling the back of her cheek and the nape of her neck. Her moans slowly grew more and more passionate. Hajime was about to take his hand away, but her eyes begged him to continue. He cast his gaze around the room, looking for some way to escape, but he still gave in eventually. She sidled up to him like a cat, and before he knew it, he was caressing the beautiful girl lying on his chest.

Once again, Hajime had lost. No matter how much stronger the monster of the abyss grew, he would never be able to win against the beautiful vampire princess

Though if the saying "the one who falls in love first loses" really was true, then Yue was the one who'd actually lost the most.

They were both losers, but at the same time they were both victors. Such was the relationship between the monster of the abyss and the vampire princess.

**FROM COMMONPLACE
TO WORLD'S STRONGEST**

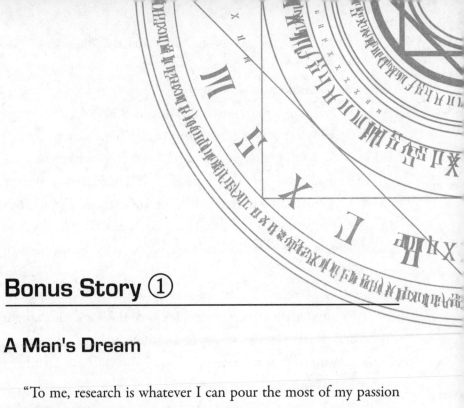

Bonus Story ①

A Man's Dream

"To me, research is whatever I can pour the most of my passion and enthusiasm into."

Those were the words written at the beginning of his research notebook. The faded gray binding and peeling yellow pages spoke of the book's age, while the numerous smudges and ink blots spoke of its extensive use. Such wear and tear spoke just as much about its owner's passion as the words written down in it.

Every single page was crammed to the margins with neat, slender handwriting. Research results, hypotheses, experiments—they were all recorded between the dull gray covers. But at the very end was a footnote whose very letters seemed steeped in frustration with the way they were written. It told of how the owner of this notebook had been unable to complete his research.

"Unfortunately, I was unable to achieve the ideal that I sought. I suspect most of it is that guy's fault. Actually no, I'm sure of it. It's all that damn bastard's fault."

Halfway through, the note went from something solemnly written to a grade schooler's whining. But if one has the forbearance to ignore such childish writing and turn the page, this is how it continues.

"To whoever ends up finding my notebook. I pray that you, like me, are one who chases after the truth. I leave all of my research behind in the hopes that you will complete what I could not. That you will be able to achieve the ideals I sought. I beg of you, don't let my research end in vain."

A faint "Hmmm" broke the silence as the boy reading the notebook finished the last sentence. He closed the book with a slight thump and gazed up at the ceiling, lost in thought.

"Don't worry, I'll clear up any lingering regrets you have. I'll inherit your will and finish what you started."

The boy's whispered mutterings were soon swallowed up by the vast silence of the room, but the determination behind them lingered. From the corner of the room, a pair of lifeless, mechanical eyes quietly watched over the boy.

Clanking noises echoed throughout the room. Hajime Nagumo was currently engrossed in putting together a plethora of newly crafted mechanical parts. He was sitting in Oscar Orcus' workshop, located at the very bottom of the Great Orcus Labyrinth.

Gouts of crimson mana illuminated the room at odd intervals as he continued transmuting. There was a golden-haired beauty sitting next to him watching the whole spectacle. At the same time, her slender fingers were skillfully sewing something. Said beauty was none other than Yue—the vampire princess Hajime had rescued in the depths of hell.

While Hajime was busy checking over his new equipment, Yue was putting the finishing touches on their wardrobe. She had sewed them some sturdy travel clothes, some more comfortable everyday wear, and even some more suggestive outfits for their nighttime adventures. Sewing had become like second nature to her after so many days spent practicing.

"...Perfect, it's done."

Hajime's satisfied voice echoed throughout the quiet room. Yue stopped what she was doing to look over at him, and saw that he was experimentally flexing his artificial arm.

"You finished your arm upgrades?"

"Yeah. I'm gonna give it a test run. Wanna watch?"

"Okay."

The artifact Hajime had created combined his knowledge of modern weaponry with his game sense and the magic of this world to create something truly fearsome. Because it all used knowledge from another world, Yue found each and every one of his inventions to be fascinating. It had been even more exciting recently, as ever since Hajime had finished transmuting all the necessities they'd need for their journey, he'd been spending a long time thinking about what else to add to his arm to make life simpler.

Hajime made a metallic fist with his hand and thrust it out toward one of the practice targets lying around the workshop. Though it was still a bit rough around the edges, his fist boasted quite a large amount of firepower.

He grinned playfully as he saw how excited Yue was.

"Here, we go! This is every man's dream! Rocket punch!" With a low bang, his left fist burst out of its socket and flew toward the target.

It left a trail of sparks in its wake as it rocketed forward. Then, with a thunderous crash, the fist pulverized its target.

Hajime grinned like a little boy and poured mana into his left arm. As if connected by an invisible thread, his hand zoomed back into place. There was a satisfying robotic clunk as it reattached itself to his arm.

"What do you think?" Hajime asked Yue. He was certain she must have been just as moved as he was. However...

"...That's it?" All he received was a somewhat puzzled reply. If anything, she seemed a little disappointed, even. Her indifference left Hajime nearly speechless.

"Wh-What do you mean, that's it? Wasn't that amazing? I just threw out a rocket punch! It's the kind of awesome move that one-shots your enemy and then comes flying back to you!"

"But...your railgun's stronger."

Hajime was left scrambling, trying to explain the appeal of his rocket punch, but he only succeeded in leaving Yue even more confused. Her unintentionally cutting reply left him mentally defeated.

At a loss for words, Hajime could only stare blankly at Yue for a few minutes before going "Wait, there's still more!" and suddenly smiling.

"It's true that it doesn't have much power compared to the railgun, but there's a huge surprise factor associated with having a fist suddenly come flying at your face."

"But the railgun's faster too. Wouldn't it be an even better surprise attack?"

Another flawless rebuttal. Hajime was swaying unsteadily, but he wasn't down yet! He refused to abandon his romantic notions of the rocket punch.

"I-It'll come in handy in case I ever lose my weapon!"

"So losing your hand as well counts as coming in *handy*?"

"......"

"Besides, even if you did lose your gun, it'd be faster to use Supersonic Step to get in close and hit them directly with your Steel Arms skill or something."

Hajime detached his left hand and threw it to the ground. He then reached into his Treasure Trove and pulled out a different left hand before smiling dangerously at Yue and brandishing his new hand.

"Fine, Yue. Challenge accepted."

"...What? I'm sorry Hajime, I have no idea what you're saying."

"You might be right, the rocket punch might just be a little too weak a weapon for me, though I'm sure for *anyone* else it would be perfect...but anyway, let me show you my other new weapon. Feel free to faint in awe at any time."

"...Umm, I still don't—"

Yue was only getting more confused by Hajime's nonsensical declarations. But for the sake of a man's dream, he couldn't back down. He started pouring mana into his arm, and his hand started glowing a hot red. His fist was burning bright with the heat of a man's dreams. This was his second new weapon.

"Heat knuckle!" Hajime's expression was as dazzling as his blazing fist. However...

"Umm...so what else does it do?" For some reason, Yue was asking for more. She was scratching her cheek awkwardly, and it was clear her soul had not been in the least bit moved by Hajime's stunning display.

Hajime's smile stiffened a little.

"...Okay, so see here, Yue. This is a fist that can melt literally anything it touches. Isn't it cool?"

"...Why melt them when you can just kill them?"

A very apt question. Hajime's brute strength and skills would be more than enough to annihilate most enemies. There was no need to add insult to injury and melt the opponent too. In fact, his vibration cannon and railgun were already strong enough. That was why most of his previous additions to his arm had been developed with convenience in mind more than anything else.

However, somewhere along the way he had let his boyish dreams get the better of him, and had started adding these useless features. Now he had to stare down Yue and prove their worth. Hajime turned off his heat knuckle and put both hands on Yue's slender shoulders.

"Think about it, Yue. What if we have to fight something that resists physical attacks really well, like that scorpion from before? If I have this, just touching it will still cause it damage. Or if we somehow get trapped inside a dungeon somewhere, this'll help us quickly dig our way out."

"...Okay."

Yue could feel the passionate fervor in Hajime's voice. But still, she thought to herself, *Couldn't you just use Lightning Field or Transmutation or something to get us out of those situations anyway?* She didn't say it aloud this time though, realizing it must be important to him somehow. And because she loved him, Yue smiled awkwardly and tried to reassure Hajime's flagging confidence.

"...Y-yeah, it's pretty cool."

"......"

Hajime wordlessly took off this hand too, then threw it to the ground. Clearly he wasn't looking for sympathy. Undaunted, he pulled yet another hand out of his Treasure Trove. He gave Yue a smile that screamed "This one'll knock your socks off for sure!" and activated it. This hand turned his arm into a drill.

"Behold, Yue, my final form! Everything you saw before was nothing more than the prelude. Be swept away in a torrent of emotion as you're regaled by my final arm!"

His speech was getting more and more cringeworthy by the second, though he wasn't aware of it himself. He then poured mana into his arm, activating the third of his "real men's weapons" series—

"This is the power of my transforming drill!"

He looked over at Yue triumphantly while his drill-arm began spinning. *This time for sure, she has to be impressed.* Or so he thought.

"...Yeah. It's cool. It's okay, you can stop now."

".....' There was an almost cruel kindness in Yue's eyes as she gently told Hajime it was okay.

As far as Yue was concerned, all of his new items seemed pointless. That being said, there was no telling what the future had in store for them, so maybe even useless-looking things might have some value later down the road. Surely their time to shine would come eventually. Deep inside her heart, Yue hoped it would, for Hajime's sake if nothing else.

However, Yue's pity only served to put cracks in Hajime's pure heart. *Don't tell me I'm actually becoming some kind of delusional idiot?*

No matter what the truth was, a bullet, once fired, could never be taken back. Half desperate, he started taking out all the other arms he'd developed. Among them were a dragon-shaped hand, one that fired water blasts from its fingers, and even one that transformed his left arm into Squall's gunblade. But the only reaction any of those ever elicited from Yue was a pitying smile.

Finally, Hajime crumbled into a sobbing heap, and Yue simply sat there patting his head, saying, "It's okay, it's okay." She comforted him until he finally regained his senses.

Just what exactly she had meant by "It's okay" was something he didn't want to think too deeply about.

❖ ❖ ❖ ❖ ❖ ❖ ❖ ❖ ❖ ❖ ❖ ❖ ❖ ❖

It was late at night. There was a single figure working in the darkness, inside a hidden room whose entrance was covered by a shelf.

"It's finally done." Hajime muttered softly. Sitting before him was a silver-haired girl. One could tell with just a glance that she wasn't human. Where her ears would have been were instead metal rectangles that kind of resembled antennas.

Her hard, metallic eyes bore no signs of sentience either. That was only natural though, as she was a cleaning golem Oscar had made long ago.

However, her features were still quite human. She had on a navy blue one-piece dress and a pure white apron. There was a headdress adorning her hair as well. In a word, she was a maid.

"Oscar. It was because you dreamed of making her real that you strayed so far from reality. That was your mistake. However, I have the knowledge granted to me by the 2D world. By making her somewhat unrealistic, she grows closer to the ideal... This is the answer you sought after for so long!"

Hajime whispered to himself triumphantly. Anyone who had seen him at that moment would have been pretty creeped out by him. However, his passion for this maid golem was real. When he had first discovered Oscar's notebook and this golem, he had decided to inherit Oscar's pure spirit of inquiry and complete what Oscar had begun. He had worked on her late into every night, making sure Yue didn't find out. He surely deserved a few moments to admire his own craftsmanship after all the hardships he went through to complete her.

However, as he was basking in his own handiwork—

"...Found you, Hajime."

Light filled the room as he heard a familiar voice call his name. He jumped with a start, then stiffly turned to look back at Yue.

"Y-Yue... What are you doing here? I could have sworn I felt your presence in the bedroom still."

"I was wondering where you were going every night. Not only did you sneak away using Hide Presence, you even left behind an artifact that faked your presence too. I didn't think there'd be a secret room here...but fortunately, this artifact helped me find you."

"So you used my own artifact against me."

Hajime ground his teeth, angry at his own carelessness. In the meantime, Yue gazed silently at the maid golem. Hajime gulped guiltily. He felt like a husband caught cheating on his wife.

"Hajime, if you liked maid uniforms, you just had to tell me." There was a little jealousy in her tone. It seemed she really was jealous of this inanimate golem. However, it wasn't what she was thinking. In order to clear up the misunderstanding, Hajime began explaining himself.

"Yue, allow me to explain. I don't actually have a thing for maid uniforms. This is about art."

"...Art?"

"Correct. A maid that's also a golem. In other words, a golem maid is every man's dream. Those two factors combined are what make it art. Just a maid or just a golem are nothing on their own. While they may have a certain appeal, only when put together as a golem maid do they become a true object of worship for men worldwide."

As he spoke, Hajime grew more and more heated with his words. Yue listened to it all seriously and nodded knowingly once he'd finished. "I understand," was all she said. Hajime let out a relieved smile, but then an instant later a blazing fireball flew past his cheek.

There was a thunderous explosion, and Hajime quickly turned around to see his precious golem maid burned to ashes.

"H-how could you..."

Hajime crumbled to his knees as he gazed upon the charred husk of what had once been a golem maid. Then he turned to Yue, who had started casually walking away, and asked in a voice full of sadness,

"Yue, why? Why would you do that? What did that poor golem ever do to you?"

"You've been acting weird recently, Hajime. You needed a little traini—Ahem, I mean, lesson."

It was true that Hajime's obsessions with things that were "every man's dream" was starting to get a bit excessive. It might have been brought on in part due to the dead end he'd hit in regards to his transmutation, but if he didn't drag himself back to reality, he'd be stuck in a fantasy land forever. The fact that he was actually sad at the destruction of an inanimate golem was proof enough that he was already almost too far gone.

Having the girl he loved tell him "you've been acting weird" to his face brought him back to his senses, though. Meanwhile, Yue picked up one of the maid uniforms lying around and brought it up to see if it would fit. She did a little twirl and licked her lips seductively as she looked at Hajime. Her sex drive was in full throttle.

Her next words blew away whatever might have survived of Hajime's reason.

"Shall I teach you just how much better a real maid is than a mechanical one, Master?"

"......" Cold sweat ran down his forehead.

For hours later, Hajime's screams could be heard echoing throughout the bottom of hell. Thanks to the loving embrace of Yue, Hajime was able to return from the depths of his delusions.

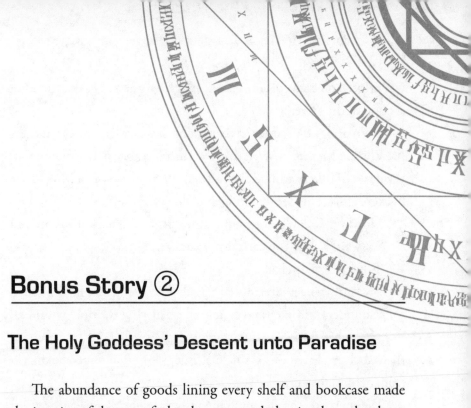

Bonus Story ②

The Holy Goddess' Descent unto Paradise

The abundance of goods lining every shelf and bookcase made the interior of the store feel rather cramped, despite the rather large amount of floor space. In the background, a popular anime song was playing, loud enough to be heard but not enough to be obtrusive. This store was famous nationwide for its selection of anime, manga, and other such products.

Naturally, the inside of the store was filled with pilgrims making the trek to this holy land. Most of them could be classified either as "warriors" or as "gentlemen." A few of them had brought their friends along as well, and the store was filled to the brim with heated arguments about who was Best Girl, or what the anime of the season was.

Within that eternal battlefield there existed a single haven of peace and quiet. At the very back of the store was a special section roped off behind a pair of curtains. A big "No minors" allowed sign was printed on each curtain. As one may have guessed, it was the adult section of the store.

No matter how hardened a veteran one was, their voices naturally grew hushed as they entered, and they instantly began worrying about the gazes of others around them. Even the anime song playing in the background seemed stifled in such hallowed ground.

However, today, that tranquil atmosphere was abruptly shattered.

"W-wait, Kaori. You can't just go in there!"

"B-but Shizuku-chan..."

Two girls' voices interrupted the silence. Their clear, high-pitched tone sounded just like the ringing of a bell. The warriors within all dropped what they were doing and timidly peeked out from behind their shelves. There was a single slender, feminine finger poking in from behind the curtains.

The men present all simultaneously thought, *Wait, don't tell me she's coming in here?! Damn, that means there's no way out!*

"No buts. The all-ages version is sold out, so just give it a rest already."

"But...Nagumo-kun's father's company made this game. What if Nagumo-kun also played the...e-eighteen plus version of the game?"

"L-Look here. You wanted to get this game so you'd have something to talk about with Nagumo-kun, right? Are you planning on talking about the s-sex scenes with him in class or something? I think he's more likely to run in the opposite direction if you try. Though maybe not for the reasons you think."

In order to have something to talk about with her crush, Hajime Nagumo, Kaori had come here today to buy the game Hajime's father had produced. However, because of its overwhelming popularity, the all-ages version was already sold out everywhere, and there were only a few copies of the 18+ version left. And even that was only because a few of the stores had accidentally ordered more stock than they had intended.

Considering her age, Kaori normally wouldn't be able to buy the 18+ version anyway, but straightforward and fearless as she was, she was still determined to try.

"I-I know. But still... Don't try and stop me, Shizuku-chan! Sometimes a girl's gotta do what a girl's gotta do!"

"Yes, but this isn't that time. Hey, no, wait, stop!"

There was a collective intake of breath as the warriors witnessed a girl burst through the curtains. For a moment everyone was at a loss for words, but then the muttered whispering began.

"Holy crap, she's hot..." and the like.

The first sight that greeted Kaori as she barged into the 18+ section was a full-size poster of a scantily-clad girl. She blushed to the tips of her ears, and then hurriedly looked down when she saw the dumbfounded gaze of every man in the section focused on her. Shizuku, who was standing behind her, grabbed her arm and tried to pull her out. However, Kaori wouldn't be deterred, and with her misguided resolution she said "I-I won't lose here!" before taking another step into the forbidden sanctuary.

Shizuku kept desperately trying to pull Kaori back, but she was too embarrassed to be able to utilize much of her strength. And so, she was unwillingly dragged along behind Kaori, like a little girl lost in another world.

"Ah. Sh-Shizuku-chan, I found it!"

"Wh-what? Can you please stop dragging me further in?"

Heedless of her pleas, Kaori continued dragging Shizuku, who had tears in her eyes, deeper into the holy land until she reached the game she sought. As she picked it up and looked at the cover, Shizuku suddenly let out an embarrassed squeal. The reason, of course, being that there were a lot of girls in suggestive poses plastered on the front.

Shizuku quickly averted her gaze, but Kaori nonchalantly flipped the box over to see what was on the backside. As she examined the illustrations, she said something terribly tactless without much thought.

"H-huh? Shizuku-chan, don't you think this girl looks a lot like you?"

"What?! D-don't be ridiculous! I would never get on all fours with my butt sticking out like that!"

Shizuku, diligent as always, made sure to actually look before retorting, even though it made her blush bright red. However, her voice had been slightly louder than intended, and there was suddenly a spray of red as someone collapsed behind a shelf. That was soon followed by a shrill scream of "Don't die on me, man! Damn, the bleeding just won't stop!" It appeared someone had a bit too overactive an imagination.

"B-besides, don't you think this girl looks a lot like you, Kaori?"

"No way! I-I'd never do something so embarrassing as get on top of a man looking like that!"

There was another fountain of red as a second man collapsed from behind a different shelf. A second later someone screamed out, "Medic! I need a medic!"

It was then that a savior descended among the gathering of hardened warriors.

"Excuse me, miss. I'm sorry, but you need to at least be eighteen to purchase these goods. Can I kindly ask you to leave?"

It was the advent of the manager. The thirty-something manager had decided it would be bad for business if a part of his store got turned into a mountain of corpses, and had wisely chosen to interfere. The remaining warriors were all certain his authority would be enough to deter the two interlopers.

However, their opponent was stronger than any of them had realized. Shizuku was bowing her head furiously in apology, her words choked with tears, as she tried to drag Kaori out of the section. However, Kaori was not so easily turned away. Even with tears streaking down her face, she still thrust the game box out at the manager and made her request.

"I-I'd like to buy this, preashe!"

The manager's expression faltered and he tried to insist that you needed to be eighteen to purchase this product, but Kaori came back with a most unexpected counter.

"I-It's for my dad!"

What kind of dad would make their daughter buy their porn! Everyone present thought the same thing. Kaori herself must have realized how flimsy an excuse it was, as she then continued, saying things like "It's his birthday present!" and "We were going to play it together!" Her excuses only made things worse, though. At this point Shizuku was so embarrassed that she buried her face in her hands, wishing she were dead. Finally, Kaori ended things with a "Please, won't you let me buy it?" Her puppy dog eyes and pleading drove the manager to his limits.

"Excuse me for a moment." That was all the manager said before running behind a shelf and spurting out a torrential nosebleed. He was just as much of an otaku as anyone else there, and thus just as susceptible to Kaori's charms. Wails of "Boooooss!" could be heard coming from the few warriors who were still left standing.

On that day, in her quest to purchase a single game, Kaori piled up a mountain of corpses of both customers and store clerks alike.

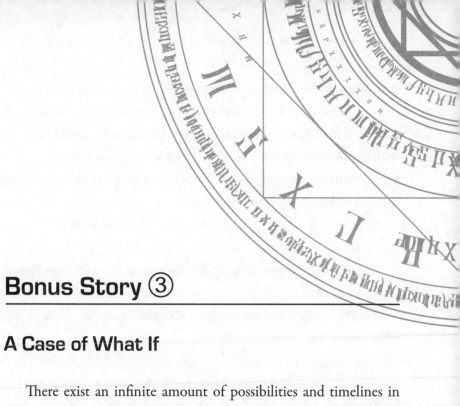

Bonus Story ③

A Case of What If

There exist an infinite amount of possibilities and timelines in this world. If we were to imagine some of those what if scenarios in Arifureta, they might go something like,

Case 1: What if, when Kouki was fighting Emperor Gahard, he did things a little differently?

"Prepare yourself, Hero. If you hold back again..."

Goosebumps coated Kouki's arms. The bodyguard's tone of voice clearly conveyed what awaited him if he held back.

"AAALaLaLaLaie!"

"What the hell?!"

Were Hoelscher's emperor a bit more like a certain other ruler, then surely all the demons would surrender and begin calling him "bro."

Case 2: What if, when Kouki was fighting Emperor Gahard, he did things a little differently? v2

"What on earth are you doing, Gahard?"

King Eliheid yelled out as he leaped in between the two fighters and blocked Gahard's blow. Gahard was thrown off balance by the fact that Eliheid had discovered his identity, but he nevertheless smiled fearlessly and prepared to charge again. Sighing, Eliheid realized Gahard had no intention of backing down.

"All things of this world, turn to ashes—*Ryujin Jakka!*"

"Wai—stop—no—"

If King Eliheid was actually the captain of the 13 Court Guard Companies, then all the demons would most likely be crying in fear.

Case 3: What if the second fight with the Behemoth went a little differently?

The Behemoth, enraged that a pair of mere humans had stopped its assault, stamped impatiently on the ground. Seeing this, the other students took advantage of its momentary distraction.

"Peerless swordsmanship that rends even the heavens—Hiten Mitsurugi style, Amakakeru Ryu no Hirameki!"

"What?"

If Shizuku Yaegashi was a master of the Hiten Mitsurugi style, she would probably be the hero, not Kouki.

Case 4: What if Kouki's sacred sword was a little different?

"Let's go! Sacred sword, lend me your power!"

"Moron, this is why I can't handle country hicks. I told you not to bother me during my afternoon tea."

"……"

If Kouki's sword was as annoying as a certain other world's Excalibur, then Kouki probably wouldn't be so nice.

Case 5: What if things were a little different when Hajime first found the Divinity Stone?

"This...is..."

The source of the liquid was a basketball-sized crystal that emitted a pale red light... A few days later after conquering his loneliness, starvation, and pain, Hajime took down his first enemy, the Twin-tailed Wolf.

"What a niiiiiiiiiiiiiiiiiiiiiiiiiice sound that was. Truly, wonderful! Is it not wonderful, O philosopher's stone?"

Had the stone Hajime discovered really been the Philosopher's Stone, he might have ended up like Kimblee.

Case 6: What if the scorpion fight had gone a little differently?

"...Thanks for the meal."

Suddenly, Yue got to her feet and brandished a hand at the scorpion-thing. As she did so, a tremendous amount of mana, golden in color, poured out of her tiny body, chasing away the darkness. Then, clad in a wondrous golden light, with her golden hair fluttering around her, she muttered a single phrase.

"Forbidden Barrage 'Catadioptric.'"

If Yue was actually the little sister to the master of the scarlet devil mansion, then she'd surely be this story's last boss.

There are countless possible timelines for every world...so why not try and think of a few yourself?

ARIFURETA SHOKUGYOU DE SEKAISAIKYOU

**FROM COMMONPLACE
TO WORLD'S STRONGEST**

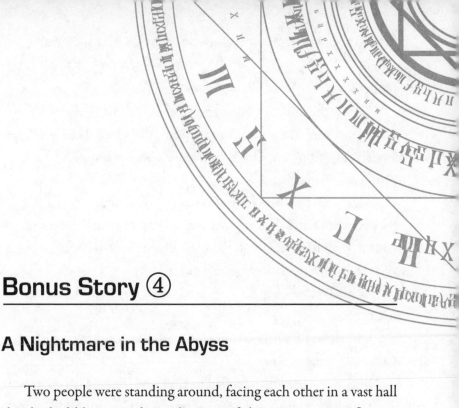

Bonus Story ④

A Nightmare in the Abyss

Two people were standing around, facing each other in a vast hall that looked like a grand temple. One of them was wearing flowing silvery robes with matching silver hair, and had in their hand a silver sword to match. The other was dressed in all black, had an eyepatch, and a prosthetic arm. The black-clothed figure had a revolver in their hands.

"I congratulate you on making it this far, Madness Parade of the Crimson Fang. Or would you prefer I call you Chaos Disaster?"

"Hmph, call me what you will. That name is naught but what others have heaped upon me. Though I am willing to admit my capacity for destruction rivals such a moniker. You shall meet your demise here, God of Origin. Or would you too, prefer to be called by your more commonplace name, Chaos of Darkness?"

...Holy crap, why do these names sound so nonsensically cringy?

The black-robed man tore off his eyepatch to reveal a dazzlingly blue eye.

"Now is the time to awaken, my steel-clad demonic arm!"

At the same time as he shouted out, the silver-clad figure grew silver wings from their back, and their silver sword glowed with a distinctively silver light.

"Very well. I admire your arrogance. Few so brazenly challenge a god. As a reward, I shall engrave eternal suffering into the essence of your very soul!" That was all the silver figure shouted back.

Oh my god, it just keeps getting worse.

As their fight began, the black-clad man screamed out an incantation.

"Oh crimson flash, heed mine call and devour thy foes—Crimson Cutter: Sacrosanct Resonance!"

The silver-haired man replied in kind, and shouted his own spell.

"Hmph, pathetic... Return all of creation to the primordial abyss—Karmic Absolution!"

They continued going back and forth like that for some time, their intense attacks creating a grand battle that would probably be the only one of its kind.

I can't take it anymore... Make it stop, please.

Finally, after the silver-clad man's third transformation, and the black-robed man had awoken to his ultimate true power, after they had unleashed not only both of their trump cards but both of their finishing moves, the black-clad figure let out a resounding cry of victory. He smiled triumphantly, covered from head to toe in wounds no mere mortal could ever hope to withstand...

"Heh, that was quite the enjoyable fight. In deference to your formidable strength, I shall grant you a gift to take with you to the afterlife. My true name, the name no one else knows... I am the Crimson Flame White Demon's—"

Please, just kill me now. Anything, anything to make it stoooooop.

"Make it stoooooooooooooooooooooop!"

"Hajime?! What's wrong, are you okay?"

Deep within the labyrinth, Hajime threw off the sheets covering him and leaped to his feet, his breathing rough. Yue also got up in a panic and gently hugged Hajime in order to calm him down.

"Th-that was a terrifying nightmare... Yue, can I ask you something?"

"...What?"

"If I ever start becoming one of those delusional crazies, use your Azure Blaze to bring me back to my senses, please."

Yue realized Hajime must still have been suffering from the effects of the nightmare, as whatever he was saying didn't make any sense. Still, she nodded in order to reassure him.

"...Okay. Leave it to me. If you ever start becoming one of those delusional crazies, I'll make sure to stop you."

Neither of them realized they had been misunderstood by the other, Hajime talking about the sight from his dreams and Yue about him becoming a monster, but...Hajime calmed down after that, which was enough to satisfy Yue, so they both went back to sleep in each other's arms.

As long as Yue was around, Hajime was safe from falling over to that side...probably.

ARIFURETA SHOKUGYOU DE SEKAISAIKYOU

FROM COMMONPLACE
TO WORLD'S STRONGEST

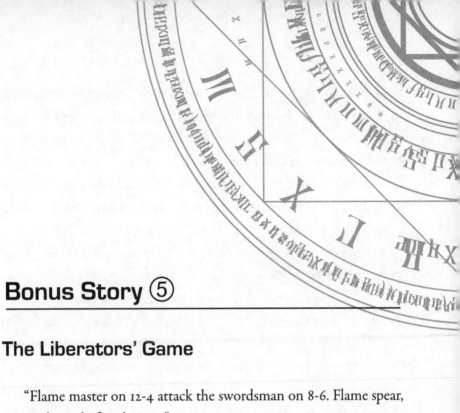

Bonus Story ⑤

The Liberators' Game

"Flame master on 12-4 attack the swordsman on 8-6. Flame spear, magical attack, fire element."

"Hmm..."

Within the depths of the Great Orcus Labyrinth, inside Oscar Orcus' private room, a young boy smiled triumphantly while the girl next to him sunk deep into thought. Her voice was oddly seductive. The two people were, of course, Hajime Nagumo and Yue. The two of them were sitting on sofas across from each other, with a transparent table laid out between them. There was a square metallic board on the table, and around sixty-four pieces lay out on various parts of it. They were enjoying a game of otherworldly chess before bed.

As one might have guessed from the different number of pieces, the rules were slightly different. For one, there were 256 squares on the board. For another, the board was split up into various terrains such as mountains, rivers, forests, hills, plains, and the like, and the pieces were categorized either as magical or physical fighters. Each piece could learn various skills, and the damage they dealt with each attack depended on the skill and element. Players also had to keep track of various resources such as mana as well.

The most fascinating aspect was that thanks to some magical contraption, the pieces all played out their actions. Even now, Hajime, who was still a beginner at the game, marveled at how his flame master fired a mini-spark at Yue's soldier, who then doubled up in pain screaming, "H-how can this be!" before collapsing. In response, one of Yue's mages moved all on its own to carry the defeated piece off the board while screaming, "So this is how your side does things, huh?!"

"I've been wondering, but is there any way to take off these little cutscene type things?"

"...If you can't do it, Hajime, I don't think anyone left alive can. This is probably the joint work of all the skilled Liberators."

It certainly was impressive. A colossal waste of skill, but impressive nonetheless. Hajime's impression of the Liberators had changed a little when he'd found this.

Now that it was Yue's turn, she sent her knight charging forward to cut down Hajime's flame master. The knight made a splendid show of spearing the flame master on his lance, crushing him to pieces. A few seconds later, the destroyed pieces of the flame master regenerated, and he cheerfully walked himself off the board.

When his flame master was destroyed, Hajime flinched a little. Not because he was sad at losing a piece, but because there was one other interesting feature built into this version of chess called Pain Trace. Each of the two players would register their mana on the game board beforehand, and whenever one player lost a piece, they'd suffer a small static shock.

"Assassin to 13-9. Attack the enemy crusader. Slash, skill, increased critical."

"Nhaah."

Hajime's assassin sneaked up behind Yue's crusader and mercilessly beheaded it. As the crusader's head rolled to the ground, Yue's queen cried out in despair.

"My dear knight!"

Next to her, the king bore down on her in an accusatory tone.

"What? My *dear* knight? And just what did you mean by that, huh, *dear*?" And so, the queen's adultery was exposed.

After a few more turns it was discovered that the king had his own bastard son, and the mother was none other than the other side's queen. Jealous, Yue's queen had an affair with her court magician, but then later on it was discovered the court magician had a secret lover of his own, and that he was a man, and that man was none other than Hajime's army's court magician. Love blossomed between them, and the whole royal family got involved. Honestly, it felt more like a drama than a chess match.

"Yue, how come you moan like that every time you lose a piece? It's not that painful, is it?"

"...You just keep attacking all of my weak points, Hajime."

"Liar. There's no such... No, wait. For some reason today the shock's always been focused on my—"

"Eeheehee, that was all my doing. I turned on the feature that probes the player's subconscious and stimulates the one place they feel it the most. I found out about it in the user's manual. By the way, you can control the voltage output too, and I set it to max today."

Hajime suddenly shivered. The user's manual was 500 pages long, so he hadn't had the patience to read more than a few of them. He wasn't sure if she just read through the whole thing, or if she found all the features she wanted by accident, but Yue now had an advantage over him.

But what was truly frightening was that every time he lost a piece, Hajime could feel his family jewels tingle. *S-So that's what she was after.* Thanks to his resistances, the shocks had been mostly mitigated, but with how seductively Yue was moaning every time she lost a piece, it was only a matter of time before his little man decided to poke its head out. No matter how superior his army was, he wouldn't be able to win at this rate. Thus, Hajime raised his voice, eager to end this as quickly as possible.

"Earth master to 16-7. Line attack from 16-8 to 16-10. Rock slide, magical attack, earth element, advanced skill."

He was sacrificing his ability to move for a few turns by carrying out this AoE attack. As the attack went off, Yue moaned once more, falling limp on the sofa after the shock finally ran its course. She was twitching a little now, and her black one-piece shuffled up a little to reveal her bare legs.

"Sorry, Yue, but I'm taking this one. I can't afford to lose when my dignity as a man is at stake."

"...Mmm, so you're finally coming at me seriously."

Beads of sweat were forming on Yue's forehead and her cheeks were slightly flushed. After thinking for a moment, she proposed something interesting.

"If you're so sure of this game, how about we make a little bet?"

Hajime warily questioned her for further details, and Yue said that the winner could make any one request they wanted of the loser. Apparently, Yue's request would be that they wear a matching set of clothes one day after they made it back to the surface.

While the mini-soldiers down below were yelling death threats at each other and waging a violent war for survival, Hajime and Yue were discussing their next date. It felt utterly surreal. It also really broke the tension. For his part, Hajime didn't want to do something so embarrassing, so he made an audacious move.

"Queen to 14-5! Activate the queen's special ability, Ruler's blessing!"

He risked sending his strongest piece into the line of fire in order to allow all his nearby pieces to do a coordinated simultaneous attack. All of his units within a certain amount of tiles began attacking at once! The king's illegitimate child died during the battle! Yue's king and Hajime's queen both lamented his loss greatly, but the battle still raged on! And lastly, Yue's moans grew louder than ever before!

That battle ended up becoming the turning point for the game, and eventually Yue was defeated. Yue's king and Hajime's queen's love story continued, and they ended up impaling each other on their swords. Finally, Hajime's king, who hadn't spoken a word during the entire play, declared his side's victory and the game was over.

Hajime breathed a sigh of relief, glad he wouldn't be embarrassing himself on the surface anymore. But because Yue was pouting, he ended up compromising anyway, and agreed to wear any one outfit she requested of him, improving her mood instantly. *So this is what they mean when they say you've won the battle, but lost the war.*

As always, Hajime could never win against Yue.

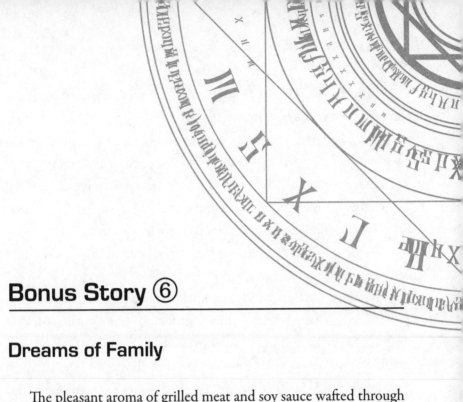

Bonus Story ⑥

Dreams of Family

The pleasant aroma of grilled meat and soy sauce wafted through the air. There was a forty-something old lady standing in the kitchen, an apron wrapped around her waist and her hair tied back in a ponytail.

The woman, Sumire Nagumo, was busy skillfully preparing a meal. She raised her head up to the ceiling and yelled.

"Hajime, dear, it's feeding time!"

After a brief silence, a pair of footsteps could be heard heading down the stairs.

"Can you please just call it dinner like a normal person, Mom?" Hajime Nagumo displayed an annoyed face as he entered the kitchen... There were dark bags under his gentle eyes. He took a peek at what his mom had made while helping her set the table, and his eyes began to sparkle.

Hajime's father, Nagumo Shuu, popped in with his two cents: "Awesome, you made Hamburg steak today. No wonder the house smelled so good." He was a slender man with short, cropped hair. Like his son, he too had bags under his eyes.

The pair finished setting the table and eagerly dug into the meal Sumire had prepared for them. They stuffed their mouths with Hamburg steak and white rice as if they were starving men. Sumire giggled as she watched them eat and muttered words of disagreement.

"No, I think feeding time suits you two just perfectly."

"Well, did you two manage to meet your deadline with that debugging?"

"Mmmgh... Mmnch... Yeah, somehow. That game's really cool."

"Gulp... It better be. The future of my company's riding on that game. Do you have any idea how much we poured into development? I'd be out of a job if that game wasn't cool. Though I guess if I lost my job, I could spend all my time playing games trying to figure out where I went wrong."

"Dad, they call those people NEETs."

"Not a NEET, son, a shut-in. Shut-ins that can make a living for themselves are what we call winners at life." Shuu riposted brilliantly. Such was his philosophy. The mother was no better in that regard, however.

"Indeed," she replied. This was the result of having a father who ran a game company and a mother who was a shoujo mangaka. Their mindsets weren't exactly normal.

In fact, when they had learned that Hajime was being bullied at school, their advice, if it could be called that, had just been along the same lines.

"Do what you want. If you want to transfer, transfer. If you want to fight back, fight back. If you want to become a shut-in, become a shut-in. Hell, get yourself expelled for all I care! I'll hire you. It doesn't matter if you're a high-school dropout or have 10 PhDs, the ones making money in the end are the winners."

Hajime was of a more practical bent, though.

"It's important to have backup plans to secure financial stability, so school's super important." Only in this household would you find a child telling their parents the importance of staying in school.

But, well, I'm glad Mom and Dad are like that, because it would have been awkward if they made a huge deal out of the whole thing.

Meanwhile, his parents were having a truly absurd conversation.

"I'm starting to think our son's got some lolicon tendencies in him."

"He certainly does like loli characters."

He quickly brought his thoughts back to the present and gave his parents a glowering glare.

"Hey hey, no need to glare at us like that. You're the one who added a blonde loli mage to the game, not me," said Shuu.

"So, that doesn't make me a lolicon. You're a grown man, you should be able to tell the difference between games and reality," Hajime replied.

"True, you're into animal-ears too. Especially rabbit ears. I'm glad my son grew up to be a patrician of such fine taste," Sumire also chimed in.

Hajime sulkily returned to his dinner while his parents grinned at him. They ganged up on their only son like that pretty often.

"I guarantee you you'd party up with a loli if you ever got summoned to another world. Just remember, attacking underage girls is still a crime. I'm sure even other worlds have laws against sex with children. They've been cracking down on it in games here recently, even."

"Don't just go around making your own assumptions. And can you please stop calling me a lolicon?"

Fed up with his parents teasing, Hajime got a little testy. Realizing he went a little too far with his teasing, his father apologized while laughing.

"But you're a healthy young boy, so I'm sure you're interested in all those fantasy worlds with swords and magic. Isn't going on adventures with a cute heroine, falling in love, and finally defeating the gods or the demon lord or whatever something you dream of?"

"That does sound like the kind of thing a lot of guys would like. And those 'reincarnated into another world' and 'summoned into another world' light novels are getting pretty popular recently. I wouldn't want our son to get summoned, though. What would we do if he couldn't ever come back?"

Sumire sunk deep into thought, taking the idea of Hajime being summoned rather seriously. Both of them had overactive imaginations, which Hajime supposed were just occupational hazards. He smiled awkwardly while watching them seriously worry over his potential disappearance into another world.

"I don't think I have what it takes to save the world, anyway."

Shuu wasn't happy with his son's self-deprecating attitude.

"You could at least pretend to be the strongest in your head, you know?"

Hajime's smile grew even more troubled, but he responded with confidence.

"I'm sure all I'd be capable of is making it back home. And if I found someone important to me, I'd probably just bring them back too. I might not be able to save the world, but I'd definitely come back."

"……"

His parents suddenly brought their heads together.

He shrugged his shoulders to hide his embarrassment before continuing. "Besides, I only like other worlds when they stay inside books and games."

For once, his parents didn't bully him, and simply smiled kindly.

"That's right. Staying safe is more important than saving the world. But if you were strong enough to save it on your way back, you might as well, right? Hmm, maybe I should make a game that has a protagonist like that..."

"Oh, that does sound like a good idea. There's a kind of surreal aspect to it when the protagonist's only interested in going home, but he beats the demon lord and the gods and all that along the way."

Their creative urges got the better of them, and their conversation turned toward how they could use this idea in their work. While he might sometimes lament that his parents only ever thought about their hobby-jobs, he was still their son, and started contributing ideas of his own to their discussion. That was just another day at the Nagumo household.

With a faint groan, Shuu opened his eyes and looked up at the moonlight streaming through the window.

"...What's wrong, dear?"

"Sumire... I had a dream about Hajime. It was about when we were talking about other worlds, a few days before he disappeared."

Sumire propped herself up on the bed and reassured her depressed husband.

"He'll come back home... I'm sure of it. No matter where he went, even if it is another world, I'm sure he'll find a way home."

"Sumire..."

"Trust me. He normally just tries to get by without rocking the boat, but if there's something he really believes in, then he'll chase after it with all his might. That's why I know he'll be fine."

"...You're right. I'm sure he'll be fine."

The two of them huddled closer together, thinking about their son who'd vanished along with an entire class full of students.

Around the same time, Hajime groggily opened his eyes, deep within the abyss. He stared off into the distance, his features illuminated by the light of the fake moon. Yue sidled closer to him, her gaze questioning.

"I was having a dream about Mom and Dad. I can't believe all those ridiculous things we joked about really came true..."

"...Hajime, it'll be okay. As long as we're together, we can do anything. We'll return to your world for sure." Yue smiled reassuringly at Hajime, her voice full of conviction. He patted her head lovingly, then nodded back.

"Yeah, you're right. We're going to make it back for sure."

For just a moment, an image of his parents hugging each other flashed through Hajime's mind. They were hugging each other sadly, both of them thinner than he remembered. For some reason, they both looked up when he'd mentioned his resolve, as if they'd heard him.

The image of his parents smiled a little, and it seemed like they'd gone back—just a bit—to their old selves...or so he thought, anyway.

AFTERWORD

To those of you who picked this up when it became a novel, nice to meet you. To those of you who've been following me since my Syosetsu days, hello again. Author of Arifureta, Ryo Shirakome, here.

Let me first start by saying that...this is a work of fiction. Any relation to real people, groups, etc. is purely coincidental. Humans of Earth cannot use magic (I think), and they definitely can't turn themselves into living railguns (probably).

All right, now that those stuffy formalities are out of the way, I'd like to take this opportunity to thank you for picking up this book.

I'm not sure if this book betrayed your expectations or fulfilled them, but I'll be glad so long as you derived some amount of enjoyment from it.

I mentioned this earlier too, but this story was originally something I put up on the novel website Syosetsuka ni Narou under the pseudonym Chuuni Lover. It's something that's been steadily edited and refined before appearing in the form you're reading now.

I'm still very much a beginner when it comes to writing, so

forgive me for the half-assed setting, overall lack of plot, and general randomness. I added things as they popped into my mind, and wrote a story that was more for myself than anything. Even now, I'm still enjoying writing this story more than anything else as Ryo Shirakome... which is why I'm truly thankful to my fans at Narou for supporting this fanfiction-tier story all the way until it got published officially. It's not every day that an author of isekai stories (narratives featuring everyday people who get transported to another world and obtain supernatural powers) gets published out of the sea of isekai works on there.

Once again, I'd like to thank my readers for letting me enjoy myself all the way through. To those of you following the web version, I still plan on posting updates there. We're reaching the end now, so things are going to start getting more and more heated. I would love it if you continue to follow the web series along with the published novel.

As I'm sure those of you can already tell by my Syosetsu pen name, I'm a huge lover of chuuni (chuunibyou—second year high schoolers who adopt a quirky hobby, often to the disparaging eye of others). Enough of one that I wrote an entire novel based on it. Enough of one that I'm going to write an entire second novel about it too.

And I'm not the only chuuni out there. I'm sure all Japanese boys—no, boys all over the world—no, every human alive—has a bit of chuuni hidden somewhere inside them. So, to all of you chuuni lovers who have to hide away because of common sense, or your age, or how embarrassing it is, or how society sees you, if this book has helped unleash your burning soul just a little...then I consider my work complete.

Ah, but please don't go around unleashing it in public. You'll cause an uproar.

Now then, I think I finally understand all those authors who resort to rambling for their afterword because they don't know what to write... Yeah. Because that's me right now. I'm out of things to write. Not good. This is just like that time I went to a job interview and blanked when they told me to write my strengths.

Anyway, before I start spouting something stupid (though I think I've already spouted quite a few stupid things in this book) allow me to once more thank everyone who made this possible.

First, allow me to thank Takayaki for his wonderful illustrations. I've been moved by his drawings ever since he sent me his first rough drafts. To have my work illustrated by someone so skilled is truly a great honor. Thank you so very much.

Next, I would like to thank my editor, S, who fought to get the publication of this novel approved against all odds because of his own personal interest in it. I would also like to thank the rest of the editing department at Overlap for all the help you've given me.

Lastly, I would like to thank you, the reader who's picked up this book. Thank you so very, very much.

Many thanks to both readers of the published edition and of the web edition. I look forward to seeing where this tale goes together with you.

May we meet again in the next volume.